Buzz Saw

A Novel by

D. James Bücher

Order this book online at www.trafford.com
or email orders@trafford.com

Most Trafford titles are also available at major online book retailers.

Note for Librarians: A cataloguing record for this book is available from Library
and Archives Canada at www.collectionscanada.ca/amicus/index-e.html

Printed in Victoria, BC, Canada.

ISBN: 978-1-4269-1850-6 (sc)
ISBN: 978-1-4269-1851-3 (hc)

Library of Congress Control Number: 2009936886

*Our mission is to efficiently provide the world's finest, most comprehensive book publishing
service, enabling every author to experience success. To find out how to publish your
book, your way, and have it available worldwide, visit us online at www.trafford.com*

Trafford rev. 09/15/09

 www.trafford.com

North America & international
toll-free: 1 888 232 4444 (USA & Canada)
phone: 250 383 6864 ♦ fax: 812 355 4082

Dedicated to:
My mother, Mary
And my forever friends, Roscoe and Dutchess,
Who are waiting with my father in Heaven.

Revelation 21:23

"And the city had no need of the sun,
neither of the moon, to shine in it:
for the glory of God did lighten it,
and the Lamb is the light thereof.

Chapter 1

THE PUPPIES WERE BORN quietly on an August night. The boxer who birthed them had apparently slipped her leash some 9 weeks previous, and found romance with another dog. Her owner had soon seen the signs of her impending state, and since the deed had already been done, now allowed her to roam free. She chose to have her little miracles under the trailer. As he walked outside that morning and did not see her bounding up to him, as was her daily custom, he knew she must have delivered, somewhere, that previous night.

Oh well, I can give 'em away, he thought. If, by some chance in a million she hooked up with another boxer, I can even sell them. Fat chance of that. People want pure breeds these days. He heard the whimpering before he thought to call out to the mother, and when he finally did call out, she emerged sheepishly from a corner of the mobile home, where the trailer skirting was gapped enough to allow entry.

My girl! What have you got under there, he thought. Did you have the sense to hook up with another of your own breed? Or was it a Dalmatian, or maybe a weenie dog? Visions of puppies with the distinctive boxer frame and the taffy-pulled look of a dachshund made him chuckle and wince at the same time. He scratched her head and went into the trailer to fix her a heaping bowl of leftover meatloaf, which she wolfed down the moment he set it before her.

Dropping pups is hungry business, he mused. Not that I would know. Well, I don't want to crawl under there just yet, he decided. Having just brought them into the world, she might be a bit protective. And even though his dog had never shown even the slightest inclination to bite the hand that fed her, he also didn't want to disturb the maternal instinct of a 50 Lb. female boxer who might be smack in the middle of post-partum protectivity. Give her some time. Then I'll crawl under there and see what canine genetics we're dealing with here.

Two days later he took time to belly crawl under the mobile home, and was rewarded with the sight of six squirming pups that had the unmistakable body of their boxer mother, but possessed rather large, round heads. Well, he mused, at least she didn't hook up with a poodle. With the shape of the heads, and the brindle coloring, he deduced that the DNA could probably be traced to a pit bull that a neighbor down the street owned. He back-crawled out from under the trailer and informed his wife that though they were not blessed with pedigree dogs, at least it should not be hard to find homes for them, as people were always looking for guard dogs. Like most women, she loved all things infant, and the next day he was ordered to retrieve the pups from under her house, and place them in a special, quilt padded box she had lovingly made in a corner of the shed.

Dolly, the pup's mother, naturally spent the vast majority of her time lying in the box, allowing her brood to suckle. The man and his wife enjoyed going out to the shed to watch the squirming group, and pet the head of their contented mother. Most of the pups were generally identical in size and color, with what seemed not to be a runt in the bunch. But in the third week of their existence, one pup emerged as peculiar, to say the least.

As they watched the ritual feeding take place, with each pup fastened securely to a teat, they saw a pup in the middle that had stopped feeding to try and dislodge his sibling from a spot he desired. What ensued made both the man and his wife drop their jaws in disbelief. The pup that had been suddenly nosed out leapt upon the one who would deny him his spot on the mother.

It was a curious sight and, at the same time, a terrible one. With his milk sharp teeth, he tore into the invader, tearing and snarling. And it was obvious that the sibling had no defense against this attack. He had never known any sensation other than the caress of his mother's tongue. The pain caused a scream of high pitched yelps to fill the air, not only from the one being attacked, but also from his surrounding brothers and sisters. It so startled the mother she leapt up, and away from the scene of the melee. Blood spots appeared on his back where he was being bitten, and to stave off this pain he did precisely what he would learn later in life not to do: he rolled over. Which put his back out of reach, but now revealed his baby-soft underbelly.

Like many other men, he enjoyed a good dogfight, as long as it didn't get out of hand. But this was no fight. It was a slaughter. And he could see that in moments it could well be dismemberment. And his wife was screaming.

"Doyle, he's killing him. Grab him for God's sake!"

With one swift move he reached down and pulled up the pup by the scruff of the neck. The small dog, not yet even 3 pounds soaking wet, was biting and snapping at the air, not yet aware he had been lifted away from the attack. It was as if he was stuck in killer mode, unable to dislodge himself from it. The sight of something so tiny, and seemingly harmless, acting out such a vicious exhibition, caused the hairs on the back of his neck to stand up. How could anything that small and cute be, at the same time, so malevolent?

"What's wrong with him?" his wife shouted, as the pup continued to bite at nothing, still being held aloft by her husband.

"Is he having a seizure?" she screamed.

"No, but he's as full of the devil as any dog I've ever seen."

With a rap of his knuckle on the pups' head, the tiny dog stopped biting, and seemed to become aware that he was being suspended by the neck. He, at once, became still. The mother dog moved to comfort the pup that had been assaulted. He was still yelping loudly, but after a few comforting strokes of her tongue his cries became less high pitched, and more sob-like.

"I've never seen anything like that in all my born days," she said. "He was ripping into that other one like a buzz saw."

"Yep," the man answered, "Just like a baby buzz saw. I think that's what we'll have to call you. Buzz Saw. That's who you are."

"Honey, didn't you say you wanted to keep one?" the man asked.

He briefly allowed his mind to dwell on what kind of guard dog this tiny pup would grow into. No one would come near the house while they were away, that's for sure.

"We're not keeping that one," she exclaimed. "He'd kill his own mother!"

With a tinge of regret he placed the pup back on the ground, cautiously watching to make sure the scene would not repeat itself. The pup waddled back to where his mother had repositioned herself, as if the incident had never happened.

He knew better than to argue with the woman. To her, the pup would forever be a murderous scourge.

"Yeah, maybe you're right. Could get us into trouble with the neighbors. But did you see that little fighter? There's a spirit there, I'll tell you."

"There's a spirit there, all right. A spirit in need of an exorcist. As soon as they're weaned Doyle, the minute they are weaned, you put an ad in the paper, or whatever you do. And make sure you get rid of that one first. You hear me now?"

"Yeah, yeah. But what a little fighter he is!" he said admiringly.

Her disapproving gaze made him stop short. There was no getting around it. Buzz Saw would have to go.

***

The boy slowly picked up the items off his bedroom dresser and lovingly wrapped them in tissue. He was not normally so fastidious. But every item here now was treasured, as it represented a link to the past. And the past was what this place was soon to become. The moment he had been told by his mother they were moving, he had lived in a state of dread. Dread over the nostalgia he knew he would eventually feel for this place. Dread over the readjustment that would have to be made: the remaking of friends, the cutting loose of old ones. The culture shock of assimilation to an alien environment, which was the view his minds eye had of Monticello, Arkansas, the place his mother and Earl had decided would be their new home.

Not that his mother and Earl had actually decided, for he knew in all reality Earl had called that shot. His stepfather Earl. The interloper who had, during the courtship of his mother, seemed so full of fatherly concern over his well being, but who now barely acknowledged his existence, and when he did, only did so begrudgingly. The man who was quick to call him "son", and had even stated he would not mind if his stepson called him "dad." This lasted only through the romance phase, not even into the honeymoon. Once the lines in the marriage license had been filled in, probably even before the ink was dry, Earl had begun to treat him like a worn out shoe. A fifth wheel.

And his mother was oblivious to it all. She still saw the pre-wedding Earl. The one who had bought him a new baseball glove, and had even taken him to the park to shag fly balls. The Earl who was going to step in and make up for a father who had decided they weren't enough, and had left to make a new family in Oklahoma. The father who was faithful to make his child support payments, and nothing more. Why weren't we enough, he wondered? If you don't like the car you're driving, you trade it in on a new one. Take the old one to the scrap yard. He and mom had been taken to the scrap yard. Left to rust in sun, while his natural father drove a new family in Oklahoma.

For a while, they were alone. Alone but happy. At least he was. He knew his mom was not. Her stifled sobs that could occasionally be heard behind the bedroom door, told him that. He wished he could be enough. Could somehow be her end-all, be-all. Could be such a spectacular son that her heart would ache for nothing more than him. And he did try so hard to be that spectacular son. Even as some of his other friends were getting in trouble at school, and even getting into minor scrapes with the law, he walked a line of obedience at home and at school.

He was therefore disappointed when she announced she had met someone. Consternated, when she confided to him a few weeks later that it might be serious. And downright depressed when, six months into it, she had come home from an evening out with Earl and told him, with the serious tone of someone announcing a life-changing event, that she and Earl were hereby engaged, and would be married as soon as her knight in shining armor could get his hands on the cash for a wedding ring, something he had insisted on. And it seemed the minute the ceremony was finished, with a local justice of the peace and a few of Earl's long-haired friends in attendance, young Robert Sinclair had gone from being "the son Earl had always hoped for," to, increasingly, like an inconvenience. Now, instead of hearing, "Lets go outside and play some ball," he often heard, "Stay away from my work shed, I got important tools in there!"

Robby doubted that Earl had important tools in the locked shed. Except maybe the shovel. That was obviously an important tool to Earl because he often left the house with it at, or near daybreak. Robby's mom had declared emphatically, from day one, that Earl's business was landscape contracting. But it was the worst kept secret in Ouachita County that Earl's actual livelihood stemmed from the cultivation of marijuana. The longhaired friends that frequented the house, the infrequent and inconsistent work hours, and of course, the tightly locked shed, did nothing to convince Robby that this was not true. Robby had no desire to go near the shed. Probably something in there that would make Cheech and Chong reach for a pack of rolling papers.

"Robby, how are you coming along in there?" his mother called out from the kitchen where she was loading dishes into boxes.

"Fine," he answered.

Moments later she was standing in the door, watching him as he held a snow-globe, shaking it again and again.

"Honey, you're not packing. We've got to get going."

"I know," he answered, but he continued to stare at globe, remembering the day his dad had bought it for him at Six Flags over Texas. So long ago. When they were a family. Leaving this place was a little like losing his dad all over again. This was the last place he and his dad had lived together. It brought the realization home that things had irrevocably changed. They had passed a time that would never be again. Leaving here was like burying something you loved. Something that was long dead, but had been neglected to be put into the ground. To bury it was to admit that it was gone. He had been trying to avoid that, since the time his father had walked out of his life. Now it had to be faced. And it hurt.

"Honey, what's the matter?"

"I don't want to move. Why do we have to move?"

"It's time for a change. We all need a change. And Earl can get more work there."

At the mention of his stepfather's name, he rolled his eyes.

"Don't look at me with that tone of voice. He loves you. He only wants the best for you."

He knew there was no sense arguing with her. She couldn't see through Earl like he could. Telling her that Earl didn't give a rat's ass about him, or probably her either, would only provoke a fight, and bring more sadness to his situation in the end. So he dutifully resumed wrapping the treasured articles that adorned his shelf and dresser, and as he did, began to mentally check off the things he was giving up. His friend Hank, who lived across the street. They had promised to write, but he instinctively knew it would not be. 15 year olds boys are usually not great at putting pen to paper. Hank would find a new friend. And, he begrudgingly admitted, he probably would too. What kinds of friends would he find in Monticello? He knew little about the place, other than they'd had some awesome high school football teams in years past. A run of state championships. The thought of football brought up another loss he was facing.

As a 10th grader, he had been looking forward to playing with the varsity at the small, class "A" school he had attended since the first grade. At the lowest classification level, Harmony Grove was not an intimidating place to participate in athletics. There would likely only be 30 or so kids out for varsity football. He would undoubtedly ride the bench quite a bit his sophomore year, maybe getting his licks in on the kickoff team. Then, when he reached the 11th and 12th grades, he'd have a full-fledged spot on the field. Two glorious years of Friday night fights. A chance for glory with friends he'd known since first grade.

He'd envisioned it so many times, and he allowed himself to go there now. He could hear the band. See the cheerleaders leaping and bouncing in hopes of motivating the team to give a little bit more. And he was there. At the tailback position. His friend Doug was quarterbacking. Another friend, Mitch, was in position at fullback, just in front of him. The noise of the crowd reached a crescendo and the defense tensed. Who was that on defense? It must be the Bearden Bears, a small town just up the road, which was a natural rival to his school, and always a hard-fought opponent. Yeah, it was Bearden, in their all black uniforms. They were waiting for the snap of the football. Waiting on him, because the play was 27 Dive. A straight hand-off to the tailback. Fullback hits the hole first, between the right guard and tackle, and the tailback follows behind him.

There was twenty seconds left on the clock. No, two seconds. Harmony Grove was behind by 5, and had the ball at their own 10 yard line. They had two seconds to go ninety yards. Who could do that? No one, except the mighty Harmony Grove Hornets, and their explosive young running back, Robby Sinclair. He'd been bottled up all game. Okay, he had over a hundred yards, but it had been gained in bits and pieces. The Bearden defense had been keying on him, knowing he was the Hornets chief weapon. But it was do or die time. A situation the coach would refer to as, "time to crap or get out of the outhouse." It was his time.

He allowed his mind to see it as a spectator would, from the stands. The ball was snapped and the lines crashed together, as they had all game. But this time it was different. This time his right guard and tackle rose to the occasion, and opened a gaping hole in the Bearden line. It was wide enough to drive a truck through. Even old lady Perkins, who taught second grade, and had glasses like the bottom of a coke bottle, could see the hole they had opened. But the Bearden middle linebacker remained unblocked, and he stepped in to fill the hole. For his team, his school, he stood in the gap.

His friend Mitch, the fullback, charged through the hole and leveled the linebacker with a block that made the kid's mother in the stands shed a tear.

The crowd saw Robby shoot through the newly opened hole, and he was into the secondary.

It was the same feeling a wild stallion feels when he is cornered, corralled, and then escapes containment. He was free. Free to run in the wide-open spaces. Only one obstacle remained: the free safety. Robby could see his eyes go wide through the facemask of his helmet, as the star running back of Harmony Grove High School barreled towards him. A juke right caused the kid to lean that way, then a sharp correction to the left faked him nearly out of his shoes, and Robby was past him. He shifted into an extra gear that all but only the best rushers possessed; Hershel Walker, Bo Jackson...and of course, Robby Sinclair. It was that almost supernatural burst of speed that had caused all the college scouts in the nation to rise up and take notice.

He allowed his mind to occupy both the field, and the radio broadcast booth, as the play-by-play announcer shouted into his microphone, "Sinclair breaks loose at the 40, midfield, 35, 20, 10…

It was at this point his mother opened the door and interrupted his run to glory.

"Robby, you've been standing in the same place for twenty minutes!"

"Okay," he said, with a sigh.

It was something he knew he'd just have to accept. This phase of his life was over. He'd have to make do the best he could, wherever he ended up.

Chapter 2

EARL COLLINS BACKED THE U-haul out of the driveway, with his wife sitting in the middle, and Robby occupying the passenger seat. He, at once, went into what he called, "auto-pilot listening mode." It was a necessary trait to possess if one were to stay married to Carol, and not lose ones mind. As was the norm, she began talking the minute he shifted the truck into gear. And she would likely not shut up until she lay down sometime that night, and sleep blissfully took over. But it was okay. He could deal with it. Just go to some interesting place in his mind, and be sure to nod whenever she seemed to be attempting to make a point.

He dealt with it because he was thoroughly persuaded that no woman ever created could control her tongue, for any appreciable time. The mindless chatter was acceptable, even if it was worthless blather. She could talk to him till she was blue in the face, which unfortunately never seemed to happen. As long as she didn't talk *at* him. Didn't disrespect him. That could never be tolerated. Would never be tolerated.

She had crossed that line once. Nagging him over money. Over his " landscape contracting job" and the fact that sometimes he had a pocket full of cash, and other times would have to resort to paying patronage to the local pawnshop for a loan. Well, he'd put her in her place right quick. Grabbing her by the throat and pushing her against the wall till her eyes bulged in fright.

It had almost resulted in a cancellation of their nuptials. But he had calmed down, and explained to her that he could put up with a lot, but he had a low tolerance for verbal diarrhea. It has to do with my upbringing, he explained. I put up with a lot growing up, he told her. And she'd tried to coax him into telling her more. Trying to get him to "explore his feelings." Fat chance of that. The only reason a woman wants to know what you're feeling is so she can get inside your head and mess with your brain. Screw with your mind big time. His mother had taught him that. She'd made a career of making his father miserable.

Now, as he so often did, fully on "auto pilot listening mode," he unconsciously drifted back to the past. To where his mother was busy berating his father. Spilling out her endless list of grievances, in an ever-increasingly shrill voice. And there was his father, slumped down in his easy chair, facing the TV. Not bothering to fight back. By that time, the fight was all beat out of him. It was no use arguing with her. Playing passive would not make her shut up. But engaging in verbal dialogue damn sure wouldn't either.

My father, he thought, went to Italy and fought the Germans. Helped run'em all the way back to Berlin. Won two purple hearts along the way. Beat Hitler, but he couldn't beat my mother's tongue. They should have sent my mother to the front with a megaphone. She'd have done in a week what it took Patton two years to do.

Oh, he fought toe to toe with her in the beginning, bless his soul. They'd had some epic verbal exchanges when he was young. But battle after battle, with never a resolution, had finally worn down the old man. Till one day he just sat down in that easy chair and let her rant. Maybe hoping against all hope that she would run out of venom. That, of course, didn't work. It only seemed to irritate her that he refused to be her sparing partner. And the onslaught increased. Went beyond an outpouring of grievances, to an outright personal attack on his character and his manhood.

"I should never have married you," she would scream. "You're a pitiful excuse for a man. You've never satisfied me, in any way. None! There were a dozen other men I could have married; any one of them would have been better than you. I don't even think you like women. You're completely worthless, you know that? Stupid, pathetic. You're a man in body only. And a poor excuse for one at that."

And there was his father. The war hero. Eyes glued to the TV. In a trance. Gone away to a better place in his mind. Any place had to be better than this. Even at the front line during the battle of the bulge had to be an improvement over this. Even sharing a foxhole with old Adolph Hitler himself would have been a step up. But he was no longer in WWII. He was locked in a battle with mother. And there would never be an armistice. Never be a cease-fire.

Till the day he came back from the doctor and announced that X-Rays had shown a shadow on his lung. And you know what was the kicker? You want to know what really took the cake? He actually seemed relieved. Seemed peacefully pleased that the cancer, which would later be revealed with a biopsy, would take him to a place where he could find some peace. Because you see, when you've faced mother's tongue for a lifetime, cancer doesn't seem so bad.

Earl was gritting his teeth now, as was his habit at this point in the recollection. In the seat beside him, Carol was going over the many reasons she hoped someday to sell Tupperware. There were many reasons. Many.

As was his custom, he now allowed himself to envision the way his father should have handled the situation. Saw his father, strong and in control, rise from the easy chair and say to her, "Woman, you will shut your foul mouth." Of course it wouldn't work in real-life, and it never did in his fantasies either. But his father was a good man. And a good man always gave warning before acting. When his order was ignored he would give her the ultimatum: "You will shut your mouth or I will do you, me, and the world a favor, and shut it for you." Once again, his mother would refuse to shut up. And his father would act, because that was another thing a good man did: He always followed through on what he said.

This was Earl's favorite part. This was what made the whole thing worth it. It satisfied the hurt within him like morphine to a trauma victim. As his mother continued to spew her verbal bile, he saw his father rise and strike her across her foul, open mouth. Due to the shock of the blow she would, finally, gratefully, stop talking. Before she could gather herself and resume, his father would quickly seize her in a headlock and pull her to the kitchen. Once there, an uppercut to her chin would send her in a heap to the floor, in a semi-conscious state.

Decisive and forceful, as Earl had never seen his father act, the old man would remove a razor sharp knife from the kitchen drawer, and bend over her prostrate form, open her mouth with the left hand, and grasp her tongue between thumb and forefinger. And because his father was a good man, because a good man always followed through on what he said, his father would slice through the fat part of the offending member, and toss it into the garbage.

She never bled to death in these fantasies. Earl wanted her to live and suffer. Live, but live mute, please. Forever silenced. She would try to talk, of course. She didn't give up that easy, not that one. But it always came out like, "ArrrUhhhArrrr..." Then she would realize he had won, and that he was a good man because he had removed her infirmity, and set her back on the proper course to being a good wife. He would be Christ-like in her eyes. He had removed her iniquities and cleansed her. He saw her forever after being the dutiful wife, silent by his side. Maybe, occasionally, washing his father's feet. Showering his father's feet with her tears in gratitude. Perhaps even Earl could, in time, love her once again, when he was certain her tongue would not grow back.

Earl emerged from his vision just in time to hear Carol say, "And that's why I want to sell Tupperware. What do you think?"

"It sounds to me like you should sell Tupperware."

"You really think so?"

"Oh yes, I think you were born to do it."

She relaxed back with a flushed glow on her face, satisfied that she'd allowed him insight into her grandest dream.

"We're looking for County Road 147," Earl announced. A few minutes later the posted highway sign came into view and he turned down the road.

"Our house is at the end of the road. We don't have many neighbors." This fact seemed to please Earl, and presently they came to the end of the street, passing their only neighbor, who happened to live next door to the small, two bedroom white frame house Earl had rented for them.

Robby noticed an elderly black man meticulously raking his yard at the adjacent property. At his feet was a toy Pekinese, with a blue ribbon tied prettily atop its head.

"Humph," Earl let out, as if in disgust. "I didn't know we lived next door to spook. Might not have rented this place if I'd known that."

"Earl, be nice," Carol said.

"I am being nice. We just raised his property values by moving in."

"His place looks better than ours does," Robby said, looking admiringly at the neighbor's house and yard. "Looks like he works on it all the time."

"Probably because he draws a welfare check and that's all he has to do."

"Please, lets try to get along with our neighbor, Earl," Carol pleaded.

"Oh, we'll get along. As long as he don't get uppity."

With the furniture, appliances and boxes lugged in by the men, and Carol busy setting up her nest, Robby hurriedly put on his running shoes and kissed his mother on the way out the door.

"Don't get hit by a car," she called out, as he stepped out into the yard. Robby had been passionate about running even before Earl had come along. Now, his stepfather's presence caused him to enjoy it even more, since it was time spent out of the house, and away from him. No one would ever say of Robby Sinclair that he was a natural athlete. He had one trophy that he proudly displayed in his room: a third place finish in a local Punt, Pass and Kick competition. And that was with only four boys competing. But he had a determined affinity for distance running, and since taking it up some two years previous had built his regular routine up to 7 miles, five or six days a week. When he felt he deserved a treat, he would do a "ten'er."

He spent a few meditative minutes stretching in their large new yard, then stepped onto the road and set off on a slow, steady jog. He passed their only neighbor and waved, silently pleased when the man waved back and smiled. The Pekinese with the blue ribbon stopped her investigation of something interesting on the ground to watch him pass by.

He hit the highway and turned right, away from town and into fresh, unknown territory. As was the norm, the first mile was spent loosening and unlimbering muscles and joints. The ground here in their new home was flat, as opposed to the rolling countryside of Camden, but he still went through the typical peaks and valleys of physical exertion that were normally experienced on a run.

At the 2-mile point he ran into a "wall" of pain: a stitch cramping his side and an annoying ache in his shins. He knew enough of his own physiology to know these were "phantom" pains. His body was literally trying to convince him to stop. To punish him into surrendering. He also knew that the proper course of action was to ignore these bodily threats. To run *through* the pain. Once the body realized he was not submitting, the pains would vanish. And, just as always, somewhere around the 2 ½-mile distance, the pain was no longer there. It was a relief, but he knew it was merely a respite. There was another "wall" ahead, and it would be more intense. His body would attack with a second wave in a more desperate attempt to subdue him into walking or stopping.

At the 3 ½-mile point he became aware of intense heaviness in his legs, as if his shoes had turned to lead. As if he were running through mud, and a great mass of it was stuck to the soles of his feet. Though his pace had not changed since the beginning, he became aware of extreme oxygen debt. In the early days of his running this usually caused him to slow down, presuming he had reached the peak of his physical exertion. But he now knew this was an illusion, and he had much more to give. It was another lie submitted by his brain. A false signal being transmitted to make him stop. Again, he ignored it, and at the 4-mile point he noticed it had passed.

The sensation of passing beyond the discomfort was almost exhilarating. He had to fight the urge to sprint. He was able to calm himself and maintain pace, because he knew what was ahead: The great wall. An all-out propaganda campaign designed to make him cease what he was doing. It would be a singular point of agony. A place where every fiber of his being was screaming mercy! Where all the smaller "walls" merged, joined forces, into a moment of suffering, indescribable to anyone who had never experienced it. And he knew what was beyond this singular point. Some called it a "runner's high." Robby didn't like to use this term. He preferred to call it "transcending." Moving beyond, to another state of consciousness.

He had, at times, tried to describe the experience to others, without success. They usually came to the conclusion that he was masochistic: a person who seeks and enjoys pain. This was not the case. It was not the pain he was seeking. The pain was only the small price one had to pay to transcend. To reach a plateau most had never experienced. It was the price of the ticket. With the second wall behind him, he steadily ran towards the final hurdle.

Just as the previous two phases had come and gone ever so subtlety, such came the final test, the one that would take him to the place he reached for on every run. He was immersed into in without noticing where it began. Suddenly he was in the midst of it, like a cloud burst that comes out of a clear blue sky. All the pains added together, the shins, the side-stitch, the oxygen debt, plus another feeling that was beyond the physical pain: an overwhelming feeling that if he continued on he would surely die. In the early days of his running he would stop at this point, if not at the earlier ones. But he was familiar enough now with the phenomenon to run through it, even eagerly anticipated it, because he knew what lay beyond it. Rather than stop, he even picked up the pace just a bit.

Using a bit of mental imagery as a tool, he imagined himself to be not a man running, but a graceful animal, a gazelle, moving effortlessly, gliding over the ground. This placed him, to a degree, outside the pain. Then, at the 6-mile point, he moved beyond. Like a mist dissipating, he moved from agony to bliss. From suffering, to triumph. It was always difficult when he reached this place to contain himself; there was always the temptation to sprint, to go with the feeling to the edge of what his body could tolerate. But he knew, just as the great wall of pain was an illusion, so was the blissful aftermath. It would be very easy to pull a muscle, or at the very least, be so sore the next day that running would be impossible. So he withheld himself, content with continuing the steady pace that had been constant.

Planning the run so that he would circle back to the house at around 7 miles, he turned back onto the street where they had moved and used the final hundred yards to cool down. The man was still in his yard, this time on the far side. The Pekinese with the blue ribbon was laying on the porch with its head on its paws. Robby remembered at that point something his mom had promised: once they were moved, he could start looking for a dog of his own. He saw no reason why she could possibly refuse. They lived at the end of a road, a quarter mile from the main highway. They had a tremendous yard, which was fenced. But parents could always sniff out the negative. He told himself not to be too hopeful, just in case.

Thus, he was elated when he broached the subject over dinner and she offered no objections. Earl, however, offered his own opinions.

"Geez Carol, we just got settled in. Do we really need to do this now?"

"I don't see why not. We've got an acre of property here. Woods all around. This place screams for a dog. What do you have against it?"

The question sent Earl scrambling for an objection. He wasn't prepared to argue against a dog. He just didn't like not being asked.

"Well, it's another mouth to feed. Dog food is expensive."

"We always have scraps leftover. Besides, Robby wants a puppy. A baby won't eat much."

Earl pushed the food around on his plate. He could conjure no more reasons to dissuade her on short notice.

"You know, I just like being consulted on matters that are this important. A dog in our lives for 10, 12 years, that's a big investment."

"He won't be in our lives for 10 or 12 years. Robby will be out on his own by then. He'll take the dog with him when he decides to get a place of his own. Right honey?"

The thought of moving out on his own with a dog, away from Earl, brought an enthusiastic, "You bet."

"Not that I want you to move out," his mother said, covering his hand with her own, "I just know young men like to get out on their own. And I don't intend to be one of those clingy mothers who try to hold on to their children forever."

"I know, mom."

Earl felt the stab of jealousy that tightened his stomach whenever Carol and Robby displayed their closeness. He felt the need to change the subject, get the attention back his way.

"I think my business is really going to take off here. It may be slow at first, I'll have to work it up."

Carol rose from the table and returned with the classified section of the paper.

"You might try the nursing homes. They usually have a lot of shrubbery and things."

The thought of actually trimming bushes around a nursing home, or any business for that matter, almost made Earl wince. In truth, he had just harvested 45 pounds of medium grade marijuana from the woods of the county they had just moved from. He intended to subsist on this until the next planting season. And, thus was the real reason Earl Collins had been so insistent on moving his family to the new county 100 miles to the East.

The local Drug Task Force in their old home had been hot on trail for the past few years. He had barely escaped out of the woods this past season with his illicit harvest. He knew his time was running out in his old stomping grounds. In this new area, with nobody aware of who he was, or what he did, Earl had plans to turn Drew County into a sea of green. A patch in every pine forest. Things had got so bad back home he could hardly drive his pickup truck down the road without getting stopped and searched. Here, he could lay low, play the role of an industrious private landscape contractor. And possibly pull off the 200-pound harvest that he had so often dreamed of, but could never quite produce in a place where he had pissed off every local law enforcement agent, at one time or another.

Robby's eyes scanned the classified section, hitting the area where he hoped someone would have a dog looking for a home. He was almost ready to give up and turn to the sports section, when a small ad caught his eye.

"Look mom, here's one. It says, 'Mixed breed pups to good home. Mother is a boxer. Call 285-4310 after 5:00 PM.' Can I call, Mom?"

Carol looked towards Earl, but he knew the decision had already been made, and it tightened his stomach thinking she had called the shot.

"Sure, call and see, " he said.

"Thanks mom, thanks Earl."

"Now honey, don't get too excited. They may already be given away."

Robby ran to the phone, and minutes later came back with a breathless report that there were still puppies available.

"Can we go see them?" he asked, pleading.

"We'll go over there in the morning," she answered.

Robby spent a great deal of time that night laying sleepless in his bed, thinking of the puppy he'd been promised. He felt friendless in this new place, except for his mother, and parents somehow didn't count. A boy didn't normally go running with his mother, didn't spend hours playing fetch the stick with his mother, and, at 14, surely didn't have his mother to sleep in his room, at the foot of his bed, which he hoped his mom would allow the new dog. When sleep finally came he dreamed of running through the woods with a dog that, upon waking up, he could not quite visualize. He only remembered that they were the best of friends, and he felt fulfilled and safe in his company.

He was awake an hour before his mother and Earl, and finally impatiently woke them by stirring loudly outside their room. When they were awake, after Earl had consumed his ritual morning coffee and smoked a number of cigarettes down to the filter, they set off to find the address listed in the newspaper.

Doyle felt guilty about the lie he was about to tell, but his wife had insisted. He had hidden the bulk of the puppies inside the house, so that all that remained was the feisty pup that had so alarmed his wife. Thus, when Robby, Carol and Earl pulled into the driveway and entered the yard, all that was available to see was the single dog to be adopted.

"Sorry, this is the only one left," he said, not meeting their eyes.

"Is he healthy?" Carol asked. "He certainly looks like he is."

"Oh, he's healthy alright. There really wasn't a runt in the bunch, and this one sure didn't fit that bill."

"You can see the Boxer in him for sure," Earl diagnosed. "And something else. Maybe Pit Bull, from the size of his head. He's got a head like a softball."

Robby felt elated. Even Earl seemed to like the bright-eyed, squirming little pup. And Earl rarely liked anything. This was a done deal, and he knew it. Robby looked to his mother, and with a sigh she shook her head yes.

Robby took the pup from the man, making first contact with his new friend. My forever friend, he thought silently. We're gonna have more fun than you can stand.

"How much do we owe you for him?" Carol asked.

"Oh, nothing. Just give him a good home. If you get back in the neighborhood, and have him with you, bring him by for a visit. I'd like to see how he turns out when he's grown. I get attached to them quick. I have to get rid of them fast or I'll keep them all; have a dozen dogs running around and my wife will leave me."

"Thanks, we appreciate it very much. Robby, tell the man thank you," his mother commanded.

"Thanks Mr., I'll take the best care of him."

They moved towards the car, and the man approached, scratching his head in thought. He knew the puppy had been emotionally adopted. From the look on the boy's face a hundred strong men with crowbars couldn't prize the dog out of his arms. So he felt safe in divulging the one fact he knew for certain about the dog.

"One thing I can tell you about that little one, he's very aggressive. Doesn't cotton to other dogs invading his space. Do you have any other dogs?"

"No," Carol answered, with a slightly worried look on her face, "we'll be a one dog family."

"Well, that good. That's just fine. He's a good little dog. I can just tell he wants to be the king of the roost. In a one dog household, everybody will be happy."

"What about our neighbor's dog?" she asked Earl.

"Is it a female?" Doyle asked both adults.

"Yeah, I think it's female. One of them little yapping dogs. A Pekinese, I think," Earl volunteered.

"Oh, you'll have no problem since it's a female. Most male dogs won't get territorial with a bitch. They appreciate her company. She's not a threat. She's a potential date on a lonely night," Doyle said laughing.

Carol blushed at the thought.

"What are you going to name him, Robby?" His mother asked.

"We called him Buzz Saw, but naturally, you can name him whatever you want," Doyle said, smiling.

"Buzz Saw," Robby said, looking down at the puppy in his arms, who had stopped squirming and appeared ready to take a nap. "I like it. That's what his name is."

"How did you come up with a name like that?" Carol asked, as they moved towards the car.

Again, unconsciously, the man felt the need to avoid their eyes.

"We named him that because he's... real sharp...yeah, that's it."

"You hear that son, you got a real sharp puppy there," Carol said brightly.

"I can tell, mom, he's gonna be the best dog ever."

Chapter 3

THE TINY DOG LIVED in a world dominated by his sense of smell. The five tactile senses in man are, for the most part, evenly distributed. But a dog's nose is over a thousand times more developed than a human being. Thus, the primary means he has to relate to his world is through smell. Just as first impressions are important to people, so are they in animals. And physical scents are not the only things available. There is an emotional scent all living creatures possess, and though he appeared to be napping in Robby's arms in the back seat, he was busy cataloging the plethora of different smells he had suddenly been immersed in.

From the boy who held him, there was instant bonding, the sure fragrance and aura of love he had, so far, only felt at the teat of his mother. He felt as safe in Robby's arms as a tiny, helpless dog can feel.

From the one in the seat ahead, the one he could sense was female, he also felt love, though much less intense than from the one holding him. There was also uncertainty, and a perception of sadness coming across. These were not emotions he viewed analytically, or with understanding. He only knew them instinctly. They were there, and that was not to be understood or questioned. From the male who sat with the female came another emotional scent altogether. It was not a pleasant odor. In fact, had he not been tightly in the arms of the boy, he would have moved away from such a fragrance. Left the vicinity of it, and not returned. But he was safe where he was, and it did not concern him. Still, he would watch the male. Stay close to the boy until he better perceived the emotions he was picking up.

Robby convinced his mother that the best place for their newest member was in a padded box in his room. She allowed this with his assurances that he would dutifully keep the area free from all the messes a tiny puppy is sure to produce. When the excitement of having a dog of his own began to wane, he turned his mind more towards the anxiety he was feeling over what was looming ahead: the new school he would be attending in the morning.

Harmony Grove High School was the only school Robby had ever known. It was a small, homey place where everyone knew everyone else. He had his clique of friends and was comfortable in it. Monticello High School was, to him, as alien as the surface of the moon. He had envisioned all the worst-case scenarios. Perhaps no one would want to be his friend. It was entirely possible in his mind that, as a 10th grader, he would languish through three years of sitting alone in the cafeteria. Not have anyone to laugh with, dream with, and horror of horrors, go to three high school proms stag: stand alone against the wall with a dozen other nervous nerds, and not dance a single dance.

All these thoughts came to the forefront of his mind on the Monday morning he opened his eyes, knowing this was the day his mother would drop him off onto the precipice of utter doom. He dressed slowly, knowing when he was fully clothed it would be nearly time to get in the car and travel the 5 miles to the new school. Carol had to knock on his door twice and urge him to hurry.

"You don't want to be late on your first day."

No, he didn't want to be late. He wanted to be absent. Absent and back at the safety of Harmony Grove. He remembered the theme song from the old sitcom Cheers, *'...a place where everybody knows your name...'* That was his old school. The new one was a place where he knew no one. Talk about being the odd man out. Even the nerdiest-nerds probably had at least one friend. Which was one more than he had.

"Mom, I feel sick. Can I stay home today?"

His mother placed her hand on his forehead and quickly removed it. She knew when he was sick, as a mother does. And she knew when he was not.

"Robby, what's wrong?"

"I don't want to go to this new school. I hate it already"

"How can you hate it already. You haven't even been there a day."

"It's too big. There'll probably be gangs. I might get shot. Do you want me to get shot? They might even make me join a gang. Do you want that?"

"Well, at least you'll have friends," she said, then instantly regretted it.

"Look Robby, this is not south-central L.A. we're talking about. There's only about 500 more students here than at the Grove. I promise you that by the end of the week you'll be more comfortable. Today will be the worst day, then it's behind you."

"Come on, finish getting dressed."

She left the room and felt a tug of compassion for her son. It was a tremendous change for him. Still, life was full of change. Change produced growth. She had been through enough change, these past few years, to last a lifetime. I've had my fill of change, she thought. Had all the growing I want to do for a while.

Meeting Earl, and the way he seemed to take to Robby, had alleviated many of her fears that things would always be upside-down. But now he seemed to have backed off his early adoration of her son. Went from being the determined father figure, to one who merely tolerated the boys' presence. Earl's just adjusting to his new role, she had concluded. He doesn't want to crowd Robby. Try too hard to be a replacement for her son's natural father. Maybe Earl was wise to back off. Perhaps he knew better than she did. But still, why was he so into it in the beginning? She shook these thoughts off and hustled Robby out to the car to get him registered at Monticello High School.

He exited his mother's car with a kiss. She had wanted to go with him to the registration area, but he declined her invitation. Better to face this alone than be typecast by the other students, from day one, as a kid who never went anywhere without his mother. As he walked down the sidewalk, through crowd of gathered kids, he noted with relief that there didn't seem to be any real gangs. Just the normal groups one would expect, only here there were more of them. There were the normal casual stares as he moved past the masses, but they were more like friendly glances. Nothing you wouldn't expect when a new face pops up.

He walked past a group of giggling girls, most wearing too much makeup to compensate for first-day jitters. On the other side of the sidewalk was a group of large boys, each distinctive by the blue letter jackets they wore. On the front was an oversized "M", with smaller patches on the sleeves denoting information that couldn't be deciphered. Closer to the door was a group of students of mixed sex. They seemed attractive and clean-cut. Maybe band members, he thought. Over across the parking lot, under a large tree, were the longhairs. There was no deduction to be done here. That was the smoking section, where the smokers, jokers and troublemakers hung out. Wonder where I'll fit in, he wondered. Wonder if I'll fit in. Will it fit? Or be a round peg in a square hole. Stop, he admonished, you're freaking yourself out.

His transcript had been mailed by his old school, and registration took up only an hour. He was advised by the public address system that all students would be expected in the gym within the next few minutes for orientation and a pep rally. Not knowing where the gym was, he followed the masses down the long hallway, out a side door which passed under a short awning, and through the doors of a spacious gymnasium, which was filled by folding chairs from back to near front. The kids were filing into the rows. Some were jockeying to sit next to their friends. Being a stranger to everyone, he simply took the seat that presented itself, and found himself next to a large girl on his left, and a clean-cut black kid on his right.

A man, who introduced himself as the principal, mounted the makeshift stage and welcomed the students to the orientation. It was the usually spiel detailing new rules for the coming year: a warning that no-sagging would be enforced, students who drove to school should not speed in the parking lot, and students with a facial piercing should be prepared to bring a note from home giving them permission. This brought a chuckle from Robby.

He had never seen a facial piercing in all his years at Harmony Grove. A person who came to school with one would be considered a freak. It only brought home to him more that he was in a different place. How much more, he wasn't sure. Robby noticed that perhaps only half the students appeared to be listening to the principal. Some talked openly to the person next to them. Others appeared to be gazing around, anywhere but towards the microphone. Even the black kid next to him had pulled out a battered paperback book and was reading. Then the principal thanked them for their attention, which was practically nonexistent, and stated they would now begin the pep rally.

Instantly, the atmosphere changed. The kid beside him closed the book he was reading. All eyes were towards the front as a tall man with salt and pepper hair walked towards the microphone.

"Who's that?" Robby asked the boy beside him, his curiosity overcoming his lack of familiarity with the kid.

"You must be new here. That's coach Byrd," the kid whispered, then went back to staring towards the front, mesmerized, as everyone else seemed to be.

"I want to welcome you to the pep rally. As you know, we did not have a successful season last year. With your support, we intend to do better. We finished 6 and 4. We can do better than that, and I promise you, we will."

Robby was confused. At Harmony Grove 6 and 4 would have been considered a good year. The coach was talking as if they went 0 and 10.

"As we do every year, we will begin with an introduction of our senior class. These are the guys who will carry our hopes on their shoulders every Friday night, so give them the respect they deserve."

The coach began calling out names, which Robby had, of course, never heard. One by one they mounted the stage behind the coach. They all wore the distinctive blue jackets with the oversized "M" on the left breast. With each name called, the student body broke out in jubilant applause. That these students were held in particular regard was evident. Robby had the impression they were seen as the elite. Almost god-like.

When the final name was announced, the coach deferred to one player standing behind him.

"Now, our team captain, and starting tailback, John L. Wilson, would like to say a few words to you."

Again, there was enormous applause as the large, muscular senior stepped to the microphone. Then, dead silence as he began speaking.

"What coach Byrd said was true. We won 6. But we also lost 4. We lost to Warren."

He paused, as if that statement had caught in his throat.

"That won't happen again."

There was a smattering of applause at this remark, then dead silence again.

"Our best season ever begins, not on Friday night, but right now. Are you ready for the best season ever?"

The crowd roared its approval, then again fell silent.

"Then lets do this thing."

It was, to Robby, as if a dam had burst. As if the whole place had gone mad on cue. A drummer, heretofore unseen, began making rhythm on a large base-percussion, and the gymnasium went from silence to delirium. The cheerleaders, both male and female, something unknown at his former school, ran to the front of the group and further whipped the students to a frenzy. Some were jumping up and down. Others were swaying back and forth as if in a trance. The atmosphere was infectious, and he was surprised to find himself clapping and bouncing. What am I doing, he thought. He looked to his immediate right and saw the black kid with the book screaming at every cue from the cheerleaders. He remembered watching a film of a religious service where people were falling out and thrashing madly. That's what this is like, he concluded.

This continued for 20 minutes, at which time a large, mounted paper machete owl was pushed to the front. Then the cheerleaders began calling, "Who we gonna beat?" "McGhee!!" screamed the students. "What we gonna do?" "Kill'em!!" They cried, over and over, until a mascot in a ram costume ran in from the wings with a blue painted Louisville Slugger. The rally exploded into bedlam as the mascot decapitated the paper owl with a vicious swing, then pummeled the body to a pulp. This must be what it was like at the coliseum in Rome, Robby decided, when the lion ate the Christian, or the gladiator cut the head off the slave. Raw, primitive abandon.

When it was over, he felt emotionally spent, even though his participation had been limited.

He was quiet on the way home, till his mother could stand it no longer and asked him, "Well honey, what do you think?"

"I think those people are crazy," he answered.

She looked over to see him smiling and was temporarily confused. These kids had a language all their own. "Tight" meant good, as did "phat." Even "bad" meant "good", as Michael Jackson had declared. She could not keep up with the variations of slang, and was often in need clarification, though she was usually reluctant to ask. Maybe "crazy" was good, she hoped.

"So...crazy. Is that good, or bad?" she asked cautiously.

He appeared to be thinking it over, then smiled, and said, "I think its good...I think."

***

Coach Don Byrd sat in his office after the pep rally, looking at the depth chart, which he had already gone over innumerable times. As if looking would change it, somehow. Looking for a ray of hope, something he had earlier missed which would brighten his outlook. He did not see it, because it was not there. This was basically the same team that had gone barely over five hundred. That would not do here. Would never do here. This town was spoiled from the success of the nineties, when the Monticello Rams had won eight district championships in ten years. Two of those eight championships had resulted in state championships. Quite a few former players from those glory years had gone on to success at the University of Arkansas and other colleges. One or two had even made it to the NFL.

He was a graduate assistant at Louisiana State University during that time. A rarity, he was a coach who had elected not to play college ball, but concentrate on coaching instead. He'd had the opportunity to go to another college and coach at the assistant level after he got his Master's. But this was his alma mater. The place he'd grown up. When the head coaching vacancy became available, he didn't even have to think about it. His wife had grown up here too, so it was a dream come true for both of them. A continuation of their adolescent years, but in a leadership role. A chance to continue what the former coach had started. The man had created a monster. Now it demanded to be fed.

And the first few years he had fed it. Stepping into the coach's shoes, picking up where he had left off, he managed an 8 and 2 season with a tie for the District title. Then a 9 and 1 campaign, with a team that went deep into the Championship tournament, losing in the semi-finals. They were rolling, and he was loved. The toast of the town. The monster was fed. And, most important of all, they had managed back-to-back wins over rival Warren. This alone was enough to make people he'd never met stop him on the street and shake his hand.

The monster's favorite food of all was a resounding victory over the Warren Lumberjacks. Even a four-loss season could be forgiven, if one didn't lose to Warren. But lose to the town thirty miles to the west, and the monster became very irritable. Lose to Warren and go five hundred, people would cross the street to avoid your shadow. There would be anonymous calls, at all hours of the night. Your children would come home from school crying, with tales of bullies who declared that their father was going to be run out of town. Tarred and feathered. He knew this was barely an exaggeration. He had experience it all the past season.

Towards the end, when it took a miracle to come out on top in the final game of the year, and salvage a 6 and 4 record, his family was showing the signs of the strain. He had noticed dark circles under his wife's eyes from worry. They were snapping at each other over trivial things. It was a blessed relief when the season ended, and this was not how it should be: he loved coaching. Could not imagine anything else he would like to do. He knew, if things continued, he would eventually be let go. Or, even worse, relegated to a "teaching only" position; a washed-up coach, spending his adult years teaching physical education students how to dodge a ball, or climb a rope.

No, he would never settle for that. They would have to leave, find a new coaching position. Which he could do with little problem. But his parents lived here, as did his wife's. This was his town, damn it. The place he'd grown up. The place he'd courted, and married, his high school sweetheart. Got his first kiss. Caught his first fish. It all happened here. But if you didn't win…the monster became angry. And eventually, you'd be eaten.

Through it all, his faith was a raft that kept him afloat. On the wall, behind his desk, was a plaque with a well-memorized scripture, Romans 8:28. But, during times such as these, he often felt the need to read it directly from the book. To drink from the spring that nourished him spiritually. He opened the well worn Bible, with its edges dark-stained from years of page turning, and read, 'And we know that all things work together for good to them that love God, to them who are called according to his purpose.' An ironclad promise, from a Father he knew could not lie. It was enough to enable him to look past the depth chart, past the schedule that loomed ahead. With his heart assured, he began making preparations for that afternoons practice.

Chapter 4

ROBBY SETTLED INTO SCHOOL much more quickly than
he had feared. Academically, Monticello was easier than
Harmony Grove, and he found himself ahead of the other
students in most of his classes. The kid who had sat
beside him at the pep rally became someone he enjoyed
sitting with at lunch, and he was pleasantly pleased to find
relations between the races to be even more relaxed than
they'd been at the Grove. Monticello was a school where
everyone shared a common passion, and that passion was
football.

Thus the mood of the entire school was subdued on
the Monday following the first game of the season. The
paper owl, which the student body assaulted during the
pep rally, proved to be much easier to handle than the one
the team ran into at McGhee. The team was 0 and 1, and
at the school, a black mood had settled over the students
and faculty.

But Robby was elated and relieved to be fitting in.
His routine became one of waking up to the bright-eyed
puppy at the foot of his bed, doing a full day at school, then

rushing home to check back in on Buzz Saw, and getting in his daily run. Then it was time for dinner, homework and time for bed.

Robby found every time began one of his runs his neighbor was in the yard and he would inevitably wave. Then, when he returned, the man would still be there, working on one task or another. No wonder his yard looked straight out of Better Home and Gardens. It felt odd, and unneighborly, not to speak, so at the end of a particularly vigorous outing, Robby strode across the manicured lawn and extended his hand to him.

The man turned to face him, and Robby was surprised to find him older than was his initial impression. From a distance he had assumed the man was in his late fifties, but up close, it was apparent that seventy was a better guess. The way the man worked all day had led him to a false assumption. But when Robby took the hand that was offered, he found the man's grip was strong. He had clear, brown eyes that sparkled when he smiled, and a humble manner that made you feel as if he was intensely interested in everything you had to say. Robby liked him immediately.

"I wanted to come introduce myself before you got the idea that I wasn't friendly, or something."

"Now why would I think something like that?" the man asked.

"Have you met my stepfather yet?" Robby answered, cautiously.

"You mean the fellow with pickup truck, rebel flag license plate on the front," he said, laughing.

"Yeah, that's Earl. He's kinda primitive."

"I understand. Some people just refuse to come along with everyone else, into the twenty-first century. They're still hanging on to things way in the past. Not just white folks either, lot of my people, too. Foolishness doesn't have a color."

"You sure do a lot of yard work."

"I'm retired. This is all I have to do. All I really want to do. This, and take care of Colleen. That's my wife. She's not feeling too well today, or I'd let you meet her."

At the mention of his wife, the man glanced back towards the house and saw, as he somehow knew he would, his wife peeking out the front curtain. The curtain moved slightly as she withdrew, but moments later parted again.

"This place is my Eden. We bought it with money from my retirement account. I used to work at an auto plant in Detroit. Ever been to Detroit?"

"No way. Monticello is the biggest town I've ever lived in," Robby answered, wide-eyed, before realizing he didn't know the man's name, and hadn't given his own.

"My name's Robby."

"My name is Fred Scott. You can call me by either one."

"Okay, Mr. Scott," said Robby, and they shook hands once again.

"Somehow I knew you'd choose that. Know how?"

"How?" Robby asked. "Are you psychotic?"

This made the man double over in a fit of laughter, and when he regained his breath said, "You mean psychic. Now, sometime my wife accuses me of being psychotic, but really I'm neither. I just knew a polite boy like you would call someone as old as me Mr."

"I don't think someone who is old could work in the yard like you do."

"Well, it's not really work if you love it. I'm just playing out here. If you look at my drivers license you might be shocked, but I don't consider myself old either. I'm somewhere around seventy going on forty."

This statement made Robby crease his brow, so the man said, "Age is just a number, and all that crap. After all, if you didn't know how old you were, how old would you be?"

"Uh, I don't know"

"If you didn't have a drivers license, or a birth certificate to tell you what your age was, you would only be as old as you felt. I feel about forty. Actually I feel younger than that, but I don't want you to think I'm a fool, or a liar," he said, with a smile.

"Oh, I don't think you're a liar. Mom says you can tell when a person is lying because they blink a lot and won't look you in the eye."

"Well, I'll try to remember that if I get a speck in my eye."

"And I don't think you're a fool, either."

"I appreciate that."

"What's your dog's name?" Robby asked.

At the mention of the Pekinese, the man's eyes brightened, and he looked around for the little dog. He found her lying on the porch, and again noticed his wife peeking out the front curtain. This time she did not bother to move back, but only continued to stare.

"That's my baby, Lu-Lu. Come here baby."

The small, brown dog jumped off the porch and was lifted into the man's arms, her ever-present blue ribbon tied prettily atop her head. To Robby, it appeared as if she had kissed the front end of a moving truck. With her smashed in nose and outrageously crooked teeth, the expression "so ugly, she's beautiful," was never more appropriate.

"I just got a little dog. His name is Buzz Saw. I'll bring him over sometime. He's just a puppy."

"Lu-Lu will love that. She never met a puppy she didn't love. I think its because we had her fixed before she ever had any pups. She'll probably adopt your baby as her own."

"Well, Mr. Scott, I gotta go do my homework. It was real good to meet you."

"I enjoyed talking with you. We'll have you over for dinner sometime. Your mother and stepfather too, if they want to come."

He could see Robby was thinking that over. Probably knew his stepfather wouldn't come. Trying to find an out for him, without embarrassing himself.

"Or, you can just come by yourself, if you want. My wife cooks better than I do yard work, if you can believe that."

"Okay, Mr. Scott. Thanks. I'll talk to you later."

Mr. Scott watched Robby run to his house, and disappear inside. He placed the rake against the corner of the house and went inside. As he stepped through the door he saw his wife standing in the center of the living room, crying softly. It so alarmed him that he rushed to her side, saying, "Colleen, what is it? Tell me!"

It was several minutes before she composed herself enough to speak to him. A dozen terrible things went through his mind during this time. Had she had a stroke?

Had something happened to one of their kids? One of the grandkids, perhaps?

"Do you remember the vision I had the other night?" she finally said, through sniffles.

"You mean the dream?"

"Fred Scott, I've been on this earth for sixty-six years. Don't you think I know the difference between a dream and a vision? I have dreams almost every night. A couple times in my life, I've had visions. There's no mistaking the two, I'm telling you."

He remembered the night in question, when she had woke him up shouting, "Hurry. Hurry up. Don't let nothing stop you."

He had assumed she was only having a nightmare, something she had rarely had in their entire forty-six years of marriage. But she had insisted it wasn't merely a nightmare. A vision, she called it. Something about a boy and his mother. And there was a man with them. Only he wasn't man. He only looked like one, because he was wearing a mask. And as she watched, he slowly began pulling off the false face...and something terrible was under it...only she couldn't see what it was...only knew it was terrible...because it had been hidden for a reason. And there was something else. Something... coming to help. An angel was leading it. It had the heart of a lion. But it was so small, and far away. And the thing behind the mask was right there, large and looming. The small thing that was coming would never make it in time. The devil had put so many obstacles in its way. When he finally got her calmed down, and she related the vision to him, she had gone into her prayer closet and stayed until dawn. But the next day, she seemed okay.

Now, she was in a fit again, and he was concerned. What if she was sick? What if this was dementia, or the early stages of Alzheimer's? If he lost her, he'd just as soon go ahead and go home to Jesus. And to lose her in mind and spirit, but have her here physically…well, that might be even worse.

"I don't understand. What's got you riled up now? Tell me what's wrong and I'll fix it."

"The boy in the vision…is the one you were just talking to in the yard."

***

Earl had been watching Robby talk to Mr. Scott, and it disturbed him. He was not one that approved of close relations between different races. He moved away from the window when Robby approached the house, not wanting to be accused of spying.

"I see you met our neighbor."

"Yeah, he's a nice man."

"Robby, I don't know if your real father ever sat you down and explained the way things work in the world. I can assume he didn't, from what I'm seeing. Your mother tells me you got yourself a best friend at school that's a… that's black."

"Uh huh, his name is Anthony."

"And now I see you chumming up with our black neighbor. Now, I don't want to jump to conclusions, but…"

Robby knew from experience that when a person followed a sentence with a "but," it usually meant he was going to do just the opposite of what he had just said he wasn't.

"…but it appears to me that maybe you prefer hanging out with…people that…aren't like us."

He didn't want to get into a scrap with Earl, especially while his mother was out, but this stuck in his craw, and he found he couldn't hold his tongue.

"What do you mean, aren't like us? Maybe they aren't like you."

"What the hell does that suppose to mean?"

"They're civilized. They're decent. They work for a living."

He regretted it the minute he said it.

"I work for a living…what did you tell that old man?" Earl asked suspiciously.

"What could I tell him? I don't know anything. You work for a living, remember?"

Robby felt a stab of fear tighten his stomach as Earl continued to stare at him with narrowed eyes.

"Look boy, there are things about this world you don't understand. Won't ever understand if you keep hanging around those people. I do some things to put food on the table, things which the sheriff is better off not knowing. So what? At least I'm not drawing a welfare check, like those friends of yours."

Robby rolled his eyes.

"Mr. Scott retired from a auto plant in Detroit. He worked hard his whole life. Now he works hard to keep his yard perfect. What's wrong with that?"

"Oh, nothing. Nothing at all. But he don't need to know nothing about what I do. You hear me?"

"I don't even know what you do. And I don't want to know."

"That's okay. You're too young anyway. Too young to know what its like to work forty-hours a week and make barely enough to give it away to the tax man, and the landlord, and every other bloodsucking leech that preys on the working man."

What a hoot, thought Robby. Earl had probably never worked a forty-hour week. Not in a place with a time clock. But he held his tongue. He knew he wouldn't be the one to enlighten Earl over anything.

"I'm gonna discuss this with your mother, son. We're not through with this yet."

"I'm not your son," he said under his breath, going to his room to do his homework and check on his puppy, glad he had a room with a door that he could retire to.

Chapter 5

CAROL CAME THROUGH THE door happy, with an armload of second-hand treasures she had rescued from three garage sales she'd located on her circular route around the county. She found Earl sitting in the living room, looking as if someone had pissed in his Cheerios. His eyes were extremely red, and she knew he'd just recently been out back smoking. She knew full well he had a marijuana habit. He'd tried any number of times to get her to partake with him, saying it would enhance their sex lives, give her a new appreciation of music, and cure any glaucoma that would dare affect her vision, but she'd always begged off. Perhaps it was harmless. But it wouldn't be harmless to Robby. She had enough bad habits, thank you very much. She would stick to her tobacco cigarettes, and hoped to quit that someday, if she ever found the strength.

"Hi, hon. How was your day? Look what I found? Do you think this will fit you? It only cost a quarter!"

"We need to talk."

"What about?" She asked. Weed usually made him happy. Cured all that ailed him. That was one reason she never objected to him smoking outside the house. She had to admit, it made him easier to live with. But he wasn't happy now, and she vaguely dreaded having to deal with whatever problem he was bringing to her.

"Your son was talking to the neighbor."

When Earl was pleased with Robby he always said, "Our boy." When he was irritated it was, "Your son." Earl obviously had a bone to pick.

"I tried to have a talk with him about things. You know, about perceptions and such. I don't know if you've noticed, but a change has come over him."

"Oh, what kind of change?" She asked, guardedly.

"Back home he had good friends, hung out with his own kind. Since we moved here he's become sort of... liberal."

His choice of words made her smile, and she felt the need to turn away to so Earl wouldn't think she was laughing at him. He was obviously taking this seriously.

"Liberal? You sound like you're worried over Robby's political affiliation."

"It's not politics I'm worried about. He has a black best friend at school. He's talking to our neighbor who, if you haven't noticed, is of the African American persuasion."

"I'm not blind, Earl."

"I know you're not blind to his color. But you may be blind to the way things work. The way kids can get stereotyped. If he's always hanging around blacks, the white kids will label him. They won't have anything to do with him. Then he'll be stuck."

"I know my son. This really doesn't concern me one bit."

"Well, tell me this: what do you do the day he brings one home. A female. And they're sitting here on the couch kissing in front of God and everybody. What will you do then?"

Her gourd was rising. She didn't like to fight with Earl. Was, frankly, a little frightened of him. But this mindless prejudice was so ugly. Like something straight off the Jerry Springer Show. It emboldened her to say what had to be said. To remain silent was to have him think she agreed with this garbage, and that was unthinkable.

"I'll tell you what I'll do: on the day when Robby brings home a black girl, who I'm sure will be lovely, inside and out, because that's the only kind of girl my son would attract, I'll love her and make her feel welcome."

"And I'm suppose to sit here and go along with this, approve of it?"

"No, you don't have to approve it. You don't even have to watch it. If it comes to that you can leave…or I will."

"I pay the rent here. I'm damn sure not leaving."

"Yeah, with your landscape contracting money," she said, sarcastically.

She'd done it now. The subject was broached. She had always suspected, even more than suspected, that Earls livelihood was not entirely produced through legitimate means. The fact that he refused to file any tax returns was one thing. And the vagueness he had in discussing which projects he had in the works. But she'd turned a blind eye to it. I've never seen anything, she reasoned. Not guilty, by voluntary ignorance. Still, there was occasionally a tiny tinge of guilt when she paid for groceries, or shopped for clothes. Where did this hundred-dollar bill come from, she would wonder?

"You sure don't mind spending it. If I didn't grow dope we wouldn't be living high on the hog."

Now the cat was out of the bag. She could no longer plead stupidity. The word "dope" made her feel dirty. She became aware of Robby in the next room. She dearly hoped he was not listening.

"I'd rather live in a shack off honest money. You don't have any of that stuff in this house do you?"

"Of course not, what do you think I am, stupid?"

You'll never be a brain surgeon Earl Collins, she thought, but let it remain a silent opinion.

"I just don't want Robby involved with the police. This is our house, not a stash spot for your…stuff."

"The police won't be coming here. Unless Robby tells that old man next door what's up!"

"Why would he do that?"

"Kids talk. They trust people. Especially sly ones like that old man."

"My God, Earl, you don't even know the our neighbor."

"I know his kind! They want nothing more than to see a white man go down. They think its payback for slavery, or something," Earl said, rising from his chair and walking around the room, gesturing wildly.

"I won't tell Robby who he can talk to, or date," she said, and sucked up her courage to say what had to be said next: "And I won't let you do it, either."

"You won't *let* me?" he said incredulously. A hundred images from his childhood reared in his mind like a hissing cobra. A small woman, with a big mouth. Getting bolder by the day. Questioning what he did for a living. Questioning his authority. Little by little. Until the day when she decided he was weak. Then she would go for the jugular. Totally emasculate him. Turn him into his father. He was tempted, almost beyond his ability to hold back, to strike her in the face. A scene flashed across his mind: he saw himself cocking back his right hand and smashing her in the center of her face, driving her nose and bone fragments into her brain. He emerged from this scene to find himself clenching, and opening his right hand.

"Woman, it'll be a cold day in hell before you have the power to *let* me do anything."

Before she had time to respond to this he was out the door and into his pickup truck, spinning his tire's backing out of the driveway, and speeding down the road.

Fred Scott saw Earl tear down the road at full throttle, and instinctively looked around for Lu-Lu.

"You stay out of the road, girl. That boy drives like he has a devil in him."

He was not surprised to see that Earl didn't wave on the way past his house.

***

Need some air, Earl decided. Take a good long drive. He was out on the road, heading towards their former home before he realized which direction he was heading.

May as well go pick up that smoke stashed behind the old house. Down to my last five hundred dollars. Move it somewhere closer, so I can get to it. Don't like to keep the customers waiting. He pulled a pre-rolled joint from the cigarette pack in which it was tucked, and slapped a cassette into the tape deck. Earl had not bothered upgrading to CD's. Most all the music he enjoyed was 80's and 90's, and he had a large collection of these tapes in a case he carried with him in the truck. A/C D/C was his choice on this occasion.

"...no stop signs..."

He struck his lighter and moved the fire towards the end of the large, round joint, took a drag and held the smoke as long as could, blowing out a blue cloud into the cab of the truck.

"...speed limits..."

I'm not gonna let her get me down, he decided. Her or the brat. I've got forty pounds of good smoke stashed in the woods. Thousand dollars a pound. Forty thousand dollars. More than most of these local yokels make working their asses off at a regular job.

"...nobody gonna hold me down.."

And I'm set up to grow even more in my new stomping ground. Just gotta get the seeds out of these pounds, so I can fill these hills with my green babies. Johnny Appleseed can't hold a candle to me when it comes to propagation.

He was feeling the first effects of the buzz washing over his consciousness. Starting to get happy, again. Amazing what a good joint could do...and forty pounds waiting in the woods.

"...hey, hey moma, look at me..."

I ought to take this smoke and stash it under that bitch's bed, he thought, and the image made him giggle, choking out the hit he'd just taken. Talk about a nest egg. Maybe stash it in the kid's room. Then call the law, and tell 'em, "Officer, I think my stepson is smoking a little marijuana. Sure, you can check his room; of course you don't need a warrant. We support our local police efforts to stamp out drugs. Just say no. That's what Nancy Reagan said do, and Officer, we intend to do it!"

Of course, Carol would tell 'em to search the room. "Oh, my boy would never do drugs, Officer," Earl imitated, in a falsetto voice. "He's a good boy! Search all you want."

"What's this leafy green substance under the bed, Ms. Collins? Holy jumpin' Jesus on a pogo stick! It looks like felony possession of a controlled substance!"

He imagined the officer pulling his service revolver and Carol fainting dead away. He was laughing so hard now he couldn't take a toke off his joint. Banging the steering wheel with the butt of his hand, causing the horn to blow. And he pulls the officer off to the side and tells him, "I don't know where he got it sir, but him and his mother go off behind the house all the time with shovels and fertilizer. You don't you think they may be growing the stuff back there, do you? Geez, I hope not. I hate drugs!"

And, of course, he would have 2 or 3 bushy plants waiting back there for the cops to find. Now its cultivation of a controlled substance. With intent to distribute. With intent to do hard time at the local state institution.

"Good bye Robby! Don't drop the soap. Good bye Carol. Hope your roommate isn't a diesel dyke named Mabel, who wants to stay up late and braid your hair!"

"...I'm on my way to the promised land..."

Of course, I wouldn't waste forty pounds on that little loser, or his square-assed mother, he concluded. But boy, wouldn't it be a hoot? That would show 'em. He flicked the small roach out the window, after sucking on it till it almost burned his fingers. I don't even know why I married her, he thought.

But Earl knew the reason he had went ahead and tied the knot with Carol. Though Earl wasn't a man blessed with remarkable self-insight, even he could come to grips with the reason he had shucked away thirty-three years of bachelorhood. He knew his inner desire was to do right what his old man had done wrong. Be the man his father never could be. And he would be that man, come hell or high water. If she gets out of line, I'll slap her back in line. "What if she gets mouthy?" a harsh voice in his head, said. You have to nip that in the bud, he thought back. Don't even tolerate that for a minute. You give them an inch, they'll take ten thousand miles.

"...I'm on a highway to hell..."

Angus Young was making the guitar scream bloody murder, and the voice came back again, harsher and questioning, "What if it doesn't work?" I'm not my father, he returned. I'm not a chip off-the-old block. He taught me. If he did nothing else, he taught me how *not* to handle it. You do what you have to do, whatever it is. It's up to her to decide what level it goes to. You tell her the consequences, and you do what you say, because that's what a good man does. He does what he says. And he follows through.

"...highway to hell..."

"What if you *are* just like your father?" said the voice.

"I'm not, I'm not and I never will be, so help me God. I'll shut her up if it's the last thing I do," he shouted, banging the steering wheel again, this time in a rage.

"...highway to hell..."

"You'll see," he said, "I'll get her right."

He pulled into the driveway of the still deserted house, checked to see that no other cars were coming down the highway, then grabbed a shovel from the back of the truck and crossed to the back of the property where he entered the woods. There was a trail he had worn getting to his stash spot. Going in about a hundred yards, he cut off the trail and headed straight for a lightning-shattered pine that easily marked the spot. Buried treasured, he thought. It always made him feel like a pirate to pick up a stash. Money in the bank. He got to the foot of the tree and saw the leaves had been disturbed. Greatly concerned, he quickly concluded that an animal must have been digging in the leaves, and this settled his mind. Couldn't get into the ice chest, no problem. The ice chest had been buried shallow, with only a couple of inches of soil covering the top. No need to bury it deep, Earl had reasoned, no one but me knows its here.

It only took a thrust of the shovel into the spot for Earl to know something was terribly wrong, but he continued to dig down, as if it might have sunk. When he reached three feet down into the dirt, he began frantically looking around. Did I bury it here? I know I buried it here. His mind was spinning. Somebody stole my stash!

Anyone within a half-mile of the area would have, at that point, heard the bloodcurdling scream of a man whose fortunes had just taken flight. He turned round and round in the spot, until he was forced to conclude that it was gone. Someone had dug it up. Who could it have been? Robby? No, the kid didn't have sense enough to be a thief. Only one name kept coming to mind: Dale. The guy he used as a middleman.

He'd never shown Dale where the stash spot was. But Dale knew he had just harvested all his smoke from the woods. He might have guessed it was hidden near the house. May have come snooping around after Earl had moved, and saw the trail. Dale was an idiot, as most of his cohorts were. But even an idiot can find something if he has enough time to look. Earl ran to the pickup truck and drove quickly to the trailer where Dale lived. When he arrived he didn't even have to get out to see that it was vacant. Dale was gone, and so was his income for the year.

***

He drove around Camden in the blackest of moods, hoping against hope he would see Dale. He knew that was unlikely. Forty thousand dollars can make a man hide very well. He prayed, to whatever god might be listening, that the son of a bitch would get busted with it. And let me read about it in the paper. In Jesus name. Amen.

His buzz had gone south the moment he realized he'd been heisted, so he pulled over to roll another joint. I've got about five more joints to my name, he concluded, looking at the bag of stems and seeds in his lap. Just a few minutes ago I had enough to last all year. Or so I thought.

Think Earl, he urged himself. Gotta come up with a plan. Could go to work, he briefly considered. This thought did not strike him as one that deserved a great deal of serious consideration. He had two problems: one that affected his immediate future, and another that would come into play later.

The first was the lack of any viable income. He had enough money in his pocket to pay their rent, and just enough at that. It would be especially hard, after his fight with Carol, to go home and tell her that they were in financial straights. He would have to swallow his pride. He'd almost rather swallow a liter of poison than do that. The second problem was that his seeds were gone, and this would prohibit him from putting in another crop. It seemed his days as a drug entrepreneur were behind him. Then, as his joint was burning down to the half-way mark, he had an idea.

He had a friend, more like an acquaintance, named Danny. Danny was a biker who sold a lot of weed. They had never done any dealing because Earl produced his own crop. But he was familiar enough with him to go by his house. They had smoked together at a couple of biker parties. Danny knew he wasn't a snitch. Maybe Danny would front him a couple of pounds. He could scarf out the seed, sell the smoke for profit, pay Danny back, then do it again. He wouldn't make near the money he would off his own homegrown, but it would be an immediate solution. And he wouldn't have to go home to Carol with his tail between his legs, and the classified section of the papers in his hands. And he could build up his seed bank. It might work. All Danny could do was turn him down. Minutes later he was pulling up outside the frame house.

The place was a wreck. Looked like it hadn't been mowed for several seasons. Towards the back of the property sat a large, old shed. Earl saw someone step outside the shed door as his car came to a halt, then quickly, furtively reenter, as if he didn't want to be seen. There was a trash barrel burning to one side of the shed, and from inside his car he could smell acrid smoke, and something else he couldn't quite place. The only redeeming feature of the place was the gleaming Harley Davidson motorcycle, which sat square in front of the doorway to the house. That's the only thing he bothers to keep clean, Earl decided. He would never do this if he weren't so desperate. But he was willing to be a dope to extricate himself out of this mess. That's why they call it dope, he mused; it makes you do stupid things. Still, all Danny could do was say no, or so he thought, until he knocked on the door.

At the point his knuckle completed its third rap, the door swung open and he was looking into the barrel of the world's largest handgun, or so it seemed from his perspective. The open end of the weapon looked as big as any Civil War cannon. It was shaking slightly in the hand of its possessor, which Earl managed to look away from long enough to identify as Danny. He looked the same. Except for his eyes, which were large, round and angry. Despite the bulge of his eyes, his pupils looked fully dilated, maybe because the inner part of the house was so dark.

"What do you want?" Danny growled.

"Hold up, don't shoot. I'm here on business."

This obviously did nothing to calm his soul, because although he backed into the house, allowing Earl the opportunity to enter, the gun never left its position, which was pointed squarely between his eyes.

"Business, huh? Okay, get out of 'em."

"What?" Earl stammered.

"I'm gonna give you thirty seconds to show me everything you came into the world with, or I'll kill 'ya."

"Easy. Easy," said Earl, but he was already stripping down to his birthday suit, and well before the time limit was reached, he stood naked before Danny. A scene from the movie Deliverance flashed through his mind: some hillbilly telling Ned Beatty, "You sure got a pretty mouth, can you squeal like a pig?" He was pretty sure he *could* squeal like a pig, if Danny applied any pressure to that trigger. Yep, this day had sure gone to shit.

Danny seemed to be hesitating, considering something. Then he said, "Give me that wrist watch."

"I can get you one at Wal-Mart for $9.95," Earl offered, but handed the cheap, digital timepiece over to the man, without hesitation.

Danny took it and looked it over as if it might be evil, then he slowly handed it back. At this point a rail thin woman, who looked as if she'd been avoiding the sun for several years, came out of the bedroom. I'm in a nest of vampires, Earl thought, noticing that all the windows were covered with aluminum foil. His eyes were growing accustomed to the almost non-existent light, the sole source of which was a lava lamp sitting on a table, globules rising and falling slowly. Probably been there since the 70's, he concluded. The inside of the house seemed even more disordered and unkept than the yard.

"Danny, when you get through having fun, I need you to help me find my U-100's" she said, and Earl wished he was anywhere but here, standing in the dim light, with a ten dollar Wal-Mart watch in his hand, butt-naked, waiting to find out what was on Danny's mind.

"I don't keep up with your needles, Charlene," Danny answered wearily, then turned his attention back to Earl.

"What do you want?" Danny asked for the second time.

"Well, I'd really like to put my clothes on. Please."

"Oh, yeah. Sure go ahead."

The vampiress named Charlene turned around in a huff and went back into the bedroom to search for her long lost syringes, as Earl redressed as quickly as he could ever remember.

"Sorry," said Danny, "you've never been by before. I thought you might be wearing a wire. Snitches are off the hook in this county. But, you know that."

Earl was beginning to feel better. His ass was covered with fabric again and Danny was engaging him in dialogue. Things had improved over the past two minutes.

Danny lit a cigarette and the flame from the lighter sparkled in his large, round eyes. They looked as if they might fall out of his head, if he opened them any wider.

"You shouldn't come by without calling. It freaks out my sensibilities."

"I'm desperate. Look, somebody made off with my stash. I'm busted." The second he said the word "busted", he regretted it, but Danny didn't seem to notice, so he continued.

"I need a front. A pound or two. I'll come pay you, then get another. I need to do business until next September, when I can get back on my feet with my own harvest. I'm really whacked. I don't even have a seed stock. If you can't help me I might have to go find a job."

"Whoa, hold up with the language. J-O-B is a dirty word around here. Go wash your mouth out with soap, you filthy boy," Danny said, laughing, revealing a mouth full of rotted teeth. The eyes looked amused, but the face remained tight and strained.

"Seriously, I don't have any smoke. I don't even have a joint in the house," Danny continued.

"Come on, Danny. I'm not a narc. You know I'm not wearing a wire. You checked everywhere but my ass." The look on Danny's face at this thought gave rise to a fear that the man might check this last remaining hiding place, but Danny just took a final drag on his cigarette, and stubbed out the remainder.

"I don't do weed anymore. That's a dinosaur high. You wanna make some money?"

"I gotta get a source of income till I can get something going. It's a long time till September," Earl answered.

"You freaked me out, coming over here like this," Danny said, moving to the window and looking out a small hole that had been poked in the foil.

"But I can do something for you, and you can do something for me." He moved away from the window and pulled a square mirror from under the couch. A cockroach scurried across the glass and Danny flicked it off with his hand. He pulled a plastic pouch from his front pocket, and poured a small amount of powder onto the mirror, with apparent great concentration. As he was tapping it out onto the surface, Charlene came slinking in with a bent spoon in her hand. There was a tiny bit of dried cotton in the center of the bowl.

"Put some in there, Baby Doll," she said, in a gravelly voice. The sharp points of her collarbone protruded through her tee shirt, which looked in the same dirty condition as the rest of Danny's world.

He tapped a portion into her utensil and she moved off, with great enthusiasm, towards the kitchen. Then, he pulled a large hunting knife from his front pants pocket and opened the blade. A faint click told him it was locked in place. Earl briefly wondered if the scene with the gun was going to be repeated, this time with a sharp instrument, but Danny used it, instead, to rail the powder into two fat lines. He then pulled a short, cut straw from the same pocket that held the pouch, and handed it to Earl.

"Uh, brother I don't think I want to indulge. What is that anyway?"

"It's meth. I know you've done meth before? Don't sit here and tell me you've never done meth!" Danny said, incredulously.

"I'm a child of the sixties. I grow, sell and smoke my weed. That's enough for me. That stuff will kill you."

"What? I've been doing it for ten years and it hasn't hurt me any."

Earl looked at the man and thought this over for a minute, but decided against any retort.

"It's up to you, I'm not going to beg you. If you don't want to make more money than you can stand, that's your decision."

"How much money?"

Danny moved closer, the mirror still in his lap, carefully balanced.

"You pay me a thousand dollars an ounce..."

"What! A thousand dollars for an ounce of powder!"

"…And you can make twenty-eight hundred off it, easy. That's if you don't cut it. Cut it, you make more. And you really should consider cutting it, 'cause the tweakers will hurt themselves with *this* shit."

Danny had piqued Earl's interest in his most vulnerable spot: his greed.

"This is a whole different deal than selling weed. With weed, they can take it or leave it. With this stuff, they come begging on hands and knees to give you their money. That's no exaggeration. Hands and knees."

Charlene came back from the kitchen holding the crook of her left arm.

"Danny, I can't hit myself. Can you do it?"

"Later. Give me a minute."

She pouted and walked back into the kitchen, out of sight.

"Okay, I'll have to forge out a new market, but I'll give it a shot. Front me four ounces to start."

"I'll front you two ounces. First, lets do this line."

"Uh, no. I think I'll just stick to my weed. Use this stuff to generate money."

"You don't want to do a line? You sure you're not a narc?" Danny said suspiciously.

"We're not back to that are we?"

Danny didn't answer, just looked at him with those bulged out eyes. Earl became aware that the knife was still open and laying on the couch beside the mans leg. One line, then I'm out of here, he thought, what can it hurt?

Earl took the mirror out of Danny's lap and position himself to inhale the line in one sucking motion. He saw the powder disappear off the mirror and felt it hit his sinus cavity. In seconds, he was absolutely certain Danny had given him Drano; such was the burning sensation. His eyes watered from the pain, and he handed the mirror back before he dropped it.

"Damn it. Damn it," he said, walking round and round the room. His eyes cleared enough to see Danny laughing on the couch. He briefly considered crossing the room and hitting him in the face, till he remembered the knife, not to mention the gun. And just like that, the pain was gone. It was replaced with a terrible, bitter taste draining down the back of his throat, but that was, at least, better than the pain. He sat back down in the chair across from Danny.

"When's this stuff suppose to work?" Earl asked. He was accustomed to the almost instant affect of marijuana.

"Ten minutes or so. It'll hit you like a freight train 'cause your system is clean."

Sure enough, on schedule, Earl felt the hair on the back of his neck standing up. Then the sensation moved onto his scalp. Like every hair on his head was dancing the mamba. The fear of what might happen to him began to fade, and was replaced with a warm, wired buzz that wiped away every worry he had. At some point, every thought that entered his mind seemed to be of special value, simply had to be spoken aloud. And he began to talk in a stream of consciousness sort of manner, saying whatever came to him. Two hours later he would vaguely recall having discussed the coming presidential election (their all liars!), his views on abortion (okay for minorities, but we need all the white babies we can get), and the best methods for making deer jerky (soak it in teriyaki sauce, and dry it in the sun). When he looked at his watch, he realized his jaws were sore and he needed to be getting back.

The drive back to Monticello was very interesting. He read every road sign on the way, and counted the number of white stripes in a quarter-mile stretch of highway because, well, just because he'd never done it before, and was curious. There were 63.

When he was through counting, and now possessed this fascinating piece of information, he simply talked to himself, and had quite an enjoyable time, since nobody was there to interrupt him.

Chapter 6

CAROL AWOKE SLOWLY, TURNED over in bed and realized that Earl was not beside her. She and Robby had gone to bed around eleven, and he had not been home. The thought crossed her mind that he may have abandoned them, and she realized, with a slight guilty feeling, that this did not cause her anxiety or sadness. Now Carol, she told herself, he has his problems, but he's your husband and you're suppose to work through things. She got out of bed, went to the bathroom and washed her face, then went into the kitchen.

There was Earl. He was sitting at the kitchen table, working intently over a pile of screws, nuts and gears.

"Honey, what are you doing? Didn't you come to bed last night?"

He looked up wild-eyed from his work. He hadn't shaved, and was still in his clothes from the previous day.

"Oh, hey babe. I came in last night and the clock was making a humming noise. I thought I better take a look at it."

The argument from the previous day seemed forgotten, and she was inclined to let it remain in the past.

"It's always made a humming noise, since the day we bought it," she said, curiously.

"Then I guess it's high time I looked at it, huh? I've been thinking I need to help you more around here. You know, with the stuff that's needs taking care of. Like the yard, the dishes…and this clock. No reason for you to have to do everything."

"So, how are you coming with it?" she said, referring to the disassembled timepiece.

"Well, I got it apart in no time, but I'll be damned if I can seem to get it back together. I've put it back together three times, but I had pieces left over, and it wouldn't work. So, I guess maybe I left out something that was critical."

"Uh huh, sounds like it," she said, now looking at him, instead of the loose parts that were occupying his attention. With his wild hair, unshaven face and intense concentration, he reminded her of a mad scientist trying to bring a creation to life.

Robby came walking into the room stretching, headed for the refrigerator, and poured himself some juice from a carton.

"Hey, wild man. How you doing this morning?" Earl said, not looking up.

Robby was a little taken back that Earl was speaking to him. Usually, he was ignored, unless Earl needed something. But he wanted to get along with Earl, for his mother's sake, if nothing else.

"I'm okay," he answered, cautiously. "Mom, can I have some eggs?"

"Of course, sweetie. I'll whip some up for you."

"Say, what's wrong with those Rams?" Earl asked. "I read in the sports page they've lost two straight. They play Warren this coming Friday. That's a big deal around here. I think it's a home game. Maybe we could go as a family? Do you think you'd like that? What about that coach? Do you think they'll fire his a…let him go, after this season? I think he's gone. They don't tolerate losing around here. This is the Notre Dame of high school football. Just win, baby. That's all the booster's care about. I remember the days back in the nineties. Nobody wanted to play Monticello. So, what do you think?"

Robby remembered being asked several questions, but they came in such rapid-fire fashion he couldn't determine which one Earl wanted him to answer. And, he was not fully awake yet.

"I'm sorry, sir. Could you repeat the question?"

"You know, you're a great kid. So polite. We really do have a great kid, don't we Carol?"

"Yes, we have a wonderful kid," she answered, studying Earl more closely now.

"And I appreciate you calling me sir, but you don't ever have to call me sir. You can call me Earl, or whatever you want. Just don't call me late for dinner." He laughed like this was the funniest thing he'd ever heard, then it shut off like a spigot.

"So, what do you think?"

"About what?"

"The coach. Do you think they'll fire him?"

"The kids love him. It's not his fault. I might play next year."

"You should. You really should. You might make it to the NFL. Go pro. Then you could buy your old man a big house. Or a new clock." He laughed at this even harder than being called late for dinner, then looked back to the mess of parts and said, "To hell with this. I'm going to town and buy a new clock. Carol, do you need anything?"

He was up, grabbing his windbreaker almost before she could answer.

"Pick up some milk."

"Okay. You guys go ahead and eat. I'm not very hungry."

Robby looked at Carol when the door closed, and she shrugged her shoulders.

***

Coach Byrd sat in his office considering his future options. Since he'd received the call informing him of a 1:00 PM appointment with the head of the school board, he had considered himself unemployed. What other reason could there be to be called on the carpet? The signs of its coming were obvious to anyone who didn't have his head in the sand: The sharp editorials in the sports section of the local paper, questioning the direction of the program, and bringing to remembrance the glory days of the past. The fact that several people he had once considered friends now no longer rang his phone, as if distancing themselves from a condemned man. And, most obvious of all: the black shirts. A group of concerned fan who had taken to sitting together in the stands with matching black tee shirts. The tee shirts were imprinted with the words, 'Give Byrd the boot.' They had taken out an ad in the local paper, offering a free shirt to anyone willing to sit with them in the protest section. It was getting nasty.

It should have been a relief that it was almost over. But it was not. He could not let go that easy. Like the captain of a ship, or a General in command of a regiment, he had a desire to go down with the ship, or die at the head of a charge. It was not fair. He had not thrown any incomplete passes, or missed any blocks. But it was his job to motivate them. To find a method that made boys act like gladiators; achieve beyond their means. And though it was not fair, he truly did not want the blame to fall on his assistants, though he knew if he were to hang, they would surely all hang together. It was almost unheard of for an incoming coach to retain the assistants from a past regime. He would want to start fresh. Bring in his own trusted advisers and friends. Wipe the foul taste of a failed campaign from the slate and start clean. They would all find other jobs. But, for him, it would be the cruelest blow. This was his home. The place he wanted to retire, die and be buried.

At 12:30, his wife called and asked him what he was doing for lunch. He lied, telling her he has a lot of paper work to finish. He cannot bear to tell her about the meeting. Not yet. Not while there is a shred of hope. Perhaps he can go in and beg. But he knows he will not. And he will not cry. At least not while in the man's office. No, better not to cause her any unnecessary worry. When this is over, he will hold her, and they will chart a new course, together. And all things will, somehow, work to a better end.

On the drive to the meeting, he recalls past moments from his seven previous seasons, like a man whose life is flashing before his eyes before death. Singing the fight song in the locker room, after a win. The same song he sang when he played here. So sweet, it never fails to make the hair on the back of his neck to stand up. He would not be disappointed to hear it on his deathbed. Let it be the last thing on this earth he hears. To anyone who has never been in that locker room, with the blue trimmed equipment bins, and the sign hanging above the door that reads 'One city, One team, One heartbeat,' that song probably is hokey and stupid. But if you've sweated, bled and held the line with 10 other brothers, as he had, and somehow come out victorious, you too would sing. You had to be there to understand. Easier to explain a sunrise to a blind man, than to make someone understand the Monticello High School experience.

It was the passion that gave life to it. For good or bad, you could never accuse Monticello fans of apathy. When it was good, they packed the stands and drove six hours, to another part of the state, for a playoff game. And when it was bad, they still packed the stands, but they were angry. It was the passion that made it what it was. And it was this passion that was calling him on the carpet.

He entered the office of the head of the school board and greeted him, trying to read his eyes, like a man trying to read his fate in the eyes of a jury. But the mans eyes did not give a clue.

"Don, good to see you. Have a seat. Want some coffee?"

"No thanks."

"How is your family?"

"They're great."

Small talk. When it's over, the man will get down to it. Either way.

"And you, how are you holding up?"

"I live and die with it. I've been dying lately."

The man shakes his head, as in understanding.

"I know. And I hate that for you. I know you put so much of yourself into it. Too much. But that's why I, and several other board members, love you so much. You're a Monticello boy. Cut you, and you'd bleed blue."

It was strange to hear himself referred to as a boy, but he could not refute it. The boy in him still lived. At the mention of their love for him, his eyes welled up. Damn it, don't cry, he told himself. Hold on to your dignity.

"There are other members on the board...very vocal members, who want you replaced. They called a vote last night, at the school board meeting, to have you ousted, and an interim coach hired for the remainder of the season."

The man paused, for dramatic effect or whatever reason, and his future hung dangling in the wind, for a moment...an eternity.

"The vote was 2 to fire, and 2 to retain through this season. I cast the deciding vote to retain you. Do you know why I did that?"

"No," Coach Don Byrd chokes out.

"Because I still have faith that you haven't given up on this team, or on yourself. I personally don't think you would ever give up. But the voices are growing louder. Winning cures everything. We play Warren this Friday, do we not?"

"Yes."

"Win that game, Don."

He saw that the president of the Monticello School Board had tears in his eyes. He became aware that he did, too. They shook hands. It was over, for now. The team was still his. Winning cures everything.

***

It is possible that everyone in the stands, for the game between Monticello and Warren, had a different perspective. Earl, sitting with his family beside Carol, mostly watched the cheerleaders. Carol did a lot of looking around for the few other mothers she had met, mostly at garage sales and at the grocery store. Robby watched the game, but also kept his eyes on the head coach. He is not a tall man, but he has the stately bearing of a general, making him appear taller than his height, until he stands next to someone else, and a comparison can be made. As expected, the stands are filled to capacity, with the overflow falling out to the circular track behind the goal posts. The town of Warren is close in proximity, and their fans have made the drive, packing their side of the bleachers.

The coach has not told his players how crucial this game is to his future. It would not be fair, or helpful, to put that kind of pressure on them. Nor has he told his assistant coaches of its importance. They do their best every week to prepare the kids, and he knows it will be the same now. As he does before every game, moments before taking the field, he talks to the team.

"Everyone of you in this room knows who we are playing. The seniors and juniors, you know what to expect. They're gonna play you like they hate you, because from the kickoff, till the final seconds of the fourth quarter, they will. They know that if they lose this game, their friends are going to give them hell all year about it. And if they win they can drive back, get a kiss from their girl friend, and all's right with the world until next year. For four quarters, they are going to try to get in your head. They are gonna say insulting things about you mother, your sister, anything to get a rise out of you and make you forget your assignment. But you are above that. Because you're from Monticello. There's only one thing I want you to do: for four quarters, I want you to line up and smack them in the mouth, and do it again, and again. Till they get tired of talking, and they get tired of fighting, and they lay down and don't get up. I know you'll never lay down and not get up. 'Cause your from Monticello. Lets pray."

A prayer is made to keep each boy from injury; that everyone will give his best effort, and they are running out onto the field. It is a singular moment the coach loves, when the quiet of the locker room is abandoned, and they run into a maelstrom of noise. What else could he do but this?

Despite his admonition to 'smack them in the mouth until they don't get up,' Warren will not stay down. The Lumberjacks have a massive tail back, a man among boys, but he does not have great speed. Play after play, they use him as a battering ram.

The coach looks towards the stands and sees the black shirts in attendance, most sitting with their arms folded, frowning. Wanting his head. He cannot blame them. They love their football. He cannot fault them for that. He looks away. Must remain focused. It is out of his hands.

As has been the case in the previous two games, the Monticello offense is unable to mount a sustained drive, and the game becomes a battle for field position. Punt after punt, by both teams. He hates to punt the football. So many things can go wrong. Almost like launching a missile, at any time it could blow up on the pad and kill the team.

But the punt team does not self-destruct, as each team show its offensive ineptitude with kick after kick.

Toward the end of the second quarter, with the Warren defense tiring, John L. Wilson, the Monticello Senior tailback, catches the opponents looking for the run. It is a simple screen pass play, but the linebackers have blitzed, trying to stuff the ground game. Wilson outruns the secondary. Touchdown. There is pandemonium on the sidelines, in the Monticello stands. Robby looks from the field to the sidelines. All the players and coaches are ecstatic, except for Coach Byrd. He remains composed with his clipboard and headset.

On the ensuing kickoff, the Warren return man takes a short kick at his own 20. The return team sets up a perfect wall of blockers. He is running in a clear path, untouched to the end zone. Now, there is madness on the Warren sideline, in the Warren stands. The Monticello crowd is stunned to silence. The half ends. The coach cannot help but notice the black shirts in the stands, as he, and the teams leave the field and head to the locker room. Some of the black shirts are smiling.

The atmosphere in the locker room is beyond subdued. The kids, every one of them, have their heads down. It is an attitude of pervasive defeat, as if they have lost already, and he knows he must shake them out of it. He usually doesn't give a talk at halftime, letting his assistants make the necessary adjustments, but this cannot stand.

"Get your heads up!" Everyone does, except for one, and he walks over and takes the boy by the chin, lifting his head, looking him in the eye, before walking back to the center of the room. He has never before touched a student, and he does not regret it now.

"We're in the same situation we started in. Score is tied. They're feeling pretty good about themselves right now. You go out there and take that feeling away from them. The first five minutes of the third quarter will decide this game. I'm proud of the way you fought, and I'm gonna be proud of the way your going to fight." This is all he feels needs to be said.

One by one, he confers with his assistants. The quarterback coach, a young man with two years coaching experience, pulls him aside.

"I want to put Bennett in for a series."

Jeff Bennett is a 10th grade student with a bright future. He is the third string quarterback, behind the starting senior and a junior. His brother played at Monticello; went on to star at the University of Arkansas. His father is a local physician. He is a very popular kid, and has shown a good arm in practice, on the scout team. But he is a pimple past fifteen. Has never been on the field in a varsity game. Coach Byrd says to him, "We'll see," then he moves around the locker room, staying busy so as not appear anxious. Then it is time to start the third quarter.

Warren takes the ball to start the third period, and they come out with a vengeance, pounding the line with their behemoth tailback, not making any long runs, but punishing the Monticello defensive line, time after time. Making first downs every third play. The starting nose tackle comes to the sidelines after one of these plays, blood streaking down his face, onto his neck, his jersey. His nose is broken. A dirty brown and green cleat mark is visible on the center of his chest. A smaller, less experienced player is hustled in to replace him. It is becoming a war of attrition, and the enemy will not relinquish the ball.

Time after time, the sideline crews move the chains, keeping pace with the Warren drive, which has reached the Monticello 10 yard line. The enemy is at the gates, and they will not be denied. The tailback plows in from three yards out, carrying two defenders into the end zone. The coach looks to the scoreboard out of habit, taking note of the score and the time. Down by six, with just over five minutes left in the third quarter. With the extra point, it will be a seven point lead. The holder for the extra point takes the snap from center, but for whatever reason, he cannot gain firm control of it. Coach Byrd watches as the kid desperately tries to gain grasp of the ball, then he is buried by blue, and the extra point fails. The Monticello defenders run off the field in high spirits, the touchdown forgotten for the moment, the score remaining 13 to 7.

Still, his team cannot move the ball. After an initial first down, the senior tailback Wilson is thrown to the ground on three straight attempts. They must punt, and if Warren scores again, it is all but over.

The fourth quarter begins. All along the sidelines players are holding four fingers in the air; an inspirational tool intended to say that the fourth quarter belongs to them, to Monticello. It is tradition at his school to do this; has been done at every game since the nineties. A few players from the opposing team can be seen mimicking the gesture, but not with passion. On the blue side of the field, every player, and coach, lifts four digits into the air.

Robby finds the coach on the sideline, clipboard in the left hand, head down, four fingers held high.

Improbably, the Monticello defense stiffens, and Warren is forced to punt. The problem with the offense is obvious. The Lumberjacks are stacking the line with eight, sometimes nine players: daring the blue team to throw, which they cannot do effectively. Coach Byrd watches his punt return team run out onto the field and senses a presence close at his right shoulder. It is the quarterback coach.

"Bennett, for one series, coach. Throw it deep on first down, just to make 'em back off. Then we give Wilson the ball, with some running room." If the move is a disaster, if the kid fumbles a snap, he, the head coach, will bear the blame. However, if the situation remains the same, they will lose, and he will also bear the blame.

"Okay," he says, knowing he is putting tremendous pressure on the boy in a very difficult situation. But all Bennett has to do is throw the first pass deep, out of reach. Make the defense back off. Then hand it off to Wilson. Surely he can do that. The offense is running out onto the field. Coach Byrd pulls Bennett back to speak final instructions: "We're throwing deep on first down to make 'em back off. Throw it as far as you can. Do not, I repeat, do not, throw the ball to a defender. Just heave it, then hand it off to your tailback." The coach notes that the tall, lanky fifteen year old does not appear nervous. He is apparently as nonchalant as if he were playing flag football in his back yard. The coach perceives this as a negative. He has the Bennett kid pegged as a slacker. Son of a wealthy man. Born with a silver spoon. Game probably doesn't mean that much too him. Just don't hurt us, son, just don't hurt us, he whispers to no one, and his offense is on the field.

The play calls for the quarterback to take a five-step drop and throw to the end, on the right side of the field, who is running a streak route, straight toward the opposing goal line. Nothing fancy. A tool to cause the defense to back off the line. Give Wilson a chance to run the ball. Bennett takes the snap and drops back the required five steps, but he does not throw it. There is the pause of a heartbeat, then another, then another. The ball should be in the air by now. Should be falling harmlessly to the turf, so they can line up and go back to the ground game. But he is standing in the pocket, and the receiver is twenty-five yards down the field, rapidly running out of the range of all but the best high school quarterbacks. He has three steps on the defender, who has been caught off guard by the streak route, but it is too far.

Just when he is sure Bennett has froze under pressure, afraid to throw the ball, the lanky 10th grader cocks the ball and releases it into the crisp, night air. A beautiful spiral, rising so high and far the coach cannot believe what he is seeing. It arcs up, straightens to level position, then noses over, textbook style. Impossibly smooth, lacking any trace of wobble, it is an aerodynamic wonder to behold.

From his position, the coach can see that the ball, thrown perhaps forty yards, is going to intersect with the receiver. It will hit his hands… and the boy will drop it. Too much pressure. He reminds himself to console the boy for the drop at the first opportunity. But small hands reach out and touch the ball, and it is like iron connecting to a magnet, firmly, smoothly drawn in. The Warren defender does not even give chase past the twenty yard line. Half the stadium has rose to standing in one motion; a collective roar of emotion erupts. The boy who caught the pass is mobbed on the sidelines. He will someday tell his grandchildren of what happened on this night. Bennett is mobbed too, but he appears no more excited than if he'd just made a free throw in a backyard pickup game. The coach comes face to face with the young quarterback as he exits. It is several seconds before he becomes aware that his mouth is open, and he has not said a word.

"I hit that one," Bennett says. Classic understatement. Then, he walks towards the back of the mob where he can smile at a certain cheerleader.

In the midst of jubilation, the coach remembers how critical this extra point is. The teams are tied. It would be crushing not to take the lead at this point. He watches the 1 point-play at all its stages, all the places where it could suddenly go all to hell: the snap to the holder, the catch. Spin the laces outward and place on the tee, kicker takes two steps and strikes the ball, never lifting the head. Extra points have not been his team's problem this year: scoring touchdowns has. But it seems too much to hope for. Too complicated to ever work. The kick sails dead center through the goal posts. They lead. Too early to celebrate. There is five minutes left on the clock.

Warren takes the ball and goes back to what has worked: smashing into the center of the line. Terrible simplicity. This time, the blue warriors cannot stop the strategy. With one minute left in the game, the Lumberjacks have moved to the Monticello 10 yard line. Then, the trash talking the Lumberjacks have been doing all game catches up with them. Something is said in earshot of the referee, and a 15 yard penalty is assessed. Personal foul. It takes most of the remaining minute for the bruising tailback to regain the lost yardage, and they are back at the 10 yard line with five seconds left, and the clock stopped by timeout. The coach mentally adds the distance: 10 yard line, 10 yards for the end zone, 7 yards back from the line of scrimmage: A 27 yard field goal. The flag near the field house says Warren has the wind at their back, gusting. It has been a good ride. A dream come true. But dreams don't last forever. He has never asked his God for a victory, and he will not now. Whatever happens...for the best.

He is too intent on watching the stages of the kick to notice that the wind has stopped, even shifted to the opposite direction, a moment before the Warren kickers foot makes contact. But others will tell him, and film of the game reveals it. The kick sails wide right by a foot. Those around him, down on their knees in the grass of the sideline, run onto the field. Just as he did not notice the wind, he does not see the black shirts in the stands pushing their way through the mob to exit.

At that moment, Robby felt as if he had only one dream in the world: to wear that jacket with the oversized "M". To stand shoulder to shoulder with that band of brothers on the sidelines. And to play for the man with the clipboard, who somehow seemed taller than he was.

Chapter 7

FOR THE PUPPY, THE world was pleasant and predictable. Sleeping at the foot of Robby's bed in a box, gave way, in the space of a few weeks, to actually sleeping curled up at the boy's feet, nestled in the covers. For the dog, nothing could be finer. He lived to be close to his keeper. A touch of the boy's hand on his head, even a casual glance from his eyes, was a moment of ecstasy.

The day would begin, on weekdays, with the puppy licking him in the face, urging him to wake up and play. There would be a long moment when the boy resisted, pushing him away and trying to put off rising, but it was futile to resist; Buzz Saw would not be denied. This would give way to a few glorious minutes of tussling on the bed. The boy would roll him over and rub his belly. He would pretend to resist and fight back with growls and squirms, but it always ended too soon. The female, the master of his master, would poke her head in the room and order Robby into the smaller room down the hall, the one dominated by the large, ceramic drinking bowl that refreshed itself when a handle was pushed. There, Robby would groom, usually with the door closed. Being separated from his master, he would run into the kitchen and check his bowl. The female would be there, and usually the man, who he avoided out of instinct.

When he had first come into the household, the man had possessed a disagreeable spirit, an aura that he avoided, just as one would move away from a foul smell. But, at some point, a different emotional scent was detected. The former essence was selfish, angry, dissatisfied and distant. That was bad enough, but the current incarnation of Earl revealed to him a man whose mind was chaotic, unstable, paranoid and unpredictable. These were not character traits the puppy spent any time deducing; he just knew them innately.

The new Earl would be awake at all hours, sometimes for 3 or 4 days at a stretch. Sometimes he called to the puppy, "Come here boy. Whatcha' doing?" Buzz Saw would just look at him, never going to him, nor backing away. This usually pissed Earl off, and he would say to Carol, "What's wrong with that dog? He's not very friendly." Then Robby or Carol would call to him, and he would run as fast as his small legs would allow, into their arms.

"Humph. Doesn't appear he knows who brings home the bacon around here," Earl would muter. Then, he would go back to what he was doing, and the puppy would be relieved that the man's eyes were off him. He did not like the man's eyes. They were windows to the soul, and gazing in those windows was not a pleasant pastime.

On school days, Carol would urge Robby out the door, and he would be allowed outside to watch the car take his master up the road, out of sight. There was always a sadness he felt at this point, although he knew, predictably, that the boy would come back home later that day in the same manner in which he left, so his sadness would be short-lived. There was too much that had to be accomplished to remain sad for any period of time. There were butterflies that simply had to be chased. How dare they flutter that way in his vicinity! Rarely did he catch one. They had an irritating, bouncing motion which made it seem they would be easy prey. But it was like trying to snare a sunbeam, which he had also tried, by the way. Couldn't be done, but he had to try every time.

And being situated near the woods, there were uncountable creatures that called the wild places their home. They had to be chased. Had to be repelled, lest they dare think this was their territory, and move into his yard. He was content to let them have the woods, unless he saw them: then the chase was on. Most of them were quite fleet of foot, and this was a good thing, because most all of them also possessed very sharp teeth, and nasty dispositions. Perhaps they didn't have a master and a yard like he did, and this made them very disagreeable. He would chase them, but was not disappointed when he was eluded.

The repelling of the wild invaders always gave way to the next stage of the day: the emergence of Lu-Lu, and her master, from the dwelling next door. At this point, all interaction with the wild creatures was forgotten, and he would swiftly forsake his own nest to be temporarily adopted by Mr. Scott and the incredible, peculiar Pekinese who lived there. Lu-Lu was not inclined to explore beyond the bounds of the Scott property, and she simply turned her nose up when he tried to urge her into the woods, but this was not a bother, as there were endless adventures to be had around her home.

Buzz Saw detected a very pleasant scent from the man who was master to his friend, and he could understand why Lu-Lu was so devoted to him. It was peculiar to him why the man was always so intent on moving leaves from one place to the other, or digging in the dirt, although he had to admit that he was also fond of digging in the dirt. But the overwhelming emotional aura that came from the man was kindness: beautiful and simple.

So unlike Earl, who exuded a complex mix of disagreeable scents. If not for the boy, Buzz Saw would have petitioned to remain with Lu-Lu and her master. But the boy would come home, and this was the highlight of his day. Like Christmas, a parade, or winning the lottery, it was a joyous event.

He would see the car coming up the road, and it was time to leave Lu-Lu and the man who groomed the yard. He would race at breakneck speed to his own domain, the car would stop and the door would open. The one he loved beyond all comprehension would emerge from the car, and the love-fest would begin. They would fetch a snack from the kitchen, then it was time to play chase the stick: the boy would throw it as far as he could. It was his duty to run to the spot and grab it. When he first learned the game, he wanted to take it and run around the yard; a game of keep away. But he found it pleased the boy when he brought it back to his hand, so it could be thrown again, and again. The boy always tired out before he did. Then it was time for a game of tussle-for-the-sock.

An old sock was presented to him as a challenge, but the boy would not let go of the end, and a mad tug-of-war would ensue. The boy always let him win in the end, and he was stroked on the head and back for participating. At some point they would foray into the woods.

The boy didn't seem near as interested in chasing the numerous creatures as he did, but did not discourage him from doing so. They would move through the woods, alone together in the primal beauty of the forest, far away from anything except each other. It always ended too soon. When the shadows began to grow long, they would head back, and it was time for something that always confused him. The boy would lace up his running shoes and he would be confined to the house. This saddened him to no end. The boy would stroke his head, speak a few words, and head out the door without him. He would stand looking forlornly at the door for several minutes, hoping against hope that the boy would return for him, but he never did.

It would seem like an eternity, but was in reality, perhaps only 90 minutes, before the boy would return, wet with perspiration, and flushed with his evening run. The puppy could not understand how the boy could leave without him, how he could bear to be separated from him. What marvelous things had he missed while being incarcerated behind the door?

When he was four months old, long legged and clumsy, Robby was headed out the door, when he looked back to wave goodbye to his mother. His eyes caught sight of the pup sitting there, looking like his heart was broke. The dog certainly looked like he could keep up for a few miles. He wondered why he'd waited so long to break him in to the road. He could wait no longer. He grabbed the lease off the top of the refrigerator and clipped it to Buzz Saw's collar. The only time he'd ever been leashed was on a few trips to the vet for checkups, but the dog didn't seem to mind, and he fell in beside Robby as he headed out.

It was a fresh experience, leaving the vicinity of the property. He soon learned to run just off Robby's right leg, a step in front. Robby cut his run short to five miles that day for the pup's sake, and Buzz Saw discovered what he'd been missing on the evening runs. New sights. New smells. The distant bark of other animals as they ran past fenced-in property. Occasionally, dogs that were untethered would halfheartedly give chase, but the pup generally kept his eyes and head forward, concentrating on the road ahead. Robby kept his body between the dog and traffic so there was no chance he might lunge out into the road. He soon found that Buzz Saw could easily keep up on the normal 7 mile outings, so he no longer cut the runs short. In fact, his dog seemed invigorated when it was over, and could even do the 10 mile runs with ease.

It was a further bonding experience for Buzz Saw. A primal feeling to be out on a run with his best friend. To him, it was a joyous task that had to be accomplished. They were out on patrol, moving everything they might encounter out of the way. Clearing a safe path for anything that may come behind them. The boy and the dog were a team on a special mission. Presently, Robby cautiously removed the leash and allowed him to run free. Just as he'd expected, the dog stayed in position, to the right, a step in front, in formation. Robby began to wonder how he'd ever run alone.

The long runs filled out the young dog, adding strong shoulders and hips to his lanky frame. Robby was sure his dog could go 20 miles if asked. When he was 6 months old, half grown, an incident occurred that would forever stand out in his mind, and change his view of his running partner.

Robby had altered their normal route, deciding instead to try an old logging road that offered some solitude, as opposed to the highway runs they were accustomed to. The dirt packed road, and lack of traffic, was a welcome change. Even the occasional puddles that had to be circumvented were not a problem. Halfway down the 3 mile stretch of road, with thick woods on both sides, a pack of what appeared to be strays stepped out of the brush, blocking the path. There were four of them. Three, each larger than Buzz Saw,

and a fourth that was comparable to him in girth, with sneaky, downcast eyes.

It was obvious who the alpha dog was: a dirty brown cur, whose ancestry may have contained a generous amount German Shepherd. He was front and center of the pack, doing the talking for the group, barking out threats. Two of his cohorts were standing at his flank, growling out their encouragement to the leader. Robby took three steps back, surprised by their appearance. Buzz Saw did not retreat. He occupied the center of the road, not returning their insults. Silent and stock still, it seemed to further agitate the pack that he would not give ground.

Fear gripped Robby in his gut. He knew if he ran they would give chase. Buzz Saw could probably evade them. But what could he do? The thought crossed his mind that he might have to seek the safety of a tree. Treed like a coon. The thought did not appeal to him, yet neither did being bitten. But Buzz Saw was not moving. He was holding his position like a statue. Robby took two more steps back and called out to his friend, "Buzz Saw, come on boy." The dog ignored him.

It became apparent what the strategy of the pack was. While the alpha dog engaged him to the front, the flanking mutts would strike from each side. They circled to the right and left, just out of reach of the half-grown pup. But it was the leader Buzz Saw remained focused on. Knowing he was being surrounded, and that the battle could not be postponed any longer, Robby's young dog left his position, and with a snarl of rage, tore into the lead dog. The side attackers were caught off guard, and wheeled to see their leader meet the charge. Such was the force, and surprise of the assault, that the alpha dog was pushed into a sitting position, with its head pushed back, trying to keep his vulnerable neck out of reach. The element of surprise, Buzz Saw's only advantage, was used with devastating results.

Sure that his dog was going to be torn to pieces, Robby stood horrified as he saw the center dog pushed back on his posterior. Then, from there, on to his back, and a sickening sight ensued: Buzz Saw ripped into the prone dogs neck, biting and slashing again and again. The brown shepherd's growls quickly turned to howls of pain. Robby could see fur flying under his dog. When Buzz Saw's face and snout were visible, as he made upward, tearing strokes with his teeth and head, the boy could see that his dog's muzzle was streaked red and wet. The two flanking dogs were barking insanely, but they did not assist their comrade, preferring to remain outside the range of what was happening to their friend.

Robby saw his dog move off the neck area and begin tearing into the shepherd's belly and groin. It was long over, but he would not stop. Ripping into the white meat of the dog's soft underside soon exposed viscera and a gray loop of intestine. Still, he would not quit. The two at the side had moved back into the ditch, unsure if it was even safe to flee.

At this point, Robby saw the fourth dog come in from the rear, intending to take hold of Buzz Saw by his leg and hobble him. His friends were emboldened by this tactic, and they moved in, ready to pounce when he was in their grip. Without time to think, Robby seized a large, knotted stick that lay at the edge of the road. Raising it above his head, he struck the sneaking mutt across the center of his back, breaking the stick. The dog collapsed and rolled into the ditch. All thought of a comeback was removed from the mob. Collectively, they took off into the woods, leaving the shepherd, who was stilled being mauled, to his fate.

It was extreme over kill. Robby could smell the sharp scent of the cur's intestinal contents, along with the coppery smell of blood, and he took a step back involuntarily. Still, Buzz Saw would not stop. The boy clapped his hands, screamed and stomped, but nothing worked. Such was the raging scene on the ground, he was afraid to take hold of his dog, for fear he'd be bitten in the confusion. He finally picked up the remaining half of the stick, and moderately struck his dog along his haunches, screaming, "Stop it."

Buzz Saw raised his head with a guilty look, checked the dog on the ground one final time, and stepped back to Robby's side. The shepherd was not yet dead, but was opening and closing his mouth like a fish. Then he grew still, and his eyes glazed over.

Horrified and drunk on adrenaline, Robby and his dog ran back down the road the way they'd came. They ran full tilt all the way home, and breathlessly burst through the front door of his house.

"Mom, mom..." he gulped out, not having breath to finish the sentence.

Carol was alarmed at the state he was in.

"What? What is it?" she said frantically.

"He killed him! Some stray dogs attacked us, and Buzz Saw killed one of them. You should have seen him. He would have killed all of them, but they ran off. One of them tried to get him from behind, but I cracked him with a stick. They thought they could get us, but Buzz Saw tore his neck out. Then he ripped his guts out, and he wouldn't stop. I thought he was gonna swallow him whole..."

"Whoa, stop. What in the hell are you talking about? Slow down."

Hearing his mother curse was unusual, and it gave made him pause to take a breath before he began again.

"Mom, we were running on the International Paper logging road. Four stray dogs came out of the woods." He paused to let this sink in to her. When she nodded, he continued.

"I was going to run and climb a tree. But Buzz Saw wanted to fight 'em."

"All four of them?" she asked, incredulously.

"He would have. But he ate the biggest one."

"He ate him?" she asked again. She looked toward Robby's dog and saw the dried blood on his face, neck and front legs.

"He tore him a new asshole!"

"Robby, watch your mouth."

"Sorry. He saved us mom. He's just a puppy, but he wouldn't let those other dogs past to get me. If it wasn't for him, I'd probably still be in a tree, or worse."

Carol appeared unsteady on her legs and she wobbled to the couch and sat down.

Buzz Saw sauntered over to her, and she recoiled as if a rabid wolf had just asked to be petted.

"Robby, go wash him off."

Earl walked in to the room. He had been asleep in the bedroom after having been awake for the past 3 days. He was not in a good mood.

"What has that damn dog gone and done?"

Robby recanted the story for Earl in all its gory details, sure that even he would be pleased with Buzz Saw's heroic effort. When he had finished, Earl looked at the dog with his still bloody muzzle, and said, "Well, we're in trouble now."

"What?" Robby said, in confusion.

"Your dog killed someone else's dog. They'll be wondering what happened to him."

"That's crazy," Robby said. "It was a pack of strays. Even if it wasn't, they attacked us. He saved me. That's more than you would have done if you'd been there."

"I'm telling you, that dog has a taste for blood now. He's dangerous. It'll be the neighbors dog next, or the neighbor. We need to take him somewhere where he can't hurt anybody. Give him to a junk yard or something."

It was hard for Robby to plead the dogs case, as he sat there with the dried brown blood coating his face and legs, an innocent look on his face, unaware that the conversation was entirely about him. For Carol, there was something creepy about the pup sitting there looking so cute, covered with gore.

"Robby, take him and clean him up," she said, again.

"Yes, mam," he responded, leading Buzz Saw into the bathroom.

"Well, what are we gonna do with him?" Earl asked. He had jumped straight out of bed and his hair was disheveled.

"Earl, we need to talk."

"Damn right, we do. We have a serious problem here. Give a dog the taste for blood, he becomes an animal."

His choice of words almost made her giggle. "I think he's been an animal for quite some time."

"You know what I mean! It's called bloodlust. He'll seek it out, now. Nothing will be safe."

"Robby will be safe. He is safe, because of his dog. Thank God for that dog. He's never shown the slightest bit of viciousness, and he won't unless something threatens Robby." She paused, unsure how to go on.

"Earl, honey…I'm worried about…you."

"What? I didn't come home fresh from a kill, covered in blood. What are you talking about?"

"These past few months…you've been different."

"How?"

The question caused her to look at him incredulously. He had been different in so many ways, in every way. She almost didn't know where to start.

"You don't come to bed with me. You're up and down emotionally. You stay up for days, then you sleep 24 hours. I was talking to my friend Millie, you know, she works at the hospital…"

"You've been talking to someone about me?" His eyes were wild, and his voice was rising.

"Just listen. She says you are showing all the classic symptoms of manic depression. She says there is medication available. That it might help you. She says you will only get worse if you don't treat it."

"You've been talking about me…behind my back?" He was walking around the living room in circles. He grabbed his hair with both hands, as if to pull it out.

"I'm not crazy, you're the crazy one if you think I'm gonna let you run to your gossip hags and spread stories about me. Have you lost your mind?"

To Carol, it was like being in the padded cell of a lunatic who thinks everyone is crazy, but him.

He released the hold he had on his hair and walked quickly over to her, inches from her face.

"I will not be the subject of two whores who think they're amateur psychologists. Two whores who can't even fix themselves."

He was shouting now, screaming himself hoarse.

Robby was scrubbing the dog in the tub. The sound of Earl shouting had startled him. Hearing his mother being called a whore had made him consider leaving the dog in the tub and going to her side. Before he could decide, the dog slipped his grip and leapt from the filthy water, running into the living room. Robby followed him as he ran dripping down the hallway. When he entered the living room Buzz Saw was standing in the entranceway, growling barely audible. The hair on his back and neck was standing upright. His ears were pinned back. He was looking at Earl.

Earl had gone from a rage, to calm and subdued the minute he saw the wet dog come out of the hallway. He was still standing near Carol, but he was looking at Buzz Saw. With his wild hair, he reminded Robby of a mad scientist who had just seen the Frankenstein monster come to life.

"Son, you grab your dog... now. Go ahead. Everything is all right. We're gonna talk about this as a family. Grab him, Robby." His voice was steady and even, but strained. Like a man trying to diffuse a bomb, afraid it might go off if he shouts.

Robby stroked Buzz Saw along the head and back, and the mood was broken.

"He's okay. He just doesn't like shouting. Or name calling," Robby said, with emphasis on the last part of the statement.

"You need to apologize to me for that. It was uncalled for," Carol said, her arms folded.

"Yeah, that got out of hand. I'm...sorry." The words were bitter bile in his mouth, but he felt relieved that the dog was no longer looking at him. "Go dry him off son, we're okay in here."

Robby reluctantly took Buzz Saw back into the bathroom and toweled him off. He had never heard Earl apologize before. Was not sure he even knew how. Obviously, he had figured it out rather swiftly.

"We'll stick together boy," he said to his dog. "You're my forever friend, you know that?" The dog wagged his tail and licked him square in the face. Robby pulled back, remembering where the dog's mouth had been, in the entrails of the mongrel. But it was joy he felt as he stroked the brindle-coated pup with the white socks on all four feet.

They slept in the same bed. Ran together, and played together. Now, they had fought together. And the dog had made his mom and Earl stop fighting. Had insisted on it, if he really wanted to admit it.

"What would I do without you?" he said, as he finished drying off the dog.

Earl was asking himself the same question. He had begged off Carol's concerns about his mental stability with promises to come to bed more often, and tell her if he felt any onset of the problems she claimed she was seeing. She, in turn, promised not to discuss him with outside sources, unless he was present. They kissed and made up.

But the situation was far from resolved in his mind. He felt outnumbered and was sure he had lost control of his household. First, it was Carol questioning the way he acted. Then, the boy calling him crazy. And finally the damn dog even got in the act. Three against one. He could not remove the image of the wet mutt standing in the doorway, dripping and growling. If that dog ever tried to bite him, he would kick him from here to doggy heaven, he thought to himself. But he had backed down. In front of Carol and the boy, he had backed down. This would never do. Something had to be done to reel them in, gain back the upper hand.

He lay in bed with Carol that night, unable to sleep, staring at the ceiling. He could well imagine sliding into the same situation as his father. Beat down. Sitting in the recliner in the living room while his wife shouted at him, "You never come to bed. You've changed. I'm gonna call all my friends and discuss what the hell's wrong with you.

Get you on some medication, so you'll get right. Oh, you'll take the medicine all right! Yes, you will. And you will never raise your voice to me again. Do you understand? Do you???"

And Robby would come into the room and say, "You're crazy. A crazy stepdad. My mom married a crazy man."

He imagined himself shouting, "I'm not crazy!"

Then, the damn wet dog would come into the room and look at him with those eyes. Those eyes that said, "You'll get right, or I'll rip you a new asshole."

And he would get right, wouldn't he? Hell no, he said aloud, and Carol stirred beside him. A prisoner in my own bed. Soon to be a prisoner in my recliner. Just like Dad. A chip off the old block. I'll die before I let that happen, he decided. Or somebody will.

Chapter 8

FRED SCOTT OPENED HIS eyes in bed, and habitually glanced over at his sleeping wife. He was pleased to see she was there, and snoring softly. It had been a week since her last "spell." She still called them visions, but to him they were frightening occurrences. He had awakened to find her gone. He searched for her, and heard her in the small room she called her prayer closet. It was actually a room that housed the hot water heater, but she used it as an enclave to talk to God.

Through the door he had heard her praying in garbled language, praying in tongues. He had hesitated to enter. Hesitated to break the holy communication between her and Father God. But her moans and cries had made him open the door. She was on her knees, an old pillow cushioning her against the hardwood floor. Tears were streaming down her face. It was not so much prayer, as a desperate intervention against something. What, she had never been able to tell him, because she herself didn't know.

It was generally the same vision: The boy, who she declared was Robby. And an adult female, who she thought likely was the boys mother, and with them a man. A man who is not a man. Because he is wearing a mask. And while she watches, the man, who is not a man, begins to pull off the false face.

It was at this point where her vision had progressed in detail. She could see what was under the mask. Something she had not been allowed to see before. It certainly was not a man. She had thought, at first, it might be a wolf. A snarling wolf. A wolf in sheep's clothing. But it was no wolf.

"What was it?" he had asked.

It was a demon, she had declared. A demon was under the mask. And something small was coming. Coming to help. It's being led by an angel, his wife had cried, her face lifted upwards in supplication, eyes drenched in tears. But it's been through so much, and it's so far away. And the devil is trying to stop it. It has the heart of a lion, she had cried loudly, looking him directly in his eyes, and he remembered feeling very afraid for a moment. Not just afraid for her, but afraid in a general sort of way. Like the fear you feel when you look into the dark woods at night, seeing nothing, but not sure of what it is you are *not* seeing. Not sure of what might step out. He had shaken off that fear. Took her and put her to bed. I'll die before I put her in a nursing home, he had vowed.

Now, a new worry had befallen them. Lu-Lu had taken sick a few days before. He'd taken her to the vet, and the prognosis was grim. Dystemper. Nothing he could do. She was an old dog. Twelve years old, he was pretty sure. She'd lived a full life. He did the mental calculation as he lay in bed, counting up age in dog-years. What was it? 14 for the first year, then 7 for each additional year? Yeah, that was it. That made her 91. With that thought in mind, he could not fault her for getting sick.

He rose softly from beside his wife so as not to awaken her, and walked into the kitchen where Lu-Lu's round wicker basket and bed lay. She did not raise her head when he approached; the head with the pretty blue ribbon his wife was so conscientious to keep there. Her bonnet, his wife had declared.

"Oh, Lu-Lu," he said, as he bent down and stroked the tiny head, now grown cold and still. He spent some time there, racked with sobs, trying to stifle them so his wife would not be alarmed and come into the kitchen. He had to be strong for her. She would be even more devastated than he was. Life's not fair, he thought. You spend your life growing close to something. Loving them more, everyday. And then they are gone. And what do you have left? Would it be better not to love? No, he concluded.

His life would have been less without Lu-Lu. And his life would have been unthinkable without his wife. Who I will also lose someday, he knew. Overwhelming sadness washed over him, but he beat it back. Got a job to do. She's counting on you not to fall apart. Plenty of time to fall apart later. Might do that when she's gone, he mused. Just fall apart. Let it all go. Tired of being strong. But not now. Not when she's counting on you to be her rock. If she only knew how weak and scared her rock was. But she will not know. You will be that rock, damn it.

Must decide what's right, he concluded. Colleen wouldn't want to see her dead. I could bury her before she wakes up. Then we could have a little ceremony, right here in the kitchen, to say goodbye. Nice and neat. God knows, that woman doesn't need to go through anything else. She might tie those visions to Lu-Lu. Think the devil took her baby. The thought made him shudder, and he got off the floor.

The sun was just beginning to brighten the eastern sky. He grabbed his shovel out of the shed and lifted Lu-Lu from her wicker basket. He started to remove the blue ribbon from her head, then decided to leave it. Take it to heaven with you, little precious one. The thought brought tears back to his eyes, but he sniffed them off.

He carried her gently to the back edge of the property, placed her on the ground, and dug a hole perhaps two foot deep. He briefly considered getting something to wrap her in, then decided against it. Better to let her go back to the soil. Her spirit was already in the arms of Jesus. Give her body back to the earth, with nothing to get in the way. He placed her down in the hole and picked up the shovel. He hesitated casting the first dirt upon her, then told himself, she's already gone, it's not her in that hole. Just a tent. She's free. Next time I see you, little one, will be in heaven.

He dumped a shovel full of dirt in the hole and watched her disappear from view. Quickly filling in the hole and tamping it down with the flat side of his tool, he went inside to prepare for how he would break the news to his wife.

She was tearful when he told her, but it went immensely better than he feared. Her faith in all things eternal helped her through it. They had a quiet breakfast, spent remembering the twelve wonderful years of life with Lu-Lu, and decided together that they would go across town and see the grandkids. Get out of the house, and away from the memories. Things rarely turned out as bad as a person dreaded, he concluded. With that, they climbed into the car and headed out.

Buzz Saw went through his morning ritual, and eagerly headed out into the yard to watch Carol and Robby leave for school. As always, next on the agenda was to head next door for his daily romp with Lu-Lu. Problem was, she was nowhere to be found. Neither was her master. She had been absent the past few days. He nosed around the neighbors yard, sniffing in the newly piled leaves and compost Mr. Scott had diligently placed at various locations. Presently, he made his way to the back of the property where an enticing mound of fresh dirt was located. Dirt meant to dig in. He began pawing out the hole. When he had dug down about two feet, he detected something in the bottom and he lowered his nose and sniffed. Lu-Lu! She was hiding in the hole! What a game this was!

He finished pawing out the hole, expecting her to jump out at any moment and surprise him, but she was playing stubborn. He had to show her she could not hide from him. He climbed into the hole and pulled her up by the scruff of the neck. He had never seen her so dirty. He spent a few moments pawing her on the ground, but she was playing asleep. He was not fooled. He knew she could not be asleep. He grabbed her by the neck again, and dragged her halfway across the Scott yard. More pawing ensued, but she was really being stubborn. In time, he dragged her all the way into his own yard, frustrated because she would not stop pretending.

Earl drove up to the house and pulled into the driveway. He had come from a meeting with a customer. They had both indulged in a sample of his product, and the neurons of his brain were firing overtime. The first thing he saw was Robby's dog in the yard, pawing at a small, brown object. He shut the truck door, and cautiously walked over to where Buzz Saw was laying prone. Since the incident in the kitchen, he'd had an uneasy truce with the dog, watching both the animal, and the way he spoke to Carol while in his presence.

"What'cha got there boy?" he said, curiously. Buzz Saw looked up in frustration, as if to say, "Can you make her wake up?"

One glance told him all he needed to know. The blue ribbon, still tied atop the head, was a clear give away.

"Oh, my God. Oh, shit. What have you done, you dirty mongrel? You've gone and done it now." Buzz Saw continued to paw at Lu-Lu, determined to make her get up and play.

Earl examined the corpse from a short distance, afraid Robby's dog might turn on him and protect his kill. Lu-Lu was caked in mud. She looked like a biscuit that had been rolled in flour. He ran into the house and grabbed the lease from the top of the refrigerator, returned to the scene of the crime, and bent down to snap the tether to Buzz Saw's collar. Bite me and I'll shoot you, he muttered, before leading the dog into the house. He unsnapped the clasp of the lease and hurried back outside to the muddy, brown lump laying in his yard.

He examined the corpse. Not a mark on her. Just cold, stiff and dirty. Must have died during rough sex, he concluded. Smothered her trying to get a little bit. Didn't matter. She was still graveyard dead. And there would be a ruckus over this. A falling out for sure. The police might be called. This thought made the neurons in his brain fire a little harder. Earl Collins had spent his entire adult life, and a good part of his adolescent years, trying to avoid contact of any kind with various law enforcement agencies. He felt some sort of subterfuge was in order, but what? He raised his head and saw Mr. Scott's car was gone.

In cartoons, when a person has a bright idea, it is represented by a light bulb. Had this been a cartoon, one would have seen a bulb over Earl's head, albeit a dim one, probably akin to a Christmas light, because Earl had an idea. Maybe not a good one, but it was all he had.

Since there was not a mark on the dog, perhaps, just perhaps, he could take her and clean her up while the old man was gone. Scrub her real good. Then, take her back to the neighbors yard and lay her on the porch. She died while you were away, yeah, that's what happened. Poor thing. A natural occurrence. So sad. Wish it had been our dog. First, he had to make sure Mrs. Scott was not home. Hopefully they were both gone. A quick knock on the Scott's door would tell the tale. If anybody answered, he would say he thought he smelled smoke. Yeah, didn't want you to burn up. Don't want to take any chances with fire, now do we? He ran to the Scott house, knocked loud, and waited five minutes before deciding no one was home. So far, so good.

He scooped Lu-Lu up off the ground, oblivious to the mud and grime, and hurriedly carried her into the house. Must hurry. If they come home, we're sunk. He twisted the knob with his left hand, cradling the dead dog with his right, and kicked the door open.

Buzz Saw saw Earl carrying Lu-Lu and thought this was some new game. He didn't like Earl, but if Lu-Lu was playing with him, he might not be all bad. He bounced around the living room in anticipation of some fun, but was further confused when Earl took her in the bathroom and shut the door.

Earl rolled up his sleeves, put her in the tub, and turned on the faucets. The water quickly turned brown with filth, but he scrubbed and dunked her until every trace of soil was removed. Then, he removed the blue ribbon, washed it thoroughly, and hung it over the shower rail. Next, he looked for a brush and found Carol's in a round holder on the back of the toilet. He stroked the dead dog with his wife's brush, grabbing a blow dryer to hurry the process. Hope this doesn't make your scalp itch, Carol honey, he thought, as he ran the bristles through the newly clean pelt, working out the knots as he went. If his wife came home now, and found him grooming a dead dog with her brush, manic depression would cease to be her diagnosis. No Earl, she would say, your not manic depressive. You're slap-dab, monkey on crack cocaine, crazy.

Sorry, Lu-Lu, didn't mean to pull your hair. Probably not your most pressing concern, at the moment. Then he shook out the blue ribbon and stroked it dry with the hot air of the blower. He tied the ribbon carefully to the head, as he had found it, and stepped back. She looked so sweet, she could be just sleeping. Yeah, he thought, and I could be the head of the Drug Enforcement Administration.

Next was the most perilous part of his plan: he had to carry her across old man Scott's yard and deposit her on the porch. If they came home while he was accomplishing this, and saw him carrying their little bundle of joy, they would naturally assume he had a hand in it, and he would be in worse shape than before. Charged with a crime he was only trying to cover up. But he had come too far to back out now.

He checked the window and was pleased to see the Scott's were still away. Cradling the freshly coffered Lu-Lu, he headed out the door and began the long trek across no-mans land. His eyes were on the approaching road as he crossed the yard, expecting any minute to see the Scott vehicle, but the road was clear. He made it to the porch and unceremoniously sat the dog down, taking a tiny moment to place her head on her paws. There, just laid down and went to sleep, poor thing. I might send flowers. To hell with that, he thought, I'm going to home to do a fat line.

Taking only a few minutes to rail out a line and further agitate his chemical imbalance, he turned to his next task at hand.

"Come on boy," he said to Buzz Saw. "You've got to go."

He clipped the leash back on the dogs collar and led him out to the truck.

"We're going for a little drive."

Buzz Saw loved to ride in the truck. Even though he thoroughly hated being in the proximity of Earl, he was delighted to be placed in the seat, with the window down just enough to allow him to stick out his head and soak up all the amazing smells that came his way as they drove.

"Going for a drive, big boy. Gonna take you to a new home. A brand new killing field, where you can find fresh victims. Don't take it personal. But, you can if you want to. I don't care. Robby will get a new pet. I think I'll get him a hamster. Something with smaller teeth. You'll find a new home. Or you can make a living raiding garbage cans."

He headed down the highway to just outside of Warren, found a cleared vacant field, and pulled the truck over. He then took hold of the leash, led the dog out into the field, and unclipped it from his collar.

"Well, goodbye, you vicious son of a bitch."

With that, he climbed back in the cab and turned the truck back in the direction he'd come. He took one last look in the rear view mirror and saw the dog standing in the field, as if he were waiting for a bus.

"See 'ya when I see 'ya."

Fred Scott was returning home a much happier man than when he had left that morning. Being with the grandkids seemed to we just what the doctor ordered. There was something about children that gave one hope for the future. It was hard to remain depressed for long in their presence. And it had seemed to buoy the spirits of his wife, although if truth be told, she was holding up better than he. Maybe its not her I need to worry about, he told himself. Maybe I'm the weak one.

They had both been close to little Lu-Lu. But it was he who spent the most time with her. She was his constant companion in the yard, and he spent a lot of time there. It was only natural he would be crushed upon her passing. In his concern for his wife, he had neglected to keep an emotional eye on himself, and thus was blindsided when his friend departed.

They'd had such a fine time with the kids that they had talked Colleen's daughter into allowing the youngest, who was not yet in school, to come with them for a visit. Something to fill the void they were expecting when they returned home. Thus Fred, Colleen and grandchild Mini, pulled up into the Scott driveway that day. Fred noticed the brown mop lying on the porch first, but it did not click in his mind.

Next, Mini saw it, and exclaimed, "Look, me-maw. Lu-Lu came back."

"Don't be silly, honey," Colleen said, "That's a rug somebody left on the porch."

But Fred, whose eyes were clearer and sharper than Colleen's, saw something else as the car came to a stop in the driveway: an unmistakable blue ribbon encircling the front portion of the brown thing, now laying on his front step. My old eyes are playing tricks on me, he chuckled to himself, as he hurriedly exited the vehicle the second it stopped. He took a step towards the porch, then another, then ran the final 30 feet to stand in front of the first step.

There was absolutely no mistaking it now. No way on God's green earth to deny it. He briefly concluded that this must be a dream, no, a nightmare. And if, at that moment, the little dog would have lifted her head and barked, Fred Scott knew he would have ran. He would have ran until he reached the ocean. Then he would have begun swimming. And he wouldn't have stopped until, most likely, he had circumvented the earth and wound up right back in the same spot.

Colleen and Mini now joined him, standing before the front step, no one daring to go another step further. Fred began to wonder, and doubt, whether the morning he remembered so clearly, even existed. I know I buried her, I know I buried her, his mind hammered.

He took off at once around the corner of the house, sprinting like he was twenty. Maybe he just thought he buried her. Perhaps his mind was slipping. Could it be possible, that the entire morning he had accepted for reality, was some joke his advanced years were playing on him? As he reached the back of the property, where his shovel had dug the hole, he knew he was not senile. Terrified yes, confused certainly. But not senile. The hole, which he had excavated a comfortable two feet down into the earth, was open, and empty. He slowly walked back around to the front of the house. Colleen now had Lu-Lu in her arms. Mini was stroking the dead dog on her flank.

"She came back, Fred," Colleen cooed, "My baby went to see Jesus, and she came back. And isn't she beautiful? Jesus gave her a bath and brushed her 'cause he loves her, too."

There was no doubt, Lu-Lu looked fabulous. Unless you looked at her eyes, one of which was closed and the other that was half open, wrinkled and collapsing in on itself. And, perhaps the tongue, which was stiff with rigor mortis, and poking out the mouth like a tiny, pink diving board. Other than that, she looked great.

It is possible I thought she was dead and she wasn't, Fred calculated. That I erroneously buried her, and somehow, someway, she crawled up out of that hole and onto the porch. But I damn well know she didn't crawl into the tub and wash herself. I buried her! In the dirt! Where's the dirt?

The sight of his wife holding the manicured Lu-Lu made him want to take the dead dog away from her, to help his wife accept what was, even if *he* did not know what was.

"Honey…, she didn't come back. Here, let me take her…"

Her eyes flashed livid. "You…are…not…taking…my…baby!!!" she screamed. And he knew for certain that if he reached for Lu-Lu, he would pull back a nub.

"Okay. Okay. Lets go in the house. Come on Mini. We're all going into the house now."

Mini was not helping the situation. "I'm so glad Lu-Lu came back from heaven, me-maw."

"Me, too. And it was so nice of Jesus to clean her up. It's a long way to heaven. She was probably pretty dirty," Colleen said, with utter sincerity.

They sat, as a family, in the living room for a moment, with Colleen and Mini continuing to stroke the stiff corpse and talk baby talk to the dead dog. Fred felt certain that if he didn't somehow get the dog out of his wife's arms, and away from them all, he was going to genuinely freak out. Maybe join them in the baby talk session. Someone would come to the house, at some point in the future, and find all of them talking goo-goo and ga-ga to a rotting, canine skeleton.

"I have an idea! Honey, lets go pray and thank Jesus for sending Lu-Lu back to us. That's the least we can do, thank Jesus."

"Oh, yes. We've got to thank the Lord, Fred. Got to praise the Lord!"

"Okay, we'll put her in her little basket so she can take a nap, and you and Mini go into your prayer closet.

There's no room for me in there. I'll do my praying in the bedroom. She looks like she's plum worn out, sweet little thing. She needs a nap. Here let me take her"

To his great relief, Colleen handed the stiff, dead dog to him, and he ushered the two girls into the room with the hot water heater. As he was closing the door he saw them kneel down and lift their hands to give thanks. Carrying the body of Lu-Lu was like carrying a rock hard, stuffed toy. He contemplated for a moment trying to push the stiff, pink tongue back into her mouth, but decided against it.

A picture flashed through his mind of Lu-Lu in his arms, raising her head and stroking him across the face with that rigid, pink member. He knew if that happened now, his heart would not survive the experience. He would scream and go on screaming, till he screamed himself dead. But Lu-Lu remained passively past on, and he quickly carried her out to the car.

He drove to a grove on the opposite side of town and removed Lu-Lu from the front seat. Keeping an eye on her, he carried her into the woods. There, he dug another hole two feet deep. Then, after some thought, he dug it another two. Now, with a four foot hole in front of him, he lowered his dog, once again, into the grave.

"Stay," he said, and the irony of the situation was not lost on him.

She was always a good girl, and eager to follow simple commands. He hoped she would be now. Then he hurriedly filled in the hole, and when it was completed, took two sticks, and some twine, and made a makeshift cross. This he planted at the head of the grave, hopefully to kill any ho-do that might still exist.

He drove back home, and prayed to his Jesus that he wouldn't see the dog lying on the porch as he arrived. He breathed a sincere thanks when he saw the porch was vacant. I'm gonna catch hell when I walk in there, he concluded. He didn't have a clue how he was going to break it to Colleen and Mini. Wing it, he thought. Just go in there, and wing it. He twisted the doorknob and stepped in, dreading what lay before him.

Colleen and Mini were in the living room. They were smiling. Before he could speak, Colleen came over to him and placed her hand on his shoulder. She had a sad, but sympathetic look on her face.

"Oh, Fred. She's gone. She didn't come back to stay. She just came to say goodbye to me. 'Cause I didn't get to see her when she left. That's why she was so gussied up. She went to the beauty shop in heaven, so I would see her at her best. I hope you aren't too heart broke, honey?"

"Uh, no. I…kinda figured she was only visiting."

"Oh, I'm so glad you aren't upset. I thought I was gonna have to comfort you. You know, she's gonna look just that pretty the next time we see her, in the arms of Jesus!"

"Yeah," he answered, "Maybe a little more lively."

"Well, sure. She was tired from her long trip. Next time we see her she'll be runnin' around the legs of the Lord, to beat all get out."

Colleen kissed his face, and he breathed a deep sigh of relief. But, all was not right with his world. There was still the distinct possibility, in his mind, that despite the distance he had carried her across town, and despite the stick cross he had planted at the head of her new home, Lu-Lu might not be through popping up. He felt the need to get his family away from this place of weirdness, for a time anyway.

"Colleen, I've got an idea. Let's pack up and go see your sister in Missouri. Stay for a while. Maybe a month. Or two."

"Well…"

"Come on…you call her. I'll pack. This is what we've been needing. It's what Lu-Lu would want us to do."

"You think so?" she answered, frowning seriously.

"Oh, I know so. In fact, the Lord told me just a few minutes ago, while I was praying, that He that he wanted us to go see your sister, and stay there…for a little while."

He instantly felt guilty about putting words in the Lord's mouth, but he had to seal the deal. And he knew nothing would seal the deal with Colleen like an order from God.

"Okay, then," she said, accepting the holy message. "I'll call and see if it's okay."

Robby came home from school and did not see Buzz Saw there to greet him. He then checked inside the house, and around the outer perimeter, still not finding his friend. He noticed a flurry of activity next door at the Scott's and walked over, sure that Buzz Saw was there.

"Mr. Scott, have you seen Buzz Saw?" Robby asked.

The man was carrying luggage, which he placed in the open trunk.

"No, I haven't. Haven't seen him all day," Fred Scott answered, and turned to go back in the house.

"Where are you going?" Robby asked, again.

Mr. Scott seemed in a big hurry, and he barley took time to glance at the boy.

"We're going to my wife's sister's place, in Missouri."

"When are you coming back?"

"I don't know. Maybe a few months. Maybe longer."

"But this is your Garden of Eden."

Mr. Scott paused and turned to Robby. The boy deserved a better response than this.

"Look Robby, the devil was in the Garden of Eden, too. And it might have been better if Adam and Eve had skeedadled when the they had the chance."

Robby appeared truly mystified by this.

Mr. Scott put a hand on both his shoulders, and said, "Son, I'm gonna give you a number where you can get in touch with me. If you have any problems, you call me at this number. Call me collect. I'll pay for it."

He hurriedly scratched out a number on a piece of paper, and handed it to Robby

"What kind of problems?"

"Anything. I'm there for you. Okay?"

"Okay. Are you taking Lu-Lu with you?"

"God, I hope not. I love you, boy."

With that, he turned and went back into the house to finish packing. Robby slowly walked back to his place.

"Mom, Buzz Saw is gone somewhere. He's always here when I come home."

This caused her to pause before she answered, as if she was considering something, then she said, "I'm sure he'll turn up. Did you check next door?"

"Yeah. Mr. Scott is going away. He won't be back for awhile."

"Hmmm. That's curious. Well, check in the woods around the house. He'll turn up."

Robby left to go check the woods, but as evening descended and the dog did not turn up, he became increasingly depressed.

After dinner, when Robby had gone to his room to do homework, Carol mentioned the subject to Earl.

"Buzz Saw is missing."

"Really? Probably found a girlfriend down the road. He'll turn up." Earl went back to reading the paper, avoiding her eyes.

"You think?"

"Sure, he'll turn up."

"I remember when I was a little girl," Carol said, looking at him, "My father took our family dog and dropped her off somewhere. Told us she ran off. My mother found out later what he had done, and she told us, years later. I don't think I ever forgave him for that."

Earl continued to read the paper, without comment.

"Anyone who would take off a kids dog and just drop him off...well, that person doesn't have much love in his heart."

"What are you trying to say?" Earl said testily.

He was now looking at her over the top of the newspaper.

Her eyes were boring holes into his, seeking confirmation of what she felt. She did not like what she saw.

"I'm not trying to say anything. If you took the dog off, go get him. We won't mention it again."

Earl Collins was confident of his powers to bend the truth upon demand. He'd had much practice at it, in his thirty-three years upon this earth. But he was extremely uncomfortable sitting there, with the woman staring at him like the truth was flashing upon his forehead. Still, it was not in his nature to admit a wrong, especially to a woman.

"I didn't take him off. He probably got himself shot killing somebody's dog. Why am I always the bad guy?"

"Maybe he'll turn up," she finally said, and left the table to wash the dishes.

"Geez, I get blamed for everything around here," he said grumpily, and went back to reading his paper, a thin veneer of sweat covering his forehead.

Robby lay in his room that night, hoping against hope he might hear the dog bark outside his window, in the yard. It was the first time in months he had been without his companion, and the room seemed empty, dead. He reluctantly prepared himself for bed, but at the last minute dropped down on his knees.

"God, I know I don't talk to you as much as I should, so I hope you're listening. I really need a favor. My dog Buzz Saw is missing. I'm sure you know where he is, since you pretty much know everything. I want to ask you to bring him back, if he's not in heaven there with you already. If he's there in heaven…" at this, Robby choked back tears. He didn't want to start crying so his mom might hear and become alarmed.

"If he's there in heaven…pet him everyday, cause he really likes that. And he likes to play chase the stick. And he likes Alpo, but he'll eat dry dog food, too. He's not very picky. I plan to make it to heaven someday, and I'll take him off your hands when I get there. If you let me in, that is. He's a great dog, but I'm sure you know that, since you made him. Well, that's all. Just bring him back. Amen."

Chapter 9

THE DOG LEFT IN the field did not understand the concept of abandonment. It never occurred to him that no one was coming back. There was much traffic going to and fro on the highway, and he watched every car, sure that the next one that pulled up would be Robby, Earl or Carol to let him in and take him home. When that did not happen the first night, he merely curled up on the ground and slept. There was water in the ditch to drink from, but by the third day hunger drove him into the woods to seek food. He was reluctant to leave the spot, since it was his only connection with his master's. So he hunted in spurts, always quick to return back when he had chased down a rabbit, or a possum that was unfortunate enough to make his acquaintance. It was peculiar to him at first, eating fresh kill, and he only did it when the pangs of hunger overrode his ability remain in his spot. But he often went without, unable to run down any prey. On those nights, he slept curled up and empty, sure that they would be back for him at any moment.

The many people that traveled the highway could not help but notice the dog in the field. He was a strange, forlorn sight, sitting just back from the ditch, silent and watchful. One of the people that traveled the road was Kyle Clary, who dropped his wife off to work five days a week at a local fence company, where she was employed as a receptionist. He then traveled back the same way to where he worked across town, picking her up again that evening. When he first saw the dog in the field the first day, it did not strike him as unusual, there being a generous amount of stray pets in the area. But day after day he began to note the dog in the same spot, and his curiosity was piqued. At around the tenth day, as they were passing, he mentioned it to his wife.

"You see that dog back there?"

"You mean the one in the field?" she said, looking back.

"Yeah, he's been there for over a week."

"What do you think he's doing out there?" she asked.

"Somebody dropped him off. Happens all the time."

They were silent for a mile and when he looked over at her there were tears in her eyes.

"What's the matter," he asked, slightly alarmed.

She was looking away from him, out the passenger window.

"That poor baby. Somebody left him, and he's waiting for them to come back. And they're not coming…" She was bawling now, and it made tears well up in his own eyes.

"What does he eat? Where does he sleep?" she asked, her voice breaking.

"He sleeps in the same spot. It was raining the other day and he was over on the edge, under a tree, never far away. I don't know what he eats. Probably nothing."

He realized, too late, that this was the wrong thing to say to comfort her.

"I'm sure he catches a bird or something. He won't starve."

"Yes he will! And he's out in the rain. And it's been ten days. He won't leave that spot. He'll die there. We have to do something."

"What are we going to do?" he said, exasperated.

"We could go get him and take him to our house. Try to find somebody to adopt him."

"And when we can't find someone to adopt him, we're forced to keep him."

"Oh, can we?" she said, through tears.

"I didn't say that. We really don't have much room. The plan was to have a baby, first. Then get a bigger place. Then, get a dog."

"Can you drive by him out there, everyday, and not do something?"

He knew, before he answered, that he had to do something, for her sake if nothing else.

"We'll go home, get the leash, grab some burgers, and try to get him in the car."

"Oh, you are my hero!" She said, throwing her arms around him, as he drove. He had a warm feeling in his heart, hoping the act of charity wouldn't turn into a disaster, possibly with him being bitten.

They retrieved the lease and bought a bag of burger, returning to the field where Buzz Saw was homesteading. He saw the car pull to a stop in front of the field and bounded up to greet his owners. He stopped short when he saw people he did not know.

Kyle had the lease in one hand, and the burgers in the other, holding out the sack to entice the dog into a close position. The burgers smelled heavenly and his mouth salivated as the aroma drifted towards him. The dog could sense that the man was tense. And the man was holding something that he associated with being led. Thus, he remained wary, and just out of reach. It was all he could do not to run up and snatch the food that was being offered, but these were not his masters. To go with them would forever disconnect him with this spot, and all he was familiar with.

The man finally grew frustrated trying to lure the dog within reach, and said to his wife, "He knows I'm gonna grab him. He doesn't want to go. All we can do is give him the burgers." He unwrapped the burgers and placed them on the ground, taking a step back. Buzz Saw took a tentative step forward, never taking his eyes off Kyle, and wolfed down a burger in two bites.

"Look at him go. I knew he was starving." Judy Clary said. "I wish we could get him in the car."

"Well, he's not going for it. We'll have to leave him here and bring him some more tomorrow."

"Maybe, eventually, he'll let us get close. Good bye, boy," she said, as they left the field. Buzz Saw wagged his tail and swallowed the remainder of the hamburgers. He then sniffed the spot where they had laid, entranced by the aroma that lingered on the ground. The car pulled away and he resumed watching the traffic that traveled up and down the highway.

Robby's mother was finishing washing and putting away the dishes, while her son sat at the kitchen table reading a sports magazine. It had been a month since the day Mr. Scott had left, and their dog had come up missing. She avoided bringing up the subject of the dog, though she knew it was still on his mind. He had been moody and introspective since that day, and she wished she could do something to bring him out of it.

"Mom, what do you think happened to Buzz Saw?"

"Oh, I don't know honey. Sometimes dogs get sick, and they go off into the woods. I guess they don't want to be a bother to anyone. I used to think that might be a good thing to do, you know, if I ever got real sick. Just go off and be alone. Not be a burden to anybody."

Robby eyed her with alarm, so she said, "Don't worry, I'm not sick, and I'm not going to go off in the woods." The boy had lost enough things in his young life. She could well understand how he might be insecure about losing the things he loved.

"Good," he said, smiling slightly. "I don't think Buzz Saw got sick and went off."

"Really?" she said, wanting to know what he thought, but not wanting to lead him on.

"No. He was too healthy. Besides, if he got sick he would have come to me."

"Uh huh," she said, hesitated, then said, "what do you think happened to him?"

Without pausing a beat, Robby said, "I think Earl took him off."

The plate she was holding slipped from her fingers and it shattered on the floor.

"Shit," she said, moving to grab a broom and dustpan from the pantry closet. When the shards and pieces were in the waste bin she sat down across from her son and gently asked him, "Why do you think that?"

"Because Buzz Saw took up for us. That night, when I thought Earl was gonna hit you, when he called you a name. Buzz Saw made him stop. I wish I could have made him stop, mama. I was scared, but Buzz Saw wasn't. He isn't scared of anything. Earl knew that. He likes people, and things, to be afraid of him. Earl was afraid of Buzz Saw, and he couldn't stand it."

From the mouth of babes, she thought, but held on to her conclusions.

"Robby," she said, slowly, "I don't know if Earl took off your dog. If I found out he did... I'd leave him. What would you think about that...if I left him?"

Robby tried not to appear too enthusiastic, but inside he was doing cartwheels.

"Oh, I'd get over it," he said, and they both broke up laughing as she saw through his act.

"It would mean a lot of changes for both of us, you and me. I'd have to get a job. I'd be away a lot more."

It was all he could do not to jump up and say, "Go for it mom." But he didn't. He knew enough to know this had to be her idea.

"I just want you to be happy, mom. But if he ever hits you or hurts you, I'll do to him what Buzz Saw was gonna do."

"What's that?"

"Eat him up," he said, and growled for emphasis. She laughed and tussled his hair. Then, she fixed them both a heaping bowl of ice cream, and had dishes to wash all over again.

***

Six weeks had passed since the day he had been left in the field, and spring was giving way to summer. The burgers continued to be dropped off, morning and evening, and it was an event he relished. It was obvious that the people who brought him his ration wanted him to come with them, to leave this spot, were even desperate for him to do so. But there was no temptation to do this, as he was sure his soul mate would show up at any moment.

One of the other people who often came down this stretch of highway was Leon Stover. He was a full time employee of the man who owned the local scrap yard, a man by the name of Bill Dollar. Naturally, this was more often than not inverted so that people called him Dollar Bill. Leon did whatever needed to be done for his boss. From pulling in the rusted wrecks that littered the 10 acre auto graveyard, to fetching him a fifth of Wild Turkey from the local liquor store. Leon barely made enough money from this enterprise to put groceries on the table. But he scarcely cared, as long as he ended up with a 30 pack of beer when the day was done. To Leon, the greatest invention of the Twentieth Century was not the polio vaccine, or the light bulb, or even the automobile. It was the decision by the brewery companies to package and distribute 5 six packs in one, easy to carry container.

And thus, when Leon Stover passed the field where Buzz Saw kept up his vigil, he did not see a lonely dog: he saw a thirty pack of beer. His boss, Dollar Bill, was a man who made his living off junk. But his hobby, his pride and joy, was in the fighting of dogs; usually of the Pit Bull variety, although it was not unusual to see any number of breeds down in the pit. Dollar Bill did not need any number of varieties, as he had long since narrowed his stable of fighters down to one dog: A huge, monstrous Pit named, sarcastically, Baby.

Dollar Bill was happy and eager to pay Leon an extra thirty pack of beer on those days when Leon would bring him a bait dog. A bait dog was any old stray that could be thrown into the pit with Miss Baby. That dog would promptly be torn limb from limb. Baby would get her training in. Leon would get his thirty pack. And one less stray dog would be loose on the streets.

The duo of Leon and Dollar Bill had, in the beginning, scavenged the local animal shelters for their bait dogs. But the ASPCA now had pictures of Leon and Bill posted all over South Arkansas, and even into Northern Louisiana. They dared not even walk into a pound. So Leon had hit the streets to pick up the local canine hobos. It was a lucrative occupation, in his mind, and it was not unusual for him to bring three a week back to the scrap yard. When he was not snagging victims and towing junkers, he was busy training the champion. He would tie a railroad cross tie to a special harness and work her round and round the rusted heaps. Thus, the off white pit named Baby had the muscular frame of a NFL linebacker.

Dollar Bill did not keep written records of fights won, primarily because the sport of dog fighting had been banned in 35 states. But he knew, unofficially, that his Baby had won over 60 fights without a loss. Of these 60 fights, she had killed over half the dogs matched against her before the animals could be separated. She was so successful, and vicious, that it was becoming increasingly hard for them to get matches in state. They had lately been traveling down to Louisiana, or over to Mississippi, just to get a match. People didn't mind losing a bet, but they were wary of losing a valuable animal. Baby played for keeps.

Leon pulled the truck onto the shoulder of the road and stepped out. Buzz Saw saw the vehicle and, as always, thought it was his master's coming to take him home. When he saw it wasn't, he naturally assumed it was burger time, although he had already been fed that morning by the Clary's, and it seemed too early for them to be coming back. He saw a rather scrawny, smelly man in greasy coveralls take a long stick with a loop of rope on the end, out of the back of the truck. The strange man then put thick leather gloves on his hands and approached cautiously.

Instantly, Buzz Saw did not like the smell of the man. Beyond the smell of automotive grease and a total lack of hygiene, Buzz Saw could smell sneaking bad intentions. But as long as he remained well out of arms reach, he felt safe. It was ingrained into his soul not to bite a master. And he would only bite those who walked upright if they threatened his soul mate Robby, or the female Robby loved. But he was sure that if this stinking, sneaking human grabbed him he might violate his most sacred rule, and take a hunk out of the man. Better to stay clear so he wouldn't be forced into it.

Leon pulled a piece of meat wrapped in white paper from his pocket and tossed it on the ground. Though he'd had two burgers that morning, he stayed in a semi-state of hunger, and because Leon was a good 6 feet from him, he lowered his head and began tearing into the steak. When Leon saw him drop his head, he stretched the pole with the loop of rope out, and towards the dog.

With the expert ease of someone who has snagged many animals, he thrust the loop over Buzz Saw's head and pulled the rope closed from the base of the pole. Feeling the loop tighten around his throat caused the dog to forget all about the meat, and a mad struggle ensued. Leon merely tightened the snare, cutting off all the dog's air, and keeping him a safe distance away with the pole.

He began walking him towards the truck, towards the open pickup bed where there was a wire cage waiting. Once at the truck, he was faced with the most hazardous part: lifting the dog into the truck bed so he could be placed into the cage. Experience had long since taught him that it was best to simply tighten the loop until the dog passed out, or nearly so, then depend on the heavy leather gloves to protect him in getting the dog up, and into the cage. The dog was fighting so hard against the loop that he didn't have to pull the cord very much, just an inch. Buzz Saw struggled with everything he had to get away from the stinking man and his stick. Then he felt his airway being constricted and the world went black. When he came to, he was in a rusted cage barely big enough to turn around in, headed down the highway, away from the field, and any connection he had with anything he knew.

Leon pulled his pickup into the entrance of the scrap yard, down a corridor of rusted automobile carcasses that had long since outlived their usefulness, to an office with windows so grimy it would be impossible for anyone to see in, or out. The entire property, even the ground, seemed to be coated in grease: the wasted blood of wounded cars and trucks. Leon did not mind this, nor even seemed to notice it anymore, since he himself was always coated in the same substance.

He walked up, twisted a grease-coated doorknob and stepped into the grease-streaked office. A calendar on the wall displayed a young female who obviously enjoyed being naked on Harley Davidson motorcycles. There were racks of alternators, distributors, starters and parts of every conceivable function lining the front of the office. Towards the back, next to a grease-coated coffee pot, was Dollar Bill. He was hunched over a stack of accounts, with his ever-present Pall Mall cigarette burning in an ashtray, and a green shaded lamp illuminating his work. At his feet was his pride and joy: the silent menace known as Baby. Though Dollar Bill kept a Smith and Wesson .45 caliber handgun at the ready in his desk drawer, it was in fact Baby who virtually assured Bill no one would be coming to steal his dollar.

Anyone who saw the dog for the first time was invariably awestruck by her massiveness. She was 120 pounds of bulging, canine muscle, from her jaws to her rear haunches. If a dog guarded the gates of hell, surely it would be in the fashion of this one. The key to her victories lay not only in the terrible pound per square inch jaw pressure she could inflict, but in her low center of gravity that made it virtually impossible for another dog to get under her. In a battle, she was always biting up.

Leon loved her more than anything in life, except for perhaps his frothy, liquid refreshment. She was his only claim to fame. To him, she was Rocky, Joe Louis and Mike Tyson, all rolled into one, and he was the trainer who pushed her to the peak of championship excellence. It was he who led her into the pit at the various blood soaked matches they frequented. It was he who fed her the precisely weighed 2 pounds of chopped, raw steak and protein mixture she received twice daily. He even administered a therapeutic post-workout massage to her shoulders and back after she finished pulling the crossties and cinder blocks around the yard.

Such was his love that he had once asked his boss if he could take one of her droppings and have it bronzed for posterity. Might be worth something someday, he'd said. Bill had told him that if he went to messing with dog shit he could look for a new job. He carried a picture of her in his wallet; right next to my heart, he would declare, patting his rear pocket.

Leon reached down and stroked the head that was every bit big as a bowling ball, and just as round. She looked up at him with adoration.

"Got one for you Mr. D."

"Did you get one that'll challenge her? She's getting tired of these patsies you been bringing," Dollar Bill said, not looking up from his paper work. The ubiquitous Pall Mall was burned halfway up in the ashtray, an inch long ash announcing its neglect.

"You're asking a lot, sir. There's not a dog in this part of the country that'll challenge her. Might have to get a bear to do that."

"Hey, there's an idea. Match her up with a bear. Bet we could get them boys to put some money on that," Dollar Bill said, chuckling.

"Somebody better get ready to lose a bear, that's all I can say. I found a mongrel out on the Hermitage highway. Looks to be a cross between a boxer and a pile of shit," Leon said, disgustingly.

"Well, ask Miss Baby if she wants to go a round. Do you want to go a round sweet heart?" Bill said, in baby talk fashion. Baby looked up to him with her thick, pink tongue wagging, smiling at the news that she would soon be fed a homeless dog.

"Baby says that suits her just fine. Did you pull that transmission out of the van, like I asked you too?" Bill asked.

"Yes, sir."

"And did you go by and pull in that wreck from the county garage?"

"Sure did."

"Okay." Dollar Bill looked down to the mass of canine muscle at his feet and said, "You go with brother Leon and do your thing. Don't strain yourself."

"It won't be no strain for her. Might be a bit taxing on the other dog, though," Leon said.

"Bon apetit," said Dollar Bill, as Leon connected a leash to her thick, leather collar and led her out of the office.

He placed her in the spacious, enclosed pen and went to the truck with the cage in the back.

"Hey there, old thing. How are you feeling? I got somebody I want you to meet. She'll like you. Her bite is worse than her bark, and she's a bit moody, but she's built like a brick shithouse. She wants to have you over for dinner."

Leon donned the thick leather gloves and picked up the snare pole. Buzz Saw shrank back to the rear of the cage when he saw the man open the cage door and push in the looping device. He shifted his head to avoid being encircled, but there was nowhere to go. Once again, the loop was tightened and his world gradually went blank. When he awoke he was being dragged toward a round pit six foot deep with corrugated iron on the sides. He was unceremoniously kicked into the hole, and landed in a heap.

The smell of the arena made the hair on his back stand up. It was the smell of blood, urine and feces, mixed with the ever-present petroleum odor that lingered over the whole place. He shook his head to clear it and took stock of his surroundings. The wall of iron was too high to jump out. Leon was nowhere to be seen. He heard a piece of the metal being moved to open a doorway, and saw the greasy man push another dog into the enclosure, then close the opening.

From his position across the pit he could smell that she was female, and had recently been in season. He took a step towards her, hoping to sniff her in a friendly gesture, but she was acting irrational: advancing toward him with her head lowered and her teeth bared. He concluded this might be a territorial matter and backed up to the rear of the pit, against the metal. This did not seem to appease her, and she continued to advance. It was not his nature to fight a female, wishing instead to be her friend, and possibly even mate her, when the time was right. But she was having none of it, and within seconds there was no space between them, and nowhere for him to go. She came at him supremely confident, intending to lock her jaws on the first bite and not let go. Not being able to retreat, he sidestepped and heard the incredible pressure of her mandible snap in the air. This process repeated itself twice before he was forced to respond, and as she thrust her face at him the third time, he moved aside and lashed into her neck.

They went around the pit. Each time she lunged, she found he was no longer there, and was rewarded with a mauling to her flank. It was a tactic similar to that used with devastating effect by Muhammad Ali: the rope-a-dope. Wait till your opponent punches, then move sideways and stick. The problem was: Baby didn't really have a neck. She was pure muscle from the edge of her eyes, to the front of her forearms. Time after time, Buzz Saw tore into the rock hard muscle where her shoulders met her head. And though she was growing frustrated, he was growing fatigued.

He was a second slow in moving, and she opened up a 3 inch gash on his shoulder. The bite felt like a steel trap closing on his flesh, before he tore away and moved right. Leon was at the edge of the pit, on his hands and knees. This was taking too long to suit him. The sooner it was over, the sooner he could get his beer from Dollar Bill's icebox. After he disposed of the mutt that is. But from his vantage point, the mongrel was not fighting fair. He was staying just outside the grasp of his champion, moving like a wisp, unable to hurt Baby, but frustrating her.

"Come on, girl. Do it. Come on Baby."

His shouts became louder and shriller. He could not remember a fight ever taking this long, especially not a sparring match against a pickup mutt.

"Quit playing with him girl. Do what you do."

It is unlikely that Baby responded to Leon's direction. She was growing increasingly frustrated due to the fact that she knew she would be rewarded with meat when she finished, and Buzz Saw was not allowing her to finish. Bleeding from the shoulder, and weary to the point where he could no longer avoid her thrust, he knew he must change tactics or die.

In her frustration, she came at him not to bite, but to pin him with her body, charging headlong. He moved safely aside once more, and her head thumped against the iron. Now, for the first time, he was fully at her flank, away from the killer jaws. It was his one chance and he knew he would not have another. He lowered his head to seek out the only soft part of her body, and went in with full force.

Leon's cries became louder. "Baby, stop that shit. What the hell's wrong with you?"

With his snout just in front of her thick, rear leg, he burrowed under and lifted with every ounce of his remaining strength, her mouth inches from his ear, crunching but unable to reach him. Then, Leon saw something he had never witnessed: like a Sherman tank being lifted up by a landmine, Baby rose into the air, and rolled. She landed on her back, and Leon would later recall the most astonished look on her face. Not a look of alarm, but the casual countenance of someone being where they've never been, and didn't expect to be. With her teats and pink belly exposed, Buzz Saw turned at once from the victim, to the aggressor. From a pitiful stray trying to survive only for another minute, to a raging mad-hound on a mission of destruction.

Leon was screaming now. "Baby…Baby…Baby!!!"

Dollar Bill heard the commotion and put down his pen.

"What the hell is going on out there, Leon?"

Leon did not hear him. His ears were filled with the growling roar of the homeless dog he had picked up in the field. Leon was now prone on his stomach, hanging over the edge of the pit, as if to reach out and stop what was happening, reaching out to his Baby.

It was amazing to Buzz Saw how hard her body had been, but how soft was the flesh he was now tearing into. He ripped into her, not in anger, but with a pure desire to survive; knowing if she got up, he would die. As his teeth tore through the flesh of her belly, she continued to try to reach him with her deadly teeth, like a snapping turtle on its back, defenseless. To Leon, it seemed as if a ripping machine was set upon his Baby's underside. Blood, and the blur of white teeth moving and tearing, made him think of a piece of lumber being eaten at a sawmill. Through it all, Baby did not cry out in pain. She continued to bite and snap in the air, until she lay still.

Buzz Saw slowly moved away from her, and Leon saw his dog on the ground, open and exposed, like a package that had been ripped open at Christmas by eager children. The dog moved to her face and licked it twice, as if in apology.

Dollar Bill heard Leon's cries go silent, and they were replaced with a strange sobbing sound. He left his desk and went around the corner of the office, to where the pit was located. Leon was prostrate on the ground, his face covered by his hands, crying in spasms.

"What in God's name is going on out here?"

Leon couldn't speak. His attempts were half-choked by grief, and Dollar Bill finally gave up on him and looked over in the pit. He saw Baby's slaughtered body. The little mongrel was sitting beside her, looking up at them as if he had come upon the scene of a horrific accident completely by chance; a dog that had been hit been hit by an eighteen wheeler and split open in the highway.

"Did he do this?" he asked. It was a nonsensical question, but he did not believe what he was seeing.

Leon tried to answer, and again was unable to form words into a sentence.

"How?"

Leon gathered himself and said, "He don't fight fair. He ran her around the pit. Then he flipped her. He took advantage of her while she was on her back. He went crazy! Oh..."

He again dissolved into a mess of moan and sobs. Then he bolted upright.

"I'm gonna get my gun. Get my gun and kill that mangy son of a bitch!" He was making an effort to get to his feet.

"You'll do nothing of the sort," Dollar Bill said.

"What? Don't you see what he did? Look at her. She's done."

"I can see that," the boss said, evenly. Flies were already starting to light on her exposed vital organs.

"It was a fair fight. More than fair. She outweighed him by 80 pounds," Bill said, his voice whispering reverentially. This was what the Philistines felt when they saw little David standing over Goliath, with the decapitated head in his hand, and four, unused smooth stones still in his pocket, he thought.

"I don't know how he did it," Leon admitted, not taking his eyes off Buzz Saw.

"It's not the size of the dog in the fight. It's the size of the fight in the dog. That dogs bigger on the inside than any dog I've ever seen on the outside," Bill said, still whispering.

"What are we gonna do?" Leon said pitifully, like a boy who had just lost his mother.

"We're gonna prosper. What you see before you is the ultimate ringer. Looks like something that was kicked out of the pound...fights like a wildcat in a sack."

The wisdom was not registering on Leon. He was looking at Buzz Saw as if the dog might leap out of the pit at any moment.

"We can take him to any fight around here. Everybody will bet against him. If he does what he does here, if it wasn't luck, then we make a killing. Was Baby hurt, or sick before you put her in there?" His mind still refused to believe it, trying to find some explanation for this phenomenon.

"No, boss. She was fit and sassy. I'm with her everyday, I know her best. Knew her..." Leon said, choking back more sobs.

"I'm not training him! He don't fight fair."

"No, don't train him. We want him to look just like he does now. Don't even give him a bath. Just give him Baby's ration. And don't cut him short."

Leon shook his head in acceptance.

"Better get your muzzle before you try to get him out."

Again, Leon agreed with this, as they both looked at the split carcass of Baby.

"Then, get a shovel, and bury our dog."

Leon nodded at the order, and wiped his nose and face on the sleeve of his shirt.

"The queen is dead," said Dollar Bill, staring at the brindle boxer, whose face and chest was stained red with Baby's blood.

"Long live the King."

Chapter 10

LEON RUDELY SHOVED THE dog into the pen formerly occupied by the deceased Baby. Buzz Saw walked around the enclosure sniffing at the scent of the female dog, keeping a wary eye on Leon, who was standing outside watching. Seeing no way to escape, he settled down to lick the still bleeding gash in his shoulder. Leon saw this and left, coming back directly with a wad of cotton soaked in a blue lotion. He tied this to a stick and thrust it through the mesh of the pen. Buzz Saw tried to move away from the stick, thinking it was going to snare him again. But Leon continued to poke at him, eventually smearing the blue lotion onto the wound. It stung, and the dog tried to lick it off, but it was bitter to the taste, so he lay down in the fartherest corner and kept his eyes on Leon.

"Lick it off it you want to, you demon. I don't care if you get an infection and die." Leon walked away to collect his thirty pack, and wash away his sorrows.

For the first time in his life, even during his time in the field, he felt something akin to loneliness; an aching emptiness in his heart. He felt totally removed from anything he knew or loved. Fully disconnected. The feeling made him want to resume trying to find a way out of the enclosure, but he was weary, and eventually sleep overtook him.

***

Carol was glad that Robby had resumed running. It had been weeks after the disappearance of his dog before he ventured back out. But, gradually he had put his running shoes back on and resumed. The Scott house next door had grown up into a jungle with the coming of the spring rains. It further served the feeling she had that they were isolated, and that the world around them was crumbling. After a week of coming to bed with her, Earl had resumed his former behavior of not sleeping. He offered no explanation for this strange behavior, other than to say that people slept too much, and he got more done this way. Actually, he rarely got anything done, preferring to sit and look out the window, and jump when his pager buzzed, which it did frequently.

She was startled one morning to see several vans pull up in front of the house. The sign on the side of their vehicle read Stewart Security.

"Earl, there's some security company outside."

"Oh, I'll go talk to them."

She saw Earl walk over and sit in one of the vans. He appeared to be reading a contract, and then she saw him signing papers. Next, he seemed to be counting out money from his wallet. When he exited the van the employees began unloading supplies.

"What's going on?" she said when he came back to the house.

"Oh, that? I'm having bars installed on all the windows."

"What? Honey, this is a rent house. What will the landlord say?"

"He won't say anything. I cleared it with him. We need security out here. We're all alone."

"How much did it cost?" she asked bewildered.

"Uh, it wasn't much. Two thousand dollars."

"Two thousand dollars? Are you crazy? You're putting two thousand dollars into a rent house?"

He stared at her for a long three minutes, which to her felt like an hour. She noticed how the skin around his face was stretched tight, giving his face a skeletal appearance with large, dilated eyes to top it off.

He finally spoke and broke the stillness.

"I keep hearing that word, 'crazy.' I'm not crazy. I cleared it with the landlord. He loved the idea, and appreciated us putting money into the place. He doesn't think I'm crazy. The people doing the work don't think I'm crazy. That just leaves you. Maybe you're the one who's crazy."

"Earl, how will we afford this?"

"Earl, how will we afford this," he mocked, in a singsong voice. "You're worried about money? Well, maybe I can calm your little mind." Earl took out his wallet and began counting out one hundred dollar bills on the table in stacks of thousands. When he had emptied the contents of the wallet, she counted five stacks of currency. And he had paid the security company two thousand.

"Where did you get all that?"

"Out of my wallet," he said, sarcastically. "And that's not all, baby." He retrieved a cigar box from a closet and began counting more money. When he was finished she counted 12 stacks. Twelve thousand cash, in hundred dollar bills.

"You see why we need bars on the windows. Hey, lets spread the money on the bed and make love. I saw that in a movie once."

It had been weeks since he had touched her, and the idea did not appeal to her now.

"Where did you get all that?" she asked again, changing the subject.

"If I told you, I'd have to kill you," he said seriously, and her heart skipped a beat. Then he burst out laughing. "It's for the security of my family; the family I love and treasure. It makes us safer."

Somehow, she did not feel safer being barricaded in with him.

"What if the police come in and find all that money? What happens to Robby and me?"

"Why would the police come here? Have you noticed anything unusual?"

"Only you installing bars on the windows," she said.

He frowned at this remark. "I'm serious, have you noticed people hanging around the house, like maybe in the woods?"

"Earl, if you saw anyone hiding in the woods we should call the police…oh, now we can't do that, now can we?" she said, sarcastically. "There's nobody in the woods."

"You're not as alert as I am. I've been staying up lately, watching"

"Is that why you're always at the window?"

"Damn right. And I've seen them. Hiding behind the trees out there. They don't know I've seen them, but I have. I'm just waiting for the right opportunity to catch them. That's why I bought this." He walked over to the couch and pulled a gleaming, black 9 Millimeter Glock out from under a cushion. She jumped at the sight of the large handgun.

"My God, what the hell else do you have in my house?"

"Our house, baby. Our house. And I am the master of my domain. The king of the castle. The cock of the walk. The duke of Earl."

He laughed hysterically at this pun, and then quickly forgot the humor.

"Anybody who comes to take what belongs to Earl is in for a rude awakening. I rarely sleep, and I'm loaded for bear."

"And what are you going to do if you catch somebody and kill them? You can't very well call the police."

"Bury them. And bury the shovel I buried them with. And go home and sleep like a baby. Well, maybe I won't go home and sleep. I'll probably go home and wait on the next sucker to try the same thing."

"That's..." she started to say 'crazy,' but consciously avoided using the word.

"That's a little irrational, honey. If you kill someone, I'm accessory to murder."

The noise from the security installation outside reminded her that she was, by the minute, being barricaded in with someone who she increasingly did not trust. It was like a prison being constructed around, while you waited patiently for it to be built. She began to question her own judgment in staying as long as she had.

"You wouldn't squeal on me would you? If I killed someone who was coming to rob us, and rape you, and steal everything I've earned? Would you turn me in to the police if I was forced to do that?" He was looking at her pitifully, as if she were Judas Iscariot and he were Jesus Christ. She felt as though she must be very careful what she said.

"If someone came to harm us, and you killed them in self defense, the appropriate thing to do would be to call the police. That would solve everything."

"I realize you've been raised to believe the police are our friends, and honey, that's not your fault," he said, in a condescending manner, "but I've been around the block a few more times than you, a few hundred more times than you. I would be placed in jail, just for defending what's mine. You and Robby would be at the mercy of the world. The next criminal who came around would not find me here, since my righteous, self-defending ass would be in the lower portion of some dungeon, and you would be a statistic on a crime sheet. The police are not our friends. The police exist to create an illusion of safety on the streets, and to stifle free enterprise and enforce unconstitutional drug laws. Whatever happens here, when those people try to come in, will be taken care of with a shovel and a bag of lime."

"What people?" she said.

He sighed at her apparent lack of understanding. "Those people I saw in the woods, at the back of the property."

He seemed so convinced of this that she went to the back window and looked out.

"Where did you see them?"

He seemed pleased she was becoming involved in the clandestine surveillance.

"They were hiding behind that big oak. The one about 50 yards back. I could see them peeking around. They jumped back when they saw me looking out the window."

"They're not there now, are they?"

"Of course not. Not with all the banging these guys are doing. They'll think twice when they see the bars I'm putting in. That's one reason I've been staying up at night, baby. I didn't want to alarm you, but I've been seeing them for several weeks now."

She found herself actually looking, and then felt ridiculous. She was sure there was no one out back in the trees, stalking them. Was there? Of course not. She looked one more time impulsively, and moved away from the window. Better to humor him, till…what? She had to make a decision, and only one seemed clear: she had to get on her feet and get Robby out of this nest of madness.

She felt ashamed at having gotten herself into this position. She should have went out and got a job long ago, but she had let Earl persuade her into staying home. Now she had no money, no car, and no real family to turn to. And they were isolated a good ways from town, and soon to be barricaded, with a man who had gained a sizable amount of cash and possibly lost his mind.

"Earl, I've been thinking…" she began, but he cut her off.

"Well, we both know that's unhealthy for you," he said, and then smiled, "sorry honey, just a joke. What are you thinking?"

"I was thinking I would like very much to go to work. I was going to wait a couple months till Robby was back in school, but why wait? It's something I really want to do."

"Uh uh, I won't have it. We have plenty of money, and more on the way. I won't have my wife working. Why do you want to go to work?" he asked, suspiciously.

She felt as if she were out on a very thin limb, and it might break at any moment.

"I'm tired of sitting home. I'm just not fulfilled."

"You're tired of being with me?"

"No," she said, guardedly.

"Then if you want fulfillment you can take up knitting. Or you can help me count our money."

"I don't want to be involved with that."

"You're already involved, sweetheart. You help me spend it. We operate a continuing criminal enterprise," he said, locking his hands behind his head in a self-satisfied manner.

"That doesn't give me any comfort."

"Don't worry. I've got everything under control. Like the putting bars on the windows. I'm a step ahead."

The sound of the workers turning the house into a secure facility echoed through the walls, and reminded her that she had to do something soon, even if she had no idea what that something might be.

***

The dog's mornings began with waking up to the sound of activity at the scrap yard. He immediately walked the perimeter of his enclosure, checking for any way out. Finding none, he would wait for the greasy, smelly man to come around and toss a thick, raw steak through the door, onto the ground. Sometime around noon, the man would come back with a shovel and a wheelbarrow, and nervously enter the enclosure where he would proceed to shovel up the droppings left by the dog. He usually talked to the dog as he did this, but it was incomprehensible to him, as it did not involve any discernable command.

Buzz Saw could only detect malice and dislike emanating from him, and he always sat at the far edge of the pen. He had the distinct impression if he were to charge the man's legs he would be brained with the shovel. Not that he had any desire to do this. The thought of sinking his teeth into the stinking flesh of Leon was enough to make him gag, and he would only do so if he were threatened. His one desire was to find a way out of the pen and escape the incredible loneliness he felt.

Leon however, did not know the dogs thoughts, and was absolutely sure Buzz Saw was waiting to tear him limb from limb. He could not erase from his mind the image of the undersized brindle dog with the white socks playing timid with his Baby round and round the pen, till he coaxed her into overconfidence. Then, metamorphasizing before his eyes, becoming, in an instant, something too terrible to watch. Something too terrible to be withstood. And Baby had paid the price. His Baby.

Leon blamed himself. He had picked up the dog from the field. How could he have known? The words of Dollar Bill haunted him: 'it's not the size of the dog in the fight, it's the size of the fight in the dog.' How could he have know what was inside that ragged looking mutt?

His Baby. Split open like a half-eaten turkey after thanksgiving dinner. The thought made tears come to his eyes, and made him want to go at the dog with the shovel.

But he knew he would not do that. Not only was the dog valuable to his boss, but also, the shovel might not be enough. After all, Baby was not enough, and she was a hell of a lot of dog. It would not be pleasant to be locked in the pen, unable to get away, if the mongrel went ballistic like he did in the pit.

Look at him, Leon thought, sitting over there just like he was sitting out in the field. Like he wouldn't eat a biscuit. It's all an act. He plays all innocent, till you're not looking, till your guard is down. Then, that other dog comes out. The one that flipped Baby like a pancake on a skillet, and went at her till her guts were steaming in the breeze.

"If I get ready to do you mister, it'll be with a shotgun!" Leon said, pointing the shovel for emphasis.

Buzz Saw looked at him quizzically, and watched as Leon emptied a mixture of crushed, dry dog food and protein mixture into his bowl. Leon was back to sniffling now, having upset himself with thoughts of the dead Pit Bull. He backpedaled out of the pen and secured the gate.

"Eat up, you son of a bitch. We got some traveling to do tomorrow."

Chapter 11

THE ROUTINE OF THE morning was broken when his ration did not come. Sometime around noon, Leon came into the pen wearing the leather handling gloves that zipped up to the elbow, carrying a muzzle.

"Hungry? Good. You're supposed to be. We got a match tonight and you're gonna make us some money. Are you gonna give me a hard time with this muzzle?"

Leon's eyes were wide round and Buzz Saw could feel the stink of fear emanating from him, along with his other odors, none of which were pleasant. His hands were shaking like a Parkinson's patient as he advanced in a shuffling motion, sure at any moment that the dog was going to do a number on him. Buzz Saw shuddered as the man drew close, and then slipped the muzzle over his mouth and face. He was greatly relieved when Leon fastened the buckle, snapped a leash to his collar and stepped back. He was then led to the truck where Dollar Bill was waiting.

"Come on Leon, get that thing in the cage so we can get on the road."

Leon seemed to be hesitating before he hoisted the dog up and into the cage in the back of the pickup.

"Leon, don't tell me you're afraid to pick up our friend here? I believe that muzzle has rendered him null and void for the moment."

Leon hesitated, then placed both arms under the dog, and lifted him up and into the waiting wire cage.

"You didn't see what he did to Baby, while he was doing it, I mean."

"Well, we're going to find out tonight if it was a fluke. We're gonna bet a hundred on him and throw him to the wolves, just to see what happens. He's already killed my golden goose, I'll be damned if I'll let him cost me a bundle in the process."

"Weren't no fluke. He don't fight fair, that's all I can say," Leon said, angrily.

Buzz Saw crouched down in the cage and tried not to let himself be thrown against the wire mesh as the truck sped around corners and braked hard. He loved to ride and feel the wind, but the uncertainty of where he was going overrode any joy he might have felt about being in the wind, and away from the scrap yard.

Leon and Dollar Bill stopped at various places along the way including a convenience store, arriving at the town of Lake Village, Arkansas around 3:00 PM. Once there, they drove to a small isolated farm with a gate, which had to be opened by a man whom Dollar Bill had called on his cell phone to say they were arriving.

They pulled up to a frame house, outside of which were several men loitering and drinking beer. The owner of the farm came over to the truck and motioned for Dollar Bill and Leon to get out.

"Don't say much about our dog. Just play stupid," Bill said to Leon, sure that his hired hand could accomplish this task.

"Bill, Leon, good to see you. Been a long time," the man said. "Where is that lovely monster you used to tote around?"

"We left her back at the house," Bill said, before Leon could speak up. She's…with child. Yeah, she's gonna have a litter. I had her bred. Been meaning to do it for some time. Her biological clock was ticking and she was moping around, so what the hell, I fixed her up."

"She wouldn't have done you much good here, anyway," the man said, "her fame proceeds her. Nobody wants to lose a dog."

"Yeah, that's why we been going out of state with her."

"What you got in the back, there?" the man asked, looking in the back of the pickup.

"That old thing?" Dollar Bill answered, "This is a dog that wandered up at the scrap yard. We ain't never seen him fight. Probably can't. Thought we'd bring him here just for laughs."

The man looked Buzz Saw over through the wire of the cage and made a disgusted face.

"It won't be funny to him when he gets put into that pit. I think my daughter has a lap dog in the house that can whip his ass."

"Well, it won't be no loss. I'm tired of feeding him anyway," Dollar Bill said, glancing at Leon.

Leon was looking at the ground like he'd just heard the worlds biggest fib, but he kept his mouth shut.

Buzz Saw was gingerly extricated from the back of the truck by Leon, and then led to a row of pens containing

151

a water bowl and nothing else. On his right and left were two other animals who nosed at the mesh as if wanting to get at him, and barked continuously. All around him was the din of excited animals, the sound of distant loud music, and occasional laughter as people milled around the farm in a party atmosphere. He lay down in the center of his pen, trying to stay as far away as possible from the strange, hyper dogs that surrounded him on both sides.

People were beginning to make their way to row of cages containing the fighting dogs, looking for an animal to bet on when the matches began. They would stop at one, scratch their chin and nod in appreciation at certain characteristics they thought assured a winner, then move to the next. The people who stopped in front of Buzz Saw's cage would, invariable, laugh and point. A few made throat-cutting gestures with a hand, signifying their opinion of his chances. The smell of them, to Buzz Saw, suggested a certain erratic nature that he could not discern, not having an understanding of inebriation. He was only glad to be separated from them by wire and several feet.

After several hours he saw Leon approach and expected his ration of meat, but the stinking man only opened the gate and fixed the leash to his collar, leading him out. Now he was away from the close proximity of the cages, but among masters on both sides. People made snide comments to Leon as the dog was lead to the fighting area.

"Hey boy, you bring you family pet here to get eaten?"

"What's that muzzle for, so he won't lick himself raw?"

"I'm betting a thousand dollars on whoever you put him in with!"

Leon kept his head down, and they worked their way to the pit, which was now surrounded with eager patrons spoiling for a spirited match, and fueled in their enthusiasm by alcohol and various other illegal substances. To Buzz Saw, it was a confusing mishmash of smells and emotions, far too many to focus on. He felt he was surrounded by madmen, as well as being led by one.

He was lifted down into the pit by Leon, and the muzzle removed. The pit smelled vaguely like the one Leon had kicked him into when he was forced into conflict with Baby, and this did not bring him comfort.

It was hard-packed dirt, and approximately six foot in depth. A man wearing elbow length leather gloves, and chaps similar to those worn by horsemen, stood back at the fartherest edge. His function was to separate the dogs if the owner of a beaten animal called for a break. Calling for a break was akin to throwing the towel in boxing, and if an owner had no concern for his animal, the fight was often to the death. Rather than give up and lose a bet, some dog fighters would allow it to continue, against all hope, till the hound was killed.

The proprietor of the farm called for his audience attention, and announced, "Thank ya'll for coming out here tonight. I think we are gonna see some good matches. We got dogs from all across the state, and some new ones for you to see. You know the rules, they ain't changed none. Owners, if you want a break just make sure you holler loud. My son will hear you, and separate. That constitutes a loss. No argument on that. Only an owner can call a break. Otherwise, we fight till it's done. One dog goes into the pit, then we get a challenger, and ten minutes to mingle and do your betting."

A woman approached and whispered something to the man.

"One other thing, the port-a-potty I rented is full and not functioning. Please go out behind the barn and do your business."

This brought a smattering of laughter from the crowd.

"Our first match will be a dog owned by Bill Dollar out of Warren. His name is…"

At that point the man realized he did not have a name for the dog in the pit, and he looked to Dollar Bill, who was standing beside Leon. Dollar Bill had not thought to name the dog either, and he looked at Leon.

"Killer," Leon barked out. "Killer…the unknown."

This caused a great amount of laughter in the audience.

"You mean killed," someone hollered, and more laughter ensued.

"He looks like he'd kill a turkey leg"

"Dollar Bill brought his family pet to a pit bull fight. Shame on you, Dollar Bill."

Bill blushed crimson and fished out his wallet.

"I got one hundred dollars on…Killer the unknown," he shouted over the laughter.

There were several dog owners standing near him and they began digging for their wallets, thrusting bills out to him.

"Hold on everybody, he can only do business with one," the farm owner said. "Give him a chance to set a match."

"I got a mangy mutt I brought just so I could get him killed and get it over with," a man standing near Bill said.

"He'll be a good match with your...dog. You want to see him before we do this?"

"No," Bill answered, taking the man's money, and giving it to the proprietor for holding, thus officially sanctioning the match. "Okay, lets have us a dog fight."

"We've got a ten minute intermission for betting, or whatever," said the owner, who had now picked up a battered megaphone so as to be heard over the audience. "One more thing, owners will be responsible for burying their own animals. We supply you a shovel and a handful of lime, please don't leave any legs sticking out of the ground, like last time. My wife thanks you for that."

Buzz Saw sat in the center of the pit calmly glancing at the crowd of faces surrounding him, the only recognizable face to him being Dollar Bill and Leon, who were waiting nervously for their opponent to be walked in. In minutes, a black Pitt Bull was brought to the edge of the arena. He had long scars on both upper shoulders and one ear appeared to be tattered down to the base of his skull. He appeared anxious to jump into the hole, and his owner was digging his heels into the dirt to hold him back. He outweighed Buzz Saw by about 40 pounds, but was not the pure physical specimen of the departed Baby. His slanted eyes, and overhanging brow gave him the appearance of a Down's syndrome child, but there was no doubt to the crowd that they were looking at an experienced fighter.

The people around the pit crowded Dollar Bill and thrust handfuls of money toward him, hoping to persuade him to make a bet with them before the match started.

"Hell, no," he said over and over again, at their offers. "I've made the only bet I'm going to make." They slunk back disgusted, putting their money back into their wallets.

"Okay, one minute," said the man with the megaphone.

"Come on," someone shouted, "ain't nobody gonna bet on this fight!"

When the 60 seconds had passed, the proprietor nodded and the black Pit Bull was lifted and placed into the pit by his owner. He was straining at the lease to get at his opponent, tongue wagging happily as he anticipated a tussle. Buzz Saw eyed him curiously, but held his position, sitting on his haunches. As he sensed it was not a female, he had no interest or fascination with the dog.

Dollar Bill glanced over at Leon and saw he had his hand over his eyes.

"What's the matter Leon, are you attached to that mutt?" someone shouted.

The leash was unclipped from the black Pit and he wasted no time in crossing the space that separated them. Buzz Saw remained passively still until the last second.

There was no rope-a-dope tactic this time. No dancing around the enclosure. When the black Pit Bull approached his face and snarled a greeting, the dog they called 'Killer the unknown' came alive, and a ferocious roar temporarily eclipsed the noise of the crowd. Those standing around the makeshift arena involuntarily took a step back, as if a bomb had gone off at their feet unexpectedly. Such was the thrust and surprise of the assault that the Black Pit somersaulted back and over, sustaining a deep gash to his nose.

He wasted no time in getting back on his feet, but made no movement to reengage his opponent. He stood at the far back edge of the pit, as far away from Buzz Saw as the enclosure would allow, looking sheepish, blood dripping from his torn snout.

"Holy shit," the man with the megaphone said audibly. "Looks like that one's through."

"Oh, hell no," said the owner of the Black Pit, and he jumped down into the hole and began kicking his dog.

"What the hells wrong with you? I didn't drive you down here to get whipped by somebody's yard dog! Get your ass over there and fight."

He continued to kick his dog until he was forced back into contact. There was a halfhearted meeting between the two, before he was driven back again to cower under the man's legs. The kicking resumed, this time with more force and viciousness. The Black Pit balled up and yelped, preferring to accept the blows from his owner's boots rather than be forced back across the enclosure. It appeared he might be kicked to death, until the brindle boxer, who had heretofore calmly repositioned himself back on his haunches, leapt from his sitting position and made a beeline for the leg of the kicking man.

For the man, it happened much too fast to register on his consciousness. He was focused on dealing misery to his dog, when he dimly saw something streak towards his lower leg like a brown torpedo. Those around the pit heard a scream that would later be recollected as "woman-like" in emanation. The man in the pit screamed and danced like a one legged Indian trying to summon rain, doing everything within his power to dislodge Buzz Saw from the firm grip the dog had on his calf.

On the edge of the pit Dollar Bill was as startled and shaken as Leon, who had at some point uncovered his eyes and also screamed, being thrown into a full fledged flashback, sure that the man in the pit was going to be disemboweled before a standing room only audience.

"Get him off," the owner of the Black Pit bellowed, "Help me, Jesus."

The Black Pit scurried away from his owner and the attacker; pleased for the moment he was no longer being booted.

The man with the break stick moved between the man and the dog attached to his leg, clubbing Buzz Saw until he suddenly let go, and withdrew to a spot on the far wall. The Black Pit moved away, apparently sure only that he wanted to be away from both.

The bitten man leapt over the edge of the pit and bellowed, "Look at my damn leg."

His pants were torn and a red stain was visible through the fabric. His dog was lifted up and out of the enclosure, but he did not appear to have any inclination to be reunited with his owner, and he disappeared into the crowd, amongst a sea of legs.

Buzz Saw walked back to the center of the ring, oblivious to tumultuous events surrounding him, preferring instead to nurse the bruises he had received at the end of the breaking stick.

The man had rolled his pants up now and was looking at an ugly, ragged tear on his calf.

"Look at my leg. That's gonna need stitches," he said, to no one in particular.

He then directed his stare to the man hosting the dogfights, who had moved down where he could look at the wound.

"That weren't no win. That mutt attacked me before my dog could handle up. I get my hundred dollars back," he said vehemently.

"Now, you know your dog was beat. He turned and refused to go anymore."

"Bullshit, he was just getting his wind. That weren't no match."

"It was a match. It was just over in the first round," said the proprietor.

"What about my leg?" he said, his voice growing shrill.

"You got bit 'cause your dumb ass jumped in the pit and stirred up the other dog. That's all."

"Well, I'm not going for this…uh, uh…no way. First thing I'm gonna do is go get my gun and shoot that leg-biting son of a bitch," said the man, shaking his head for emphasis and pointing at Buzz Saw.

The owner of the farm just raised his hands as if to say, 'what can I do,' and the wounded man limped off, presumably to get his weapon.

"Leon, take possession of Killer the unknown," Dollar Bill said hurriedly, as he accepted the hundred dollars from the proprietor. Leon jumped into the pit and cautiously placed the muzzle on the dog, then lifted him out of the pit to the cheers of the onlookers.

"Better get out of here. He's a might sore, and I don't just mean his leg," said the farm owner.

"Thank you. We'll be leaving now. Come along Leon," said Bill.

They walked through a corridor of people who opened up to let them pass, and ignored several calls from potential buyers wanting to know the asking price they would take for the dog.

They half jogged to where the truck was parked, and Leon stuffed the dog into the cage, in back of the pickup. Dollar Bill climbed into the passenger seat and looked back to see a limping man emerge from the crowd 50 yards to their rear, carrying an object in his hand which looked ominously dark and heavy.

"Better hurry, brother Leon, better hurry."

Leon sidled into the driver's seat of the truck, simultaneously turning the key and stomping the gas. The truck fishtailed out of the parking area and onto the loose gravel of the driveway exit, then straightened out as the tires grabbed hold of the road. They then heard the booming sound of a large caliber handgun. The sound of the next shot did not reach them, as it shattered the rear window of the pickup, and the sound of breaking glass was the only thing evident. They both ducked involuntarily, with Leon trying to keep the vehicle on the road, and not get shot at the same time.

When they turned onto the highway and both rose from a stooped position, Leon looked over at Dollar Bill, the whites of his eyes showing, gestured back towards Buzz Saw and said, "Boss, that dog is more trouble than a car with a bent frame."

***

"Mom, I need you to take me by the field house at the school so I can pick up a permission slip for football," Robby said to his mother, on a day towards the end of July.

"Earl, is that okay with you? We won't be long,"

Earl had lately been increasingly reluctant to let Carol go anywhere alone in the vehicle. His excuse was that the vehicle had a bad universal joint, and could leave her stranded at any minute. She found this reasoning suspicious, since he was making no effort to get it repaired, and he obviously had the money to do so. Perhaps it was a control issue, or maybe he didn't trust her to come back. In her heart, she considered the relationship fractured beyond the bounds of healing, and she had been looking for an opportunity to get Robby away from Earl, so they could talk.

Earl looked at her a long moment, trying to read her, then said, "Okay, don't stomp the gas or that U-joint might give way. And hurry back."

"We will. Just to the school and back."

She gathered up her purse, which as always, contained only a drivers license and some makeup. Then, she and Robby got in the truck and pulled out on the highway.

"So," she began, "when does football start?"

"The second week of August, about 2 weeks from now."

"You're really looking forward to it, huh?"

"It's gonna be great. Its a lot different here than at the Grove."

"How so?" she asked.

"It's a lot harder I hear. The kids say the only thing worse than two a days under Coach Byrd is Marine Corp boot camp."

"And you're looking forward to that?" she asked, looking at him incredulously.

"Well, it makes it matter more. If you make it through that, and get to wear a Monticello jacket, everyone knows you've paid your dues. They start with a big turnout, and the ones that can't cut it drop out."

"Do you think you'll make it through all that?"

"Oh, I'll make it through. I'd crawl through broken glass to play for Coach Byrd."

She looked at him with alarm. "That's not part of the program is it?"

"No, mom," Robby said, shaking his head at her question. "That's just a figure of speech."

"Good, otherwise we'd need a lot of iodine and Band-Aids." She sighed, and was silent for a moment.

"I guess we'll have to stick it out here for a while," she finally said.

"What do you mean, mom?"

"Robby, have you seen anyone hanging around the house, like in the woods?"

Now he was really confused, and the emotion registered on his face.

"Of course you haven't. You'd have said something about it. Earl has just got me freaked out lately. He claims someone is stalking us, hiding in the woods. He's convinced of it."

"Earl is crazier than a soup sandwich," Robby said with conviction.

"Yeah, or a screen door on a submarine," she responded.

"Or a space heater in an igloo," he shot back, and they both laughed.

"Seriously, I've let us get into a situation that...that can't persist," she said, with conviction.

"But you've got football coming up and you really want to play. And I don't have any resources available to get us anywhere. Tell me, what you think…would it be stealing for a wife to take some of her husband's money and leave. If she didn't help earn it, I mean? And she didn't have any other options?"

He appeared to think on this hard for a moment, then said, "Mom, I would like to tell you it's okay, but I have to tell you what you'd tell me: if its stealing, its stealing. Better to ask God for help, and let him do it. You believe God would help, don't you?"

She felt momentarily ashamed that her son had given her advice that she herself should have already known.

"Sure, I believe God would help. Sometimes I forget He's available. Sometimes I make Him my last option. I hope you don't follow my example on that," she said.

"Mom, when Buzz Saw came up missing, I asked God to send him back, if he wasn't dead. Buzz Saw didn't come back, so I guess he's dead."

It was the first time, in a long while, that the subject of the dog had come up, and her heart broke a little remembering how her son was affected by it; was just now getting back to himself.

"Do you think there are animals in heaven?" he asked, and the question took her aback.

"Well, I don't know. I don't know near enough about heaven to give you an answer." She was silent for a long moment, and then said, "I know this: God can do anything. And if you wanted Buzz Saw to be there, God can do it."

Robby was looking out the window of the truck, away from her eyes, and she hoped he was not overly sad, thinking about his lost dog. At once he turned towards her and she was relieved to see him smiling.

"I believe in heaven. And I don't think heaven would be heaven unless you and Buzz Saw were there. So I know he'll be there," Robby said, with confidence.

"That's good enough for me," she said, happy to see him smiling.

They pulled up at the school and she watched him enter the field house. Five minutes later he emerged with the permission slip in hand, and they headed back towards the house.

"We're going to try to tough it out here until the end of the school year. I'm going to ask God to help us find a way out of this situation. I want you to ask him too, okay?"

"It must be bad between you two, huh?" Robby said, looking at her.

She returned his gaze briefly but did not answer his question.

"I hope you forgive me for getting us in this situation."

"I forgive you, mom. If you want, I'll quit school and get a job so we can get out. I can walk to work and Earl can keep his truck."

She was touched by his offer, and again regretted her decision to marry Earl.

"You're not quitting school. I'll find a way for us to leave. If he doesn't straighten up."

"I think Earl is as straight as he's ever going to get, mom."

She sighed, knowing her son often showed more wisdom and insight than she did. And he was only 15. I used to change his diapers, she thought silently, when did he catch up with me in brains?

A week after the match in Lake Village, Arkansas, Dollar Bill called Leon into the office.

"Leon, I like what I saw the other day with our friend, out there."

"You mean your friend."

"He'll be your friend when he buys you a few more beers," Bill responded. Leon appeared to think on this a minute, before Bill continued.

"Although that was a no count dog he got put up against, I see where he gets his gumption, or at least I think I do. He sits there looking like any old ordinary dog, and then when the other dog comes up to take a bite out of his ass, he goes plum, mad-dog crazy. Startles the other mutt so bad, his ass is grass before he can get his feet under him. Sort of like the quiet kid in school who lures the bully into picking on him. Then…wham! He's on his ass, and the other kids are laughing. Pretty clever. You saw him sitting in that field looking all hungry and lonesome and…wham, he lured you in," Dollar Bill said, chuckling.

"Don't remind me," Leon said, still hurt over the loss of Baby.

"Well, I've just about seen all I need to see before we go bet the farm on…Killer the unknown. I like that name Leon, you done good there."

Leon just looked at his boss, sure he didn't like anything about the dog, even his name.

"We just need to do one more thing. I want to see him go round, one more time. Go out and get me another bait dog. Don't go to the same field, though." Dollar Bill's eyes said he was having fun with Leon, but the humor was lost on the man.

"Never mind. Just go out and pick up some worthless mutt. Throw him to Killer."

"Okay, boss," Leon said, happy to garner another thirty pack at the expense of a stray.

Later that day, Leon took Buzz Saw to the pit and removed his muzzle. Due to his prior experience at being in this situation, he did not relax, but paced nervously back and forth, keeping his eyes on the door leading into the enclosure. Presently the rusted. corrugated iron doorway was pulled back, and a rail thin collie was kicked through the opening. The hair bristled on Buzz Saw's back as he eyed the other dog, certain he was going to be attacked.

A couple had adopted the collie shortly after he was weaned, and brought into their home amid much affection. He was the sole dog in their household. His bowls for food and water were always in the same place, next to the stove, but he, as often as not, ate directly from their hand, begging scraps as they took dinner. The female half of the couple bragged to her friends how easy he had been to house train, and this assured his place in the house as an "indoor dog."

The couple took him to the vet at the age of three months for shots, and was faithful to have him checked for heartworms every six months. At Christmas, his owners fastened a red ribbon to his collar, and took photos of him standing next to the tree, looking up at the camera with a goofy smile. When the female owner's friends brought their young children over to visit the dog was always patient with them as they pulled his tail and ears, even when it caused pain. He was a good dog, no could dispute this.

His one great joy in life was in pleasing his owners. The sound of their voice in praising him was music of the sweetest kind. The touch of their hand on his head, when he managed to please them in some way, was an emotion a human could understand only in terms of winning the lottery, or the academy award: it was joy of the highest order, bliss at the highest level, nirvana.

When he was approaching his fourth year, knowing only peace and pleasure his whole life, his owners had a crisis. The man had been hired for a lucrative job in the city. They were moving to an apartment; one that did not allow pets. There were calls made to members of his family. No, they could not accommodate another dog in their household. Her family said the same thing. So sorry, we just can't do it. None of her friends, or his, could find a way to take the dog known as Buddy. They had other pets that wouldn't appreciate another animal's presence, or they just couldn't find room for him.

There were tears on her part. Maybe they should take him to the pound. Perhaps someone would adopt him? No, the man assured her. He would languish at the shelter because people wanted puppies, or purebreds. Then, when the allotted time for adoption was past, he would fall under the policy for euthanasia, and be put down. Better to drop him off in a good neighborhood. Someone would be quick to take him in. He was sure of it.

So, on a cold day in January, Buddy was driven to a pleasant area of town and pushed out of the car. He remembered the woman looking back at him as they drove off. This was a peculiar game to him, though not unpleasant at first. He was confused by his new surroundings, and by the fact that he'd never been away from his owners, but excited to be free to roam and explore.

He was almost run down by automobiles twice the first day because he had no fear of cars, and was careless. The second day, hunger set in. He found bowls of food sitting at the backs of some houses, but was always run off by the occupying dog, or the homeowner. He was startled by their anger, having never known any reaction from humans, other than love. He found garbage cans to be enticing, but this invariably produced more hostility.

The loneliness he felt proved to be more debilitating than the hunger. He often curled up near the spot where he'd been dropped off, because it was his last connection with his owners. Sometimes he would dream he was back in his home, surrounded by all things good. Then he would awaken, shivering and hungry, and be forced to move just to stay warm and alive. His past life became a distant memory, but he never entirely forgot his owners.

Thus, when Leon saw him scurrying along a sidewalk, and called out to him, he did not hesitate to come. No loop stick was used to snare him. No food was even needed to entice him. He came because he was called, and he was taken and placed in the cage, in the back of the truck. It was frightening to him riding in the back of the strange vehicle, but at least he was in someone's charge, perhaps going to a place where there was food and love. Perhaps going back to his owners. Maybe they had been missing him, as he missed them. What a reunion this would be!

Buzz Saw looked to the top of the pit and saw Dollar Bill and Leon standing at its edge. The situation was identical in nature to the other times he had been matched. But the dog that stood before him was not like the others who had come in spoiling for a fight. He advanced on the starving collie with uncertainty, but quickly read the eyes of the animal. He saw fear and confusion. The way the dogs eyes darted here and there, trying to keep one eye on him, but also desperate to find a morsel on the ground, revealed to him that this creature was suffering from extreme, stomach gnawing hunger. But the overwhelming emotion he could read in the collie's eyes was pure, simple loneliness. A heart made hollow by loss.

The collie cowered before him, tail tucked tightly between his legs, expecting at any minute to experience the wrath of the dog whose territory he had dared invade.

"This'll be over quick," Leon said to his boss.

Buzz Saw stood before the dog and sniffed his head, their noses touching. All the emotions the dog was feeling, he himself had felt. This was not a threat, but a kindred spirit. Buzz Saw's tongue snaked out and passed over the muzzle of the collie, he then sat on his haunches, and resumed watching the men on the upper side of the pit.

"That son of a bitch never misses a chance to disappoint me," Leon said, in disgust.

"Get him out of there, Leon," Dollar Bill said, walking back to his office.

"I still get my thirty pack, don't I?" Leon called out to his back. Dollar Bill did not answer, but disappeared around the corner.

Leon left the pit area and the collie began making circles around the arena, and around Buzz Saw, looking for a crumb of any kind to slake his hunger.

Presently, Leon reemerged at the top of the pit holding a bolt action, single shot .22 rifle. He called out to the collie, "Hey boy, here's a bone for you."

The starving dog stopped and looked up at him, hoping for something to be thrown so he could wolf it down.

Leon raised the rifle and shot. He had been aiming at a spot between the animal's eyes, but he was a very poor marksman. The bullet passed behind the head, into the neck, and severed the spinal cord. Very much alive, but paralyzed, the dog fell to the ground and cried out continuously in long, shrieking yelps.

"Shit," Leon said, concerned more for the din the animal was creating than for its

pain. He fumbled in his pocket for another bullet, dropped it on the ground and, with a curse, picked it up, blowing the dirt off it while looking it over carefully. He then casually loaded it into the chamber, shouldered the weapon, and fired another bullet, which struck the collie, this time, mercifully in the brain. The dog, who was known as Buddy in his former life, lay still in the dirt.

The silence that permeated the air was abrupt. Buzz Saw flinched and moved away when the report of the rifle echoed through the scrapyard. Now he stood still, looking up at the man. Leon shuddered at the look the dog gave him, pointed the empty .22 caliber bolt action rifle at the dog, and said, "pow."

Chapter 12

EARL SAT AT THE kitchen table compulsively chopping and rechopping a pile of powder on a mirror. He had been awake continuously for 6 days. The house was quiet, or should have been. Shortly after Carol and Robby had gone to bed, the sounds had begun. Distant music coming from…somewhere. It seemed to come from all directions, and he had, at first, walked around the room trying to pinpoint the source of it. At first, he was sure it was coming from a central air vent in the ceiling. Was even tempted to take a screwdriver and extricate the cover to find a speaker. But as he stood under the vent, he determined that, no, it was coming from the living room. He crawled on hands and knees around the room, moving the furniture quietly so as not to wake the woman and the boy. He did not want them to see him searching. That would tip them off to the fact that he was on to them. But again, he was unable to locate any source.

So he now sat quietly, listening to the faint sounds of music. Classical music. He hated classical music. She knew that. That was why it was being piped in…somehow.

To drive him to distraction. Very clever. Then, he had an idea. It was in the attic. The sound system was in the upper loft. Again quietly, mustn't awaken them or it would be moved, he fetched a ladder and started to carry it to the attic opening located in the ceiling of the kitchen pantry. As he was carrying the ladder across the kitchen, he glanced out the back window into the woods.

There was a bright moon filtering through the trees, and despite the light from the kitchen, which made it difficult to see out, he saw a shadowy figure jump back behind a tree. Uh huh, he thought. He leaned the ladder against a wall and moved to extinguish the light in the kitchen. Now, the darkness of the kitchen made it much easier to see out into the woods. Be patient, he thought, I'm comfortable in my own house. Whoever is out there is fighting mosquitoes and hoping not to step on a snake. I have all night. At once he felt a great desire to have his Glock 9 millimeter in his hand, and he quickly retrieved it from its place, under a cushion in the couch.

When he came back to the window, pistol in hand, he saw the figure again. This time behind another tree, closer to the house. The figure jumped back again, out of sight. It was advancing, getting closer. Tonight must be the night he, whoever he is, has chosen to assault the house. To steal his money. Steal his drugs. Harm his family? No, he doubted the silent assassin was here to harm his family. He was likely a friend of Carol. Friend and lover. As the thought burned into his brain, the music stopped, but another sound took its place: laughter. He could hear laughter. Faint, but unmistakable. High, lilting laughter. Mocking him. Mocking his soon demise, as the shadowy figure crept closer and closer. His attention to the woods had been interrupted as he listened to the sounds, and he focused his eyes to the trees just in time to see the shadow move behind another tree, closer again.

He ran to the back door and checked the latch. Locked. Then ran to the front door, and saw it was securely locked also. Back to the rear door, and checked it twice more. Good. They were all locked. But maybe he should unlock one of the doors? Allow whoever it was in his backyard to try the door, find it open, and come inside, so he could blow the stalkers brains out, and get this over with.

As he was considering this, the laughter ceased and was replaced by someone calling out his name. It was a female voice. Carol. She had a microphone in her bedroom, and was doing this. He left the kitchen and, carrying the pistol in front protectively, entered her bedroom. He stood over her bed. She was snoring softly, or she was faking. It was impossible to tell. He could still hear the voices, ever so faintly. He had to listen very hard to hear. The sound of her snoring made it difficult to discern.

He remembered the silent creeping form outside his house and sprinted back to the window. Two shadows, one a ways back, and another terribly close, jumped behind the safety of the trees. So, there was more than one. And if there were two, who was to say there were not three. Or four. He imagined the house coming under siege from the front and back simultaneously. Very hard to defend. And, as the front and back door were assaulted, Carol might pop up from her bed with a hidden weapon to distract him further. Attacked on three sides. Impossible to defend. Even Robby might get in on the act. Flanking him from all sides. He strained his ears, listening for the sound of anyone just outside the house, and the sound of the female voice once again became the focus of his attention.

He knew the voice. It was faint, but shrill and accusatory. The voice of his mother. How had they done that? His mother was in a nursing home in Oklahoma and she rarely spoke to anyone, even the nurses who changed her diapers. One of life's little blessings, he mused. But still, it was her voice. Talking as she had talked to his father. Only she was not talking to his father. His father was dead. She was talking to him.

He felt his jaws clench and heard the sound of his teeth grinding. He couldn't make out every word she said, but at spaces in her discourse he could hear his name being thrown out. Oh yes, she was talking to him. Very clever of Carol. Besiege him physically and mentally. If one doesn't work, perhaps the other will. Probably hoping he would turn the gun on himself. Save her the trouble of betraying him. Save them the trouble of assaulting the house.

There was a solution to all this. He could go into the bedroom and put a bullet into her brain. Then, quickly go into Robby's room and finish him. The attackers outside would hear the shots and know they had been foiled. They would know Earl Collins was not to be messed with. She was probably sleeping with one of the men stalking the house. He was certain of that. Maybe all of them. The mental image that came to mind made him cry out in anguish, and he bit his hand to stifle any noise that might wake up his wife and stepson. They would be very sad when he heard the gunshot, heard the sound of her dying.

But what if it was the police outside the house? What if she were in cohoots with the Drug Task Force? He would be playing into their hands by killing her. Capital felony murder. Caught on tape, while they staked him out. Must decide what to do. Before they crash through the doors. With the gun in his left hand, he snorted another large line of methamphetamine, keeping his eyes on the window and his ears attuned to the distant voice of his mother, trying her best to drive him over the edge.

At the scrap yard, the dog slept and dreamed. He was at the foot of Robby's bed. There had been no separation between them. He had never been dropped off in the field. Earl had never placed him in the truck and taken him away. Perhaps he and Robby had ran that day, as they usually did on most days. Whatever they had done, it had been a perfect day, he could be certain of that. And tomorrow would be another fine day. All was right with the world, in this world. In Robby's world. At the foot of the boy's bed. Nowhere else he could ever want to be. And it would never end. He could not even remember when it had begun. In his mind, it always was.

His nose suddenly picked up a noxious smell. It was foul and foreign in this place of peace and happiness. It was getting stronger. And he could now hear something coming down the hallway. He rose and faced the door, summoning all his rage toward what would dare come at his master. He was barking with everything he had, making a terrible racket, but improbably, Robby slept undisturbed. It was just outside the door now, he could hear its breath coming in ragged drafts, and the smell wafted in with every exhale. His fear was not of the thing outside the door, but that he would fail in stopping it. That he was powerless to prevent it getting at the boy. It wanted the boy. Just as the door began to swing open, and he braced for an onslaught, he awoke on the ground of the pen.

Dollar Bill, who often stayed late at his place of business and slept on a bed in back of the office, awoke to the din of the dog in the enclosure barking madly. Such was the continuous intensity of the noise, he was sure someone was lurking outside. He grabbed his .45 Caliber handgun from a desk drawer, quickly dressed and headed outside into the night. He made his way to the pen and shined the light on the dog.

Buzz Saw was running from one corner to the next, desperately looking for a way out. The dog, who rarely barked, was making such a racket that the man placed both hands to his ears before leaving briefly to make a sweep of the property, looking for an interloper. Finding none, and at a loss to explain why the dog was acting in such a bizarre way, he returned to the office and called Leon.

"Leon, come over here and help me with this dog. I believe he's gone loco."

Leon arrived twenty minutes later with his hair disheveled and a scowl on his face. They stood in front of the pen watching the dog run from corner to corner, searching for any way out of the area he was in, still making a deafening racket in the otherwise still of the night.

"What the hells wrong with him?" Dollar Bill asked his flunky, who was still slightly intoxicated from his nightly liquid diet.

"He needs a bullet. Want me to get one?"

"No. Maybe he needs somebody to comfort him. Go in there and pet him, or something."

"Like hell I will!" Leon answered, his eyes wide in the moonlight.

The caged dog was howling now, his head thrown back, wailing like he'd seen the devil. It raised the hackles on the necks of both men.

"I pay you to deal with this dog. He needs... something.

"I told you what he needs, and it comes out the barrel of a shotgun."

"I'll never get any sleep at this rate. Leon, get in there and put that muzzle on him"

"I'd just as soon put a suppository in a grizzly bear than open that cage door, right now."

Leon turned to go back to his truck and Dollar Bill called out, "Come on, Leon. I'll give you a case of beer just to muzzle him."

"Uh, uh," he said, continuing to walk.

"Then you're fired."

"At least I'm alive."

Dollar Bill heard Leon's truck fire up and leave the scrap yard. He went back to his office and put thick wads of cotton in both his ears. At some point he managed to drift off to sleep, and when he awoke in the morning, the dog had resumed his thankfully quiet demeanor.

For Earl, the voices had dissipated sometime around daylight. No one had tried to enter the house, and he could only assume they had been frightened off by his vigilance. Nevertheless, when the sporting goods stores opened at 8:00 AM, he had gone out and bought the most expensive pair of night vision goggles available.

Carol slept in that morning, arising around 9:45 AM. She looked in on Robby and found him still buried under his covers. She entered the kitchen and found Earl sitting at the kitchen table tinkering something that looked like a high-tech pair of binoculars.

"Hey. Whatcha doing?" she said sleepily.

He looked at her angrily with a sideways glance, and said, "Working on a pair of binoculars I bought. Might do some hunting. Might do some night hunting."

"When did you decide to take up hunting?" she said curiously.

He cast her a withering glare containing so much malice she found herself unable to keep his gaze.

"Sometimes its necessary to get rid of pests around the house. They like to creep at night, when they think you are most vulnerable. But I'm rarely ever vulnerable. I'm well aware of the threats that exist outside…and in. And how did you sleep?"

This cryptic comment spun around in her head. He was still looking at her like she'd killed his firstborn child.

"Uh, I slept great."

She started to ask him how he'd slept before she realized that, once again, he had not.

"Did you now?" he asked.

"Sure. Why do you ask?"

"Because I looked in on you. While you were *sleeping*, I mean. You appeared to be sleeping very soundly. Looks can be deceiving though. People can appear to be asleep and not be. They can deceive you."

She had no idea where this was going.

"There was a time when I could be deceived," he continued, "because I was naïve." He chuckled at the accidental poetry.

"But that's behind me. That was the old me. I've transformed, evolved if you will." He was speaking to her as if trying to explain a higher concept to a child, in a condescending tone.

"It is very strange to me that most people lay down and remain motionless for eight hours, or more. Think of all the things people miss by this wasteful habit: the things that go on in the night. I no longer miss these things. I no longer miss anything. Oh, I usually break my sleeping fast around the sixth day. I believe I can extend that eventually. Perhaps do away with sleep altogether. Would you like that? Would you like it if I was awake and alert all the time?"

The question struck her as so insane she had no immediate response, so he continued, "I don't think you would like it very much: because then you could get away with nothing. Nothing would escape my attention."

"What am I getting away with?"

"Nothing, Carol. Absolutely nothing."

Against her better judgment she felt a wave of pity for him, and moved to sit across from him at the table.

"Earl, nobody can go without sleep forever. You've been staying awake for days, and then sleeping for twenty four hours to catch up, that's all. You're having some sort of problem and I want to help you with it. But you've got to let me in before I can help."

Her response threw him off guard and suddenly made him very uncomfortable.

"And what happens when I let you in? Oh, no. No, thank you very much, honey," he said, his voice dripping with sarcasm. Then he was up and out the door, leaving her at the table, shaking her head in confusion.

***

Having been fired by Dollar Bill on numerous occasions before, Leon showed up at the scrap yard at his normal time, as if nothing had happened. He walked into the office to get a list of his duties for the day.

"Morning boss," Leon said, gauging the mans mood, and seeing he was his normally surly self.

"Uh, huh," he responded as usual. But then he pulled out a wrinkled pack of Pall Malls and lit one, forsaking the one in the ashtray already burning. This was a signal to Leon that the man had something on his mind. He leaned back and inhaled deeply, then blew a column of smoke into the air.

"Leon, we will pull out of here in the morning for a road trip. We'll take our friend out there for a little tour down south. Money's better down there. Start off in Monroe. Hit all the best fight spots till we get to Morgan City, then maybe work our way back up. We'll move quick from match to match, before the word gets out on what we got."

"That dog has a demon, boss. That's what we got. A dog with a devil in him."

"Well, if the devils paying, I'm accepting. Take care of everything around here so we can be gone for at least ten days. Just like with Baby, I'll pay you ten percent of what we take in."

Leon stood there trying to convert this into how much beer he would be able to buy, before finally saying, "Okay, boss. Be good to get away from here for awhile."

"Feed our friend double portions today. He's gonna earn it. What in blazes do you thing was wrong with him last night?" Bill asked.

Leon's face drained its color slightly at the memory.

"I think he wanted me to open that cage. I think if I had, he'd of done both of us."

Dollar Bill leaned his head back and laughed riotously.

"Leon, you got one hell of an imagination. Where do you come up with this shit? He's just an undersized mutt with a real bad fighting temper. That's all."

"You know what an anointing is?"

Bill felt a little miffed that Leon knew a word that he obviously did not, but he bit the bullet and said, "No, what is an anointing?"

"It's a spiritual gift. Allows you to do things you couldn't do otherwise. It's a touch from the spirit world. That dog has an anointing on him. I don't know if it comes from God or the Devil. I really don't care, either way. What he did to Baby...no other dog could have done that. No dog's gonna beat him, boss. You ain't gotta worry about that. I just don't want to get on his wrong side when that anointing gets on him." Leon appeared to shudder when he said this, and Dollar Bill remembered his thoughts the night his champion Pit Bull was torn asunder: this must have been what the Philistines felt, when they saw David kill their warrior. The anointing. A big spirit, in a little package.

"Oh, bullshit Leon," he said, shaking off the goosebumps he felt crawling up his arm. "Get that badass mutt ready and we'll go make us some money."

"Yes, sir," Leon said, walking out the door.

Chapter 13

ROBBY AWOKE THE NEXT day in a bright mood. Regular football practice did not begin for another week, but unofficially this day marked the beginning of the Monticello High School football season. It was tradition for all would be players to meet at Coach Byrds house on this day for what was called The Gut Run. It was not mandatory by any means, but everyone usually showed up, hoping a good effort would put them in special graces once the season began. It was all very simple: a ten mile run for the sake of camaraderie and fitness.

Being an avid runner, no one had ever come close to beating the coach. Most of the players on the team could probably outrun him at a hundred yards, save the fattest linemen. But the ten mile course belonged to him. This didn't dissuade the young men from hoping and trying however, and they always showed up with high ambitions. Many of the runners would walk the last half of the race. Some would even stop along the way and call their mothers for a ride back to the coach's house. There would be good-natured ribbing about this, but no one really expected to beat him. The run would conclude with sandwiches, refreshments and bonding for all.

Robby was elated to finally be together with the team. It was a chance to rub shoulders with kids he looked up to at school, and be a part of something he considered great. His mother dropped him off at the front of the coach's house and he scanned the faces that were gathered on the front lawn. Jeff Bennett, the kid everyone expected to be quarterback this season. He had played well as a backup, including the Warren game. Darryl McDaniel, an outstanding defensive back. Chuck Hoover, a kid they called a "headhunter," out of pure respect, due to the fact he would clean your clock if you dared run the ball towards his middle linebacker position. And many others whose names he did not know. He had never had the opportunity to run in the same circles as these kids, and he already felt different about himself, just being able to stand in same group.

And there was the coach mingling with the players, in his running gear. Robby noted the worn running shoes the man was wearing. He obviously had put a lot of miles on them. The slender, toned legs and bunched calves also spoke of someone who ran seriously. Coach Byrd finally made his way over to Robby and introduced himself.

"Hi, haven't seen you out before," said Don Byrd.

Robby swallowed the lump in his throat. He felt he was speaking to royalty, and he was very self conscious.

"Yes, sir. This is my first year."

"I'm Coach Byrd."

"Yes, sir. I know," Robby said, and could only stand there gawking.

"And who are you?"

He realized he had not introduced himself and felt foolish.

"Oh, sorry. My name is Robby Sinclair, sir."

"Have you played organized football before?"

"Yes, sir. At Harmony Grove High School in the ninth grade."

"The Hornets."

Robby felt proud that this man knew the mascot of his old team.

"Yes, sir. The Hornets."

"What position?"

"I played defensive back, sir."

"That's great. I always preferred defense to offense when I played, a thousand years ago. I always felt it was better to do the hitting than be hit."

"Yes, sir."

"Well, were getting ready to do a little running. A short stretch of the legs. You can do as much as you want, no pressure. We meet back here when it's over for the food. Great to have you here." Then he was gone, leaving Robby feeling as if he'd had a brush with greatness. He was greeting other players and Robby could tell they were much more familiar with him, as there was good-natured joking and tussling going on.

About thirty minutes past and it was decided that everyone who was coming had arrived. The group moved to the road and set off in mass. As was his custom, the coach ran with his boys for the first three miles. At this point the linemen and overly out of shape boys fell away. Robby was running in the front, and he looked back to see the group had thinned. He had not yet even passed the first "wall" of pain, and he was running comfortably.

Many others along side him were gasping and showing the signs of fatigue. He was ten feet behind the coach, who was running alongside a group of seniors.

At the five mile point the coach shifted into serious mode and moved out to point fifty yards in front of everyone. Robby looked around and saw there were only fifteen boys remaining. Nearly all of them appeared as if they would die at any moment. Only a black kid by the name of Quincy Ross, who had the long legs and body of a distance runner, and Jeff Goff, who was also a runner on the cross country team, seemed as if they were going to hang in for very long. Robby saw the coach look back to check out who was still with him and he felt a wave of pride wash over him.

At the seven mile point Ross fell back, and though he continued to run the race, he mentally gave up any hope of catching the coach. Goff was still beside Robby, running steady. Sometime in the seventh mile, Robby hit, and passed beyond the final "wall." Now he was stretching out, loving the knowledge that the misery was left somewhere on the road behind him. Goff's face and demeanor remained impassive as he ran stride for stride with Robby, but his comfort level was revealed when he broke his pace near the eighth mile and fell back.

Now it was only he and the coach. Don Byrd craned his head around expecting to see an empty road, as he always did at this point in the yearly run. What he saw was the kid from Harmony Grove, keeping pace at a steady hundred-yard distance. Hmph, he thought, kids got some legs. Time to leave him behind. The coach stretched out his stride a bit, careful not to use all his resources. See you later, kid.

Robby did not know the exact distant point he was at in the race, but was able to calculate, from the point he had passed the final "wall", that they were close to the final mile. The coach was a good hundred yards ahead and appeared to have lengthened his stride. Robby knew he had to make up ground. He decided to begin an alternate running method to gain it. Using the telephone poles alongside the highway, he began sprinting between the gaps of the poles, then slowing back down for a distance of two poles. Sprint, then normal stride, then sprint again.

At the nine mile point the coach looked over his shoulder, sure he would see empty highway, or at the very least, Robby Sinclair a solitary point in the distance. There was the kid, now fifty yards back. A wave of panic gripped his gut. He had never lost one of these season opening runs. It was a matter of pride to him, more so than he had imagined. No one had ever kept up with him to this point, and the kid was obviously gaining ground. He had to be extremely careful not to exhaust himself foolishly, but he had to speed up. He lengthened his stride a bit more. He knew the course they were running well, thus he knew they were in the final mile. Should be able to hold him off, he told himself, nothing to worry about. Just stretch it out. Who is that kid? No problem. Just stretch it out.

With a half mile to go, the coach no longer had to look back to know where Robby Sinclair was: he could now hear the sound of the kid's shoes on the pavement behind him. He passed a telephone pole and heard the boy speed up into a sprint. Good God, he's twenty feet behind me, he thought. Robby sprinted between the poles and this placed him just behind Don Byrd. No reason to hold anything back now, the coach reasoned, bust your gut or lose this race.

They were on the final stretch now. The coaches' house would be visible on the flat, straight road at any moment. They were running stride for stride; both pushing one another at a pace neither had ever run at this distance. The house came into view. Players who had given up and hitched a ride back were along the side of the road. When they saw someone was running with the coach, and it was a race, they began shouting, waving and jumping up and down. The torrid pace had exhausted both runners to the point of collapse. Robby was running for the thrill of beating his hero. The coach was running for the pride of never having lost the run he hosted every year. In the final fifty yards, pride won out. The coach pulled ahead several steps and reached the finish line as the winner.

After running such a distance the prudent thing to do would have been to walk a ways and cool down, but both competitors fell into the grass gasping for their breath as the spectators clamored around, excited but trying not to crowd the spent runners too much. When Coach Byrd decided he would indeed not die on the ground, and finally rose to his feet, he approached Robby, who was being congratulated profusely by the other boys for his effort. He stood looking at the boy for a long moment, and then extended his hand.

"Kid, you almost killed this old man. Harmony Grove, huh?"

"Yes, sir," Robby said, flushed with pride.

"Here's a stupid question, but have you ever run that distance before?"

"Sure, I probably do a ten once a week."

Over food and Gatorade they discussed their favorite routes, and found they often overlapped.

"Look, I need someone to push me a little. Not like you just pushed me I mean, just a little," the coach said, laughing. "You'd push me into a grave if you did that everyday. Give me your phone number and we'll meet at a halfway point a couple days a week, after two a days are over, I mean. You probably won't be able to run during two a days. We do enough running during practice." Robby hurriedly found a pen and a piece of paper and scratched his number for the coach.

The day ended and his mother came to pick him up. As he climbed into the car and they left the house she asked him, "Well, did you make any friends?"

He smiled serenely at her and said, "That was the best day of my life."

***

On the same day of the race, Leon, Dollar Bill, and the dog they called Killer took to the highway. They traveled to Monroe, Louisiana and found a cheap motel that allowed pets.

"Get our friend out and bring him inside, Leon," Dollar Bill said, as they carried the luggage into the room.

"What? He's not sleeping in the room with us!" Leon bellowed.

"That's our moneymaker. He can't very well sleep in that little cage all night. Take the muzzle off of him to feed him, then put it back on if it makes you feel any better."

Leon did as he was ordered and they settled in for the night, with the each man in a twin bed, and the dog curled up on the floor, still wearing the muzzle. After lying in bed for a sleepless hour, Leon rolled over and saw that Buzz Saw was still awake and alert. The dog appeared to be looking directly at him.

"Oh, hell no," he said in frustration, as he arose and began putting on his clothes.

"Boy, what are you doing?" Dollar Bill said groggily.

"I'm sleeping in the truck. I got no desire to die in my sleep."

"He's got the muzzle on."

"It ain't enough. He might chew through it. I wouldn't sleep in the same cage with him, and I'm not sleeping in the same room with him. If you're dead in the morning, I'll shoot him in your memory"

Dollar Bill managed a short laugh as Leon stalked out the door, headed for the safety of the truck cab.

When morning came, Bill dressed and checked on his hired help still sleeping curled up in the front seat of the vehicle. Leon had a severe crick in his neck, but was happy to have survived the night. They drove south out of Monroe, arriving at a large poultry operation being used on this night to host a large meeting of dog fighting enthusiasts.

The dog in the cramped cage at the back of the truck knows, by now, the routine that will unfold. He is not fed his normal ration on the day of a fight, which is his clue as to what is to come. He is taken to a pen area populated with numerous cages and the dogs they contain. The din is deafening, not only from the other animals, but from music, raucous laughter and general hell-raising. There is a tension of excitement in the air, and the other animals around him seem to enjoy every minute of it. But the dog they have named Killer finds no enjoyment in the ritual. It is good to be taken out of the small cage by the nervous Leon, but it is small consolation for what will come next.

He knows he will be led through a phalanx of masters, all of them behaving wildly, and he will eventually be lifted down into an enclosure from which there is no escape. There he will come face to face with another of his species, an animal bred and encouraged to kill him in sport. He will not encourage the conflict, but neither will he back down from it. The joy of fighting will be evident in the eyes of the dog he is pitted against, and they will meet in battle. At some point, he will see the joy in his competitors eyes fade to confusion, then fear, and finally shock as he senses he is losing, and will not survive the encounter.

All goes as he has expected. He is matched against what appears to he a reddish Rottweiller, Pitt Bull hybrid. Dollar Bill has brought five thousand dollars stake money, and quickly all his money is on the line. His opponent is led into the sunken enclosure through a sliding door. He is a massive dog, but slow as a result of his weight. He likely has a stronger pound per square inch jaw than the deposed Baby. And he is chomping at the bit to get at the dog opposite him. There is joy in his eyes and he is dragging his handler. He sees an insanely small dog standing across the pit. He feels this will be great fun. He will charge at this pitifully small enemy and dispatch him with haste. Then, he will be rewarded by a happy owner, and fed all the meat he can stand. The voices he hears cheering, though he cannot understand them, must be for him. It excites his soul to be here, and when his lease is untethered he bounds with all his massive weight towards what will be his victim.

For Buzz Saw, the dog, though massive, appears to be running in slow motion. It is childs play to dart to the side and rip the dog from the flank. This happens twice, and when the dog turns to him again he sees in his eyes, no longer the look of joy, but the look of confusion. The large reddish dog is now bleeding on the upper body, just behind his front left leg. His owner, on the edge of the pit, is calling to his dog to change this tactic, to fight smarter. His voice is beginning to show the strain of mounting anger. Other voices are chiming in, but many, who do not have money on the red hybrid, are beginning to cheer for the obvious underdog.

A chorus of, "Get him little dog. Move and rip him. Don't let him pin 'ya," further enrages the red dog's owner.

After five minutes of hit and run tactics, the red Rottweiller is bleeding profusely from both sides of his body. Buzz Saw no longer sees confusion in his opponent's eyes, but fear and great fatigue. He has chased the smaller dog for the entire match, and has been gashed every time he tries to attack. It is like fighting the wind, and the wind is winning. Due to his great fatigue, and perhaps because he still underestimates the smaller dog, he turns his back and heads for the far wall of the pit to gain his wind. He has made many mistakes in the fight. This will be his last.

His owner cries out in horror as the brindle boxer charges from the rear, and seizes the leg of the red dog. A whip of his head to the left dislocates the leg from the hip socket. A tear to the right severs the long tendon. Now his enemy, like a crippled battleship, is dead in the water.

All his hatred at being in this place, at being taken from his true master, at the myriad of drunken voices calling to him, is turned upon the Rottweiller in a fury of retribution. To the crippled dog, it feels as if he is being struck from all sides at once. His master is hanging over the edge of the pit, almost to the point of falling in.

Unlike many here, he truly loves his dog. He is screaming, "Stop it! Stop it!" But the word "break," must be specifically called out, and in his grief he does not realize why the man in the pit with the thick stick does not move to separate. His dog can no longer here his master's voice, as his ears are filled with the sound of his ripping flesh, and his own pitiful cries. When the man gathers his senses, and calls for a proper end to this, his dog is prostrate on the ground, unmoving, and it is over.

The breaker disengages the attacker and the man leaps into the pit to do what he can for his animal. He is crying and cradling the dog's head, but his blood pours into the dirt as he holds him, and he will not survive long enough to be taken from the poultry farm. A vet would be out of the question, as the man could possibly be reported to the authorities for allowing his dog to engage in illegal activities. So, it is just as well when the dog looks up at him with eyes wide in the throes of shock, and dies.

Leon and Dollar Bill have learned from experience that it is best to gather their animal, collect their winnings, and depart posthaste. They have doubled their money and their dog is unscathed.

Later that night, in the motel, Bill is awakened by a dream he cannot quite recall, and he lies there unable to reclaim sleep. His thoughts turn to the matches he has witnessed. Watching the brindle dog is glorious for him in its monetary gain, but disturbing in another way. It is like watching a mystery. Something seen with ones own eyes, but illogical and unfathomable. Like watching a mongoose take down a wildebeest, or a mountain lion single handedly take down an elephant. It shouldn't be, but it cannot be denied. What was it Leon said the dog had? A mojo? No, an anointing. A spiritual touch.

The room is deadly quiet, the only sound being his own breathing. Leon is torturing his neck and back on the front seat of the pickup truck. Suddenly, Dollar Bill feels he is being watched, and the hairs on his arms and neck stand straight up. He sits up in bed, and sees that the dog is awake also. The dog's eyes are upon him. He has a mad urge to rise and check the integrity of the muzzle. Upon inspection, he finds it is secure; has not been breeched. The dog looks up at him with large, wet eyes, as if to implore him to remove it.

"Uh, uh. Not for a million dollars, old boy," he says, rubbing his arms.

Chapter 14

ROBBY ARRIVED AT THE Monticello High School field house for the obligatory physical examination, which marked the actual beginning of the football practice season. It was identical to everything he had already experienced at Harmony Grove. A lot of time spent standing around self-consciously in your boxer shorts with other self-conscious young men. The dreaded moment when you were asked to drop your shorts. The doctor jams a finger rudely above the testicles, and tells you to turn your head and cough. Surely, nothing could be worse than this. The day passes, to Robby's relief, quickly. He is issued a pair of gym shorts, a gray tee shirt, and ordered to report back the following morning.

His mother drops him off at the field house at 8:00 AM the next day, and after a short welcome speech by Coach Byrd they are ordered out onto the practice field. The friendly welcome speech quickly becomes a distant memory, as the attitude of all the coaches' changes. There is no longer friendly encouragement, but the harsh demanding voices of would-be drill sergeants.

Everyone is lined up for calisthenics, which at Harmony Grove would have been a time to loosen up and goof off. It is not the case here. After a fairly easy round of jumping jacks, they are ordered to run in place, knees up high.

A number of coaches prowl the ranks, screaming, "Knees up. Higher! Higher!" They have no problem getting in a boys face, inches from his nose. This is mostly done by the assistant coaches, but Coach Byrd is prowling nearby with a scowl on his face. No one wants to displease him and just a glance is enough to make Robby lift his legs a little higher. After what seems like an hour they are ordered to stop running. But it does not end here; in fact, it is only beginning. Now they are ordered to belly flop and get to their feet, time after countless time. Robby has come into this with the perception that his high level of conditioning will give him an advantage, but as the belly flop session concludes he is hurting. He looks around to see if anyone else appears winded, and is relieved to see that they are.

The calisthenics session ends and there is a short reprieve, very short. The boys are broken up into groups of five and lined up at the far goal line.

"Gassers," one of the boys says, his eyes weary as if he is about to be sent to the front lines of a battle.

"What's a gasser?" Robby asks, a little afraid. But the question is not answered, and it soon becomes obvious what a gasser is: run to the twenty yard line, then back to the start. Without stopping run out to the thirty, then again back to the start, then out to the forty and return to finally sprint out to the fifty. With all the starting, stopping and changes of direction, it would be bad enough. But the coaches have declared that the trailing person in the five-man group must then do a lap around the track. Thus, no one wants to be last, and each boy pushes the other. In fairness, the linemen are paired together, as are the backs and ends.

This is pure running, Robby concludes, surely I will have an advantage. But it is a different kind of running altogether. Do to the group aspect, it is perhaps three minutes between rounds, and after the first gasser he is very glad to have a short respite. He is in a group of fairly fast young men, and must struggle not to come in last. The boy who ends up trailing his group is separated and forced to do a lap, thus he gets no break. The minute he rejoins his group it is time to line back up. When the boy in Robby's group comes in last twice, and it appears he will collapse, the coaches intervene and angrily direct him to a slower group. Now Robby fears he will be the slowest member of the group, and this proves to be true. He gets no break, and a coach screams into his face to take a lap. He arrives back at the session just in time to line back up and do it again.

Several boys are standing doubled over, and nausea sets in. This appears to please several of the coaches. Robby has never puked from exertion, but on the fifth gasser, after having two penalty laps added for coming in last, he turns his body away and empties the contents of his stomach, his gut retching in agony. Finally, mercifully, the gassers come to an end. The practice is scheduled to last three hours. No one, by order of the coaching staff, is wearing a watch. Robby finds himself wondering what time it is, how much longer this will last, can last. He looks upwards towards the sweltering, morning sun, trying to judge how much time is past. He cannot judge. It seems they have been here forever. Robby worries what demented torture will come next.

Now they are broken up into squads of linemen on one side, backs and ends on the other. The middle part of the practice is rigorous, but not brutal in intensity. It mostly involves moving through footwork drills and agility workouts. A ball is brought out and the three quarterback vying for a job throw passes to the boys as they run routes. Robby runs a post pattern, down ten yards then slant towards the sidelines. Jeff Bennett, the kid everyone expects to be the starter, streaks the pass towards him. It is on target, but comes in with deceptive velocity, bouncing off and stinging his hands. He is berated by a coach when he returns to the group, and he again checks the sun, trying to determine when this will all end.

The practice is drawing to a close now, but to his dismay it will close with more gassers. Now, a large portion of the boys are in a line at the back with exertion sickness. It must end soon, he tells himself. Hang on. Everyone is hurting. You're not alone. A whistle blows and everyone drags to the field house for a shower. The time is 11:00 AM. Practice will begin again at 2:00 PM, and last until 4:00 PM. I want this, Robby reminds himself as he showers. He crawls into Earl's truck in the parking lot, sure he has never been this tired.

"Did you have fun?" she asks, bright eyed. He can only look at her, too tired to respond.

He makes it through the first week of two a days and notices, as the practices close on Friday, that there are ten less boy here than when they started. He feels a certain pride that he has lasted. It is indeed easier towards the end of the week than when he started, not due to any respite by the coaches, but because his conditioning level has risen. He is enormously happy to have a weekend to rest. The dreaded two a days are half over.

Come Monday morning it is raining, and he is joyous they will not be on the field. He reports to the field house, wondering how the coaches will fill the day. It does not take long to find out. The players are crowed into a long hallway for a bear crawl session. Down on hands and feet, they are made to traverse up and down a long hallway, between the coach's offices and the weight room.

The hallway is packed with participants. To slow up is to be crowded and pushed over by the boys to the rear. A coach prowls the line of boys with a wooden paddle. The boys who are impeding progress are given a sharp lick to their raised posteriors, as encouragement to speed up. In minutes, Robby has blisters on both hands at the palms. After an hour of this the blisters have broken to reveal red, raw flesh. It is ninety minutes of screaming, crawling madness, punctuated by the smack of the board being applied to their raised backsides. The coaches seem to be enraged by the fact that it is raining; taking it out on the players. Robby now finds himself praying it will stop raining soon. The bear crawl session ends, and they are allowed to stand up.

Next comes a special game. They are herded into a room with mats on the floor. A towel is rolled up and secured with rubber bands at each end, making in effect, a limber club. Two boys are picked from the crowd and made to each hold on to an end. On the go signal, each boy tries to make his opponent let go of the rolled towel. The round lasts for five minutes. If one contestant lets go of the towel after the first minute, the one who now has control is allowed to whack him for the remaining four minutes.

The towel, when rolled, is a soft, heavy weapon. And it stings like the dickens, as Robby finds out when he loses his grip with two minutes remaining. This must be something invented by the Nazi's, Robby concludes, as he is struck again and again by his triumphant opponent. But the next time he is paired up, the pain he has felt makes him hang on as if his life depends on it, and he is rewarded with the towel now secure in his hands. With the shoe on the other foot, he gleefully whacks the loser for the final minute. This games not so bad, he concludes, applying a sharp smack to the cowering back of the boy he has beaten.

As the week progresses, he finds he no longer dreads waking up in the morning to the two awaiting practices. Somewhere around fifteen boy have stopped showing up for the twice daily torture sessions, having decided that band, or the tennis team, might be more to their liking. Robby feels an increasing sense of pride at having made it this far. With what he has been through already, nothing short of a gun to his head would make him leave the team now. The worst is well behind.

When it all first began, he questioned the necessity of the twice daily misery sessions, but as it comes to a close, at the end of the second week, it all begins to make sense. The boys that were not truly committed have been weeded out. Those that remain are meshed together by suffering, by the common knowledge that they have each passed through the fire, and been found worthy. The screaming coaches, who were hated to a man in the beginning, now feel a certain level of appreciation from their young charges. They made it hard. Damn hard. And that has made it worthwhile.

Looking back, Robby thinks of enumerable times when he was sure he could not go on, but somehow he did. Therefore, he concludes, there must be more to me than I thought. He has upgraded his own opinion of what he can accomplish. Who know what I can do, he wonders. He makes a conscious decision to no longer sell himself short. It is a moment of growing, and that in itself has made it all worthwhile.

The attitude of the coaches on this final two a day practice has now changed. They are no longer spoken to as harshly. There is more individual instruction and encouragement.

Instead of, "What the hell's wrong with you?" he often hears, "Good job," or "That's okay, try again."

He finds himself wondering why he ever hated the taskmasters, with their scowls and whistles, but in thinking it over he knows the answer. He had no idea what they were trying to accomplish. What he saw as pure punishment and madness, had a method behind it. What he could not see then is crystal clear now. He has joined a band of brothers, and has earned the right to wear the jacket with the oversized "M".

***

In a period of two weeks, the duo of Dollar Bill and Leon had entered the dog in a total of six fights, in five different cities, headed steadily towards the southern portion of Louisiana. They had effectively doubled their money at each event. Dollar Bill was beginning to have much faith in the words of his hired hand, who had declared, "No dog will beat him."

Thus, when they pulled the truck into the parking area of the farm north of Baton Rouge, Louisiana, the scrap yard owner with the brindle colored dog in the back was feeling very confident. This was the largest such event they had yet to attend, and there were dogs and owners here from five states. Leon secured their muzzled canine in the provided area, and the two men mingled freely among the hundreds of other hopefuls here to enter an animal in a match, or just make a wise bet. The vast majority of the men, some of which had women on their arms, were dressed casually. One man, however, stood out from the rest, and Dollar Bill poked Leon excitedly on the arm when he spotted him.

The man was dressed impeccably in a tailored suit, with stylish alligator boots and expensive sunglasses. His dress and demeanor screamed of money. He was flanked on both sides by handlers, or body guards, and Dollar Bill could well imagine them fulfilling both roles. Even his hired flunkies were well dressed. He was talking to a stunning woman and holding an unlit cigar, that from their vantage point, Bill guessed was Cuban of origin.

"Look, Leon. Do you know who that is?"

"Who? The movie star?" Leon asked.

"That ain't no movie star. He's more impressive than that. That's Bob Lucky."

"He's lucky, alright. Look at that chick he's with," said Leon.

"Forget her. I want his money, not his girl. That fellow owns the top fighting dogs in the southern United States."

The man with the last name Lucky had indeed lived a charmed life. Born into moderate wealth, the son of a nursing home entrepreneur, he had taken his inheritance and established a successful chain of luxury car dealerships that spanned three states. He had retired at thirty-five, and now occupied himself with what he considered the true sport of king, the breeding and fighting of dogs. He was a rarity among his peers, in that he was not in it for the money.

It was pride that drove him. His dogs all had bloodlines that could be traced back to mother England, from the days when a dog would often be matched against a bear or other similar animal. He only attended the largest events, and if a dog he owned lost, and survived, it was quickly disposed of, so as not to breed again. His palatial house and breeding farm just north of Biloxi, Mississippi contained what many considered the best fighting dogs in the United States. It was not unusual for him to travel to Europe just to see a special animal, and if it fit his fancy, no price would dissuade him from its purchase.

Though he had brought one fighting dog with him to this event, he was really here to mingle and watch other people fight their inferior animals against one another. He considered it his duty to rub shoulders with the common man occasionally, and perhaps bring some class to an otherwise drab event.

"Leon, we're about to hit the big time. Come with me and don't say nothing stupid."

The two men approached the man and his entourage, and stood at his shoulder for a moment trying to get his attention, without appearing rude. Dollar Bill finally grew impatient and cleared his throat, gaining the eye of the immaculately dressed man. Bob Lucky looked at the scrap yard owner for a long moment through his designer sunglasses.

"Can we help you?" he finally said, in the tone of one addressing a homeless person begging for a nickel.

"I think we can help each other. My name is Bill Dollar. My assistant here is my handler and trainer, Leon Stover."

"Good day, sir," Leon said, extending his hand, and it dangled in the air for a good twenty seconds before he realized the man was not going to make fleshly contact, so he withdrew it, and quickly dropped his eyes to the ground.

Dollar Bill realized the situation was growing more awkward by the minute, and he tried to establish their credibility before they were rebuffed.

"No need for you to introduce yourself. Your reputation proceeds you, and it is an honor to make your acquaintance."

"I think he wants an autograph, honey," the stunning woman said.

"No, we don't want no autograph," Dollar Bill said. "I mean any fan of the great sport of pit bull fighting would love to have your autograph, sir. But we have bigger fish to fry. You see, I have in my possession what I feel is a champion fighting dog, and he's looking for a challenge."

"And he told you that, did he?" Bob Lucky said, and his entourage chuckled appreciatively at his humor.

"Uh, no. But he's a gamer, I tell you. I was thinking the other day of retiring him because nobody can beat him, and he's getting mighty bored. But then me and Leon saw you standing here, and I said to Leon, 'Leon, there's a fellow who probably owns a dog who could give Killer a challenge.'"

"Killer?"

"Yup, that's his name. Killer the unknown, because... its...unknown if anybody can beat him," Dollar Bill said, improvising.

"Killer. How original. How long did it take you to come up with that?" Bob Lucky said, engaging the seedy man now only for the amusement of his audience.

"Oh, it weren't hard to come up with that name, because you see, he kills everything we throw in there with him."

"Probably defeated all the dogs in your neighborhood, I'll bet," Lucky said, and again his friends laughed politely.

"He's won 75 straight matches," Dollar Bill lied.

"If you've won so much money off him, you should consider buying yourself some new clothes," Lucky said, now being outright rude in hopes the man would take the hint and leave.

"Oh, we dress like this to throw people off. So they'll think were poor and we won't get robbed."

"You had me fooled. I thought you were a redneck rube, with a mangy mutt, probably carted down here in the back of a pickup truck." Lucky's small group laughed riotously at this, and Dollar Bill blushed at the accuracy of the assessment.

"I'm willing to wager whatever you feel is appropriate, that my dog will kill your dog."

Bob Lucky was growing weary of this exchange, and one of his handlers made a move to grab Dollar Bill by the arm. Lucky waved him off, preferring to dissuade the man with economics.

"I don't uncage my fighter for anything less than ten thousand dollars, so with that, we'll bid you a good day."

Bob Lucky began walking away, but stopped when Bill said, "We'll match that ten thousand dollars, unless you're afraid you might lose?"

Lucky looked at the man with cold malice, and said, "Lose? To you, and whatever dog you may have, somewhere, leashed on a clothesline rope? I don't believe you even possess ten thousand dollars."

Dollar Bill had sense enough to know he had riled the man, so he decided to push his luck.

"I've got ten thousand dollars. Maybe you don't. Maybe you spent all your money on those fancy clothes."

Lucky smiled at this comment, and directed his question towards his female companion.

"Baby, would you like to see my fighter go a round tonight?"

"He won't get hurt will he?" she said, concerned.

"I doubt that very seriously."

"Yeah, that sounds like a blast," she said, snuggling up to his arm.

He turned back towards Dollar Bill and Leon.

"Bring your dog to the main pit area in one hour. And I expect you to have the money."

With the last comment he turned to look towards his handlers, who Dollar Bill saw were looking at him hard, and the reference did not go unheeded. They both looked like they could climb into the pit and fight, if the dogs chose not to.

"Oh, we'll be there. Give your dog my regards," Dollar Bill said.

"Yeah, *last* regards," Leon shouted out, and Dollar Bill punched him in the arm after the men walked away.

"Don't go stirring them up any further. Jesus, Leon, we just bet ten thousand dollars on a mutt you picked up in a field." The man appeared to be having severe anxiety over his wager.

"We're gonna need plenty of your mojo shit to win this."

"Anointing," Leon said, simply.

"Whatever the hell you call it. I hope it ain't run out, or we just lost a pile of money."

"If Baby was here she'd tell you. No dog's gonna beat him." Leon appeared very sad when he said this, but the moment was forgotten in getting Buzz Saw out of the holding pen, and in position for the money match.

The hour passed quickly, and the duo were waiting by the largest of the three fighting pits when Bob Lucky approached with his crew and female friend in tow.

"Where is your dog?" he asked, seemingly oblivious to Buzz Saw's presence at their feet.

"This is him here!" Dollar Bill said, proudly. Buzz Saw looked up at all of them, still wearing the leather muzzle.

"Good God, you must be joking," Lucky said, looking at them as if they'd brought a leprechaun to fight against Joe Louis.

"No joke. And here's the money," Bill said, producing an envelope stuffed to bursting with hundred dollar bills.

Bob Lucky slumped his shoulders and looked towards the ground.

"Look, why don't you save your dog. Save your self some money, which you obviously need. And we'll call this farce off."

"We're here to bet. Our *champion* is here to fight. You seem awful hesitant to put up. Maybe you have a reason to back out of this, now that you've seen our dog?" said Dollar Bill.

"And this is the dog?" Bob Lucky said, making sure there wasn't some sort of mix up.

"Oh, that's him alright. He's left a trail of bodies all the way from Arkansas to here."

Lucky again looked down at Buzz Saw. He stared at the medium sized, brindle colored mongrel, who looked like he'd be quite comfortable chewing on a newspaper, or chasing the postman around somebody's neighborhood. The situation he was presented with was uncomfortable. He could not have cared less about the ten thousand dollars he was about to win. But he had allowed himself to be goaded, by a pair of hicks, into turning his fighter loose on a common yard dog. It was sure to be a grisly scene. The woman, who was his companion on this night, would be horrified at what was about to happen. It certainly would not enhance his reputation to participate in such an obvious mismatch. All he stood to gain was the money.

"I'm sorry, boy," Bob Lucky said towards the dog at their feet, "they're leaving me no choice. Alright, it's a match." He watched Dollar Bill hand the envelope of money to the matchmaker, and one of his handlers counted out an equal of cash.

It was at this point Dollar Bill and Leon got their first look at Bob Lucky's fighter. Off-white in color, he was of the American Pit Bull variety. Not gargantuan in size, but chiseled from his rear haunches to the front of his head, he tipped the scale at perhaps ninety pounds. The most striking aspect was in the brown eyes that revealed a deep intelligence. He was obviously a champion, as his father had been a champion, and his father before that. He had cost Bob Lucky more than many of the people standing around the pit made in a year, and his diet was as balanced and scrutinized as an NFL athlete. Thus, Lucky never referred to his canines as "dogs". To him, they were much more than that, and he always referred to them as "fighters."

Leon brought Buzz Saw into the pit arena and removed his muzzle. Minus the leather mouth guard he looked even less intimidating. To those standing around the pit, he looked rather lost, like he'd gone out to fetch a bone and ended up in the middle of a blood sport. There were catcalls and laughter mingled with hoots from some of the more drunken spectators. Bob Lucky felt the blood rising in his face. If they were laughing now, just wait until they brought his animal into the ring.

One of Lucky's handlers walked the dog named Victor into the fighting area, and the matchmaker, with a portable microphone and sound system, called out the already familiar instructions and introductions regarding the dogs ownership.

"This should be interesting," said the female at Lucky's side. She had never been to a dog fighting match, and didn't know what to expect. She assumed it might be similar to a boxing event, where two combatants pummel each other for a time, then shake hands and go home. Lucky wanted to brace her for the carnage they were almost sure to see.

"You might not want to watch this. The little dogs in for a rough time. I don't think he'll survive it. We can step away if you want."

"No, I want to see your hobby."

"My hobby isn't always like this. It's usually more evenly matched. I didn't want this match. I let myself be talked into it. It never should have happened."

"You don't think the small dog has a chance?" she asked, wide-eyed.

"Not a chance in hell. He'll be ripped apart. Come on. We'll come back and watch when they match two better dogs."

"No, I want to stay. I can handle it."

"Okay. I hope you have a strong stomach," said Lucky, seriously. She took his arm as Victor was unleashed, and the handler hurriedly exited the pit.

All things, up to this point, where familiar to Buzz Saw. But the dog he now stood across from in the arena was markedly different, in his perception. There was none of the goofy exuberance he'd seen in all the other dogs he'd fought. This dog was not rushing toward him overconfident. He was calmly, coldly sizing him up. It was several seconds before Victor even made a move in his direction, and it was paced and measured, step by step. Unable to judge a specific strategy the dog was using, Buzz Saw remained still until they were almost nose to nose, and a brief melee ensued which did damage to neither.

"He's a brave one, I have to give him that," Bob Lucky whispered to his female companion.

"Whose winning?" she shouted over the noise of the crowd.

"Victor's sizing him up. That's the way he was trained. When he's sure of the tactic of the other dog, it'll be over quick."

Victor moved forward again, this time with force, and Buzz Saw was backed up to the wall. He tried to step right, then left, but quick blocking moves prevented him from sidestepping. During one attempt to step aside, the brindle boxer's ear was ripped badly, and blood began to drip into the dirt off his face and neck. Victor broke off the attack and stepped back, apparently inspecting the damage he'd done. His well-honed instincts told him that his best strategy lay in an aggressive, overpowering attack to quickly finish off the small dog. He could both see, and smell the fresh blood he had drawn. He was unscathed and barely winded.

Buzz Saw had desperately searched for any tactical error the dog might make, and had found none. He had been prevented from a flank assault by cleverly taught blocking tactics, and he was at a tremendous disadvantage in strength and weight. The coppery taste of his own blood running into his panting mouth told him he had been wounded. He had to lure his opponent into a mistake, somehow, or he was finished.

They had, to this point, been eye to eye, each dog unwilling to break visual contact, which signaled submission. But Victor suddenly saw his opponent lower his eyes and tuck his tail between his legs. Then, Buzz Saw hunkered down like a whipped puppy that had been beaten with a rolled magazine.

"It's over," Bob Lucky said, "Victor's broke his spirit."

"That poor baby," the female said in pity.

"Damn it. Damn it," Dollar Bill said to anyone listening, and turned half away.

Victor however, had no pity. Standing a foot back from the brindle dog, he crouched and coiled his hard, muscular body into a posture that everyone knew meant the kill was coming. With his ears pinned back, he leapt with all his might at the cowering dog on the ground, intending to rip him to pieces. When his feet hit the ground, he found nothing to bite but air.

It was an amazing transformation, seen but not registering on the senses of the onlookers. The cowering brindle mongrel came out of his submissive posturing a split second before the dog reached him, and leapt deftly to the side. And he was no longer cowering. The roar of his rage seemed too expansive to have come out of such a small form, and it caused Leon to unconsciously shield his eyes from it, in remembrance of his Baby's moment of death. Dollar Bill, who had seconds earlier been in a state of mourning over the lost ten thousand dollars, felt his jaw drop open, and he staggered back a step at the sound of the growling menace that had emerged off the ground.

The damage that was done to Victor's flank in a matter of seconds defied anything Bob Lucky had ever witnessed. One moment his dog was preparing to execute his victim, and in the blink of an eye he was fighting for his life. The off-white Pit tried to spin away from the raging meat grinder on his flank, but Buzz Saw spun with him, step for step, not willing to relinquish his position. They went spinning in circles, with Victor craning his neck, snapping and biting, as Buzz Saw steadily opening a gaping, ragged tear from the back of the left shoulder, to the front of the muscular rear leg. Round and round the pit they went in a dizzying movement, until Victor stopped his attempt to reach the other dog. They spun another 360 degrees before he stopped turning, and slowly lost his footing, falling into the slick puddle of his own blood on the ground. A pair of glistening white ribs were visible through the hole in his side, and blood continued to pulse out in weak spurts from a torn artery. Buzz Saw backed against the far wall of the pit, as Victor raised his head and growled in his direction, before his chest heaved twice, and he died.

"What the hell just happened?" Bob Lucky shouted to anyone who was listening. He became vaguely aware that his female companion had turned away and was vomiting, but he was, at this moment, too stunned to comfort her.

"What happened?" Lucky said, turning to one of his handlers. "What was that?"

He felt stunned to the point of idiocy, and he could only look for someone to explain to him what he had just occurred.

Dollar Bill grasped Leon's wrists, and pulled his hands away from his face.

"We won," he said quietly. "He did it."

Leon only shook his head, acknowledging he had heard his boss, but still unable to gather himself to retrieve their dog, who was licking the dripping blood off his left shoulder and leg.

The silence of the crowd had given way to a buzz of conversation, as everyone questioned what they had just witnessed. Everyone seemed to have temporarily forgotten the two dogs in the pit. The matchmaker finally jumped down into the enclosure and checked Victor for signs of life, while keeping one eye on the other dog.

"He's dead. The white dog is dead. That's a match," he said, announcing what was already obvious to all.

Bob Lucky had given up trying to determine what he had just seen. He stood with his hands on his hips looking toward the dog that had killed his fighter. Dollar Bill and Leon approached him, and they stood there in silence for a long moment.

"I don't know..." said Lucky, finally. "That was amazing"

"I taught him everything he knows," Leon bragged.

"That's a very special dog you have," he said, still looking not at them, but at the dog that was still attempting to clean the blood from his torn ear off the lower white part of his leg. It was still oozing dark red, but appeared to be trying to clot.

"I would like to purchase him," Bob Lucky said, still ignoring his female companion, who was holding her stomach and gasping for air, with the remnants of her sickness coating her chin and dress.

This statement brought Dollar Bill out of his trance and he said, "No way. He ain't for sale."

Lucky ignored this, and said, "I'll give you fifteen thousand dollars for him."

"He ain't for sale."

"Name your price. I can do more for him than you can. Sell him to me and I'll hire you to train him. You can remain with him and handle him."

"He ain't for sale," Dollar Bill repeated.

"I think I'm gonna be sick again," the woman moaned, but Lucky ignored her. Dollar Bill and Leon walked away to collect their money from the matchmaker.

The well dressed man never left the edge of the pit, as Leon muzzled and removed Buzz Saw from the enclosure. He watched as Victor was lifted out limp, and carried to a burial pit for disposal. He then watched the two men as they left the match area with his money, and made their way to the parking lot, where Buzz Saw was loaded into the cramped cage.

"Can you take me home?" the female said, her face ashen from nausea.

It churned a knot in his gut knowing someone else owned a dog that could defeat his personally trained fighters. He had offered a magnificent price and been rebuffed. By two ignorant, undeserving hillbillies. He had always been able to buy what he wanted. They were just being stubborn. Stubborn rednecks. Probably lose the dog in a dice game. Or get down on their luck and sell him for whiskey.

"If I can't buy him, I want him dead," he said, to no one in particular. He left the woman standing by the pit with vomit clinging to her face and dress, as he and his handlers made their way to their vehicles.

Chapter 15

ROBBY ARRIVED AT THE field house in an excited mood. Today they would be issued pads and equipment. Two a days were over. The physical conditioning they had begun with was, for the most part, at an end. It was time to begin football in its truest sense.

Being new, and not established in the mix of things, he assumed a position towards the back of the equipment line. The starting players were at the front of the line, getting the choicest shoulder pads, helmets and accessories. When his turn came, he was glad to get a helmet that fit. He noted the deep scars on the outer plastic that spoke of head-jarring collisions the previous owner had encountered. They were issued a locker, and the obligatory athletic supporter.

He sat in front of his locker putting on his freshly issued equipment, and listened to the bantering going on, some of which was quite crude in nature, as boys have a way of acting in the midst of athletic activity, when their parents are home and far out of earshot. The pads felt cumbersome and heavy, especially the ones he wore over his shoulders, and he hoped he would be able to catch passes while wearing them.

Coach Byrd sat in his office, awaiting the equipment manager's signal that said his players were adorned with everything they needed, and regular practice could begin. His eyes dropped to the schedule that lay in front of him.

They would open in ten days at McGhee, on the road. They had lost that game last year, but he knew this Owl team was not predicted to be as good. He mentally marked that down as a win.

On to Hamburg, at home. In a normal year, this would be penciled in as a win, with Hamburg being a traditional doormat. Not so this time, however. They had a major college prospect at wide receiver. The kid had offers from schools as far away and diverse as Michigan and Notre Dame. He had been unstoppable the last time they had played, and was the main reason they had lost to the Lions. Reluctantly, he marked this down as a loss. Next, the big one. Actually, one of two "big ones" on the schedule. Warren. On the road. This would be a problem. It was always difficult to beat the Lumberjacks, but to try and do it twice in a row was asking a lot. And to do it on their home field…he penciled this in as a loss.

Hermitage was next on the schedule. They were normally not a talented team, but they always fielded a group of huge boys. Country boys. Corn fed. The game was on the road, and the Hermitage field, remarkably, had stones which washed up through the turf after each heavy rain. It was similar to playing on a sandlot. Always a lot of injuries to account for after a trip to Hermitage. Still, this looked like a victory.

Unfortunately, they would likely bring those injuries with them to face Dollarway the next week. The Dollarway Cardinals ran the spread offense. After a season spent trying to mainly defend the run, they would be forced to shift gears, and stop an all out passing attack. If the enemy quarterback, and receivers, were in synch, it would be a nightmare. If they went in with a depleted secondary, well, it would not be pretty. He sighed and marked it down as a loss.

The yearly game against Woodlawn High School was a welcome relief. It was a small school, and Monticello had taken a win from them the past six years running. He happily penciled this in as a win before the home crowd.

Lake Village. He personally had a successful record against this delta school situated a few miles from the Mississippi river. But the team he would face this year was senior laden. They would be improved, and they had beaten him the previous season. He marked an "L" next to Lake Village.

Star City. The second of two "big ones". They were, traditionally, the most talented team in the league, and it was on the road. They had a creative, committed coaching staff, and a rabid fan base that craved and expected success, much like his own. Go into Star City without all your ducks in a row, and you'd likely go home embarrassed. He well remembered his own embarrassment, when his team had been beaten 30-0 the past year. He would be lying to himself to mark this down as a win, and he added an "L" next to this game.

White Hall. This game could go either way. He marked it a win, simply because they would be playing on familiar home turf

They would finish up at Dumas. He had beaten the Bobcats previous season, and they were not expected to be much improved. He placed a "W" next to their name, and did the math: it added up to a probable 5-5 season.

He slumped in his chair and let his head fall back, staring at the ceiling. If things went as he'd just planned them, he would be looking for another job, come November. He remembered being in this similar situation the past year, and suddenly felt very weary. It was like running on a treadmill, or working on an assembly line. If you fell behind, it was very hard to catch back up. And he'd fallen behind.

He pulled out a chart listing the likely starters for this year's team. The improvement he needed just wasn't there. He felt good about the defense, and there was a temptation to focus his eyes on that aspect. But he knew deep in his soul that the key to great improvement was in a vastly upgraded running game. The kid Bennett, who would surely inherit the quarterback role, could help the team. He had a major college arm, but his work ethic was questionable.

Still, in this league, with a lack of sure handed receivers, you had to have a running game. They had Steve Karnes marked for tailback. He would never break a big run. Great young man, excellent grades, honor role. Someone you'd love to date your daughter. But he would certainly never play a down of football after high school was over. The fullback, Juan Tucker, was a fearsome short yardage specialist. He was built like a Mack truck, and a stalwart at the outside linebacker position. His presence made other teams run in the opposite direction.

On the defensive side, Chuck Hoover at middle linebacker was cause to smile. The kid was small, but he played large. On the field, he seemed to forget he was only 5' 7" and 165 lbs. Come running through the line with the ball, on a trap play, and he'd leave a lasting impression on your mind, as well as on your helmet. Darryl McDaniel, at the safety spot, terrorized opposing receivers who dared run across the middle. The defensive ends needed work, but he felt they could be brought around.

It was frustrating, in that this defense deserved a potent offense. They needed a homerun hitter. He was sick of losing games 14-7, or 7-0, due to a lack of offensive punch. They had a good group of new players he'd never seen in pads. He checked his watch and saw it was time to get his first look at them. The equipment manager poked his head in the office and announced all the necessary items had been handed out. He picked up his silver whistle and walked out of the office, towards the field where his players were waiting.

After watching young men form a mass group, and do stretching and warm-ups, they were separated into their various position groups, and put through specialized drills. For the linemen, it consisted of pushing a sledded blocking machine, while the line coach stood on its back and screamed encouragement and instruction. The offensive backs took handoffs, and practiced running past a pair of assistant coaches who smacked them with a hand-held blocking pad. The ends were at the far end of the field running routes, and catching a ball thrown by the staff. And the two kickers on the team were separated from everyone else at the other end, practicing their kicks through the goalposts.

At the halfway point of the practice, the first team offense was gathered together. Robby stood on the sidelines and used the respite to catch his breath. A mock scrimmage was quickly organized, with the first team offense going against the second team defense. Robby wasn't sure where he stood in the pecking order, but it was obviously not among the starters or the second stringers, because he was not included in the action.

He watched as Jeff Bennett and the starters had moderate success running the ball against the backups. This was to be expected however, and the coaches did not appear to be overly pleased with the result, Coach Byrd included. They repeatedly stopped the exercise to correct mistakes, and chew out players who were in the wrong position, or not giving what they considered a sufficient effort. Thirty minutes into the scrimmage, it became clear that the backups on defense had gained the upper hand. They had stopped the starting offense from gaining a first down, time after time.

After one particular frustrating sequence in which the offense actually lost yardage on three consecutive plays, Coach Byrd conferred with his assistant coaches, and several key position changes were made. Robby saw a kid he recognized as Ellis Owens, inserted at tailback. He was a compactly built young black kid with a big smile who had transferred to Monticello from somewhere in California. He had a bright nature one would associate with being from the sunshine state, and he was constantly making jokes. It was obvious from the start that he would be popular, as he was friendly to everyone. Besides his locker room demeanor, Robby knew only that he was usually near the front of the line in the speed sprints.

With the changes in place, the coaches in charge of the offense gave the ordered play to Jeff Bennett, and he carried it to the huddle. It was a simple off tackle play to the tailback, one the starters had already run numerous times. Watching from the sidelines, Coach Byrd was looking for any sign to give him encouragement. Thus far, he had found nothing that gave him any real hope. The backups were doing quite well against his potential starters. If the Monticello second string could consistently stop his offense, it stood to reason they would not score many points once the season started.

He watched as Bennett took the snap and handed the ball off. The smiling kid from California hit, and was through the hole in a flash. He was past the linebackers, and into the secondary before anyone on the defense could react. The safety made a vain effort to cut off his angle, to no avail, and he sprinted into the far endzone. This appeared to rejuvenate the slumping offense, and they showed more enthusiasm getting back to the huddle. Run it again to the opposite side, came the order from the assistant coaches. This time, Owens barreled over the middle linebacker who was unblocked, and attempting to plug the hole. The safety squared up to make the stop ten yards from the line of scrimmage, but the tailback faked left, and left him grasping air, then again sprinted into the endzone. This brought cheers from the backups on the sidelines, and the dejected defense was left with their heads hanging. A sweep right netted 25 yards before he was forced out of bounds, and the defense was beginning to think this was a moral victory.

It was all highly impressive to the head coach watching from the sidelines, but perhaps the defense had worn down. On a normal day, the starting offense would never be matched against the first team defense because of injury concerns, but he had to find out if what he was seeing was for real, or a fluke.

"Coach Baker," he shouted to his defensive assistant, "put your starting defense on the field."

"Are you sure?" the assistant coach said.

"Do it," Byrd said.

"First team defense, on the field."

The starting defense, that was languishing on the sidelines and spoiling for action, sprinted out, while the second stringers, exhausted from chasing Owens, trotted off.

"Run option left," Coach Byrd told his assistant, and the play was relayed to the quarterback.

The cocky defenders took their positions and prepared to get in their first licks of the year. Bennett took the snap, and reading the linebackers movement, exercised his option to keep the ball, leaving the fullback to crash into the line empty handed. He then rolled left to read the defensive end, and seeing the end commit to him, pitched the ball to the trailing tailback. Racing for the corner, Owens made it a split second before the corner back and appeared to shift into another gear. He gained thirty yards before the secondary made the tackle.

"Do you see that?" the backs and ends coach said, excitedly.

Coach Byrd nodded appreciably.

"I think he runs faster with the ball than he does without it," he said.

It was a rare phenomenon that the best backs possessed, and it was apparent that Owens had it: the ability to actually move faster with the ball in his hands. It defied rational explanation, but it was showing up on the field every time he touched the ball.

"Play action, fake the dive and throw to the H back on a slant," Byrd told his assistant.

Bennett faked the handoff to Owens, and the entire defense, aware they had been burned on the last play, reacted to it. Quincy Ross, the speedy flanker, drove up field 5 yards and slanted in. Bennett pulled the ball away from Owens and threw a perfect strike to his receiver, who streaked past the fooled secondary. Touchdown. The offense was clicking, and did not want to leave the field, but the coaches called a halt to the scrimmage, and ended the practice with a short round of gassers.

"I think we found our starting tailback," Byrd said to his smiling assistant. For the Monticello coach, things were looking infinitely better.

***

With their winnings, Dollar Bill and Leon paid a months rent on a house with a fenced in yard, just outside New Orleans, so their dog could heal a bit from his last match. The left ear was, for the most part, torn off at the base of his head, but it was mostly cosmetic in the scope of the injury. Secured in the backyard, he was allowed to run free without the muzzle, and the men could both sleep soundly in real beds. The plan was to attend a large match at Morgan City, Louisiana, then work their way back up on the western edge of the state. At the end of the week, his wound had closed sufficiently and was free from infection, so they began making preparations for the next fight.

"We hit Morgan City, then work our way up to Shreveport," said Dollar Bill. "Who knows, we might even swing over into Texas after that. What do you think?"

Leon was cleaning his fingernails with a pocketknife, and seemed to think on that for a moment, before answering, "I think we should turn him loose here in New Orleans and head home."

The suggestion was so ridiculous to the boss he ignored it entirely.

Dollar Bill walked to the window, and looked into the back yard where their dog was lounging under a tree. He looked perfectly at home in the back yard, like a typical family pet, and it further perplexed him over the things he'd seen the dog do.

"Leon, have you ever seen a dog do what he did at that match? That was real deceptive. I mean, I don't think there's any other way he could have tricked that Pit into letting his guard down. But he did. He tricked him. Then he turned into...something else. Something else..." he said in wonderment. "How do you suppose he came up with that? And don't give me any of your twilight zone shit."

Leon just looked at the man and continued to clean his nails with the knife.

"Well, he had me fooled. I thought he was begging for his life. But he was really begging for that other dog to misjudge him. God help the dog that misjudges him," Bill said, shaking his head and pouring whiskey into a glass on the table, until it was just over half full, "or the man, for that matter," he added, and shuddered a bit at the thought.

"I think we should let him out the gate, and just drive off," Leon repeated.

"I thought you hated him?" Bill said, beginning to feel the whiskey glow creep from his stomach to his head.

"I don't think I hate him anymore. I was just upset over Baby. You were right. He killed her in self defense. I believe in the anointing, even if you don't. My grandmother told me about it. It can make a man who stutters preach as smooth as Billy Graham. Or make a short man seem ten feet tall, to his enemy."

"Or help a boy kill a giant with a rock," Dollar Bill said, and finished half the glass with a flick of his wrist.

"What?"

"David and Goliath."

"Yes!" Leon shouted, and Dollar Bill flinched at the sudden noise, sloshing a bit of his whiskey.

"Damn it, Leon, you almost scared me sober."

"Sorry. But that's exactly what I'm talking about. I know I'm not ever gonna be smart enough to be rich. But I'm smart enough to know there's things in this world that defy explanation. That's one of them," said Leon, pointing towards the backyard.

"Yeah," Bill said, looking back out the window at the dog, "he defies explanation, alright."

"And God doesn't put an anointing on somebody...or something, for no reason. I believe we're getting in the way of it, doing this to him. We should just turn him loose and let him get on with his business."

The man at the window was busy calculating how much money they might make on the return trip to Arkansas, fighting at every big event.

"No. Maybe God put him in that field for us. So we could get rich. Yep, maybe that was it."

"It's a higher calling than that," Leon said, simply.

"What's a higher calling than getting rich?"

"He's not fighting to make us rich. He's fighting 'cause we keep making him. He's fighting for his life."

The dog looked up from his place under the tree, and made eye contact with Dollar Bill in the window. The man stared at Buzz Saw for a long moment before turning back to Leon and going for the bottle on the table.

"His ear is healed good enough. There's a fight tomorrow in Morgan City. We're gonna be there. With him."

The two men left the outskirts of New Orleans, and drove due south over the vast Lake Pontchatrain Bridge, heading even deeper into Cajun country. They crossed numerous points of highway where the road was bordered on both sides by dense, dangerous looking swamps. The humidity of New Orleans had been stifling, but they found it could get worse as they drove down the State.

Leon was quiet, and Dollar Bill had his familiar hangover headache from over-consumption of alcohol, so they drove mostly in silence. An hour and a half after leaving the Crescent City, they reentered a point of civilization that told them they were near Morgan City.

They stopped at a combination gasoline/liquor store, and got directions from a man with a nametag that said Jean Pierre, who they could barely understand. He seemed reluctant to give them directions to the dog fighting farm, until Dollar Bill purchased the most expensive liter of whiskey he had available, and showed him the brindle dog cramped in the cage at the back of the truck, looking dangerous in his leather muzzle. They were then directed to head east, and briefly left civilization again, to arrive at an expansive sugar cane plantation with a large antebellum house situated at its center. The sound of barking canines somewhere towards the back of the property, and the many cars and trucks parked wherever they could find room, told the men they had likely arrived at their destination.

As was normal, they left Buzz Saw, for the moment, in the sweltering heat of his cage, and made their way to find whoever was sponsoring this event. It didn't take long to work their way through the gathered crowd, finding a man with a spiral bound notebook, and a walkie-talkie hooked to his belt.

Dollar Bill extended his hand and introduced Leon, inquiring where they could house their dog until the matches began, which usually took place at, or near dusk. The man seemed to be scrutinizing them closely, then abruptly asked to see their animal. This was not a normal reaction, as proprietors at these events where usually too busy to care what dogs were brought in. Most were just glad to have another dog to match up, as the more betting that took place, the more money they would make.

"It seems he may have heard of our famous Killer," Dollar Bill whispered to Leon, as they walked back to their truck. He felt a flush of pride that the man would want to take time to see their fighter, being a celebrity of sorts.

The man reached the pickup, and stood looking at the dog in the cage for perhaps a minute, before saying, "Sorry, this 'un can't fight here."

"What do you mean, he can't fight here?" Dollar Bill said, incredulously. "We came a long way to get here. Is it 'cause you heard he's too good? Lets put him in the pit and see if anyone steps up. That's how we do it, back where I'm from. I'm sure there's somebody here that's not scared to fight him."

"Not a matter of being scared. I've been told you fed that dog something, most likely gunpowder. Can't have that around here."

Dollar Bill's mouth dropped open, and he stared at the man like he was looking at a lunatic.

"Gunpowder? Mister, first of all..." he seemed genuinely, momentarily, at a loss for words, before he gathered himself and said, "You know, and I know, that gunpowder don't make a dog mean, and it sure don't make him a good fighter. It makes him sick. And a sick dog don't fight good. That's an old wives tale. You're a smart man. You know that. So what is this shit?"

The man sighed and looked off, before answering, "Look, I was told, by a very influential source, that your dog was doctored by...gunpowder. I'm not in a position to question it. This...source, is very reputable. It's in my best interest to follow what he says. Go up north, maybe you'll have better luck up there."

"Could you direct me to this...source," Dollar Bill said, spitting out the last word.

"No, I couldn't direct you," he said, hesitant, "but...I've been told he will be in attendance tonight. He's usually well dressed, kinda stands out from the normal clientele, if you know what I mean."

"Expensive boots, cigar, has a couple of goon handlers with him. Maybe a movie star looking woman on his arm?"

"I can see you've met. I didn't tell you anything. You came to that deduction on your own," the man said nervously, and walked off without another word.

The string of expletives uttered from the mouth of Dollar Bill lasted a good three minutes, before he turned to Leon and said, "Get the dog out of the cage. Walk him around till this evening. I may get shot, I may get arrested, or I may just get a good old fashion ass whipping, but I'm gonna speak my mind to Mr. Lucky." Leon did as he was told, and they settled in, hoping Bob Lucky would show up.

The immaculate Mr. Lucky did indeed decide to attend that particular sporting event, on that particular night, but he was fashionably late, arriving close to 8:00 PM, well after the matches had already begun. And Dollar Bill was well into the liter of whiskey he had purchased at the roadside gas station. When Dollar Bill saw the man, he fairly rushed up to confront him, alarming the body guards into seizing him by his arms, before Lucky ordered him to be loosed.

"You've besmirched my good name, with a bunch of bullshit, at that," Bill spit out.

"I don't think your name is in any worse shape now, than when we last met, Mr. Dollar."

"And you've besmirched my dogs good name. Gunpowder my ass!" he shouted, and people around them turned to look, and move a step away at the same time.

"Come walk with me, Mr. Dollar. Would you like a cigar?"

He looked at the fat, brown exotic tube of tobacco Lucky was offering to him, and said, "No, thanks. The only thing you can do for me is to clear up that lie you told."

"I think I can do much more for you than that. Come walk with me."

Mr. Lucky turned to walk away from the throng of people, and reluctantly Dollar Bill followed behind a short distance, still fuming. They arrived at a champagne colored Lexus with dark tinted windows, and Lucky opened the rear door, beckoning his handlers to remain outside.

Dollar Bill hesitated entering the vehicle, before Lucky said, "Please get in. I promise you won't regret it."

They both slid into the car and Bill smelled, and felt the leather interior surrounding them.

"Would you like a drink?" said Lucky, producing a silver flask from a pocket mounted on the back of the front seat.

"No, thanks," Dollar Bill slurred, and Lucky poured three fingers of brown liquor into a small crystal glass that was also in the seat pouch.

"I want to ask you one more time, will you sell me the dog?"

"He ain't for sale," the scrap yard owner growled.

"No, I didn't think you would change your mind. The problem is, as I see it, that you have an eye like mine. We both know a special dog when we see it. And that is obviously a very special dog. The fighter that your dog defeated, Victor was his name."

Dollar Bill grunted an affirmation, and Lucky continued, "There may not be ten dogs in the continental United States who could occupy a pit with him. Yet, your dog, uh fighter, excuse me, did just that. Not only did he hold his own, he destroyed him in short order. I hate to lose a fighter like Victor, but I would not have missed that for a fortune. Your fighter possesses a rare combination of cunning and…ferocity. Ferocity is not even the proper word. I don't have a word for what I saw. If he were trained, I have no doubt he could take down a tiger."

"Well, I wouldn't go that far…" Dollar Bill said, flattered but still not thoroughly swayed to like the man.

"Oh, make no mistake. I know fighting dogs. I own dogs from all over the world. I seek out the best. The very best. That was why I was so anxious to purchase him, I think he's the best I've ever seen."

Dollar Bill started to speak, and Lucky beat him to the punch.

"Oh, I know. He's not for sale. And I understand. I wouldn't sell him either. And, I'm willing to concede that I don't own a dog who can beat him, and probably never will."

The flattery was beginning to swell Bill's head, and he said, "You know, I will take a drink." Bob Lucky handed the flask to the man, and when it was determined that no glass was available, Dollar Bill turned the whiskey container up and felt the expensive, hot liquid burn it's way down his throat.

"Damn, that's good whiskey," he said, attempting to hand the flask back to the man, but was waved away. He cradled the liquor in his lap, as Lucky continued his spiel.

"So here's what I propose: you come to my kennel in Biloxi. It's a short drive from here. I will invite a carefully chosen group of friends to witness, what I consider, not a dogfight, but an event. The best fighting animal in all of North America, going against three of my fighters."

"All at once?" Dollar Bill said, incredulously, fingering the flask in his lap.

"No, not all at once, of course. In consecutive matches. Spaced say, thirty minutes apart. You see, I want to see him fight again, but as I said, I don't have a dog that can possibly beat him. No one does, Mr. Dollar. You know that."

"Uh," he grunted in response, remembering Leon's words when he said, 'no dog can beat him.'

"Thus, it isn't sporting to fight him against one dog. That wouldn't be worth watching. Fighting three in succession would even the odds, though I'm still not convinced he will be defeated. But it will be spectacular. And that is what I want my friends to see: a spectacular match. One that will rival any sporting event since Ali verses Frazier. Twenty years from now, they will still talk of it. The night Bill Dollar's champion dispatched three opponents in succession. Your dog will be more than a champion. You could then legitimately call him a super champion."

Dollar Bill had now forgotten his anger, and was intently listening to the man's words.

"And what would I have to put up?" he said, preparing to take another stiff swig from the flask.

Bob Lucky leaned close until he was leaning on the arm of the other man.

"You would have to put up absolutely nothing. Just bring your champion. I will wager twenty five thousand dollars, to make it worth your while, of course. And I have every confidence that I will have to pay. But, it's worth that to me, for my friends to see this phenomenon you possess in action."

"Let me get this straight," Dollar Bill said, now himself leaning toward Lucky. "I have nothing to lose, nothing whatsoever? And you put up twenty five thousand dollars?"

The now thoroughly intoxicated man appeared to be trying to wrap his mind around the figure, but he gave up, and turned the flask up again.

"What if I say no. What if I just leave here with him, and head north?"

"Word travels fast, Mr. Dollar," Lucky said. "You could take him home and engage in backyard matches for a few hundred dollars. But another major event? No, that would be over."

"Uh," Dollar Bill grunted, and he knew it was futile to argue further. It was a deal he could take or leave, and if he left, they were out of the big time money game for good.

"Let me talk it over with my partner," he finally said, and finished off the whiskey with a flourish. Then he handed the flask back to Lucky, and exited the vehicle, staggering. Leon was standing by their truck with the muzzled dog.

"Well, I think I worked something out to our satisfaction," said Dollar Bill.

When he saw Leon was not going to respond, he continued, "Mr. Lucky is enamored with our dog."

"He's what?"

"He likes him. Very much. Wanted to buy him, but I said, hell no. So he wants a personal match, an extravaganza, I believe he called it. Our Killer, against some of his dogs.

You said no dog could beat him, so I think I'm gonna say yes. Twenty five thousand dollars if we win."

"He must like losing money," Leon said.

"It's a three dog match," Dollar Bill said, gauging the reaction of his trainer before continuing. "One right after the other, till he kills them all."

To this Leon finally showed emotion.

"Jesus, what do you think he is?"

"I think he's the best fighting dog in the country," Dollar Bill said, angrily. "Lucky said so, said he could take down a tiger if we got him ready."

"You come out of his fancy car with a lot of faith in his words," said Leon, and Dollar Bill suddenly couldn't look the man in the eye.

"I know what you said, and I know what I've seen. Hell, I forced him into it by refusing to sell the dog," Dollar Bill said, folding his arms and looking back towards the sound of the current matches.

"Why would he risk losing all that money, and three more dogs if he thought he would lose?" Leon said, with finality, and the logic of the man further angered his boss.

"Because," Bill said, as if trying to explain a simple concept to a child, "he's a sporting man, and it's the only way it will be fair."

"He's not the devil," said Leon, referring to Lucky, "but they may be related. You know how I feel. If it was up to me, I'd just unhook this lease and give him a kick towards the highway. Call it even. He killed Baby, but he made us a pile of money. I don't think nothing good can come out of dealing with Mr. Lucky. He thinks we're stupid, and he may be right. You're the boss, but that's my advice."

"Well," Dollar Bill said, "I think you've gone soft on the dog. Probably take him home and have him in your lap, if I let you. Change his name to Spot, or something. But he's a moneymaking fighting dog. And he's gonna go to the match of the century in Biloxi, and he's gonna relieve Bob Lucky of twenty five thousand dollars. Then, we can go home, and you can bronze one of his turds if you want to."

With that, Dollar Bill walked away to reconvene with Bob Lucky.

Leon stood there for a long moment looking down at the muzzled, brindle colored dog at his feet. He had never touched the dog in kindness. Never put his hands on him, other than to muzzle him, or lift him in, or out of the pit. The dog was looking up at him with large, wet eyes. It did not seem like the same dog that, somehow, transformed himself when in the midst of a life or death struggle to…something else. It did not look to him, from where he stood, that this *could* be the same dog. Slowly, he reached his hand down and stroked the dog's head, and was rewarded with a wag of his tail.

A still, small voice whispered quietly to him, "Just let him loose. Unhook the lease. Let him go. And walk away." Leon considered this thought for a moment. Then he dismissed it, and leaned against the truck to wait on the return of his boss.

Chapter 16

ROBBY SAT BY THE phone, wanting to pick it up and call the coach, but nervous as a boy calling a girl for a first date. The coach had asked him to call and arrange a run together, but perhaps he was only being polite. He sat there, wavering between calling, and forgetting the whole thing, before finally picking up the phone and dialing the number.

It rang four times, and Robby was about to hang up the phone, semi-relieved no one had answered, then he heard the receiver click, and a voice said, "Hello?"

"Uh, I'm trying to reach Coach Byrd."

"This is he."

For a brief moment, he considered hanging up, but instead said, "This is Robby Sinclair. I know you're busy, but I'm gonna be passing about two miles from your house, and if you go running today, I'll be at that point around 6:00 PM. But I understand if you can't make it…sir."

The coach could hear the nervousness in the voice of the boy, and he felt he better speak before the kid dismissed himself and hung up.

"I was wondering when you'd call. You're still running, aren't you?"

"Well sir, I slacked up during two a days, but I'm back at it now," Robby answered.

"You say 6:00 PM? If you can run by the field house, we can join up there and do a loop."

"I can do that," Robby said, excited.

"Okay, see you there."

At 5:55, Robby had jogged the three miles to the field house and stadium area, where the coach was already waiting out front. They left at a moderate pace, with the coach asking him to take it easy.

For Robby, it was strange to be running with a partner. Since the disappearance of his dog, he had run alone. Even now, there was little conversation between them, both focusing on the rhythms of their breathing, and the feel of the road under foot. It seemed to end too soon, as they made a four mile circuit, and the field house came into view. They stood in the shadow of the stadium, cooling down and catching their breath, before the coach said, "Come with me."

Robby followed the coach as he opened the gate to the stadium entrance, and they made their way slowly out onto the track surrounding the field.

They walked for a short distance, basking in the silence of a place that would be filled with noise on gameday.

The coach broke the silence by saying, "I love this place, the field when it's deserted. I come here and imagine victories. I'm not sure if it helps, but I guess it can't hurt."

Robby imagined the man, probably here often when no one else was present. Walking the track, standing at the 50 yard line. Looking at the empty scoreboard, dreaming of it with his team ahead. He suddenly was able to see the man, not as a heroic figure to whom he could not relate, but as someone who simply had dreams he hoped would be fulfilled. They had this in common. This was a man who had once been a boy, and someday he would grow old. He felt privileged to be in this place of ghosts, with him, at this time.

"Football's different here," Robby said, wanting to say something to contribute to the conversation.

"How so?" the coach asked.

"It matters more. People care more. At Harmony Grove it was something to do for fun. Just for fun. Here it's like we're..." he paused, temporarily at a loss for words, "we're defending our honor, or something."

"You know, we really are," Byrd said, agreeing, "we're defending what's been established. Good people, good kids, set a precedent. We're struggling to hang on to that. Tradition is hard to achieve. It takes time, and in the case of football, blood and sweat. It can all go down hill in a couple of years, if you let it. All of a sudden, people don't equate your town and team with winning. It's time to turn it around, get it back to where it belongs. I don't want to be the one to let it get away."

The coach was looking towards the bleachers now, remembering the black shirt section. It would be larger this year, if they didn't win.

"Passion is a two edged sword," the coach continued, "It can drive you, but it also can kill you, if you don't fulfill it. I wouldn't want to coach at a place where there's no passion. I guess I'm addicted to it. Without it, I suppose I'd just as soon sell insurance, or used cars. Before we go any further, Robby, do you know what a dual relationship is?"

The quizzical look the boy gave him told him the answer was no.

"A dual relationship is where you have one sort of relationship with a person in one setting, and a different relationship in another setting. Like on the field, and in practice, I'm the coach of the team you're on. Don't freak out if I ever shout at you. I'm just being the coach. But here, when we run, we're just brothers. Got that?"

"Sure, I understand that," Robby said. "You mean running brothers, right?"

"That, and spiritual brothers. I believe all men came from one man. That makes us brothers in ancestry, too."

"So you don't believe in evolution?"

"I believe in the Bible. It doesn't take a blind leap of faith to say that. DNA evidence suggests that all men came from a common female. But that's not the main reason I believe it. The main reason I believe it is this: two thousand years ago, a man claimed to be God. He said the ancient scriptures Jewish scriptures were true and accurate. Then, he was put to death, and he came back from the dead, proving he was God. If I believe he was God, then I must believe what he said about the scriptures. I believe in a literal creation, a literal savior, and a literal afterlife."

This brought many questions to Robby's mind, and he didn't know where to begin asking, so he only said, "I believe in God, but sometimes I wonder about things. Sometimes I wonder if it's true."

"In every man's life," said Byrd, "there's a defining moment. A point in time when his destiny is changed for better, or worse. The defining moment of my life was when my faith went from believing, to knowing. When I took a hard look at the facts, not just the words of the Bible, but other historical sources, that make it clear Jesus rose from the dead. There were over five hundred witnesses that walked with him, talked with him, even ate with him. It's so undeniable he appeared alive after the crucifixition that critics have come up with outlandish explanations to cover what they don't want to accept. Such as, maybe he had a twin brother, or maybe he only fainted on the cross and the Roman guards thought he was dead. It takes more faith to believe those things than to just accept that it happened. Anyway, that's what changed my life radically, when I achieved heart faith. It changes everything."

Robby looked at the man. It was obvious he was sincere, not just pitching some religious spiel to try and get him to join a church.

"I wish I had heart faith. How do you get it?"

"You seek it, and keep seeking with all your heart. Don't believe what anyone tells you. Not even me. Get into the Word and search. Jesus said, if you seek, you will find. If you seek sincerely, he'll make sure you succeed. He wants you to know the truth."

Robby thought back to the night he'd prayed for his dog. That was the last time he had talked to God.

"Do you ever feel like when you pray, that God doesn't hear you?"

"There were times in the past," the coach answered, "when I wondered if he heard me when I prayed. That was when I viewed God as far away, sitting on a distant throne. Then I came to the knowledge that He actually, literally, lived inside me. Now, I know my prayers don't have to go any farther than the tip of my nose for him to hear me.

The enemy will tell you that God isn't listening because he wants to disrupt your lines of communication. He doesn't want you to talk to God, because that's your power source. He doesn't stand a chance unless he separates you from the Father. I don't want to put too much on you at once. It's just I can't talk to the kids at school about my faith. Separation of church and state, you know. I tend to get excited when I have a chance to share it."

"Do you think there are animals in heaven?" Robby asked.

"In the Book of Revelation, Chapter 19 I think, Jesus is seen riding a white horse. Like I said, I believe in a literal Bible, so there must be animals in heaven."

"I'll look that up when I get home."

"Yes, always look up everything anyone tells you. It's too important a subject to just trust what someone tells you."

Robby noticed for the first time it was getting very late, and his mother would be worried.

"I've got to be getting home," he said, reluctantly.

"I'll give you a ride, really I don't mind."

A few minutes later the coach pulled his car into the driveway, and Robby thanked him for everything.

"No, thank you. And I'll see you at practice tomorrow."

Robby started to get out of the car, and felt the desire to ask one more question.

"Coach, do you think we'll win this Friday?"

He hated to make predictions, almost felt it might jinx the result, but he felt the need to be honest.

He hesitated, and said, "I'll know a lot about this team after the first half, but yes, I think we'll win this Friday."

"I do too, coach. See ya." Robby said, and exited the car.

He went in the house and his mom, who was doing dishes, pulled his plate out of the microwave.

"I was getting worried about you. Who was that man?"

"That's Coach Byrd. He's the best. Did you know there are animals in heaven?"

***

Dollar Bill and Leon left Morgan City, Louisiana and initially headed north, up the boot of the state, then connected with Highway 10 in New Orleans. There, they made a turn due east, and arrived in Biloxi, Mississippi two hours later. From there they turned on highway 90 north, and followed the simple, written directions Lucky had given them, to pull up at the gates of a palatial enclosure. There was short period of waiting, during which a posted guard communicated to someone, and the gate opened, allowing them entrance to the twenty acre facility.

Bob Lucky received the call telling him the two men had arrived with the dog. He gave instructions to his household staff regarding their sleeping accommodations, and then called the manager of his kennel, which was an expansive area occupying a full acre of the property. He had felt there was a chance the men would not show, and had waited until this moment to finalize his plans.

"Tom, yes, they're here," he said, into the phone. "We'll need the dogs ready tomorrow night. Yes, three. We want to go in this order: I want the most intelligent fighter to open up. That would be Cleo. If by some chance he gets by her, he'll be wounded. Then we go with size and strength, that would of course be Sampson."

"What dog do you want in the third position?" his manger said.

"I'm certain we won't need a third fighter," Lucky said, "but, just in case, have Lobo prepared to go."

"Boss, Lobo isn't even a dog," the manager said.

"This isn't a sanctioned match. This is my pit. I make the rules. I arranged for three successive matches. Nothing more."

"He hasn't been out of the cage since he was trapped, but we'll get him there," the manager said.

"Don't let it concern you. I don't think he'll get past Cleo. She's smarter than Victor."

"I'm curious, Mr. Lucky. What type of dog are we dealing with here?" said Tom, perplexed that three fighter might even be needed.

Bob Lucky sighed, not sure that he could put what he had seen into words to make the man understand.

"Victor was a fine dog, was he not?"

"One of the best. Trained him myself," said the manager, matter of factly.

"And you trained him well, Tom. I know that. But you couldn't have trained him for happened there. I saw it, but it's difficult to put into words. He was deliberately lured into miscalculating. Then, the dog turned into...a lion."

"What?" Tom said.

"No, not literally, of course. But I'm sure that's what Victor thought before he died. There was no fixing him, no reason to try and bring him back here. He died in the pit. I watched it. It took less than a minute from the time he was flanked, to the time he was ripped open. What can do that?"

"I gotta see this dog," the manager said, impressed.

"That's just it," Lucky said, "you won't believe it when you see him. I was there. And I was sober. I saw them carry Victor out of the pit. He could not survive what was done to him. That's all I can really say."

There was silence on the phone for a moment.

"The men, a Mr. Dollar and his handler, are bringing the dog to the kennel in the next few minutes. Give them the best accommodations. Don't underestimate the dog, Tom. I saw what I saw," said Lucky, and hung up the phone.

Dollar Bill and Leon secured the dog into the kennel, standing in awe in front of the sprawling training area, and the enclosure housing the fighters, which in itself was roofed, and large as a gymnasium. Remarkably, it was free from the din one would associate with an area housing dogs. Buzz Saw was placed in a large cage away from any other animals, and they watched as the handlers fed him sumptuous, raw steak through an opening in the pen. The handlers took time to show the men an elaborate watering system that fed the dogs specially cooled spring water.

"Damn, it might not be too bad, living here," Dollar Bill said, "what do you think Leon? We could still sell him, and go to work for Mr. Lucky."

Leon remained silent, content to look around at the sophisticated operation. Satisfied that their dog was well cared for, they were led to the main house, which was situated on a man made lake. Entering the house, the men felt their feet sink into a carpet several inches thick.

The house was mostly empty, except for a cleaning staff busy in other parts of the mansion. They were shown the Jacuzzi area, and the weight room, which interested neither man. Dollar Bill did find the wet bar quite impressive, and made it a point to commit its location into his memory. They were then taken upstairs to adjourning rooms, both of which offered a stunning view of the lake.

"Please avail yourselves of the amenities," they were told by their escort, "and if you desire to prepare your animal, Mr. Lucky has asked me to inform you if will be open at any hour. If you need anything, just press this button on the wall." The man pointed to a call center.

"First, we need a bottle of the same whiskey me and Mr. Lucky drank in the back of his car," Dollar Bill said. "And some ice, and glasses."

"As you wish," the porter said, leaving to accomplish this task.

"Well, Leon, we have finally hit the big time."

Leon just stood there, moving to look out the window at the lake.

"You've been mighty quiet lately. What's eating you?" his boss said.

"It feels wrong…somehow."

"Nothing wrong with winning twenty five thousand dollars."

"What if we don't win?"

"Nothing ventured, nothing gained. He's got us blackballed. I'm not going back to the small money. No reason to. I think Killer can do it. Damn, where's that whiskey? Stay here and drink with me. You haven't had a drop in two days. What's wrong with you? You sick?"

"Maybe," Leon answered. "I'm going to lie down a while." He left Dollar Bill's room and went to his own, lying down in his clothes.

"Fine time to quit drinking," the scrap yard owner said, as the servant brought an unopened half gallon of Kentucky's finest to the room, and left the man with his spirits.

Leon awoke to the deathly quiet of the room, still dressed in his clothes. His thoughts went, at once, to the kennel area, and without considering, he left the room and followed the staircase down to the first floor. Just look in on him, he thought. No harm in that.

He quietly exited the house, hearing loons call out somewhere on the water. The kennel area, being well lit and conspicuous on the western edge of the property, was easy to find. He was relieved that the door, as promised, was open. He walked past row after row of cages, some occupied, and others empty. Wonder which ones he'll fight tomorrow, he wondered. He was again impressed that none of the animals barked. Disciplined bunch, he reasoned, no silliness here. Everybody's all business, just like their owner.

The brindle boxer was at the far end, and he saw the dog raise his head as he moved to stand in front his cage. He was unmuzzled, and his missing left ear gave him an unbalanced look, but otherwise he gave no impression of being a threat. Leon felt his hand move towards the gate latch, and he slipped inside the door, shutting it behind him.

"I really don't care if you kill me, old boy. I don't care."

The dog saw Leon approaching and keened his senses to pick up his intent. There was no muzzle in his hand. No looping stick. The man did not have food, and he had been well fed already, so this was also ruled out. As he entered the cage, there was an incredible emotional sadness that emanated from the man, overpowering in its aura. It reached the dog as he lay there, and he remembered his own loneliness, his own isolation and heartache. He felt the desire to explore out the source of the pain, to eliminate it if he could, and he slowly rose up and crossed the cage to where the man stood.

His senses told him this creature was in too much pain to be any threat to him, and he moved his nose from man's shoes, to his knee, where he stood looking up at Leon.

Leon was not at all sure of the dog's intention, and he stood stiff, until the dog gazed up at him.

He was suddenly taken back to a point in his childhood; something he thought was long forgotten. He had owned a dog. A beagle dog named Skippy. A silly dog with long ears. Skippy loved Leon, and he loved hunting squirrels more than he loved life. Skippy had taken sick, and he told his father, hoping the old man would, somehow, fix the situation. His father had a fix for it, all right. It involved a shovel and a .22 rifle.

"He won't get any better," his father had said. "We got to do this. You got to be a man," he told the eight-year-old boy.

Leon wanted to do the right thing for the dog. He wanted to be a man. He and his father took Skippy out into the woods that day, the same woods Skippy loved to hunt in. They toted Skippy in a wheelbarrow because, by that time, Skippy could no longer walk by himself. The squirrels were calling in the trees, and Skippy heard them. He perked his ears and by God, he wanted to get out of that wheelbarrow and chase one. He tried, bless his heart. Leon tried to get his dad to let him push Skippy around on one more hunt, but his old man said, "No. We got to do this." So, they went on into the woods, with the squirrels barking, and Skippy looking up at them with his eyes all bright, convinced he was going hunting.

Then, they came to the spot his father said would do. And he made Leon dig a hole, because it was his dog, and he had to be a man. Then his father lifted Skippy out of the wheelbarrow, and put him on the ground by the hole. His eyes were still shining; that was all he had left alive in him, those shining eyes. The rest of him wouldn't work.

His father handed him the gun and told him, "take it off safety, son, and put your dog out of his misery."

Leon did as he was told, and moved the safety switch to the fire position. Tears were rolling down his face by then, and he hoped that didn't mean he wasn't a man, because Skippy was depending on him to be one.

"You do it now," his father said.

And he did it; he pointed the gun at Skippy's head and pulled the trigger. But his hand was shaking, and there were tears in his eyes, and the shot went bad. It didn't hit Skippy in the head. It hit him in the abdomen. And the dog was howling. His eyes weren't bright, anymore. They were wide with shock. And Skippy knew they hadn't come out here to hunt squirrels. They had come out here to hurt him bad.

Leon's father grabbed the gun away from him, and tried to move another bullet into the chamber with the bolt, but the gun was empty. They had only brought one bullet.

And Skippy was howling, and Leon could only cover his ears and scream, "Do something Daddy. Do something Daddy." And his old man briefly considered bashing the dog's head in, but he didn't have the stomach for it. So he kicked the still screaming dog into the hole and shoveled the dirt in like a madman. The dog continued to scream in the hole, but with each shovel of dirt, it became more muted, until there was only quiet in the woods. And the sound of his eight year old son, who had to be a man, sobbing.

Leon became aware, at this point, that he was standing in the pen with the dog, and he was quietly crying; big, wet tears rolling down his face, landing on the concrete of the enclosure. He could feel the dog nuzzling his knee and he felt, at that moment, if he didn't find some comfort, he would die right there.

I'm losing my mind, he thought, as he knelt down and rubbed the dog over his head, carefully avoiding the still healing wound of the missing ear. A thousand transgressions came rolling over his mind as he stroked the brindle boxer. The innumerable strays he had thrown into the pit with Baby. Shooting the collie. It all flooded into his consciousness, and leaked down his cheeks.

The dog was licking his face now, desperate to subdue his pain, knowing no other way. Make it right, something whispered to Leon. This time, he did not ignore the request.

"Come on, boy," he said, and unlatched the door to the pen.

The dog followed him out the door and down the corridor of enclosures. Several of the penned fighters rose from prone positions to stick their noses through the wire as the pair moved past, and one dog yipped, but for the most part it was quiet except for their footsteps. Thank God they're not all barking, Leon thought, as they reached the door. Leon twisted the doorknob and felt the humid night air sweep in over the air conditioning of the kennel. When he stepped out, his path was blocked by two handlers.

"Going for a walk, Sir?" they asked.

Chapter 17

ROBBY HAD SPENT THE week on the scout team, wearing a red, mesh vest identifying him as a facsimile of a McGhee defender. He had taken his lumps against the first team offense, offering his body for their further development. There were countless times, at the cornerback position, when he was run over by the leading blockers, or beaten on pass routes. It was a humbling experience, but he soaked it in, knowing it would probably be his only opportunity to play, as he was listed third string.

Coach Byrd had been true to his word, cutting Robby no slack during the week leading up to the game. He was thrilled when, prior to the pep rally, he and the other players were issued jerseys and led to a special seating section. It was a new season, and the school was buzzing with excitement. There were even several young ladies he had noticed looking his way, who had previously ignored him the past year.

As the week progressed, the players became increasingly nervous and introspective. Everyone, except Jeff Bennett. He remained laid back to the point of lethargic. When they arrived at the field house to dress and prepare for the bus ride, there was a tense quietness to the atmosphere. The only boys who seemed unaffected were Bennett and Owens, who attempted to engage the others in horseplay, but were ignored.

The coaches moved through the field house trying to solve any equipment problems before they got on the bus, and generally attempting to gauge the mood of their charges. Mostly they were nervous, and had nothing to do to pass the time, till it was time to go. In truth, everything that could be done had been taken care of the previous five days. There was nothing to do but wait, and it was tortuous.

Coach Byrd tried not to show his fear. To his players and assistants, it was imperative he maintain a confident front. If the leader had doubts it would spill over to the others, and could well be disastrous.

It was not that his team was without talent. The new kid, Ellis Owens, had terrorized the defensive coordinator. But he had coached other kids who were spectacular practice players. When the lights went on, however, they seemed to put on a different persona; they could do nothing right. He hoped Owens would not be one of these.

What he feared most was losing the first game of the year and going into a skid. Despite the talent he saw, he knew it was possible to lose confidence with an early loss. Then the thing could snowball, until it all came apart at the seams. He had earlier penciled this game in as a win. It was imperative to win the ones they should win, and take a few they shouldn't. This was, therefore, a must win game.

It was a welcome relief to load up and head out, for players and coaches alike. Being on the bus seemed to break the tension, and a few more players engaged in good natured bantering during the trip. Coach Byrd looked back over the row of seats at the kids who were carrying his future. Only a few of them were shaving everyday. What a peculiar business I'm in, he thought; my fortunes in the hands of children.

The forty minute bus ride concluded as they entered the town of McGhee, and pulled up to the field house and stadium area. They were shown to the dressing area, and the round of mundane, last minute checks ensued. In the distance, outside the field house, the coach could hear the opposing teams band striking up, signaling that the time was very near. The players were seated on a row of benches, each with the Monticello helmet at his feet. Most of the young men had distant looks on their faces, visualizing what was to come; each seeing himself making a tackle, or a block, or catching a pass. Willing himself to succeed. With five minutes to go, it was time for Byrd to say something inspirational. Speak a word that would cause a boy to give up his body for his city. Give until he had nothing to give. The coach never scripted these times, and he did not now. He took the center of the room and opened his heart.

"Look up. This is why we ran ourselves sick in the August heat, to be here. I can promise you this: they didn't outwork you. I made sure of that. It's up to you not to let them outplay you."

An official in distinctive striped clothing stuck his head in the room and said, "Ready, Coach."

"Let's put a licking on them."

The room erupted in a flood of emotion, and the coach felt confident for the first time that day, standing in the midst of the screaming, blue clad boys. I hope they can hear us in the next dressing room, he thought. Anything to get in there heads.

They ran from the dressing room, into the early September evening. The stands that were empty when they arrived are now full. He notes that the visitors section is perhaps half full. In past years there would have been standing room only for a game this close, but he does not begrudge the fans this. They have no reason to expect anything different, and in truth, he has no reason to expect it either.

The emotion of the run onto the field subsides and the coin toss is conducted, which is won by McGhee. They opt to go on offense first. Good, he thinks. If he were playing his team, he would have put the Monticello offense on the field first, that being its weakness.

The kickoff is uneventful, and the McGhee Owls take the ball at their 30 yard line. On the first play from scrimmage a good size hole opens up on the left side, but Chuck Hoover, the "head hunter", lives up to his name and plants the ball carrier. He is slow to get up. Very good, Byrd thinks, smiling. He'll think about that next time his number is called. A short pass garners a first down, but three runs into the line force a punt. He has seen the defense in action, and has been pleased. Now it is time to look at his offense. Bennett, Owens and the rest run onto the field.

Robby is standing two players to the left of the coach. His theory is he wants to be easy to find if the coach decides to put him in. He searches the stands and is pleased to find his mother and Earl. He waves, but she does not see him in the midst of the other players.

The play is a simple dive to Owens, into the middle of the line. Bennett takes the snap and a hole appears to open. The handoff is made to the smiling kid from California, but he hesitates, and the hole closes. The gain is one yard. Two more attempts net the same result, and they are forced to punt.

"What's he doing?" an assistant coach shouts in his ear. "He's not hitting the hole." The offense runs off the field, and Owens is no longer smiling.

The Monticello defense is snuffing out everything McGhee does, and a short pass is nearly intercepted by the safety, McDaniel. Another punt, and Monticello once again has the ball.

"Keep giving it to him," Byrd tells his assistant coach, and the order is carried out onto the field.

Time after time, the tailback appears to have running room, but he is not blasting through the line, as he did day after day in practice. Maybe not a game player, Byrd thinks, sadly. He is obviously trying to break it big, when he should just hit the hole, and it results in another punt.

Midway through the second quarter, disaster strikes and Bennett mishandles the snap. The Owls have the ball at the Monticello 17 yard line, and they take full advantage, crashing into the endzone with 2 minutes left in the half. There is elation on the opposing sideline. The coach knows if they can't find their running game soon, they will be forced to pass. This was not in the game plan, and any change from what is expected is a bad portent, especially on the road. The half ends and the teams exit the field to their dressing rooms.

Byrd stands in the locker room with the backs and ends coach and assesses the mood of his team. The room is quiet, disturbingly quiet. In the next room, through the cinderblock wall, the muted noise of the McGhee Owls can be heard. One of their coaches is pumping up the team with inspirational talk. Now they're in our heads, he thinks. Owens is sitting there, with his head down. His sunny disposition is overcast. He honestly doesn't know, or see, what is so obvious to the coach. Byrd calls him to a back corner of the locker area.

"You're not hitting the hole. You are trying to break it big every play. Just hit the hole. Take what they give you."

Owens stands there like the words are not registering. I've got to take the pressure off him before I can make him see it, the coach realizes.

"Play this game like it's a scrimmage. Have fun, and get the first down. Can you do that?"

There is pain of confusion on his face, then he nods affirmatively.

"Have fun. That's what I want you to do."

Again, Owens nods a yes.

"Good man," the coach says, and he heads back into the locker area. He feels the defense deserves credit for a half well played, and he goes to each starter, patting them on the arm, moving down the line. He notices Bennett sitting there smiling, trying to engage the kid next to him in a joke. It is slightly disturbing, but he passes on it. Once again, the official inserts his head into the locker room, and it is time to take the field for the second half.

The home crowd is more animated this time than at the start of the game. The McGhee band even seems to be playing louder. Amazing what confidence can do, Byrd considers, and the second half begins.

Monticello takes the kickoff and begins at the 30 yard line. No reason to panic, Byrd tells himself. Give the kid a chance to work out his kinks. He directs the offense to run Owens on a straight dive play. Nothing fancy, just put the ball in his hands, let him figure it out.

The line fires out hard on the first play, but again, the tailback hesitates and gains nothing. Byrd sees him slam the ball to the ground and get up slowly. Another series, or two, then he will put Karnes into the tailback spot. Or go to the pass, depending on the score at that point. They are only seven points down, but the offense is dead in the water. Must make the proper decision at the proper time, he reminds himself. Run it again to the other side, he directs his assistant.

Again Owens takes the handoff and he has room for a moment, but he is dancing east and west, not running up field. He doesn't get it. It's not his fault, the coach reminds himself. Seen it before. Marvelous practice player. Can't do it on Friday night. What can be done to correct it? It's a psychological matter, the coach realizes. And I'm not a psychologist. Off tackle right, the coach directs.

This time, Owens takes the ball from the quarterback and plows through the hole for five yards. On an option right Bennett keeps for another five, and they have a first down. A dive to the fullback Tucker garners six, as the big bruiser carries three defenders four yards down field.

On second and four, Owens gets the ball on a counter play, stepping left at the snap, then moving right. The Owl linebackers have bit on the fake left, and his line has sealed the defenders out. Owens takes what they have given him, and they have given him plenty. He is in the secondary and the stunned linebackers are craning their necks to locate him, but he is past. It is as it was on the practice field, and the only McGhee youngster who has a chance at stopping him, the free safety, is forced to try and make an open field tackle. It is an embarrassing attempt, and he ends up on the ground without laying a hand on the Monticello tailback.

Byrd watches his player, wondering how he will react to his first touchdown. He is pleased when the young man hands the ball to the official and heads back to the sidelines. He scores points with the coach for this, and he is smiling again, accepting congratulations from his teammates.

The defense is energized by the long run, and stuffs the Owls on three successive plays. The mood of the team has shifted; even the assistant coaches on the sidelines are more animated, sensing the momentum has changed. The offense runs back onto the field invigorated.

Owens gashes the Owl defense for 7 and 9 yards. Byrd watches the tailback as he gets up off the ground, looking for any fatigue. The kid bounces up off the ground and sprints back to the huddle. A good sign.

They are at the 50 yard line, and the home crowd has grown quiet. Even the McGhee band is strangely out of tune as they play an up tempo number. A called pass from Bennett to the fullback nets 12 yards, as three defenders ride Juan Tucker down cowboy style, unable to tackle him any other way.

The pass play sets up the draw, and Bennett drops back as if to pass. At the last moment, he hands off to Owens, who is squared up to pass block. On the sideline,

Robby sees the kid from California pass through the line of scrimmage untouched and into the secondary, where he splits two Owl defenders and races for his second touchdown.

When the game ends, Owens has run for 175 yards and three scores. Monticello has won their first game 28-7. Robby sits in the locker room between two other players, both of whom have seen action. Their uniforms are stained green and brown from the battle, and one has a red bloodstain on his upper thigh. But even though his blue pants and white shirt are unmarked, he feels a part of it all, and they sing the fight song. It is stirring to him, and he is slightly sad, but elated, when it is over. He wishes they could stay here and sing it all night.

***

For Dollar Bill, the day is spent enjoying the ambience of Bob Lucky's palace. He was awakened the night before by his host's staff and told of Leon's apparent attempt to steal his dog.

"He weren't trying to steal him," Dollar Bill tells them, "he was trying to save him. Don't worry, I'll take care of it."

He asks the men to stand guard over the dog, and goes back to sleep. He had not seen Leon all morning, and he finally goes to the man's room and knocks on the door. Leon opens the door. He seems quiet, but unapologetic, not avoiding his boss's eyes, and not offering any explanation.

"Leon, they told me what you tried to do last night. Now you might think I'm pissed off at you, and I am a might miffed. But, I understand that dog has put some sort of spell on you. It ain't entirely your fault. I've seen it coming. Hell, you ain't even had a drink in over a week. That in itself tells me you ain't yourself. Now, lets just put last night behind us."

"I can't handle the dog. Can't put him in the pit."

"Well, shit," Dollar said, "I can just get one of Lucky's men to put him in. All that will do is cost you your ten percent of the winnings. Don't let some dog-voodoo get in the way of your payday. Does that make any sense?"

Leon pulled two chairs out from the table and beckoned his boss to sit. Dollar Bill hesitated for a moment, then plopped down. He sensed a marked difference in the man, and could not put his finger on what it was. It was surely an improvement, he hated to admit. Leon was less fidgety. He had showered and shaved. But most of all, Dollar Bill realized, the change was in Leon's eyes. They were meeting his own, and it was spooky because this was so unlike Leon. Leon never looked anyone in the eyes. Probably didn't even look himself in the eyes in the mirror. But he was looking straight at Dollar Bill, and it gave him a whole different persona, like he wasn't even the same man.

Dollar Bill found himself checking Leon's arms for familiar tattoos, just to see if this was the same man. Of course it was the same man, with the same cheap, blue ink tattoos on his forearms. Must be the attention to hygiene, Dollar concluded. I've never seen him clean before.

"Whatever you do is up to you," Leon said evenly, still looking directly at him, and Dollar Bill felt himself look away.

"But I won't have a hand in it. I know you think I've lost my mind. Maybe I have, and maybe it's a good thing. Maybe the mind I had needed losing. I never knew an animal could have a soul. Never considered it, to tell you the truth. I lost a lot of things last night…and I'm better for it. I can't explain what happened to me last night. I don't even know why I'm trying. If you put that dog in the pit, you'll regret it. It's as wrong as wrong can be."

"Since when have you started considering what's right and wrong?" Bill said, growing very uncomfortable with the conversation.

Leon looked at his boss for a long minute, considering his response, before saying, "since he healed the hurt in me."

He had said it with such utter sincerity that Dollar Bill managed a laugh, but only a short one. He looked back at Leon and saw he was not joking; he was not even smiling. He just sat there serene, and that was something Leon had never been. Nervous, usually. Shifty eyed, intoxicated and unwashed, always. But never serene, and it gave Dollar Bill pause to consider what the man was telling him.

"You mean the dog healed your hurt?"

"He did."

With that, Dollar Bill rose from his chair and headed for the door, but stopped just before his hand reached the knob. He spoke not turning around because he felt more comfortable facing away from Leon. Not wanting to look at the man who was so utterly sincere, but talking such foolishness.

"Brother Leon, you've suffered some sort of breakdown. Or that dog has hexed you, or something. I got a dogfight to go to this evening. I hope you change your mind and go with me."

"I won't be there. I'm hitching a ride home. Look, I got a piece of property my moma left me just north of Little Rock. It ain't nothing but a couple of acres of pine trees, but it's worth about ten thousand dollars. Let him go, and I'll give it to you."

"You're shitting me? You'd spend ten thousand dollar to free that pooch?"

"And I'll work for you free for a year. I'll pick up cans or something to eat on and put gas in my truck. What do you say?"

"I say I hope whatever that dog put on you, stays away from me," Dollar said, and he walked out of the room without looking back.

Around 4:00 PM the staff informed Dollar Bill that Leon had left the premises, walking towards the highway.

"Well, good riddance," he said, and went back to nursing his whiskey.

The match was scheduled to begin at six, and an hour before, the scrap yard owner noticed an assortment of expensive cars begin streaming into the property, moving past the lake to park near the back of the large house. At 5:30 PM, he called the staff and notified them he would need a substitute handler to assist him in getting his dog to the pit area.

He checked his appearance in the mirror and left the room to take the short walk to where the fight would take place. He sized the crowd up to be around thirty people, most standing in small groups. Lucky called him over and introduced him to several people before pulling him to the side.

"I would still like to purchase the dog, Mr. Dollar."

"Hell," he said, suddenly feeling very inebriated, "everyone wants to buy my dog today. Makes me think I should hang on to him. We got us a dog fight to put on. Lets do this thing."

"Very well," Lucky said, and nodded an affirmation to a man holding a communication device.

Lucky walked over to where his kennel manager Tom was standing.

"I want you near me when this happens. Give me your impressions," Lucky said to the man.

"My pleasure," he said, and the brindle boxer with the torn ear was brought in.

"I took a look at him last night in the holding area. I thought it was some sort of joke on me," Tom said.

"No joke. That's the dog that killed Victor."

"How?" he said, simply.

"I don't know," Lucky said, and the kennel manager noted he'd never heard his boss utter this particular phrase before.

"Should be interesting then," Tom said, as the boxer was left alone in the pit.

The reddish brown Cleo was then brought into the arena, and the handler unleashed her and quickly exited, leaving only the two dogs and an outfitted break man in the ring. The man was standing against the wall, well back out of the action that he anticipated would unfold.

She was of the same breed as Victor, though slightly heavier. She had shown a great mastery for tactical training at an early age, and was one of Tom's favorites fighters.

"Is the second dog ready?" Lucky said to his manager.

"He's ready, but surely we won't need him."

Lucky held his eye for a moment, before both men turned their attention to the impending action.

Cleo wasted no time crossing the distance between herself and Buzz Saw. It looked to the crowd like a heavyweight champion about to pummel a junior high student. Several of Lucky's friends called out to him and raised their hands questioningly, as if to say, what is this? He motioned for them to watch, curious himself about what was going happen. They met in the middle of the pit and began brawling, with the brindle fighter not wanting to give ground, but he was forced back to the wall before Cleo disengaged. His right ear was now in tatters, and a small amount of blood could be seen issuing from his upper shoulder. Cleo paused to catch her breath only for a moment, and Buzz Saw declined to keep his back against the wall, meeting her half way.

"He has heart," Tom said, "but that's all he's got. This is a mismatch."

"Keep watching," Lucky said, as the dogs tangled up again.

A furious exchange developed directly under Lucky and his handler. This time when the dogs disengaged it was apparent that Buzz Saw's face and mouth had been ripped. The left side of his face was dripping blood, his teeth exposed on the injured side.

The brindle boxer shook his head twice and viewed the female with a lowered head, never taking his eyes off her. She charged full tilt at the wounded dog, and he met her attack with heretofore-unseen ferocity. This time there was no break in the engagement, and they battled just off the wall, neither giving ground. Droplets of blood were flying through the air and landing in the dirt of the pit, and

Lucky assumed it was from the boxer's injuries, until ever so slowly, Cleo begin to be forced back. The dogs circled, locked up face to face, and he could now see she had been gashed under the eye. Still, she was savvy enough not to turn. She tried to disengage by backpedaling but Buzz Saw followed her, step for step.

Lucky became aware, at this point, that he was standing, as was the man at his flank. The entire crowd was screaming, leaning over the pit towards the action. It was impossible to tell for whom they were cheering, such was the cacophony of noise and emotion. Lucky himself was not sure whom he was screaming for. He had forgotten his wager, and was immersed in the moment of the underdog. They were caught up in the feeling one would experience at the sight of the skinny kid punching out the schoolyard bully, or a high school basketball team driving for a fast break on a group of NBA All Stars. To not cheer for the boxer would have been unsporting, unthinkable, and they were lost in it.

Maintaining his level of incredible rage, Buzz Saw backed up Cleo and she felt her rear haunches strike wall, which prevented any retreat. Lucky saw his fighter lose her concentration momentarily; glancing back at what was blocking her movement. In this moment, Lucky and his manager witnessed the intensity of her opponent grow exponentially in its terrible fierceness. With his ripped face and teeth moving like a blur, he tore into the frontal portion of Cleo, shredding whatever was in his reach.

"Good God," Tom shouted, "he's killing her, he's killing her…"

Still, Cleo would not turn, until she fell at his feet, and Buzz Saw continued to open her neck and back. The wall of the pit was splattered with blood. Even the man in the pit was stunned and he made no move to disengage the boxer from the red Pit. It was uncertain to the onlookers when she expired. When the brindle boxer ceased his attack and walked to the far wall, with the left side of his face torn, and his shoulder hemorrhaging in a stream, she lay dead.

Lucky realized then that he was standing, had been shouting, and he wondered to himself when this had occurred. He felt a similar feeling he had felt at the previous match with Victor: having seen something with his eyes, but not being able to fathom it.

"What did you see?" he asked the kennel manager to his left, who was still on his feet, looking toward the now dead Cleo. The man only shook his head, never taking his eyes off Buzz Saw, who was now feeling the pain of his torn mouth.

The dog lay fatigued and bleeding near the wall of the pit, panting and swallowing his own blood. From his past experience, he knew he would now be removed from the enclosure. He had done what they placed him here to do. He would go back to the loneliness of the pen, until at some point the cycle was repeated. He was therefore confused when the routine was broken, and he was not lifted out of the pit.

"What did you see?" Lucky again asked Tom.

"He became a lion," the kennel manager whispered, still staring into the arena.

Lucky remembered then that the event was not over.

"Bring in Sampson," he told an assistant, and the man hustled off to perform the request.

Lucky saw Dollar Bill standing to his right, a quarter ways around the arena. Several people were clapping him on the back. His dog was still on its belly, red drool dripping from the injury to his mouth, looking spent. Two of Lucky's men carried the ripped Cleo out of the area, one eye glazed and lifeless, the other torn from its socket and hanging by the thread of a connecting nerve. She looked to Lucky as if she had been the victim of an industrial accident.

The buzz of conversation had not died down completely, when the massive Sampson was escorted into the arena. There were sounds of astonishment from the crowd at his entry. Lucky had originally purchased him for his sheer size, hoping to breed that characteristic into a more agile offspring, but with agility conditioning and strength training, he was found to be able to carry the weight effectively. Lucky's handlers had turned him into a tank with teeth. To the dog on the ground just gaining his wind, Sampson looked like a black wall of grinning teeth and muscle.

Buzz Saw barely got to his feet before Sampson was on him, his shadow dwarfing the boxer. He backpedaled, purposely moving back and to the side so as not to be pinned. The tactic allowed him to stay alive, but he was suffering further injury with every second. Blood now coated both legs and chest, obscuring the white socks, turning them red with his gore. Unable to advance an inch, he was denied any opportunity to inflict damage on the dark giant, staying just out of his opponents death grip. Sampson tried to hem him in, but Buzz Saw deftly sensed what was behind him, and backed pedaled to the side at the last moment.

The brindle dog was now leaving a trail of his own blood in the dirt, giving aggression only to stop an all out advance.

"He can't keep this up," Lucky said, "he's finished."

A profusion of blood from a gash to his head had now blinded the smaller dog on his left side, and he was forced to steadily move right to keep Sampson in his view. It was at this point he did a 90 degree turn and appeared to take flight, keeping to the edge of the pit.

"He's broke. He's done for," Lucky's manager said, punching him in the arm for emphasis.

"No...not yet," said Lucky, warily.

Sampson wheeled his massive frame to give chase and made two circuits around the enclosure, attempting to cut him off without success. To the onlookers it was a tragic, slightly comical scene, with the giant chasing the small brindle boxer, who was a bloody mess, and fleeing for his life. After the second pass, the giant appeared to figure out the game, and turned the other way to catch Buzz Saw as he continued in a rightward loop. It seemed to Lucky and the crowd like the logical thing to do.

Buzz Saw, with his unobscured right eye, saw the black dog's rear come into view for a split second, and he altered his path straight for Sampson's blind side, seizing him by the trailing leg. Hanging on as the huge dog drug him in the dirt, he locked his jaws in desperation, chewing and tearing. Sampson continued to spin, trying to loose his leg from the boxer's grip.

Everyone was screaming, excluding Lucky and the manager, who stood slack jawed at the development. It was apparent that the small dog would be summarily dispatched if he let go of the leg, but he did not let go, instead chewing and climbing until the leg was a mangled mess, and he chewed his way up the leg, to the thigh, and onto the back of the giant. Sampson howled his indignation at the attacker he could not reach.

Looking much like a mangled cowboy riding a bull, he turned his attention to the black fighters neck and back, unleashing a terrible attack. Lucky dimly remembered later how the frenzied voices of his invited friends were eclipsed by the frightful mad roar of the smaller dog. It was rage amplified beyond what seemed possible, both terrible to watch, and impossible to turn away from

"Do you see it? Do you see it?" he screamed repeatedly to anyone who would listen.

With his back and neck literally being removed in chunks, all thought of tactics and training went by the wayside. His only thought was to remove the offender from his blind side; to dislodge the flesh-eating nightmare causing a pain he'd never before experienced. With a howl of indignation, he sank to the ground and rolled. It appeared momentarily that the small, bloody mongrel might be rolled under, and the crowd craned to see what might become of this tactic.

Buzz Saw loosed Sampson at the first sign of his roll, and bounded with lightning speed back onto the belly of his enemy. Bob Lucky and Tom watched their gargantuan animal leave his feet, and capsize like a doomed luxury line. There was a split second when the men knew not how the small dog would react to this, but he quickly dispelled all doubt, and unleashed a totally unabated blitzkrieg to his enemies' underside.

"Oh, God...my God...my God," the manager said, and even before the giant had breathed his last breath, and lay still, Lucky was screaming into his walkie-talkie.

"Bring me Lobo...get Lobo up here, now!" he said, wildly. It is unclear anyone else heard his words, as the noise from the brindle dog was stifling out all other noise. When it was clear to everyone except the small dog that Sampson was eviscerated, the break man moved his stick between the two, and Buzz Saw staggered off the bloody mess of a corpse and collapsed in the dirt.

In the excitement of the battle, no one had noticed the smaller dog's condition. Now the brindle boxer's wounds became apparent to the onlookers. There was scarcely an exposed point on his body that was without injury. His true color was no longer discernable, and he lowered his head and appeared to lose consciousness for the moment. The dirt around him was turning into a mix of blood and mud, as his breath came in ragged gasps. Only the right eye was visible through the mess of his own injuries, and it was closed. He lay there, fully alert, waiting to be taken from this place of pain, certain it was now over.

Bob Lucky pulled a Cuban cigar from his pocket and stroked the end with a silver lighter till the ember glowed. His manager was silent next to him, and he saw the man looking at the ground, unmoving.

"What are your impressions?" he asked, unable to resist the question.

Tom sighed and looked up at the sky.

"It is not my responsibility, as your employee, to tell you what you should do. It is my responsibility, as a sportsman, to tell you that you should cancel this wager. Take that dog from the pit; give him the best veterinary care you can give him. He's already earned his owner whatever sum you've bet against him. I personally wish I could forget what I've seen here. On the other hand, I hope I never forget it. If I owned that dog, he'd never fight again."

With that he threw his hands in the air in frustration, knowing Lucky would not heed his advice, sorrowful at the condition of the boxer that lay in the dirt. Such courage as he had seen deserved better, and it hurt his heart knowing his boss would not cancel the match; would proceed on to its conclusion.

"I've lost three fighters to that one," he said, pointing at the dog in the dirt. "A bets a bet. It will be concluded here, tonight."

"Yes, sir. It will be," he said, simply. He looked to the small dog lying in his own blood, and wondered if he could even rise when his final opponent was brought in. The manager stood there mute for a moment, then walked over to Dollar Bill.

"You can stop this. Call it a match. Haven't you seen enough?"

"He can still win it. One more to go. We're smelling the money, now," said Dollar, looking around for anyone to back him up.

"You don't know what's coming."

"You're just trying to save your boss some money. Better get that cash ready, mister," he said, poking the kennel manager in the chest for emphasis.

An audible murmur swept through the spectators near the pit entranceway, and they could be seen parting to allow the next opponent a wide berth. On the ground,

Buzz Saw could smell Lobo before he ever laid eyes on him, and the hair on the back of his blood encrusted neck stood straight up. It was the smell of something wild, something that moved by night, and howled to his brothers by the light of the moon.

The timber wolf, weighing in at perhaps one hundred fifty pounds, had been captured in the Alaskan wilderness as an adolescent. His mother had been shot by one of Lucky's hunting buddies, the pup transported illegally back to the states, and given to him as a gift. He was a novelty at first, considered for possible breeding purposes to create a super bloodline. This had never panned out, as Lucky's females had preferred to fight to the death rather than be his mating partner. Thus, he remained secluded in a far corner of the kennel, where he grew into adulthood.

Buzz Saw looked through his clear right eye at the silver streaked, yellow-eyed menace that entered the arena, and began growling even before he was unleashed. Slowly, with great pain, he rose to his feet.

Dollar Bill saw the wolf enter, and began shouting and jumping up and down.

"Foul, foul! That ain't no dog. You've forfeited." He ran to where Lucky was standing and his dank whiskey breath washed over the man, causing him to turn his head.

"What kind of shit are you pulling here? This was supposed to be a dog fight!"

"You made a deal for three matches in succession. This is the third," Lucky said, not looking at the man.

"Stop the match," Tom said, looking directly at Dollar.

"Hell, no," he said, shaking his head, "he can do it, I know he can."

The kennel manager looked toward the small dog, whose blood was running freely down all four legs, and who now stood facing the wolf. It was obvious he could no longer see from the left side, as his head was cocked strangely in that direction, using one side of his vision. He looked like a bloody soldier standing in front of a tank, daring it to run him over. The man is blinded by greed, Tom concluded, and he waved the scrap yard owner away.

Lucky nodded to the handler tethering the wolf, and Lobo was unleashed. He moved stealthily, circling. Buzz Saw turned in the center of the pit, keeping the wolf in view. With two bounding steps the timber wolf closed the gap, and he was met with all the malice the small, bloody dog had to give. It appeared to catch him off guard for a moment, this wounded animal putting up such a fight, and he backed off a step before charging once again headlong towards the scent of fresh blood. It appeared for an eternity, which was actually two minutes, that Buzz Saw would hold his ground, meeting rage with rage. And during this period the kennel manager found himself wondering, can he do it? Can the little dog really pull this off?

As they broke off the furious melee the wolf backed from the encounter. Fresh blood could be seen streaking down his muzzle from cut to his nose. Buzz Saw stood in the center of the pit staring in the general direction of Lobo, not entirely at him, but up and beyond. Blood covered both eyes, and his countenance was unrecognizable.

"He's blind," said Tom, to Lucky at his side.

"Finish it!" Lucky screamed at the silver wolf.

Lobo shook his head once to clear the pain in his snout, and seemed to realize the small dog was sightless. He began moving in a circling manner. Buzz Saw could only smell the lupine killer, and spun in his general direction, but not fast enough. Lobo hit the small dog from the side, knocking him from his feet, and the form of the mangled boxer was hidden by the body of the wolf, as he sought to destroy him with vicious tearing strokes, to eat him as he would a rabbit or small deer in the wild. When the wolf stopped and stepped back, the small, bloody form in the dirt was unmoving, a lump of bright red.

"Stop! Enough of this!" Tom screamed with all his voice.

The break man looked toward Lucky and he nodded his head in affirmation. The wolf was forced back with the breaking stick and he stood there panting, his face and breast coated with his opponents gore, satisfied that he would be allowed to feed shortly.

A great sadness swept over the onlookers, and some could be heard sobbing in the stillness of the place. Dollar Bill stood with his hand covering his mouth, his lost fortune temporarily forgotten.

Slowly, with the greatest exertion, the small bloody form in the center of the pit began moving, and raised its head. The sound of those crying temporarily subsided, and those standing around the sunken arena could hear a faint noise. It was the sound of the little dog growling. With his head now up, he could be seen trying to place his front legs under his body to lift himself.

"Stay down," Dollar Bill whispered, then shouted, "Stay down!"

But he would not stay down. Like a scene from Night of the Living Dead, where the corpses come to life, the unrecognizably mauled dog slowly rose and lifted himself on front paws, then painfully pulled himself into a teetering, standing position. Standing slightly askew from the wolf, knowing not exactly where the killer was, but seeking to reengage with his last bit of life, he made a stumbling step in his general direction, only his white, bared teeth visible through the sheen of his own blood.

The timber wolf, delighted that the game was not yet finished, pushed past the break stick and seized the blind dog by a rear leg, pulling him completely off the ground, and swung his head side to side in an attempt to disengage the limb. He then threw the small form to the ground and mauled him again for several moments, before backing off.

The break man again moved the wolf from the mangled mess on the ground, and this time Buzz Saw did not move. A length of white, glistening bone was visible halfway up the leg. Otherwise, the profusion of blood prevented one from determining his back from his front.

There were a number of people in the viewing audience who would never again attend another dog fighting event, having been witness to what they had seen. Dollar Bill was one of those people. He shuffled over to Bob Lucky and stood silent for a moment by the man's side.

"Damn, he was something, wasn't he?" was all he could finally say. He stood there feeling empty and lost, suddenly stone sober despite having consumed a vast amount of whiskey throughout the evening.

Lucky watched as two of his staffers lifted Buzz Saw from the pit, and Lobo, frustrated that he would not be allowed to feed on the corpse, was escorted out of the arena.

"Our business if finished, Mr. Dollar. You know your way out."

Dollar Bill turned to see the two men, one holding the front paws, and the other holding the rear with gloved hands, carry the dog out of his sight. The body was carried a short distance to a slope and dropped. It rolled, leaving a trail of blood on the leaves and grass, before coming to rest at the bottom, among the bones of other animals long dead.

Chapter 18

COLLEEN SCOTT KNEW, BEING a normally heavy sleeper, that something unusual had awakened her. She craned her neck to check the form of the man sleeping beside her, and finding him snoring softly, dismissed him as the source of her rousing. She keened her senses inward toward her inner spirit, and heard the clear, calm call: pray.

They had now been at her sister's residence in southern Missouri for five months, and she knew they were welcome to stay as long as they liked. Her sister had a large, pleasant house near the Arkansas border with several empty spare bedrooms, and she and her husband Fred got along splendidly. They had originally planned to stay for a month or two, but this had, day by day, stretched to September. She missed the house in Camden that was surely overgrown with neglect, and Fred had said they could go home any time, but neither she nor he had voiced a concern to leave.

The visions she had experienced were a rare occurrence, but it was not at all uncommon for her to be summoned awake for intercessory prayer. During these times, like now, she was not given instruction on who, or what to pray for. There was only the call to rise and let the spirit pray through her, in tongues. She moved silently in her slippers to the quiet of the living room and found a wooden rocking chair. There was a worn Bible sitting on a table beside her, and she impulsively picked it up and cradled it to her breast. She opened her mouth and felt the strange syllables pour over her lips, the familiar feel of something coming up from her belly, almost like water, spilling out. With her eyes closed, she uttered mysteries into the stillness of the room.

The dog found himself moving through a realm of shadows. There was a presence beside him, moving strong and steady. He could not make out its form, but somehow knew it had been with him his whole life, from the time he suckled his mother, to his time through the fighting pits, until now. He did not question its presence, and knew it would not leave him. He was happy to be away from the blinding pain, and there seemed no sensation of time, as they drew away from what had been, toward what was, and a feeling of utter joy swelled within him.

It was a feeling akin to running with the boy. The feeling of being with another who loved you more than life, sharing a primal bond. Being complete in the moment. Simply being. The memory of what was had not been lost in this realm. He remembered everything with perfect clarity.

He could still recall his time of waiting in the field, a time of confusion for him. Being pressed into blood sport by the two men, and an endless succession of violent encounters and death. And the yellow eyes of the wolf. He felt there were no such spirits in this vicinity, and none where he was headed. This made him even more joyful, and he willed himself to somehow move faster, toward what was to be.

Colleen felt her prayer rise in pitch and a feeling of ecstasy washed over her. The phenomenon had never been this intense, and she relaxed and allowed it to flow, determined not to interfere with it in any way. Her lips stammered in response to what flowed out of her, and her hands gripped the arm of the rocker, letting the Bible slide down into her lap.

The dog, and the presence reached a kind of boundary, a border between the realm of shadows, and the beginnings of light. He felt himself slowing, as did his companion. The light ahead, he somehow knew, contained perfect peace, and it was tantalizingly close. The aura of the light was a sweet fragrance to him; containing in its entirety all the good things he had beforehand only known in pieces and fragments. And it was forever, never ending, waiting to surround him if he continued. He also sensed he could continue if he choose. Then why had he paused? It was clear to him that he had a choice. He was being asked to choose. And on the surface it would seem like an easy choice.

Ahead was joy in all its fullness, pure and simple. Behind was the blinding pain, and the souls of those whose mission was not to heal, but to hurt. The ones who made it their daily mission to add pain to the world. Those who, out of their own pain, gave pain to others.

He paused, perplexed why he would even be offered such a choice, and he heard the presence beside him whisper, "Something remains…."

As there was no time to his perception, it could not be said how long he considered this, but his mind was filled with thoughts of the boy, and he knew the boy was not ahead, but behind, in the realm of pain.

Again he heard, "Something remains…"

At this point, with no more deliberation, the conscious decision was made within him, and he was moving back, the ever-strong presence at his side.

Fred Scott emerged half awake and rolled over, as he was of habit to do, to reach for his life companion; to place his arm around her, and comfort himself in the knowledge that she was there and safe. It was something he loved to do in the night, or upon waking in the morning. With his arm around her he would meld his body next to her, attempting to not disturb her sleep best he could, but immersed in the feeling of oneness. But when he reached for her, the bed was empty. The door to the bathroom was ajar. He could see she was not there, and this slightly alarmed him, causing him to come fully awake.

It had been quite some time since she'd had one of her visions, and he credited being away from the house in Camden for this. Maybe the house had gone "bad". With what they had experience with Lu-Lu, who could know? He only knew she slept peacefully here, and that was enough for him.

He swung his feet over the side of the bed and found his house slippers. He quietly cracked the door of Colleen's sister and saw that his wife was not there. Padding through the hall, careful not to crack his shin on a hidden object, he heard the squeak of the rocker and entered the living room. She was sitting with her back to him, and he softly said, "Colleen." She did not respond, and a wave of panic washed over him.

A variety of scenarios passed through his mind, none of them good. He imagined her sitting there with the corner of her mouth fallen on one side, the victim of a massive stoke. He saw, in his mind, her holding her chest, experiencing a crushing chest pain, unable to even call out to him. It could be any of these things, or a hundred more, and he felt the grief of it even before knew what actually was.

He hurriedly shuffled to where he stood in front of her. She was smiling and holding her Bible securely to her breast.

"Colleen," he said again.

"Yes, Fred," she said. She was looking at him, but seemingly not seeing him; looking through him. Fred felt suddenly afraid. More afraid than when he thought she might be sick, and it was a nameless fear, which made it somehow more terrible. He would later recall that her face looked like an angel. There was an unearthly glow to her, and he was, at first, hesitant to touch her. But his concern for her overpowered all the fear he felt, and he reached out and gently touched her face. A passage from the same Bible she was holding flashed through his mind. Something from a long ago sermon he had heard. Moses coming off the mountain after being in the presence of God, and the Israelites were afraid to come near him because…the glory of God emanated in his countenance.

"Are you alright, honey?" he choked out.

"Oh, yes. I've never been better. Never been better. Jesus was here, Fred. He was standing right there where you're standing."

Fred jumped when she said this, and unconsciously moved a step back.

"He explained everything to me, yes He did. He told me what the small thing was that's coming, and I ain't worried no more. Told me to look up I Corinthians 13:8."

"What's coming, Colleen?"

"Love's coming. And that explained my vision, 'cause you see, love may seem like a small thing, but it never stops fighting, never stops trying, till it does what it came to do. Everything is going to be all right, oh yes. You can't stop love. Might as well try to stop the wind from blowing, or the sun from rising. The devil keeps trying. I don't know what he's thinking. My Jesus … you should have seen him, should have seen him…the marks are still in his hands."

There were no roses in or outside the house, and his wife had never worn a scent even vaguely resembling it, but Fred detected it briefly, ever so subtly in the room, and he looked around wildly before focusing back on her. He wanted to move her, take her safely back to bed with him. But she looked so gloriously happy he could not bear to take her from this spot.

"I'm gonna get a drink of water, sweetheart. Do you want anything?"

"No, I'm just fine. Thank you."

Fred left her sitting there and went into the kitchen. He then remembered there was another Bible in the bedroom and he suddenly felt a mad desire to retrieve it. He hesitated a moment, fighting the urge, then walked back down the hall on the balls of his feet, and found it sitting on the table by the bed. He opened the book and thumbed past John, Acts, and Romans, finally coming to I Corinthians.

He located the thirteenth chapter, ran his finger down to verse eight, and read, *'Love never fails…'*

Consciousness began to awaken within the dog, and with it the all-encompassing agony of his torn body. He lay there a while, gathering a sense of his present reality, feeling the rise and fall of his chest, and the pressure of the ground beneath him. Then he attempted to open his eyes. The blood had crusted and welded the lids shut, and it took a vast amount of his remaining energy just to force them open. They finally broke the bond of plasma holding them, and he cringed from the brightness of the day filtering through the branches of the trees. To his immediate left he detected a dark shape sitting a foot away from his head. He willed his eyes to focus in that direction and found himself staring into the black pupil of a vulture. Drawing on what strength he could summon, he managed a low growl and the bird lifted off with a squawk of protest.

It seemed impossible to take stock of his injuries. His entire body was alive with pain. There was a sense that his consciousness was not uninterrupted because, at some point, he opened his eyes again and the day was late. Now he was able to move a foreleg and lift his head for brief moments. Thankfully, the bird had not returned. There were other animals around him though. He could not see them, but could sense their presence. He became aware of burning thirst, and this, together with the unseen creatures surrounding him, convinced him of the necessity to move. It seemed but a moment had past when he looked out at his world, and found night had fallen. Now he was able to move both front legs, and not only lift, but also hold up his head.

This gave him a fresh perspective on his world, and in the darkness he determined himself to be in a shallow depression. He could both smell and see the whitish outline of bones and skulls around him, and it gave him further incentive to remove himself from this place of death. Of his many injuries, the damage to the left leg was the most severe. It had been stripped of flesh to the bone, but miraculously unbroken. He found he could pull himself with front paws and push with the right leg. The incline he was facing was the first great challenge, and he began inching toward where it sloped up. He was able to wet his tongue on the dew from the vegetation around him, and it was glorious to his parched mouth. Another moment seemed to pass, and when he opened his eyes the morning sun was just beginning to illuminate the eastern sky.

He had paused at the very bottom of the incline, and he sensed his strength was sufficient to attempt the climb. The gravity of moving uphill seemed to be an enemy that was angry at his escape, and it was as exerting as moving up the slope of a mountain. After an hour of struggling, he crested the top of the six foot embankment and collapsed along its edge, careful not to allow himself to roll back down.

After an undetermined period of rest he opened his eyes and looked back down at the valley in the daylight. It was no wonder the vultures frequented this place, as it was littered with skeletal remains. He could see the brownish red trail he had left on the opposite bank when he had rolled down it, and the depression in the grass where he had landed.

His existence became one of pulling and pushing himself along the ground, and collapsing from sheer exhaustion, to awaken and do it again. Pain was his constant companion, save for the periods of blissful unconsciousness. It was with him at every move, and with him as he opened his eyes to his world.

To the old man, sitting in the woods with his rifle was therapy. He had no need to hunt for meat, as his monthly disability check supplied his grocery needs. And he was not of a mindset to kill for sport. It just seemed natural to take a gun into the woods, and since the death of his wife eight months previous, walking in the woods had become the glue that held his mind together. The house without his wife seemed vastly empty, and he found himself spending every available moment away from it. Too many memories of her there, yet financially he could never hope to move anywhere else, except perhaps a retirement village, with a supplement from the government. Rather be in the woods, he concluded.

Being in the woods surrounded by life, albeit of the wild variety, seemed utterly preferable to sitting home. A hawk flew overhead, and he found his mind wandering to an increasingly recurrent theme. He could, so easily, remove his shoes and socks. Then, with the big toe of his foot on the trigger, position the rifle so that it squared up to his forehead. Have to do it carefully, he reasoned. Wouldn't want to mess around and do it halfway. Blow the side of my head off and leave myself alive. Wouldn't I feel stupid then? Straighten up the leg, apply tension from the ankle and then...and then I'm up there flying with the hawk. No more waiting for the grim reaper to come calling, no sir. Beat him to the punch. Cheat him out of his stipend.

Probably wouldn't hurt, surely not. Wouldn't even hear it. One minute I'm here, the next minute, I'm there. I'll bet there is better, he concluded, and he was more convinced of this fact every time he dwelt on the subject, which he did nearly every day now.

Are you afraid to do it, his mind asked? Hell no, he came back. Actually, I'm afraid not to. Then why put it off? I don't know, he reasoned, maybe things will get better. Sure, just like your health. Getting better everyday; you're not getting older, you're getting better. I wonder if my toe will even reach the trigger, he wondered. Well, take your shoe off and see, came back the response. I guess it wouldn't hurt to find out, he concluded. No one out here but me and the wildlife. He scanned the forest for sign of another human, knowing he wouldn't see anybody. There was never anyone else out here. Still, he thought, I wouldn't want someone to see me and run up and snatch the gun away. Maybe have me committed to a psychiatric ward.

He was just about to lower his eyes from the wood line when a black shape caught his eye. It was perhaps seventy yards away, and he could not have seen it through the vegetation had it been any further. From the distance, it appeared to be stationary, then disappeared just as he noticed it. It piqued his curiosity and he tried to dispel it from his mind, then decided what the hell, its not like I'm on a schedule or anything.

He tried to fix his eyes on the last point he'd seen it, thoroughly convinced he would find nothing when he arrived. Probably a coyote, or a dog out for a romp in the woods. He moved past the shrubs and deadwood, being careful not to twist an ankle on the rough ground, not letting his eyes leave the spot.

He saw it when he was perhaps twenty feet away, and cautiously stopped. It was an animal, no doubt about that, though what kind was impossible to determine from where he stood. He advanced in measured paces until he was standing over it, though far enough back to flee if it decided he was a threat.

It was a dog. A mangled mess of a dog. And he could see it was alive because its eyes were open and staring at him. Buzz Saw sensed the presence of the man and keened his nose to detect the scent. There was the scent of tobacco and aftershave, but he could not pick up the smell of alcohol that he associated with erratic behavior. He allowed his instincts to probe deeper, and detected a painful, almost unfathomable loneliness. He had just finished moving and had collapsed at this spot, unable to go any further without rest. Regardless, he would not have fled from this soul had he been able. He may even have moved to comfort him, if he perceived any invitation to do so. At present, he could only lie there.

"Good God," the man said aloud, "What did this to you?"

He looked around and checked to make sure the rifle was off safety, unsure if a marauding animal was nearby. When he spoke to the dog there was the faintest wag of its tail, and it moved him to approach within arms reach. Must be careful, he's obviously in great pain; can't survive this. No way.

"Hey, boy," he said, and the tail twitched a bit from side to side.

It appeared the dog had been dipped in blood, like an apple dipped in caramel. It was dried to his coat and beginning to flake off. Underneath he could see punctures and tears running the length of the body. His ears were gone, leaving only the holes atop his skull. The mouth was ripped on the left side, giving him the appearance of a permanent sneer, the teeth exposed and visible. The back legs were splayed and he could see bright white bone showing through on the left leg.

I should put him out of his misery, he concluded, and took a step back to ready himself for the shot. He glanced back in the direction the dog had traveled and saw the draglines visible in the leaves. They went back as far as his vision would allow.

"You been dragging yourself a long ways, huh?" he spoke, and again there was a slight movement of the tail. The scene that had obviously unfolded flashed through his mind. The dog had encountered something in the woods. He had obviously put up a terrific struggle, maybe even killing the thing that had attacked him. But he had barely survived. He could have stayed in the spot where he had been wounded. Just lain down and succumbed. But his spirit would not allow that. Despite catastrophic injuries, he had dragged himself through the wilderness, towards nothing, towards anything.

The dog had now closed its eyes, his breath coming in quick convulsive movements. Despite his fear of being bitten, the man crouched down and reached his hand to a small area on top of the dog's head that appeared unlashed. A millimeter before his hand made contact, the dog opened his eyes. I should not be doing this, he told himself, then his hand was touching the wounded animal, and large round eyes were looking up at him.

"Its gonna to be all right," he lied. "What in the world did you run into? You got away, so I guess he got the worst end of it. Hard to imagine, though."

He searched for any other area he could touch in comfort and found none. To Buzz Saw, the touch of the man was puzzling, but not unpleasant, and it momentarily diverted his attention away from his pain.

"Well, I can't just leave you here like this. I can either put you out of your misery, or try to take you home. What's it gonna be?"

The dog closed his eyes and appeared to fade out of consciousness. If he's struggling this hard to survive, what right do I have to shoot him, the man concluded. I could walk back to the house, make a travois out of cardboard, walk back here and sled him home. It was two miles to where he lived, and then two miles back, then two pulling the dog. A six mile trip. He'll be dead before I get back. What the hell.

"Hang on," he said, and gave the dog a final pat on the head.

To Buzz Saw, it seemed like only seconds before the man returned, minus his rifle. In all actuality it was a rather long walk there, then back again, before the man returned with a rectangular strip of cardboard. He approached expecting to find a dead animal, but found the dog very much alive, and resting.

"Okay, here comes the hard part. I'm here to help you, okay?"

The dog gave him another twitch of the tail and he laid the cardboard down beside him. He then began sliding the stiff brown paperboard underneath best he could. When it was halfway under the dog, he found it would not slide any more, and he positioned himself over the animal to place his hands on him and finish the procedure.

"I'm a fool, and I'm gonna get bit, I know that," he said, "but here goes."

It was painful being placed on the makeshift stretcher, but no more so than crawling, and the dog perceived the man meant him no harm. He whimpered audibly, but allowed himself to be positioned, then the man moved to the front of the cardboard, lifted the front, and set off on a bumpy trek through the woods.

After the tedious slow pace of crawling it seemed to Buzz Saw as if they were flying over the ground. He could hear the breath of the man ahead coming in ragged gasps as the travois lifted and fell over the rough ground. The man stopped several times and caught his breath before continuing on. Presently, the board was sliding over a very smooth surface and then it stopped near the front step of a wood frame shed.

The man left the dog on the cardboard and made a soft bed of old quilts, placing a water bowl and a dish of raw hamburger near it. Then he returned to Buzz Saw and tried to decide how to get the dog into the shed. He finally ripped off the front part from the makeshift stretcher, grasped both ends of the cardboard, praying it would not rip and drop the dog on the ground, and carried everything through the doorway, sliding the dog off onto the quilt. He then collapsed into a lawn chair sitting in the corner and lit a cigarette, trying to regain his breath.

"It's been a long time since this old man did that much work," he said to the dog.

Buzz Saw took stock of his surroundings and immediately the mouth-watering scent of the hamburger wafted to him. His most pressing concern however was water, and he was attempting to move towards the water bowl when the man saw his need and crouching down, moving it within his reach. The dog drank greedily, a good bit of the water spilling out his injured mouth. When he had finished the bowl the man left and refilled it. Then he pinched off pieces of the raw meat and hand fed them to him. He noted how the dog was careful not to bite his hand, and licked his empty fingers after every bite.

"Good, huh?" he said, and the dogs eyes emphatically declared that it was.

When the burger had been consumed the man sat back on his haunches and again looked the dog over. The leg was the most serious concern. Should be cleaned, bound to develop into a serious, bone deep infection, he concluded. But any of the other laceration could kill him as well, if infection set in. He went into the house and returned with some cotton gauze and a jug of distilled water.

He dipped the cotton into the water and rung it out over the exposed area of bone on the leg. The dog whimpered and tried to raise his head, but otherwise did not interfere with the man.

"Hurts like the dickens, I know," he said. "Got to at least get the dirt out, old boy." He noticed as he said this the eyes of the dog. They were not the eyes of an older dog, but were clear and bright despite his trauma. The teeth on the left side of the mouth that were permanently visible due to his injury were strong and bright white. He concluded the dog was not very old, was perhaps even very young.

"Mighty nice set of choppers you got there. Bet you could do some damage with those. Bet you did some damage, actually. Thank you for not damaging me with them," he said, and the dog, having sated his hunger and thirst, dropped his head onto the quilt and fell fast asleep. The man quietly left the shed, disposed the cardboard in a burn barrel, and went inside the house to rest from his long journey.

The man's habit had been, since the death of his wife, to lie in bed for as long as he could stand in the mornings. Then, when he could it could no longer be put off, to rise, grab his rifle, and exit the house as quickly as possible. Now when he awoke, his thoughts went to the dog in the shed, and he immediately rose from bed and dressed quickly. Probably dead, he thought. I'll grab my shovel and bury him out back.

But when he went to the frame out building the dog was very much alive and alert. He looked at the leg and found it crusted and inflamed around the edges where the bone was exposed. He realized it was not the trauma of the injuries that threatened him, but infection.

"Lets get you outside so you can do your business", he said. The dog could still not support himself, so he made a sling with two towels looped and tied, then inserted a stick through the open holes. Placing the dog in the center of the towels, he was able to hold the stick up and walk him outside. The dog looked slightly ridiculous dangling in the air, but it was effective. He walked him to all the places in the yard that he felt a dog would seek out, and accomplishing the mission, brought him back to the shed. After placing him back on quilt, he was given more food and water and left to rest.

He repeated this pattern three times daily, and often entered the shed to talk to his patient. He found himself eagerly looking forward to the feeding times. The dog listened intently as he spoke, and he could almost convince himself the dog understood what he was saying.

On the fifth day as he entered the shed the dog did not raise his head to greet him. He hurried to where he was laying and saw the leg was swollen, and angry red around the edges. A large amount of pus was exuded over the exposed bone, coming from the edges of the wound. Upon close examination he could detect a foul smell coming from the injury. Not good. He rushed into the house looking for anything that might be effective. A tube of antibacterial cream was the only thing he could find.

He took the cotton gauze and smeared it copiously with the cream, then applied this to the wound. The dog was awake, but listless, and did not protest when he touched the wound. Also, not a good sign. Petting the dog for comfort, the man went into the house and called a local veterinarian. It would cost one hundred dollars just to bring the dog in, plus any other procedure that was necessary. He hurriedly took out his wallet and found it contained only sixty dollars, and this had to last him through to the end of the month. He asked if this could be billed to him, and the answer was negative. Neither could he write a check to be held until he deposited the money. Guess we're on our own, he concluded.

When he checked on the dog that afternoon, the wound had a slight greenish tint and the leg felt hot to the touch. The beginnings of gangrene. A vet would probably want to amputate the leg. He vaguely recalled a dog in his neighborhood that had lost a leg chasing cars. He had recovered remarkably, and even learned to run on three limbs. They had changed his name to tripod. The memory made him smile. Animals were so resilient. Never giving up on life.

As he sat in his kitchen he saw the rifle sitting in the corner. It had remained untouched since he had brought the dog home. In fact, he had not even thought about it. Being in the house was no longer painful. The dog had taken his mind away from himself, given him something to care for, something to live for. His thoughts went back to just moments before he had seen him.

Sitting in the woods, feeling sorry for himself. Just like every other day since his wife had died. Surrounded by the life of the forest, thinking only of death. And he knew, on that particular day, he probably would have taken his shoes off and ended it all. While seventy five yards away a small dog was struggling mightily to live, he would have been stretching his toe out to reach a trigger and murder himself. What would his wife have thought had she seen it? Could she see it? Was she looking down somewhere, watching? He felt deeply ashamed that he had ever let himself get into that position, that he had even considered it.

On impulse, he rose and took hold of his rifle, carrying it to a spot where he split wood. He retrieved a sledgehammer from the shed and placed the rifle flat on the hard ground. With a high arc, he raised the hammer over his head and smashed the rifle again and again until it was broken in pieces. He did not stop until the rifle was an unrecognizable mess and he was winded. A five hundred dollar weapon lay shattered on the ground, and he felt at peace, felt downright giddy about it.

When he went back to check on his friend for the final time that evening, the leg was horribly swollen and distended. The white bone, usually visible in the opening of the wound, was almost lost in the swelling. He touched the dog on his head and got no response. His breathing was shallow and rapid. I did all I could do, he thought, sitting in a lawn chair looking at the animal. And you did all you could do. Would have died in the woods if I hadn't brought you here. At least you found some kindness in your last days. And you gave me much. Much more than you'll ever know.

He rose and went inside the house. His mind searched for solutions. There were none to be found. Around 10:00 PM he drew back his cover and crawled into bed.

The dog had entered into a long, dreamless sleep. Suddenly, all at once, he seemed to be awake. There was no transition to this, as it was seamless in nature. With the return to consciousness he became aware of eyes in the darkness, drawing closer. They were all around, and they were decidedly not friendly. When they had drawn close enough to be discerned in the darkness, he could see they appeared to be wild dogs.

The door to the shed was closed, so it was not apparent how they had entered. It was apparent that they were intent on attacking him, perhaps devouring him. Somehow his position had shifted from against the wall where the quilt lay, to the center of the room, and they were surrounding him. He snarled a warning at the closest one and it drew back, but another on the far side moved in and he swiveled his head to repel it. They were close enough now to be discerned in detail. They had yellow eyes, like the wolf, and enormous sharp teeth designed for tearing flesh.

Though he was immobile, he felt confident he could put up a terrific struggle against one, but they were moving in slyly. When he faced one direction, the ones on the blind side would advance.

They appeared to be gaining confidence, and as he snapped at one particularly close attacker, he felt the hot breath of another behind him, smelling his flesh to determine if it was worth the battle it would take to overpower him. He turned his head and summoned all his rage, attempting to convince it he would fight to the death and take several with him before he went. They were close enough now that he could smell their breath. It was the smell of rotting meat left in the sun, hot and fetid.

The man lay in bed unable to find sleep. A constant phrase persisted in his mind: I've done all I can do. He had searched himself exhausted for an answer. Had he done all? I've done everything humanly possible, he concluded…all I can do. I've done everything but pray to God. Why haven't I done that, he suddenly wondered? It had been years since he had prayed. He wasn't even sure he remembered how. He realized he felt angry with God. Angry for taking his wife. Angry for the loneliness he felt. Angry for almost allowing him to blow his brains out. Then, he realized God had not allowed him to kill himself. A miracle had intervened. The miracle of something small and helpless that needed him. He'd had no thoughts of suicide since the dog arrived. And the destruction of the rifle was a vow to himself that he would not allow himself to ever go there again, even if the dog died. The miracle had happened, and it would not be taken back.

He tried to think back to any sermon on prayer that would help him reach God. The twenty third psalm came to mind, but it did not seem to fit the situation. I've done all I can do, he thought again, I might as well try this.

"God," he began, then decided it would be better on his knees, more effective. So he left his bed and knelt beside it, with his elbows on the mattress.

"God, you're gonna have to cut me some slack, because I'm an ignorant old man, and I don't know the proper methods that are probably listed in your book. I am on my knees, so I hope that counts for something. Look, I know your busy running the universe and all, so I'll make this short. I've got little friend out there in the shed, and he's fought all he can fight. I know he wants to live 'cause he drug hisself for God knows…well, you know how far he drug hisself. He's already done a lot for me, and I can't do nothing more for him myself, except ask you, so I'm asking. Help him."

The man felt hot tears flowing down his face, and the next thing he knew he was prostrate, face down on the floor, still crying, whispering, "Help him, Lord. Help him."

The wild dogs were so close around him now their nostril looked like large, round black holes. He could see them flaring with each foul breath. Suddenly, the dimness of the shed was illuminated from all sides. His attackers pulled back, desperately searching for the source of the light, but they were perplexed, as it seemed to come out of every molecule of matter. And it became apparent they were very afraid of the light. They no longer looked fierce, but pitiful and beaten. If he could have moved, he would have leapt off the quilt and scattered them, but his leg was numb with swelling and smelled foul like the wild dogs breath. He realized that the same poison they contained in their being was alive in his wound.

Like shadows, his attacker seemed to be consumed by the light, unable to stand in its presence, unable to exist in it. They were there, and then they were gone. And the light coalesced out of the matter, into a somewhat discernable shape. It had a body with arms and legs, much like a master, and though it was every bit bright as the noonday sun, somehow it was not impossible to look at. In fact, the dog found it was impossible to look away. He felt no fear of the light, even when it reached out what appeared to be a hand, and touched his leg.

At some point, the man had left the floor and got back in bed. He felt foolish for crying on the floor, but decided with all he'd been through the past year, to cut himself some slack. When I go out there in the morning and he's dead I will not cry, he promised. I'll give him the best burial any dog ever had, and I'll thank him for letting me run across him in the woods. That's what I'll do. Then he fell peacefully asleep, finally assured he had truly done all he could do.

He got out of bed the moment his eyes opened, and he dressed slowly, convinced he would have to dig a hole and give his friend a proper send off. He felt peaceful regarding the situation. Guess I got all my crying done last night, he reasoned. When he had put on his shoes and tied them carefully, he headed out to the shed and swung back the wooden door. To his surprise the dog was alive. He raised his head, and his tail swung back and forth in wide strokes. Then, before the man could enter the shed, the dog gathered his limbs under himself, and pushed himself creakily off the floor. He took a testing step in the man's direction, then another, and finally stood at the man's feet, looking up at him as if to say, good morning.

Chapter 19

COACH DON BYRD SAT in the quiet of his office reviewing the season that had unfolded thus far. There had been some anxious moment in the opening game, at McGhee. The first half had been a disappointment. He had been counting on the new kid Ellis Owens to make a major contribution, and it seemed the boy had frozen up; unable to do in a game what he so easily did in practice. But they had worked it out. Actually, Owens himself had worked it out. Till that glorious point in the second half when it all came together for him. When he discovered the talent he possessed, and he took what was given instead of trying to take it all. After that, there was no stopping him. The coach had prayed he would not lose what he learned the next time they played, and he was not disappointed. The next week, at home against the Hamburg Lions, Owens had broken the hearts of the opposition with a coming out party of sorts: 220 yards rushing, and a 60 yard pass reception from Bennett. The smattering of black shirted fans left over from the previous season had fled the stadium like cockroaches running from the kitchen when the light is turned on.

And the next week, at Warren. No matter the records, no matter the talent, you could take it all and throw it out the window when you played the Lumberjacks. His team was confident all week, maybe overconfident. He'd preached to them over and over not to take anything for granted. In truth, he himself expected his team to fall. To fight hard, but to come up short in this yearly pivotal game. It was, in fact, settled shortly after the opening kickoff. Ross, the H-back who ran a 4.4 second 40 yard dash during time trials in the summer, took the kick and broke the orange clad warriors hearts, going 85 yards for a score. They led 7-0 with only 20 seconds off the clock, and they never looked back, winning 42-0. There were bricks tossed at the bus as they pulled out of the parking area, and all his kids were instructed to put their helmets on. Sweet. Unforgettable. Their pain was his pleasure. His religion taught him it was wrong to hate, but it was so easy to hate the rival.

"Sorry Father," he said, looking heavenward. "I promise to only hate them on the Friday's we play."

Hermitage, another road game. With his team up 14-0, Owens took a hard shot and went down to the turf. The coach had stood there for what seemed an eternity, waiting for him to get up, but he stayed down. The season had seemed to crash and burn like a pilotless plane, on a rock strewn field in a backwater town. To a team that fielded less than 30 players. They had brought Owens to the sidelines and asked him various questions to determine if there might be a concussion. What is your name? What team do you play for? Who is the president of the United

States? To this, he answers Herbert Hoover, and breaks out in a big smile. He goes back in the game, and Monticello wins 30-0. But, it is determined after the game he has a mild concussion, and a team physician advises him to sit out the following week. The next game is against the Dollarway Cardinals.

He had done everything in his power to prepare his team for the offensive onslaught that was coming. Running the spread formation, deploying 4 and 5 receivers, it would be unlike anything his defense had seen, or would see. They might be forced to outscore their opponent. It might turn into a track meet. And the engine of the team would be watching from the sidelines, in street clothes. Byrd knew they likely be forced into the passing game. Their hopes resting on the arm of Jeff Bennett.

There was no doubt the kid had all the talent in the world. But things had come too easy for him. He loafed through workouts, sat on the sidelines making eyes at the cheerleaders while the defense was on the field, and generally goofed his way through life. Byrd had called him into the office on the Monday before the game. Told him how much his active participation was needed for the coming week. Told him if he, the coach, was not impressed mightily with his work ethic during the week, he would not start. Bennett had sat there looking at him with a sly smile. Like it was all a big joke. But Byrd had not been joking.

After another listless week of effort from his talented quarterback, Byrd had announced at the last possible moment that he was starting the backup. And it almost backfired, as they fell behind 14-0. But as he glanced back at his junior quarterback, he was pleased to see Bennett with his eyes on the game. And when he inserted him in halfway through the second quarter, the lanky kid with the rocket arm who never seemed in a hurry, had sprinted onto the field. The ploy worked, and he engineered a comeback. Monticello ended up winning the game 33-32. Thank God Owens would be back the following week.

His team routed Woodlawn and Lake Village the following weeks, shutting out both. They were rolling, but Star City loomed large. If there was a stumbling block, it would be there.

They were 7-0. Every cliché he'd ever heard kept coming to mind. Take it one game at a time, week to week. Don't look ahead. Stay focused. And despite himself, he found he could not help but pass these on to his team. But in private, in the sanctity of his office, when all the assistants coaches were out performing other duties, his mind invariably drifted to his greatest professional ambition: an undefeated season.

He dared not dwell on it for long. Though he was not superstitious, all the clichés he threw at his team came back at him, and he feared he might jinx the dream, somehow. But it was always there, in the back of his mind. And the dream, at the present time, was still alive and well.

He checked his watch. He had arranged to run with the Sinclair kid at 6:30 PM. It had proved to be a pleasant mentorship for him. The kid was full of questions, and it was refreshing to be away from campus where they could talk about anything that interested him. Byrd had soon noticed their conversations invariably turned to spiritual matters. He wasn't sure if this happened due to his direction, or if Robby initiated it. Probably a little of both, he concluded. He was more than willing to talk about things he felt were important, and Robby seemed hungry to know.

Poor kid, he had no one else to talk to regarding the serious issues of life. He could talk to his mother about things on the TV, or girls, or a hundred other things. And from what Robby said, he couldn't talk to Earl the stepfather about anything. So it was only natural, when he'd met someone who seemed to understand basic truths, he was open and curious. Fine with me, the coach thought. Nothing in this world I like talking about more than Jesus. Out of the abundance of the heart, the mouth speaks. What you store up in your heart will eventually make its way out to the mouth.

He picked up a half finished Bible study he had been working on through the week. It was a course dedicated to the many names of Christ, and how each name corresponded to an aspect of his character. There were many, and each one revealed a different side to the Savior.

He was called 'a friend that sticks closer than a brother,' and Bryd recalled the Lord saying, "I'll never leave you, nor forsake you." John the Baptist called him 'the lamb of God that takes away the sins of the world.' This revealed his willingness to be a sacrifice, to leave heaven and willingly die for us. The moniker 'Lion of the Tribe of Judah,' caught his eye. This revealed the strength of the Lord. It was amazing to him the number of people who bought into the typical cinematic version of the "weak Jesus." How ridiculous. It was impossible to be a carpenter in the first century and be a weakling. And it was certainly impossible for a weak man to descend into the pits of hell and return victorious. Jesus had done all that. He truly was lion-like, only assuming the role of a lamb for our sake.

Revelation 19:11 stated he was called 'Faithful and True.' How beautifully simple. I want to be that in my life, Byrd concluded. Toward the bottom of the list, he ran across what was probably his favorite name: The Rose of Sharon.

This spoke of the all-encompassing beauty of his character. Byrd knew it was not a physical reference. The scriptures made it clear the Savior was not indifferent from other men physically; he did not stand out to the carnal eye. People who met him, who were not looking for the coming of the redeemer, did not know who he was. His beauty was in his heart. He was the desire of the ages. The rose without a thorn. The Rose of Sharon. Byrd felt uplifted, as he always did when he allowed his mind to dwell on the Lord. He checked his watch again and saw it was time to meet Robby, so he closed his study guide and left the office.

***

Earl Collins was a man on a mission. He had been suspicious for some time that his wife was cheating. As he thought on it night after night, always alert for the lurking shadows creeping outside his house, he became convinced it was true. And he made it his mission to catch her in the act.

It wasn't just the fact that she no longer seemed interested in him sexually, although this figured in somewhat. It was the little things. The fact she sometimes changed the sheets while he was away, before he came home. The looks exchanged between her and that brat of a son. They were in collusion, no doubt about it. The boy probably sat at the window and kept watch for them, warning them if he came home. He imagined the interloper running out the backdoor when he arrived, to a car that was parked at a safe distance. The fact that she never complained about his absence. Of course she wouldn't. She welcomed his leaving. More time for him.

But the thing that sold him on the idea one hundred percent was not her at all. It was his mother. His cheating mother. In the later days of his mother and father's marriage, she had even given up all pretense of fidelity. Her suitors would come by the house and whisk her away while his father sat nearly catatonic in his easy chair. Poor guy, he was so beat down by then he didn't even care. Probably grateful to them for taking her out of the house so he could have some peace.

And on those nights when her "friends" came by, she would doll herself up, speak a few disparaging words to his old man, and with a honk from a horn outside, she'd be off on business. It was always business. She speculated in real estate. There were always clients to entertain. Sometimes she entertained them all night. There were lame excuses in the beginning. Then she stopped bothering with them. Not even bothering to lie.

The fact that Earl had a number of customers he regularly bedded was not relevant to him, and did not even enter into his logic. Men were different. They had a greater sex drive. Man was not meant to be monogamous, and any man who said otherwise was only trying to placate his wife. Put up a front for the little lady. There were always strung out females wanting to have sex for a ridiculously small amount of dope, and Earl availed himself of it. It was a fringe benefit of being "the man." They would do anything for some of his product. He had respect, and people eating out of his hand. Something he had never had before. But a rooster was raiding his nest, and he became obsessed with catching the rooster.

Thus on this night, Earl told Carol he had business to attend to. Of course she didn't object. Once again, there was the sideways glance to Robby, as if to say, "the cats away, and its time to play." The boy ought to be ashamed. Helping his mother commit adultery. Perhaps her suitor even brought him a date.

Earl got into his truck and backed out of the driveway, waving at his wife as he pulled out onto the road. He glanced back in the rearview mirror and saw she was watching him leave from the porch. Uh, huh. Planning her rendezvous even before he was out of sight. Okay dear wife, you're in for a surprise tonight.

A quarter mile away from the house, he pulled the truck into a dirt road he'd already picked out. Need to fortify myself, make sure I'm good and alert, he decided, so he tapped out a small pile of methamphetamine onto the dashboard. Then, taking a hundred dollar bill from his wallet, snorted the pile without measuring it into a line. The burn that had been so painful in the early days of his usage was now sweet to him. It was a precursor to the buzz that was shortly to follow, as was the acrid bitter drain that rolled down his throat. He felt the psychological effects even before it entered his bloodstream, as his pupils dilated and his heart thumped a bass rhythm in his chest. By this point in his addiction, his body was reacting to what it knew was coming before it ever reached his brain, a type of placebo effect. He secured the remaining speed in a pocket and exited the truck. No telling how long I'll have to wait, he surmised. How ever long it takes.

He set off into the woods back in the direction of his house, planning to wait on the backside in the general area where he always saw the shadows. There was any number of trees he could hide behind, just as they did. Two could play this game, he thought wryly. In ten minutes the house came into view through the woods and he ducked down so as not to be seen. He could watch standing back from a distance, and move closer as night fell.

While in the woods, Earl began to think on just what he would do when he caught her in the act. His first thought was to pistol whip both of them to a bloody mess, but on second thought he dismissed this. The police would be called. He would go to jail, and she would be left free with her lover. No, that would not do. He suddenly felt himself in a quandary. Just what could he do? What could he say, other than get the hell out of my house?

As he stood in the woods, he kept thinking back to something Danny the Biker had said. Something about, "If anyone ever crossed me, I'd just dig a hole. Get a bag of lime and put them in it. Bury them and bury the shovel I buried them with. Over and done with. Nice and neat. No body, no charges."

The world was indeed a big place. The lime would consume the body in a matter of weeks, even the bones. Not to mention covering any smell. That was one solution. Kill them both and bury the bodies. Then bury the shovel I buried them with. And the boy? He'd have to go with mommy dearest. No choice in that. He's on their side anyway, so what the hell. Wait a day or so, burn their clothes to make it look like they ran off, and bada bing. Call the police and report her missing.

"Officer, please find my wife. I'm worried sick over her. And my stepson. I miss them dearly."

Several days later the guy she was with comes up missing too and, suddenly it all makes sense. The cheating wench ran off with some other guy. Couldn't shoot them in the house. CSI would be all over that like a fat kid on a cupcake. Tie up the kid at the house, then take momma and the rooster to the gravesight, do them there. Then come back for junior, rinse and repeat. It was the only way.

He felt butterflies migrating in his stomach, as he realized it could well happen tonight. Probably would, in fact. She thought he was going to be gone for quite a while. He'd purposely left her with that impression. The enormity of it all hit him, and he began wondering if he could really go through with it. Would he punk out at the last minute? And how could he not go through with it? The only alternative was to take a seat in the recliner and go catatonic like his old man.

"Bullshit," he said a little too loudly, and his voice echoed in the stillness of the forest. Have to dig a hole. A deep one. At least six feet. Make it eight. There would be three bodies, stacked like cordwood.

Night fell, and with it came the shadows. A limb fell somewhere behind him, perhaps the result of someone coming to this very spot? Wouldn't they be in for a cruel surprise. The insects that were droning their wavering tone seemed to cease momentarily, and he braced for an intruder. Then they resumed. He pulled out the handgun he had tucked into the waistband of his pants and checked the safety. It was on. Good, he certainly didn't want the gun to go off in his pants. Might leave me half the man I used to be, he thought.

He tried to remain still, giving him all the advantage over anyone creeping up, but it was difficult. He was jumpy and wired. Suddenly, the lights of a car could be seen turning onto his road. There could be no doubt it was coming to his house. It couldn't be a customer. Most of them didn't know where he lived, and the few that did wouldn't dare violate his most sacred rule, upon fear of being cut off from future purchase. The car could be seen crossing in front of the house, and from his vantage point a distance back in the forest he saw the lights of it swing into his driveway.

The house itself blocked the view of the car, so he could not see who exited the vehicle, but momentarily it pulled back out and left the same way it came. So that's how they do it, Earl thought, gritting his teeth. Someone drops him off. Virtually no way to get caught that way. If the husband happens to come home, just run out the back and call for a ride with the cell phone. Sneaky. Probably how I would do it. Well, it takes a rat to catch a rat, and buddy, there is a big fat rat sitting out here in the woods. He has a bullet with your name on it. And two for the accomplices.

Robby and Coach Byrd had finished talking shortly after dark, and as usual the coach gave him a ride home. Robby said thanks and the coach pulled away and left.

"Hey, honey. Did you have a good time?" Carol asked.

"Excellent. Wonderful. Fantastic."

"Well, good. Doesn't sound like it can get much better than that," she said, happy for his enthusiasm. "What did you talk about tonight?"

Robby paused, considering if he wanted to let her into his and Coach Bryd's personal world, then decided quickly that he did. "We talked about the season, and about different running shoes. Then we talked about the different names of Jesus."

"Oh," said Carol, "I didn't know he had any other names."

"Yeah, he has other names that help us know him better. Descriptive names, Coach Byrd says."

"That's very interesting. You know the more you tell me about this coach, the more I like him. It's nice of him to share this stuff with you. I'd like to meet him someday."

"Yeah," said Robby, "Maybe you can come to a PTA meeting or something."

In the woods, Earl again checked his pistol, this time moving it off safety. Give them a few minutes. Let them get comfortable, maybe pull back the covers and crawl into our nice, soft bed. While that little sneak Robby is watching from the front, Daddy is coming up from the rear, under the radar. Earl hurriedly went over the details of his plan in his mind.

First comes the surprise entrance. Damn, where did he come from? Carol, and the rooster, scrambling for their clothes. First I have to make sure Robby doesn't bolt out the door. Sit your little ass down or I'll blow your head off. Grab the duct tape, and make the boyfriend wrap Robby up like a Christmas package. Then, its Carol's turn to tape up Romeo. Now, both the guys are bound. Bound for glory. Bound for something, and you're not gonna like it when you get there. Finally, I take my time and secure my lovely wife. Don't spare the tape, it's cheap. Good. They're all wrapped up, waiting to be delivered.

Carry them out, one by one, to the truck. Lay them in the bed. Grab a tarp and cover the happy new family. They're not likely to be too happy at this point, but at least they're together. Going on a little trip. Drive out into the wilderness. Going to a new home. Oh, home on the range. Drag them out of the truck, don't bother to be gentle. Lay them out side by side, facing the direction of the excavation. They're gonna want to see this. Oh, yes.

Earl is digging a hole. Why is Earl digging that hole? Could it be because he plans to put us in it? Oh, shit. We really messed up. We messed up messing with Earl. How does it feel to be the rooster now? Was it worth it? Why weren't you watching better, Robby? You should have been watching the back yard. Where the shadows lurk. Earl tried to warn you they were back there, but you wouldn't listen. Wouldn't heed the warning.

Now, Earl is putting down the shovel. And he's pulling out that gun. That damn big gun. The one Carol is so scared of. It's dark out here, but she can see it in the moonlight. The rooster is the first to get it. Pow. There goes the rooster. Gone home to roost. She would be hysterical now. But don't faint. There's much more to come. Got another bullet for...lets see, how about Robby! Robby, come on down. You're the next contestant on: Lets mess with Earl! Pow, Robby bites the bullet. Now it's just you and me, honey. Alone, together in the dark. Lying there beside your two favorite men. Although they don't look so good now. They came to creep, and went to sleep.

She's probably begging me to shoot her now. Tired of laying there waiting. But the waits not over yet. Watch this Carol, darling. Watch while I push the rooster into the hole. He lands with a thunk. He's waiting for you in your new wedding bed. Next comes the lookout, young Robby. Lookout below. Robby lands in the hole with a muted thunk. The rooster broke his fall. Now Carol would be waiting for her bullet. Desiring it. Please, please, please Earl. Shot me in the head and end my terror. Oh no, darling. I'm not wasting a bullet on you. You're going in the hole alright...alive.

Earl imagined himself pushing his duct taped wife over the edge of the hole. Boy, wouldn't she love to scream right now? If only her mouth was free. Her lying mouth. On second thought, Earl decides, I might take the tape off her mouth. There's no one out here but me, my wife, and two of her favorite people, who are waiting for her to join them.

Sure, why not. Take the tape off. Rip it off slowly, inch by inch. Ouch. She's begging. Then, blubbering. Then praying. Then, blubbering some more. Enough of this. Get in that hole, you cheating wench. She lands right on top of dead Robby. The family that lays together, stays together. And you're gonna be laying there for quite some time. Time to fill in this hole. Can't leave a big hole out here. Somebody might fall in it and get hurt.

What a pleasure it is to fill in this hole. Much easier than it was to dig it. Much more enjoyable. Carol is trying to spit the dirt out as it covers her face, but there's so much! It finally covers her eyes and her world goes dark. Then it goes into the nostrils when she tries to breath, and that can't be pleasant. Heavens, no. Can't see, can't breath.

What's a woman to do? Hug your son, dear wife. This is the price of messing with Earl.

He'd given them time to get involved in whatever they were doing. Earl threw all caution to the wind and sprinted from behind his hiding place behind the tree. It was a short run to the back yard. He looked at the bedroom window as he neared the house. They were, in all likelihood, in the bedroom. In his bed. In their bed. He began running faster as he neared the house, then he bounded up on the porch and kicked in the rear door.

In the kitchen, Carol screamed when she heard the door crash in, completely caught off guard. She heard Earl's voice as he turned down the hall and entered their bedroom.

"I got you now, you son of a bitch."

There was an interlude of several seconds, before she heard him shouting again, "Where are you? Where are you, you son of a bitch?"

It sounded like he was searching the room, and she gathered her senses and ran to the bedroom. Robby ran behind her, a few paces back. As she reached the doorway, Earl emerged. She had seen Earl in the midst of a variety of emotions, ranging from giddily stupid, to downright angry. But the Earl she met in the hallway was almost unrecognizable. His eyes were bulging out of their orbs. His hair contained bits of twigs and leaves from his jaunt through the woods. His hand contained the 9 millimeter handgun, and he seemed to be trying to point it everywhere at once.

"Where is he?" Earl roared.

"Where is who?" She could only scream back, and she was suddenly convinced he was going to shoot one of them by accident.

"Your boyfriend," he screamed, inches from her face, and Robby took a step towards both of them. Earl swung the pistol up, pointing it at Robby. To the boy, it looked like a huge black hole, staring him in the face. He could see it shaking in Earl's hand.

Carol consciously tried to modulate her voice, seeking to bring calm to this insane situation.

"Earl, put the gun down. There's no one here but us. Please honey, put the gun down."

It seemed to break the tension for a moment, and he lowered the gun. Then the thought screamed in his mind: he's going out the front door. The rooster is ducking out the front. They're occupying me here, while he gets away. With a growl of indignation, Earl left them in the hallway and sprinted out the front door, looking up the street, and around both corners of the house. He reentered the living room, and saw Carol and Robby come out of the hallway and stop before entering the room. They stood there looking at him.

"Come sit here," he said.

When they made no move, he said again, "Please, I obviously overreacted. Come sit here, lets talk this out."

Slowly, Carol made her way into the living room, watching every move he made. Robby felt the need to stay close to his mother, and as he saw her take a chair, he too sat down across from Earl. Earl seemed to realize he was holding the gun, and he looked at it once and tucked it under a cushion.

"Now, everything is calm. We can talk as a family."

Carol sat there, unable to imagine how he might explain this; afraid to talk for fear he might blow up again.

"Robby, I apologize for pointing the gun at you. I was obviously very upset at that moment. It was inexcusable. I won't ask you to forgive me, but I am sorry."

"What were you thinking?" Carol managed to say, summoning her courage in the face of repentant Earl.

Earl had long held the opinion that when one was faced with admitting the truth, or telling a lie, it was usually preferable to lie. So he opened his mouth and made it up as he went along.

"My truck broke on the road, on the way home out on the highway. I left it there and walked through the woods, taking a shortcut. I saw the car pull up in the driveway. I thought someone was here in the house. With you."

"You thought I was entertaining another man?" she said, slowly. "It was Coach Byrd bringing Robby home."

Earl decided, at this point, to mix a little truth with the lie, hopefully making the whole thing believable.

"It would help if you understood: My mother was unfaithful to my father. I saw this as a child. I never forgot it. Never got over it. When I saw the car, I felt I was back in my childhood. Losing everything all over again. Not losing my mother, this time, but losing my wife. It was more than jealousy, although I was jealous. It was also grief."

Earl felt his eyes welling slightly at the memory of his mother and father, and he made sure Carol and Robby saw him wipe at his eyes with the heel of his hand. Despite herself, Carol felt pity rise up inside herself, and she left her chair and sat beside Earl. He covered both eyes with his hands, rubbing them red to further the effect. When he took his hands away, it appeared as if he was deeply, emotionally upset.

"I'm sorry. That's all I can say. I can fix the back door. But I can't repair my family with hammer and nails. And I can't fix myself with carpentry tools. All I can do is throw myself on your mercy."

"You've never told me about your mother and father," said Carol.

"No. Too painful. Maybe I can someday. I can't bear it now."

"It's okay, we understand," Carol said, looking at Robby for confirmation. He only looked at her, preferring to leave the melodrama to the adults. He was halfway convinced that most adults were crazy, and his mother was not always immune from this.

"I can only get better with your help. I can only overcome this if you guys are with me," Earl said, in a pleading voice.

"We're here Earl," she said, and she placed her arm around him in comfort.

"Okay, I'm gonna patch up the back door, best I can. I'll go get my truck in the morning." Earl got up from the couch and went to inspect the damage he'd done when he made his grand entrance.

Carol leaned close to Robby and whispered, "How many games are left in the season?"

"Three," he whispered back.

"We're getting out of here just as soon as it's over. Even if we have to go to a shelter."

At that moment, Robby knew his mother was not as crazy as he'd feared.

Chapter 20

THE MAN WAS INCREDULOUS when the dog rose from his quilt, left the shed, and walked stiffly to greet him. He sank to his knees and inspected the rear leg that had clearly been in a deadly stage of infection. It was far from healed, as were his other wounds. In fact, they were barely scabbed over. But the swelling was gone, and there was no evidence of discharge. Further, the dog was putting weight on the limb, whereas on the previous days he was unable to walk.

It became painfully obvious in the light of day, with the dog standing there before him, just how disfigured the poor animal was. With the missing ears, the lip and mouth ripped into a permanent sneer, and the body that seemed from all appearances to have been hit by a shot gun blast, he did not fully resemble a dog. More like a cancerous miscreant, somehow walking on four legs. Anyone coming upon him would be convinced he had some sort of deadly plague.

"You're beautiful to me," the man said, and he gently hugged the dog to him, and was rewarded with a lick to the side of his face. He sat there holding the scarred animal for a long moment, wondering if he'd really diagnosed the condition of the leg properly. A small part of his mind did not want to accept it. Gangrene did not go away by itself, thus the need for amputation. It wasn't like the flu, running its course in time. But it was gone.

"Miracle," he said, conclusively. "That's all there is to it, and we just need to believe it and rejoice. Thank you, God," he said, and the dog licked him across the face again.

He allowed the dog to exit the shed, telling him, "Don't over do it now."

The dog seemed overjoyed to be mobile again, and quickly went around the yard, visiting the favorite spots the man had previously carried him to in the sling. Then he was invited inside the house. The man cooked up a sumptuous breakfast of eggs, bacon and sausage and split it in half with his friend, letting him eat off a plate on the floor.

"Wish you could tell me what got a hold of you," he said, as they ate. "Bet that's some story." The dog merely looked up at him with his mangled face and head, and then went back to eating.

When they had finished the meal it did not seem as if the dog wanted to go back to the shed, so he puttered in the yard, taking care of things that had been neglected for some time. Buzz Saw nosed around at his feet and at the perimeter of the property. It reminded him dimly of Mr. Scott working diligently, and the dog sniffed around for any scent from Lu-Lu, or one like her.

When evening came, they sat on the porch together watching the sun go down. The man thought back to other days, when he would sit on the porch with his wife and strum on an old guitar. He'd always said he could only play good enough not to run her off, but she had seemed to enjoy it. He tried to remember the last time he had played it. Sometime before she died, that was for sure. He suddenly had a strong desire to retrieve it from the closet where it was stored.

"Want to hear something awful, my friend?"

Buzz Saw rose with him, wondering what fun the man had in store for them next. The man entered the house, and emerged momentarily with the six string instrument. The guitar was horribly out of tune, and it took a good ten minutes of picking and tuning to synchronize the strings, but presently the man applied a "C" chord, and was rewarded with a clean, clear sound.

The dog cocked his head at the peculiar vibrations emanating from the box. It was completely indescribable to him, combining the tone of a whistle, with the melody of a songbird, and he could only sit there and attempt to fathom what it was the man was doing. It was not at all unpleasant to him, even when the man seemed to dislike the noise he was making. But it seemed to make the man happy, and he grew more joyful as he played. Though totally confused with exactly what the man was doing, he could sense that it was bringing peace to his soul, and that made it a good thing, indeed.

Thus, the next night, when the man fetched his guitar, Buzz Saw associated it with peace and pleasure, and eagerly sat at the mans feet, soaking up the emotional joy he felt washing off his friend.

Living in this place with the man was heaven for the dog, and there was nothing more he could have wanted in life. His overwhelming desire, his consummating passion, was to give pleasure to his master, and it was very apparent that even his upward gaze towards the man was pleasurable to him.

***

The dog awakened in the shed at daybreak with a burning restlessness. It would be several hours before the man emerged from the house, but he knew in his soul that he must leave the comfort of this place today, and it pained him. He had lived with the man for six weeks and felt at home here, but to remain was to deny what he felt, to deny the very reason he was alive. He knew instinctively that something else remained for him, something else other than comfort and pleasure. It would be the hardest thing he had ever done to walk into the unknown, not only for the pain it would bring to him, but also for the pain it might cause his friend. There was not a complex rationalization to this thought process. Things were as they were, and could not be denied.

Thus, when the man emerged from the house, the dog met him at the door, and he saw the dog looking down the path away from the house, and then back to him.

"What is it, boy?" the man said, but somehow he knew. He had known since shortly after the dog began walking that he might have a home somewhere. Someone was almost surely missing him. The dog did not belong to him on a permanent basis. Their paths had crossed as a mutual healing miracle, and this had been accomplished.

"You need to go home. I understand. It's okay." He bent down and carefully hugged the animal whose wounds were still scabbed, but trying to close.

"I promise not to cry, if you won't," he said, and though his heart was breaking, he felt great peace with allowing him to leave.

"One thing. You've got to let me send you off on a full stomach." With that, he brought the dog into the house and repeated the breakfast of eggs, bacon and sausage, this time giving his friend the greater portion.

"I hope you don't have to travel far. And please, stay out of the woods, okay? If you get back near here, you stop in. Promise?" The dog looked up from the plate long to acknowledge he had heard, and then went back to wolfing down the breakfast.

When they had both eaten, he walked the dog onto the porch and they stood there for a long moment, looking at each other.

"Go on, now. I'm fine, and somebody's missing you like crazy. I'm not gonna give up on myself. You taught me that, and I'll never forget it."

He gave the dog a final caress, and Buzz Saw knew it was time. He had no idea where he was going or why, he only knew something remained for him, and it was not here. So he left the porch and walked to the point where the road met the driveway. When he looked back, the man had brought his guitar out onto the porch and was strumming a tune. It was a happy song, and the sound drifted out to his ears, still peculiar, but sweet. He stood listening for a long moment, then looked left and right. Right felt better, so he began walking, staying well off the scarcely traveled road.

Though he was alone and his heart ached from leaving his friend, he did not feel lonely. He continued to follow a leading that could not be interpreted with his physical senses. While a part of him would have loved to remain with the man, another part of him was happy to be moving. He had no concept of destiny or divine mission, only a drive to put one foot in front of the other, in the direction he was heading.

Highway 90 runs the length of Mississippi like a spine, from the Gulf Coast to Memphis, Tennessee. Five miles from where he left the man's house, Buzz Saw came to the juncture of this highway. He had seen very little traffic up to now, but the cars that were traversing this road was dizzying.

Again he looked left and right, south or north, and he chose north, staying as far away from the cars as possible, setting off at a steady trot. The left leg had given him pain two miles into his journey, but had now loosened up. He was ten miles outside of Biloxi, Mississippi, a small, scarred form on the right side of the road, limping slightly. Most people who passed him heading north out of Biloxi gave him no notice. Those who did see him as they passed probably assumed he was a stray, or came from a home nearby on the highway. Most people were to busy in their own lives to notice him for more than a moment.

He occupied himself with the myriad of sights and smells surrounding him. As afternoon drifted into evening he had been walking for ten hours, traveling 20 miles without stopping. He was growing very hungry, and a convenience store set back from the highway provided tempting smells. He left the edge of the highway and walked into the parking lot, soon making his way to the trash dumpster, where various pieces of leftover discarded food littering the ground.

He was moving from piece to piece, generally ignoring the people in the parking lot exiting and entering the store. He heard voices shouting above the din of engine noises and looked up as a beer bottle crashed a few feet from his head, scattering glass in all directions.

"Get out of here, you mangy mutt," a teenager in a low rider truck shouted, laughing. He took hold of the largest piece of food he saw and bolted around the corner of the store, emerging back on the edge of the highway from the far side. He paused long enough to drink from the ditch, and then continued on his course, stopping later that night when he was too exhausted to go further. He curled up under a tree amongst a pile of fallen leaves, far enough back so he could not be seen from the road, and drifted off in a dreamless sleep.

***

Robby, and the entire team, had noticed the intensity level of the practices ratcheted up during the week. The coaches were tense, attempting to micromanage every aspect. On Tuesday and Wednesday they had stayed at the field house until 7:30 PM watching film. It was the week of the Star City game, and both teams had identical 7-0 records.

As the starting offense punished the scout team defense play after play, Robby found himself wondering if the opposition could possibly be preparing as thoroughly, or working as hard as his team. Not since two a days had ended had the practices been as brutal, or lengthy.

On Thursday, there was a respite from the coaching staff who worried a late-week injury might destroy their chances. The team did stretching minus pads, and finished with a film session. Robby watched the flickering images on the screen showing the distinctive SC on the helmets. They had been repeatedly drilled all week concerning their opponent. Star City had skilled players at key positions. They were disciplined and boasted the lowest penalty per game average in the league, a credit to their coaching. They did not talk trash, preferring to let their play on the field speak for itself. They came at you and they never gave up.

The team watched a synopsis containing pieces from three of Star City's victories. They did not look physically larger than anyone they played. A few of their players had great speed, but neither did this seem to be the reason they were undefeated. To Robby, it appeared they were simply in the right place at the right time. Time after time. Anyone watching this team for a series of downs, or even for one game, could come to the conclusion they were lucky. But the film montage made it obvious this could not possibly be the case. It came into play week after week, game after game, and down after down. Thus, it could not be simply the result of good fortune, but pure preparation.

The Thursday night film session ended with Coach Byrd addressing the team. To Robby, he looked worn, like he hadn't been sleeping well. And all eyes were on his as he spoke.

"We've worked you hard all week for a purpose. We have something special that's within our grasp. I haven't allowed myself to say this word, and I hesitate to do it, but I'm gonna say it now: undefeated. When I was in the ninth grade, a thousand years ago, when they played with leather helmets and no face guards..."

The players laughed at this exaggeration, and he continued, "I was on a special team, and it was right here at Monticello. We went undefeated. Nine and zero,"

He seemed to choke up emotionally at this point, and the stillness of the moment was palpable. No one moved or even coughed.

"Sorry, I still get a little emotional talking about it. That's because it's such an important thing to me. Something I'll never forget, and I know the other guys on that team with me also remember it. We'll take it to our graves with us. It was the year we were the best. Week after week we left the field victorious, and no one can ever dispute it, because no one could beat us. It's a rare thing. I've never experienced it as a coach, and I never experienced it again as a player. I want you to experience it. Many times, at this point in the season, a team already has a loss, or more than one. So here we are. And it's within our grasp. There are seven other teams that met us on the field of battle, and when it was over, they left with their heads down. As of now, we're perfect. Star City is coming in here tomorrow night, and they want to take all that away. Somebody is gonna leave that field tomorrow night with a sick feeling. Not because seven and one is bad. That's a fine record. But because the dream of perfection is gone. And there's no hope of getting it back, until next year. When this game is over, I want the dream to still be alive. I don't know how bad you want it. I don't know if it means a lot to you. But I do know how much it will mean to you, later. And that's why I want it so bad for you. Go home and get a good nights rest. I'll see you back here tomorrow."

With that, the team was dismissed. The tension at school the next day was evident. Teachers made lame jokes, but it seemed as if everyone was too keyed up to laugh. The tension was broken during the pep rally, at the close of the school day. It was a raucous letting of emotion, surpassing anything Robby had yet seen. The coach took the podium and discussed their perfect record.

Sitting with the team, every one of them resplendent in their blue jerseys, Robby felt like a member of a team of knights on a quest. They had come too far to let this slip away. Three Friday's from perfection.

An hour before the start of the game it begins raining, cold and miserable. The team gathered at the field house at the normal game day 5:30 PM time. Several players were there early. The silent, tense atmosphere that had been present during school was again present in the locker room. They had spent so many hours watching film, and discussing at length their opponent, that Robby could not wait to see them on the field. They had been elevated in his mind to a god-like status. Were they really just boys such as he? Did they really have homework and pimples and curfews to be home at a certain time? Coach Byrd had made them out to be almost superhuman. But, Robby reminded himself, their record was no better than that of his team. Both had achieved, thus far, a level of perfection in this particular form of athletics.

Robby had no illusion that he would play in this game. Through seven games he was yet to step on the field. There was always a temptation during his runs and talks with the head coach to broach the subject. To perhaps ask him if there was any chance he might play in the next game. But Robby intentionally avoided this, feeling it might put his mentor on the spot. Coach Byrd knew where he was at on Friday nights, and if he wanted to insert him into the game he would.

Byrd had, in fact, appreciated Robby not discussing his playing time. He knew full well Robby wanted to play, and it pained him not to be able to play the kid he had so much love and respect for. But out of love and respect for his team, and his personal integrity, he could not play Robby just because he had a relationship with him off the field. It was the dual relationship they had discussed. Robby was third string corner back. There were two other boys who had shown more skill, who could benefit the team more. He knew Robby was a junior and had hopes he would improve enough in his senior season to play more, perhaps even start. For now he could only watch the kid work his tail off in practice, and hope he improved and didn't quit.

6:30 PM. The beat of the band can now be heard through the walls of the locker room. The kids know outside the stands are already packed. Everyone has been talking about this game all week. It is predicted to be standing room only. Players are taping up and checking their equipment. In the adjourning locker room a Star City coach can be heard giving a barely audible pep talk. His voice rises to a pitch, and can now be clearly heard. The words 'undefeated season' come ringing through the walls, into the Monticello locker room, and young faces look around the room, each trying to see how the other is reacting to the words of the enemy.

It is a moment of revelation. The others, the invaders who are coming to steal all that is dear, feel precisely as they do. It means every bit as much to them, this quest for perfection. Coach Byrd knows his players are waiting for him to give the pre-game speech. Up to now, he had no idea what he would say. He felt he had said it all during the pep rally. But the opposing coaches words have given him voice.

"You all heard that. You know what they're playing for. You know how much it means to them. It may sound like something you've heard in a hundred pep talks, but I have to say it, because it's true: the team that wants it more is going to win. I can't want it for you. If I could, we'd win a hundred to nothing. When the lights go out, I want to be eight and zero. Undefeated."

Now he is shouting so the team in the other locker room can clearly hear.

"I want an undefeated season. Are you with me?"

Forty seven boys stand and scream in a deafening outpouring of emotion. As he screams, Robby wonders what the reaction in the Star City locker room is to this.

They are told it is time, and Byrd's team takes the field with emotion. It is a shock to the system coming from the dry, warm field house, to outside where it is pouring, but in minutes everyone is soaked and it becomes easier to bear.

Just entering the stadium is an experience, something to be remembered. Just as they knew it would be, despite the weather, the stands are packed on the home side with a wall of blue, every seat filled, spilling out to the end zones where people are standing, unable to find a seat. But what makes it so unusual is the visitor's side. Here too, it is packed, but with the black and gold of the Star City bulldogs. They are truly surrounded on all sides by emotion.

As Robby stands with his team doing warm-ups and stretching, he gets his first look at the athletes who have occupied his thoughts all week. There is a distinction to them that goes well beyond size or the uniforms they are wearing, and at first Robby cannot place it. Even at the distance of a football field they seem to exude a cocky confidence and bearing that is hard to identify, but it is clearly there. They look as if they expect to win. Robby wonders if his team has this aura, and he stands up straighter, hoping they will think he is confident also.

On this same night, on a highway fifteen miles north of Starkville, Mississippi, it is also raining torrentially. The ditches along side the road are full and rushing, and it has forced the dog to walk on the shoulder, uncomfortably close to the traffic. He is freezing cold and shivering, but there remains within him the desire to move forward at all costs.

He has traveled somewhere around 120 miles since he left the house of his friend five days ago, walking till he is stumbling with fatigue, seeking scraps of food at the truck stops and convenience stores, and collapsing in any soft spot when he can no longer go on.

The wind howls in his face, pushing the rain into his eyes, into his nostrils. It is like an enemy seeking to break his spirit, pushing him back. The wind from the streaming traffic buffets him off the highway shoulder, but it is impossible to walk in the ditch, so he must remain on the pavement, though the roaring cars and trucks are frighteningly close. There are short periods of silence, when he can only see the ground at his feet, and the rain streaming out of the night sky. Then the world ahead of him is illuminated by any number of vehicles approaching from the rear. Their lights stretch out, showing him where he is headed, which shows nothing but highway and an endless deluge of falling water. Then their roar is upon him, the gust of their turbulence pushing ahead and to the side. They file by in a rushing roar, and then there is quiet again, until the next line of traffic catches up to him.

There is so much liquid in the air, sometimes blowing horizontal into his face, sometimes buffeting around him like a cyclone, it seems as if he could drown on dry land. Occasionally he passes houses close enough to the highway where lights can be seen. He knows there are masters in these places, and some of them are angry with him.

As he was passing through Starkville, Mississippi the previous day, there were many people out and about. Most did not notice the small, torn figure passing by on the sidewalk in front of their house. There were two children, however, who did notice him. They were throwing a Frisbee back and forth, laughing and running in the autumn day. When he was passing one of them, the boy, called out to him.

"Hey puppy. Whatcha' doing? Come here boy."

His instincts told him to pretend he did not hear, to keep his head down and continue onward. But the laughter of their voices, and the beauty of the day, caused him to look in their direction. The wonderful purity of their innocence and joy was like a magnet to his soul, and before he could dissuade himself, he was running onto their lawn to engage in play.

"He looks funny," said the little girl when Buzz Saw drew close. "What's wrong with him?"

"Nothing," the boy said, "He probably got hit by a car, or something. I like his mouth. It looks like he's smiling all the time. Come on boy, let's play Frisbee."

They resumed their game, this time with the dog running back and forth between them, trying in vain to catch the flat, flying disk that was always just out of reach. In the midst of the mood he forgot his fatigue, jumping and running while the children laughed uproariously at his antics. It is a glorious moment of joy. When the children have run and laughed themselves to exhaustion they collapse on the lawn.

"Do you think mom will let us keep him?" the boy asks his sister.

"Maybe we can hide him in the garage," she says conspiratorially, and giggles, rubbing the dog between the wounds on his head.

At this point, the mother emerged from the front door of the house.

"Bobby, Lisa, get away from that dog. Get away from him!" she screams.

Buzz Saw is already up, sensing her anger.

"Oh my god, he's horrible. Get away from here you dirty thing," she says, running in his direction.

"You know better than to play with stray dogs. He probably has rabies. Did he bite you?" she asks both children, as the dog scurries back onto the sidewalk and continues on a northward path up the street.

Star City has won the coin toss and elects to receive the kick. In the steady downpour, Byrd stands hoping they will fumble the return, giving his team excellent field position. This does not happen, and the opponents take the field with the ball at their 30 yard line.

Robby watches ever nuance of the black and gold warriors. They sprint onto the field as a group, no one lagging behind. In the mess and confusion of the downpour, even their offensive huddle seems structured and impressive. They break the huddle the same way they came on to the field, together in mass, and the drive that commences is a frustrating thing of beauty.

The field becomes a quagmire after a few plays. Footing is difficult, passing seems impossible, but this does not seem to bother the opposition. Sticking strictly to the ground, they grind out first down after first down, gaining just enough each time to bring the crews out for a measurement, and then move the chains. They reach the Monticello 20 yard line and half the first quarter has been spent. Byrd looks at his offense in frustation. Their uniforms are wet, but clean. They have yet to step onto the field in this game.

The Monticello defensive end loses containment, and an option play goes for 12 yards. Byrd realizes his defense is exhausted from having been on the field for so long, and he calls timeout. The bedraggled, filthy group slogs off the field.

Robby sees the defensive end, a tall black kid named Antonio Willis, approach the waiting defensive coach. The kid's uniform is no longer blue, but muddy brown from head to his cleats. As he leaves the field he is crying out, "I'm getting it coach. I'm getting it. They won't take it on me again." Through the opening of his helmet his eyes are wild and pleading. The defensive assistant grabs him by the facemask and pulls him to within inches.

"You've got to contain the tail back on the pitch. Don't go for the fake. You got that?" the coach screams, and pushes the kid back onto the field.

Byrd is standing nearby. He is disturbed by the coach's actions, and makes a mental note to talk with him after the game. Passion is good, but we must remember these are kids, he will tell him.

The timeout seems to last only seconds, and then they are back on the field, with Star City at the Monticello 8 yard line. Robby watches as the enemy runs the option to Willis's side again. This time he moves to cover the trailing tail back as he was instructed, but the quarterback keeps, and takes the ball to the three yard line. Three gut runs up the middle take two minutes more off the clock, and the Star City tailback breaks the plane of the end zone for a touchdown. The disciplined group in black and gold exit the field as they entered it at the start of the game, with no celebration or dancing. They have taken the ball down the opposition's throats, just as they expected. They lead 7-0.

On the highway, the rain slacks up, then ceases, but the dog cannot leave the shoulder of the road since the path to his right is still flooded. Glass and sharp rocks abound under his feet, and along with the ache in his body is a sharp stinging under his paw pads. He must be careful in his weariness not to veer left onto the highway, and he uses the edge of the grass as a guide to keep himself on keel. His instincts have told him that in the rain he needs to keep moving to maintain blood flow and not succumb to hypothermia, but with the rain ceasing, he will stop soon and find a tree to rest under.

Out of the darkness behind him come the lights of an approaching car, one of thousands that have passed him on this night. Just as it is almost upon him, something screams into his spirit, "Move right!" He jumps into the water-filled ditch a millisecond before the car sweeps by and misses him by inches. Someone is hanging out the passenger window shouting and laughing, "Get out of the road, you damn dog." For whatever reason, they tried to run him over. He climbs out of the flooded ditch and resumes walking, the tail lights of the car receding in the distance ahead of him.

It is, to him, as if the world of the masters is a sea of madness, a world populated with unfeeling, uncaring zombies, bent on the destruction of themselves, or others. In this sea are scattered points of light, people with a degree of enlightenment and peace. There is no hatred within him for the zombies. There are too many of them to hate, too many of them to consider. Best to avoid them and seek out the ones with whom he can relate.

After standing on the sideline so long, the Monticello offense is chomping at the bit to get into the game. They take the field with great enthusiasm. A call to run into the middle of the line gets nothing, and after one play the offensive team is also coated head to toe in the wet, brown mud. On option right, Bennett keeps for 3, making it third and seven, then a draw to Owens loses a yard, forcing Monticello to punt. It is obvious after one series that the Star City defense is keying hard on the star tailback, and they now have the ball.

A nightmarish repeat of the first enemy possession begins playing out on the field, with first down after first down being achieved. The first quarter ends, and the Star City bulldogs have the ball at the Monticello 50 yard line. For Coach Don Byrd, it is an exercise in maddening frustration, his defenders making the tackle a second too late. Three plays and first down. Three more and another first down. Keeping the ball on the ground. At the 8:00 minute mark of the second quarter, the enemy is again at the gates, in the shadow of the goal line, and the

Monticello defense has no clue how to stop it. It is almost anticlimactic when the muddy black and gold warriors slosh into the endzone, and the score is 14-0.

"Get us a first down," Byrd screams to his offense, as his team takes the field for only the second time. There are 6:00 minutes left in the half.

"Got to get to the locker room and stop the bleeding," Byrd says to an assistant. "Got to get in there and make some adjustments." But even as he says it, he is wondering what kind of adjustments they can make. His team has been one-dimensional all year, counting on Owens to overpower the opposition.

Thankfully for the coach, the Monticello offense manages to gain some ground using screen passes and dive plays to the fullback, but the drive stalls at midfield, and Star City takes over with 2:00 minutes remaining till halftime.

Byrd knows 14-0 is bad. 21-0 would be a death knell. He calls timeout and tells his defense, "Give us a stop. That's what you have to do to give us a chance."

He tries to look each boy in the eye to underscore the importance of what he is saying, and then releases them to take the field.

Like a machine, the enemy does what they have been doing all game, but this time the clock is against them, and as they cross the Monticello 30 yard line, the half ends. Demoralized and confused, Byrd's team heads to the locker room.

On the highway, the cessation of the rain has brought an increase in the wind and cold. The dog is about to leave the highway and seek shelter among the trees, when across the road a house comes into view. The lights are out, and his hunger emboldens him to head for it, hoping he can find sustenance in a garbage can. As he enters the front yard he senses another small animal in the back yard. He cautiously skirts the front corner of the house. In the dim light he can now see it is another dog tied up to a small shelter. The dog yips once at him, but otherwise does not bark.

As he draws closer it becomes clear to his senses that it is a female. He creeps closer, and when he comes into her view she bristles at the sight of his mangled appearance, but her posture and demeanor tell him she is friendly. They sniff each other freely, the human equivalent of a handshake, or a hug, and she moves aside to offer him what food she has in her bowl. He is too ravenous to be a gentleman, and cleans the bowl with great sweeps of his tongue till it is empty.

After the succession of dogs bent only on fighting and killing, it is delightful to be in the company of another of his species who is friendly. They romp and play to the extent her rope will allow, and then his body begins to remind him of all it has been through. The doghouse seems dry and inviting, but he will not enter her space without invitation. When she senses his hesitation, she goes in first and turns to see if he will follow. Now, with permission given, he enters the small dwelling and curls up with her to fall fast asleep. It is warm, and it is divine.

After the dirt, mud and moisture of the field environment, the locker room seems sterile. It is also quiet. Through the walls Byrd's team can hear the voices of the enemy as they relate portions of the game that have been memorable to them. The boys sitting in a circle, most of them filthy even to the skin, are looking at him, waiting for him to give them the answer.

It is obvious that Owens has been shut down. It is also apparent they had some success throwing the ball towards the end of the half. Before addressing his troops, he pulls the assistants aside and informs them of the direction they must take.

"Open it up," he tells his assistants. "That might work. But we have to fix the defense. We do that by crowding the line of scrimmage. Move nine defenders into the box. If they want to move the ball, make them do it through the air."

"I believe we can throw," he tells them, "I don't think they can."

Now it is time to address the team. It is imperative that he make them believe, even if he isn't sure.

"Look up," he says, consciously keeping his voice low so his voice will not carry through the walls to the opposite locker room. Owens face looks as if someone has stolen his pony, and Byrd speaks to him first.

"Ellis, they're keying on you. It's not your fault. We've rode you all year and it's just not going to work tonight. We may be down by two touchdowns, but we still have an advantage. We can throw the ball. We've done it in practice. It's time to do it for real, when it counts. We haven't used the spread offense all year, and they won't be ready for it. So we go to the spread package. We *will* score. We put nine defenders in the box. That means the corners and safeties are out there alone. If they burn us through the air, it's on me. Do you understand? This is my call, my decision. We can still win this."

As he finishes speaking he looks at Bennett. For the first time this season it will all be on his shoulders. He is pleased to see the young man concentrating, not making a joke about it. Nor does he look scared or nervous.

"This is your time to shine, son," he says to the junior quarterback, and receives a nod in return, then a smile. Byrd feels immensely better than he thought he could down by two touchdowns, and it is time to head back out onto the field.

The rain has ended, but it has been replaced with a stiff cold wind. It is not a night for any team to unveil a passing game, but there is no other choice. Exiting the warmth of the locker room is a painful experience, and when they reach the sidelines it is apparent that the crowd on both sides of the field has thinned out. Monticello, which began the game on defense, will have the ball first in this half. Byrd watches his kick return team field the ball and whispers a prayer of thanks when Ross, the return man, gathers it in cleanly and returns to the Monticello 30 yard line.

The beleaguered blue offense runs onto the field. It's obvious the black and gold player are still keying on the tailback, as they crowd the line of scrimmage eight deep. But they are seeing a different formation this time, with Monticello employing four wide receivers instead of the typical tailback-fullback formation. There is some confusion in their ranks before the ball is snapped, as the safeties and cornerbacks try to clarify their assignments.

Bennett play actions to Owens, pulls the ball from the tailback with a deft fake, and hits the H-back Ross on a slant. The defense is undermanned in the secondary and he catches the ball cleanly. Only an open field tackle by the strong safety prevents a touchdown, as he jumps on the speedy flankers back and rides him down after a 20 yard gain. It is only the third Monticello first down in the game, and they are at midfield.

This time, as Monticello lines back up in the "I", it looks for all the world as if they will go back to the run, and again the defense crowds the line. Bennett drops straight back and hits the end on the right side of the field on a 10 yard out pattern. A perfect throw in the swirling wind, and another first down.

Now the defenders are looking toward their own coaches on the sidelines. No answer to change tactics is forthcoming, and the blue team breaks the huddle. Back in the spread with a single running back, and four wide receivers, Bennett sees the impending signs of an all-out blitz. The play called is the same slant pattern ran successfully on the first play, but he audibles to his teammates, changing the play to a tunnel screen to Owens.

On the sidelines, Byrd hears the quarterback calling out the play change.

"What's he doing? Did you tell him to do that?" he screams out to the offensive assistant standing at his side.

The assistant's hair is blowing wild in the wind, and his eyes are wide, matching his appearance.

"I didn't call it. I swear I didn't," he says, and they turn their eyes back to the field just as the ball is snapped.

The black and gold linebackers leave their positions and sprint toward the tall, lanky quarterback who has taken the snap and is backpedaling. They have one assignment and purpose: to smother him in retribution for daring to not hand the ball off. To attack unmercifully for daring to pass again and again. There is no fear or thought of a running play, because Owens, the only blocking back, is squared up to pass block. But there is only one of him, and there are three determined young men rushing inward who are bent on the destruction of this particular play. From the sidelines it looks like annihilation, an absolute catastrophe.

At the last second, before the attackers reach his position, Owens comes out of his pass blocking stance and trickles out into the flat. With him is the right guard, who has pulled in preparation to block. Bennett continues to backpedal, pulling the defenders in further. It looks as if he is trying to avoid being sacked, but he is luring the enemy in, further and further away from the true source of the action. At the last second of impact with the onrushing enemy, he wheels and hits the waiting tailback.

In the time it takes the ball to travel 20 feet, the tables have turned. Owens has the ball in his hands, and practically everyone wearing the back and gold color is behind him. The wet, muddy field ahead seems strangely empty to him, and with only himself and his blocker at his side, he uses the speed that has been moot to this point. The lone safety that must somehow make the tackle looks every bit like a deer in the headlights as the duo rush upon him, and then they are past, and into the end zone.

The blowing cold wind, the mud and the damp, are all temporarily forgotten by all on the blue clad sidelines as they greet the triumphant offense coming off the field.

Byrd sees Bennett coming and steps to him.

"You changed the play," he says.

"Yes sir, I saw the blitz."

"Good job," the coach says, and pats him hard on the back.

There is a transition moment before the kickoff, and Byrd uses it to rally his defense, calling them together as a group on the sidelines.

"Remember what we discussed, eight men in the box. Stuff the run. Get us the ball back."

The muddy young men nod as a group, and then it is time to take the field. At first, it does not go well. Despite crowding the line of scrimmage, the Star City offense continues to move the ball and reaches the 50 yard line, before Byrd's squad gets a break. A rare holding penalty by the disciplined group on offense stalls their drive, and they are forced to punt.

"Do it again," Byrd says to Bennett as he is taking the field with the offense.

Now they have abandoned the "I" altogether, offering no pretense of a running game, but the enemy has not prepared for this, and they are slow to adapt. Throwing short strikes, Bennett moves the offense to the opponent's 20 yard line. Now there is outright confusion evident in the opposing ranks, as Byrd sees the coaches across the way conferring desperately to solve this wrinkle he has thrown at them. They are trying to get the attention of the referee, wanting a timeout, but Bennett gets the snap off before it can be given. He lofts a perfect spiral through the cold windy air, into the end zone for a touchdown. The extra point kick ties the game, and Byrd looks to the scoreboard. The third quarter has just ended. There is an eternity to go in this ball game, but they have a chance.

Despite their best efforts, despite moving eight men to the line, the massive Star City line opens up creases in the defense, and begins another long march. Standing at the 50 yard line, Byrd watches time after time as they gash his defense with power running and move to midfield, directly across from where he is positioned. From this vantage point, it becomes apparent his defensive line is woefully inadequate to stop the onslaught. With every snap of the ball, his boys are pushed 4 yards back. In a match of strength versus strength, they are outmanned.

By the time the drive reaches the Monticello red zone, inside the 20 yard line, the blue defense is completely beat down, helpless to stop what they know is coming. When Star City scores and moves ahead by 7, there is only four minutes left in the game.

Bennett is standing a few feet down from Byrd, attentive to what has happened. There is a calm confidence radiating from him. It makes the coach want to stand next to him, hoping some of it will rub off, and Byrd moves to speak with him before they take the field for what will surely be the final possession of the game.

"What are you thinking?" the coach asks.

"Decide whether you want to go for the tie, or go for the win," Bennett says simply, "After we score, I mean."

It is an absurd thing to say, but seemingly lacking in bravado or cockiness. To him, there seems to be no doubt in the outcome. Byrd can only smile at the young man's optimism. Kids, he says to himself, shaking his head. We need more of whatever it is they have. More faith, or blind stupidity, or whatever you want to call it. Then the offense runs back onto the field and there is no more time for philosophical musing.

They have a slightly dejected look until Bennett huddles with them and they break. Whatever he has said seems to have made a difference, and they take the line of scrimmage with enthusiasm.

Burned by the long pass on the previous possession, the Star City defense has elected to go into a prevent defense, designed to give up the short routes underneath, and deny the long play. They are counting on the fact that time is on their side; a bend but not break philosophy. Byrd finds himself wishing they'd spent more time on two minute drills in practice, but Bennett seems to have an idea what is needed, as he takes what the defense is giving and begins hitting short passes. More importantly, he gets the offense back up to the line quickly, conserving time.

Byrd watches the quarterback with wonder. He is not the same kid he was when the season started. He has taken command of the situation, and he has the others with him believing. The coach on the sidelines finds himself believing, too. But the clock is a serious enemy. With one minute remaining in the game and no timeouts they are at the Star City 20 yard line, and the defense continues to drop back, denying anything deep. It has been a drive committed strictly to passing, and Bennett has completed eight straight throws. Byrd calls the order for another pass, this time a post route to the left end, going for broke. He prays it will not result in an interception, sealing the game for the enemy. Let it be complete, or at the very least, fall harmlessly away.

As Bennett positions himself under center, it becomes obvious to the Monticello staff he is changing the play. Again, as he did before, Byrd feels wildly out of the loop, unable to control what is happening on the field. But it worked before, maybe he sees something I don't, Byrd tells himself. Wait and watch.

Bennett takes the snap and begins and dropping back with Owens held in to pass block. To Byrd, the positioning and execution look like a draw play, but it can't be, he tells himself, not in this situation. To the coach's dismay, Bennett curls around the waiting Owens and tucks the ball into his gut. In the midst of mud-streaked black and gold defenders, Owens begins weaving through the dense traffic. There seems a moment when they are blind to what has happened. So fully are they expecting a pass, they cannot believe a running play is developing. They reach for him in the backfield, but he is just beyond their grasp each time until, improbably, he finds the light of a hole in the line of scrimmage, and streaks into the secondary.

Now the defensive backs, who have retreated into the end zone to defend the would be receivers, are rushing forward madly to stop what has become a run. The closest ones make contact with him at their own 7 yard line, and Byrd watches as a violent collision takes place between Owens and two Star City defenders. It seems likely these two forces will cancel each other, bringing him down where they meet. But somehow the power of his driving legs dissipates their forward power, and they are pushed back; back to the point they desperately do not want to go, and Owens carries them into the endzone.

Madness ensues along the Monticello sidelines for a brief, wonderful moment. The offense trots off the field and Bennett is staring at Byrd. At first, the coach does not comprehend why his junior quarterback is looking at him this way, then he regains his composure and realizes their situation: they still trail by one point. A decision must be made, and without further thought, he turns to Bennett and says, "Go win it."

The quarterback breaks out in a tremendous smile, and it is then that Byrd knows. The play has not been run, nor has Bennett even reached the huddle, but he knows the game is theirs. They have won. The smile on the quarterback has told him. He will not be denied. It is the smile Babe Ruth probably had on his face before he pointed his finger to the wall at Ebbots Field, then stepped up and gave the Yankees the game. It is the smile of a winner who knows he has won before the game begins.

Bennett is standing by the huddle waiting for the play signal. Byrd gives him the wave that means, 'you call it,' and again he smiles, then steps to huddle his offense. I can't believe I let him call the play, Byrd thinks. At this most crucial point, I've given total control to a 16 year old boy. What was I thinking? But in truth, he knows where the call came from. He had no choice but to go with that smile. To ride it for all it was worth.

Bennett takes the snap and rolls right. Owens is ahead of the play waiting for the option pitch. Bennett fakes the pitch and the entire Star City defense goes with it, sure the star tailback is going for the win, but Bennett keeps the ball, and crosses the goal line. Byrd looks up at the scoreboard and sees it still reads Star City 14 Monticello 13. He is being hoisted upon the shoulders of his players and his eyes are still there, waiting for it to change. They have carried him to near midfield when he finally sees it move in their favor.

Chapter 21

THE DOG LAY IN the comfort and warmth of the doghouse awake, but unmoving. It was the sound of a door opening that persuaded him it was time to leave. He left the side of the female, and thrust his head into the bright daylight just in time to see a man emerge from the house carrying a rifle. He had enough experience with firearms and their effects to know this was not a positive development.

Buzz Saw had enough time to sprint out the door and head for the corner of the house before he heard, "Get the hell out of here."

The sharp snap of a bullet passed over his head before the blast reached his ears, and it gave further speed to his gait. He was halfway to the highway when the ground to his left splattered, dirt raining around his head, and again the blast from the rifle roared through the air a split second later.

He hit the edge of the highway without looking back, running past a sign that said, 'Jackson, Mississippi 70 miles.'

"Mom," Robby said, as he climbed in Earl's truck after school, "Coach Byrd wants me to go to a revival tonight at his church. He wants us all to go, even Earl."

Carol Collins looked at her son, taking her eyes off the road for a moment.

"What kind of church are we talking about?" she said warily.

"It's non-denominational. Coach Byrd says it jumps. He says it's on fire."

"What does that mean?" she asked.

"It means things happen. Good things."

This answer did not seem to comfort her. She had always attended churches where things rarely "happened." Churches where you knew what to expect, even if that was nothing. But he seemed so eager, so excited to be going. It would break his heart if she said no. And she knew her son didn't need any more heartache.

"Well," she said slowly, "I wish I knew more about it, but if you want to, we'll go. I wouldn't put too much hope in Earl, though."

"That's okay," he said, and the light in his eyes told her she had done the right thing.

As they walked into the house Earl was sitting at his familiar place, at the kitchen table, by the window.

"What took you so long?" he said, sullenly.

"I was just there and back. We're going to church tonight. You wanna go?"

"And sit with a bunch of hypocrites? You must be kidding."

"Well, I just thought I'd ask," she said, "Robby's coach wants me go. It'll be good for him. Mr. Byrd is helping him so much. I want to meet him and tell him thank you."

"Is this guy married?" asked Earl, still looking out the window, away from her.

Carol looked at her husband, realizing the direction he was taking this.

"He's married, Earl. This is not a date. It's a ride to church. If you want us to take the truck we will."

"No, I may need it. I assume his wife is going with you."

"I didn't ask Robby. That would be a ridiculous question. I'm sure Mr. Byrd attends church with his wife. It would be good for us if you would go."

"Why would it be good for us? So I could be *holy?* I know plenty of people who go to church who are more screwed up than I...than most people." He glanced up her as he said this, judging her reaction.

"Well, I'm going with Robby. You're welcome to go if you want to," she said, laying a hand on his back as she walked away to get ready.

At 6:30 PM, Byrd's vehicle pulled up outside the house. Carol kissed Earl on the cheek as they went out the door, and they walked to the vehicle. They saw he was alone in the car, and Robby introduced the coach to his mother.

"We'll have to go by and pick up my wife," Byrd said, "She wasn't through putting on her makeup, so I told her I'd swing by here and pick up you guys."

At the window, Earl saw his wife and stepson get into the car with the man, then he spun in his chair and punched the wall, cracking the sheet rock. His fist hurt like hell, but the pain was soon lost in his anger. The images swirled in his amped-up brain like a swarm of wasps bent on hurting him.

The very same car he had seen coming to the house when he'd hidden behind the house watching, had just come and taken his wife away. The utter nerve of the guy was astounding. He must think I'm a fool. Must think I'm a weakling.

"Going to church," Earl said out loud, and laughed bitterly while rubbing his bruised hand. Last time I checked, adultery was frowned upon. What commandment was that? The first? The tenth? I know it's in there somewhere. I won't make a scene this time. Won't tip my hand. Won't be a fool. Got to get out of here for a while, he decided, leaving the chair and heading for the truck.

Byrd pulled up outside his house and his wife came out wearing her finest. Carol left the front seat where she'd been sitting, and got in the back seat with Robby. Very attractive, Carol concluded, in a conservative sort of way. Then she unconsciously looked to her own mode of dress to make sure it was appropriate. Robby, now sitting beside her in the back seat, saw her giving herself the once over, and said, "You look great Mom."

She declined to accept his opinion, and when introductions where concluded she asked Byrd, "Am I dressed appropriately?"

"You can dress anyway you want at our church," he said, looking at her in the rearview mirror. "People come in jean sometimes. Even on Sunday mornings."

She felt a little better hearing this, but was still a little apprehensive. Robby sensed her nervousness and placed a hand on her arm.

"Thank you for coming with me, Mom," he said, and with the simple sincerity of his words she felt her eyes moisten slightly.

"I'm a little nervous, but it'll be okay," she said, moving close so only he could hear.

"Yeah, it's gonna be okay."

Earl drove his truck to the only place he felt safe, away from traffic, out on the dirt roads of the county. I'm not letting anybody take what's mine, he thought. If I send her away, that's one thing. But nobody's taking anything. My old man let everything he had be taken. Just sat there while the roosters came to the door of the hen house and robbed him blind. I'm not my old man. I'm not my old man.

"I'm not my old man," he shouted, and banged the steering wheel causing the truck to fishtail in the gravel. He had to grip the wheel with both hands to bring it back under control.

The Byrds, with Robby and his mother pulled up at the large church with a sign that read Victory Word Center. When they exited the vehicle, the music could be heard outside where they stood.

"It's loud," Carol said, standing outside the car looking toward the building. Her nervousness was apparent to even the coach and his wife. He felt moved to somehow make her feel more comfortable.

"Praise and worship is a big part of the program. It's a celebration."

"What are we celebrating?" she asked, genuinely confused.

"Jesus," he said simply, and smiled.

"Okay, that's a good thing," she answered, feeling foolish for asking. They began moving and entered the foyer. They milling about, and before they entered the sanctuary she had shaken hands with over a dozen people of all colors and nationalities.

"Very friendly here," she said to her son.

A balding man in glasses, standing at the podium, was leading the worship. They made their way quickly to four empty seats and settled in. Behind the worship leader sat a distinguished looking black man holding a Bible.

"Who is that?" she asked Robby. He shrugged his shoulders and whispered the same question to the coach sitting next to him.

"That's the evangelist," he said to his mother.

"Good thing Earl didn't come. He'd have a stroke," she whispered back.

Carol noticed the Byrds had gotten involved with the praise, singing and clapping. She mouthed the words to the songs as they became familiar to her, and it helped that they were being projected onto a screen behind the worship leader. She felt a little self-conscious, but she noticed Robby was doing just fine, singing and clapping with vigor.

The worship portion ended and the evangelist took the podium. He thanked the audience for attending and launched into the message, which dealt with the covenant names of God.

"Jehovah's Covenant names are, literally, what God does for his people, expressed by His names. We'll go over these quickly, until we get to the one I want to focus on tonight. If you are taking notes, please write these down, because they are important."

Robby found himself wishing he'd brought paper and pen. He made a writing motion to his mother, and she produced a pen from her purse. He then began copying the names into the back portion of his Bible, where a blank page was located.

"Jehovah Sabaoth, meaning 'the Lord of Hosts,' he continued. From I Samuel 1:3, it represents God as the sovereign ruler of the heavenly realm."

"Next is Jehovah Rapha, from Exodus 15:26, it means 'the Lord healeth.' To all those who need healing tonight, aren't you glad we serve a God who is a healer? A God who brings healing? Malachi 4:2 states, 'But unto you that fear my name shall the Sun of righteousness arise with healing in his wings...'"

The congregation shouted joyfully at this, with many raising their hands toward the ceiling and shouting, 'Amen,' and, 'Praise the Lord.'

Earl had drove to a secluded area in the county, and pulled his truck into a logging road, where he killed the motor and sat there in the darkness. I've got to reel her in somehow, he thought. Got to get her back under control. Shock her into seeing I'm not to be messed with. She obviously thinks I'm stupid. Thinks I'm gonna let her run free, till I wake up one day and she's gone. Then where would I be?

The solitude and stillness of the place spoke to him. If I was hide somebody, he decided, it would be a place just like this. Perfect place to put somebody who won't do right. What if I dug a hole right here? A hole that looked like it was ready for a person who is bound and determined to betray you. I bet I could take her out here for a little drive and show her that hole, I'll bet that would straighten her attitude up quick.

Earl poured a generous amount of speed onto the dashboard and used his drivers license to rail it into a line. Then he pulled a hundred dollar bill from his wallet, slowly rolled it into a straw, and snorted the chemical. Before the burn had even dissipated, he decided he *would* dig that hole. Dig it right here. Come back and place a bag of lime on the edge. Then, if she kept messing around, he'd bring her out here. Show her where it was all going to end up, if she didn't get right. It suddenly seemed like just the thing to do. He was not his old man. He was taking action. He wasn't sitting in a recliner while his world fell apart. He was going digging.

At the church, the evangelist continued his message.

"Next we see, Jehovah Nissi, which means, 'The Lord our Banner.' Exodus 17:8-15. When pressed by the enemy, Moses called on Jehovah Nissi."

"Jehovah Shalom, meaning, 'The Lord our Peace.' Judges 6:23-24. Like Gideon, we call upon Jehovah Shalom when we are cumbered with care, and need the peace of the Lord. How many of us here need the peace of the Lord?"

And again, there was a chorus of agreement from those gathered.

"Isaiah 26:3 states, 'Thou wilt keep him in perfect peace, whose mind is stayed on thee: because he trusteth in thee.'

"Jehovah Raah, which is translated, 'The Lord My Shepherd.' When you understand this aspect of the living God, you *know* all your needs will be met."

"Jehovah Tsidkanu, 'The Lord our Righteousness.' Jeremiah 23:6 reads, 'In his days, Judah shall be saved, and Israel shall dwell safely: and this is his name whereby he shall be call, The Lord Our Righteousness.'

"Jehovah Jireh, 'My Provider.' When in need, be like Abraham; Abraham needed a lamb for his son, a ram in the bush…the Lord who provides."

"And finally, the name that we will study tonight, Jehovah Shammah, meaning, 'The Lord is there.'"

Earl left the truck and grabbed the shovel from the back. He walked off the logging road for approximately 50 yards and began clearing the leaves away from a spot that was free of brush. He then tested the softness of the ground, and finding it suitable, began making an excavation. This looks like a get right spot to me, he thought. No honey, we don't need counseling. We don't need a marriage manual. We don't need church. What we need is a shovel and a bag of lime if you don't get your ass right. Despite the damp chill in the air, he felt himself sweating under his flannel shirt.

How many people do you think find their way to this spot, over the course of a ten year period, Carol honey, he said to himself, as the dirt piled up on the edge of the hole. The moonlight filtering through the trees illuminated the accumulated dirt, but the hole itsef was a yawning center of blackness. Probably none? You would be right. I don't believe in divorce, sweetie. For better or worse, till death do we part. Sooner or later. Do you want it to be sooner or later? I'll bet she chooses later, Earl concluded, looking at the pit he had dug thus far.

It was getting deep now to the point where he had to step into it to continue. He stepped carefully into the sloping dark hole and saw it just over knee deep. Want it a least four foot deep for visual effect, he decided. Deep and dark. Cold and lonely. He wanted her to have a true, life changing experience when she looked over the edge of her potential new home. It's there for you honey, if you choose to continue on this path. The road you're on leads to here. Better exit while you can. Standing knee deep in the darkness, he began shoveling again.

"Jehovah Shammah," the evangelist continued, and Robby hurriedly wrote this on his note page in the back of his Bible.

"From Daniel, the third chapter."

The evangelist was perspiring freely, his voice building in pitch gradually as he related the passage.

"Three Jewish boys, Shadrach, Mechach, and Abednego, were ordered by King Nebuchadnezar, that at the sound of the musical instruments, to fall down and worship the golden image. They chose not to do this, desiring only to serve the living God, Jehovah. The king ordered them thrown into a fiery furnace. He was so mad, he ordered the furnace heated seven times greater than normal. It was so hot, that when it was opened it killed the men that opened the door, and the three Jewish boys fell into the furnace. When the king looked into the furnace, he saw they were not burned, and there was a fourth presence with them…who do you think that was?"

When there was no response to this, he said quietly, "Jehovah Shammah, *God…is…there*, in the midst of the trouble. And here's the part I like best…"

The evangelist reached for a handkerchief and wiped his brow that was glistening with perspiration.

"When they came out of the fiery furnace…they didn't even smell like smoke!"

There was a thunderous release of emotion from the audience, and Carol saw Robby beside her raise his hands, along with Byrd and his wife. The evangelist was jumping up and down in a joyful manner, and for a moment Carol felt like everyone but her was caught up in the moment. She had the desire to raise her hands and join in, but felt something holding her back.

In the hole, Earl was waist deep in his plan. He began taking dirt off the sides, making the hole more square and easier to stand in. This is just to scare you honey, he thought, I'm doing this to get you right. So I don't have to do it for real. So you'll know I'm not to be messed with. It's the only thing women understand. Sometimes you have to get them right to the edge of death to make them see. Then everything will be all right. I'll leave this hole open, just in case she needs a refresher down the road.

"Matthew the fourteenth chapter, Jesus told the disciples to take a boat and cross the open water. Told them he would meet them on the other side. In the middle of the journey, there came a terrible storm, and they were sore afraid. They were in trouble, but in the midst of the trouble, who showed up?"

The congregation was onto his theme now, and shouted out, "Jehovah Shammah," in unison. Carol found herself shouting it too, and she looked around self consciously to see if anyone was looking.

"Jehovah Shammah, *God…is…there!* The children of Israel had left bondage, but Pharaoh wouldn't let them go. Even after all the plagues God had brought down on his people, he decided to pursue the Israelites. They came to the Red Sea, and there was nowhere to go, Pharaoh's chariots were coming hard to wipe them all out. But you know the story...Pharaoh didn't wipe them out. Why?"

"Jehovah Shammah," roared the worshippers, and the evangelist was dancing on the podium.

To Carol, there seemed to be an electricity in the air. She wanted to raise her hands high in the air, but was self-conscious, and settled for holding them waist high.

"Jehovah Shammah showed up, and parted the Red Sea. They walked across to dry land, and when Pharaoh was foolish enough to pursue them...can you imagine? The man's already seen the Red Sea part, he's already seen all those other plagues, and he's so stubborn, he still chases them between those walls of water. Well, you know the rest. The water came crashing down. Exodus 14:28 says, '...there remained not so much as one of them.' Jehovah Shammah...God is there...when you need him...in the midst of the storm...in the fiery furnace...when the armies of hell are pursuing you. *God...is...there!*"

In the church, a spontaneous session of praise erupted. To Carol, it felt like a wave of joy had crashed down upon her. She felt herself jumping up and down, clapping her hands, and suddenly she didn't care who was watching. The evangelist called out through the noise for anyone to come forward, and Carol saw Robby move to push past her. He caught her eye as she moved to let him by, and they both smiled.

Earl looked up from his digging and saw that his eyes were just above the rim. Good, he thought. I'm 5-9, so this suckers about five and a half feet deep. No need to go for regulation. Any deeper, I'll need a ladder to get out. He threw the shovel over the edge, pushed himself up onto the rim and rolled out, then stood there looking downward into the chasm. He tried to imagine someone bringing him to this grave at gunpoint. What would he feel? I'd sure as hell wish I was somewhere else, he reasoned. What would Carol feel? I bet she'll feel guilty about messing around on old Earl. I bet she'll get right. And with that, he picked up the shovel and made his way back to the truck in the moonlight.

Robby stood in a line worshippers as the music from the pianist swelled around him. A tiny black lady, who he learned later was the evangelist's wife, was making her way down the line praying with each person. As he waited, he quoted the Covenant names the evangelist had mentioned, committing them to memory. Jehovah Sabaoth, Jehovah Rapha, Jehovah Nissi, Jehovah Shalom, Jehovah Tsidkanu, Jehovah Jireh and Jehovah Shammah, he whispered, as the lady made her way towards him. She was carrying a large Bible that made her seem even smaller by comparison. She finished praying with the person to his right, and moved to stand facing him. Her eyes were sparkling and she had a strange, beautiful smile, like a little girl that has a secret.

She took both his hands and said, "Whoa…honey, I see Jesus all over you."

Robby just stood there, not sure if she said this to everybody.

"God's given me a word of knowledge for you, and I want you to accept it. Take it and run with it, because it's from him, just for you." She moved close and was looking him straight in the eye. He felt, at that moment, as if they were the only two people in the world. It was a kind of tunnel vision, and despite being surrounded by people, she was somehow the only person he could concentrate on.

"There's a call on your life. Strong. So strong, I'm trembling just standing near you. I see a great number of souls who are gonna cross your path and enter into the Kingdom. I see them stretched out, like on the side of a road, as far as I can see, and they're happy, because they made it. And you helped them. You're a soul winner," she said, as if in awe.

This confused Robby, and he said, "When did I do that?"

"Oh, you haven't yet honey, but you will, if you let it happen. God doesn't do nothing against our will. He'll let you go your own way if that's what you want to do. Jeremiah 29:11 says God has plans for us. And His plans are wonderful. That's my word of knowledge for you. Do you want that? Do you want what God has for you?"

Robby could only nod, and she let go of his hands and placed them on his forehead.

"Father God," she began, "I'm giving this one to you and I want you to release your power into him, to do what you want him to do. Don't let nothing stop it. For your glory, Lord. In Jesus name, Amen."

She took her hands from his head, and he said, slightly disappointed, "I didn't feel anything."

"Oh, honey, you don't have to feel anything. Just believe and receive."

"Okay," he said, "I believe and receive."

She moved down the line and Robby walked back to where his mother was sitting.

"Was it good?" his mother asked.

"Very good," he said, wanting to keep what the lady had told him in his heart for the moment.

***

Three days after nearly being shot, the dog was entering the metropolitan area of Jackson, Mississippi. The traffic became more congested, but the weather was dry, and he was able to stay well off the road, out of harms way.

On the preceding night he had passed a roadside rest stop and the sound of voices had drawn his attention. He was very hungry, and had eaten only crumbs and bits of sandwiches where he could scavenge them at the various truck stops lining the highway. A group of traveling women stood near a sandwich machine, and the smell of food drew him within their sight. As it was dark, they could not make out his form.

One of the women called out to him, "Look, there's a doggy. Someone must have let him out for a walk. Do you think he wants a piece of sandwhich? Come here, puppy."

They certainly seemed friendly, and he approached them without hesitation. He emerged into the light of the vending area, his earless visage, torn mouth and body illuminated. They began screaming and running for their car. To his delight, three of the four dropped their sandwiches on the ground, and he helped himself to what seemed a feast. They pulled out of the rest stop craning their necks to see the dog from hell that had come out of the darkness.

The roads running right and left became more numerous, but he followed his leading on a straight path north. Before entering the downtown section of Jackson, he passed a sign that read, 'Interstate Highway 20.' It was much larger road than the one he was skirting, and he passed it by and traveled a hundred yards up highway 90, before stopping and looking back. He stood there several seconds before taking off at a run back towards the highway marker. Crossing the road was perilous, as the traffic was almost non-stop at this section of highway, but he found a gap in the stream of cars and bolted across four lanes. He ran down a grassy embankment, crossed an exit ramp, and began heading west on the shoulder of Highway 20.

It was night when his nose picked up the scent of water ahead. From his side of the road, he could see the lights of the cars rising up as if to meet the sky, then disappearing from view. He gradually made his way to the beginning of a bridge, and could now clearly see a vast expanse of water. Thankfully, there was a pedestrian walkway across the mile long bridge, and he was in no danger of traffic. He walked at a steady incline for a half hour, the water of the Mississippi river rushing so far below his feet that its sound was lost in the traffic noise. He then reached the peak of the bridge, and began walking the downward slope. An hour after he had stepped onto the bridge his feet touched land on the other side, and he entered into the state of Louisiana.

Chapter 22

It was Tuesday evening at the Sinclair house. Earl was out on his business, leaving Carol and Robby home alone. She tried reading a novel, but was unable to concentrate. She then turned on the TV, but the mindless programming made her even more restless. She finally got up and went into Robby's room.

He was seated at his desk working on a poster.

"Hey, honey. What are you working on?" she asked.

"It's a poster," he replied. From where she stood, looking over his shoulder, she could see it contained all the Covenant names of God set in a circular pattern, with Jehovah Shammah set prominently in the center.

"I felt like I needed to remember these, so I'm gonna hang them on the wall, where I can see them."

"That's good. I guess you got a lot out of the service."

"Yeah, I did. Did you?" he asked.

"Yeah. It was different. I think once I got used to it, it might be good. It's so different from what I'm used to. I think the word is…dynamic."

"Dynamic," Robby said, slowly. "Like dynamite."

They both laughed, and she tussled his hair.

She stood behind him silently for a moment, and he sensed she had something on her mind.

"What are you thinking, Mom?"

She sighed, and said, "I'm thinking you have ten more days until your football season is over. And I still don't have a plan, other than going to a shelter. I don't want to take you to a shelter. I don't see any other way. What are we going to do?" she said, and Robby heard the desperation in her voice.

He turned around in his chair to face her, wanting to help her some way. Feeling frustrated for his mother. He was really the only male she could turn to, and he had no answer.

"You're sure you want to go, huh?"

"Yes, I'm sure I want to go. And I'm sure we need to go. Honey, he pointed a gun in your face. He could have killed you. You probably don't know this, and maybe I shouldn't tell you, but...Earl has problems, other than what are apparent. He has a drug problem."

She hoped her 16 year old son was mature enough to handle this information, but regardless, she had laid it on him. She stared into his face, judging his reaction.

"Mom," Robby said, slowly, "I know you think I'm a kid, and I still kinda am. But I'm not stupid. The only people who act like Earl are maniacs and drug addicts. Earl may be both, but he's definitely on drugs. A blind sixth grader could see that."

Once again she had misjudged her son, and she nodded to acknowledge her error.

"When I think that I allowed a drug addict to point a gun in your face..."

Her eyes flooded with tears, and Robby moved to comfort her.

"You didn't allow it Mom, we're going to get out of here. You're not putting up with it."

"How…are we going to get out of here?" she said, in frustration, and the tears began rolling down her face.

Robby stood and wiped the tears with his hand as they streaked down her face.

Grasping for anything he could say to comfort her, Robby remembered the number Fred Scott had gave him.

The man had said, "Call me if you need anything." And he appeared sincere in saying it. It was an idea pulled from his mind in desperation, but the more he stood there and considered it, the more it seemed to make sense, till he could no longer hold it in.

"Mom, you know I got to be good friends with Mr. Scott before he went to his sister's. He gave me his number before he left, and said to call him if I needed anything."

"Honey, he was just being nice…"

"No, mom. I don't think he was. He looked me in the eye when he said it. And he's the kind of guy who means what he says. If I ever needed help, and you weren't around, I'd call him. Well, we need help, don't we?"

"We sure do." She said, seriously. "What if he says he can't help us?"

"Then he says no. Nothing lost. He sorta knows how Earl is."

"You told him about Earl?"

"I didn't tell him he was on drugs or anything. He just knows Earl is primitive. If he didn't think we might have problems, he wouldn't have given me his number."

"I hate to impose on anybody," Carol said, shaking her head.

"Would you rather move into a shelter?" said Robby abruptly.

"No," she answered, wide eyed. "Those places can be awful. Especially with kids."

"Well, I'm not exactly a kid, but I know what you mean. Let me call him, Mom. Let's see what he says."

She sighed and looked up at the ceiling. She had no other idea to offer, so she looked at her son and said, "Okay, go ahead."

"Yes!" he said, and pulled the number from his wallet. He punched the numbers into the phone, and after three rings a female voice answered.

"Can I speak to Fred Scott?" he said, excitedly.

"Just a minute," came the response, and within seconds Robby heard the familiar voice of his neighbor.

"This is Fred."

"Mr. Scott, this is Robby Sinclair."

"Robby Sinclair, how in the world are you doing?"

"I'm doing okay Mr. Scott. You gave me your number and told me to call if I needed help?"

"Yes, but there was one stipulation."

Robby was confused for a moment, and said, "Yes sir, what was that?"

"I told you to call me collect."

Robby felt a flood of relief that he was not going to be put off, and he said, "It's okay, Sir. We can afford it."

"I hope so, and I'm glad you called. How is my house looking?"

"It's grown up sir. I started to go mow it, but I wasn't sure you wanted me to."

"No, you didn't have to do that. We've been meaning to come back at any time, but we keep putting it off. It's so nice staying here near the Ozark Mountains, and Colleen loves being near her sister. Let me ask you something Robby, you haven't… seen Lu-Lu around have you?"

Robby was momentarily confused, and said, "No sir. I haven't seen her."

"Okay," Scott said, relieved. "A friend's been keeping her, she got loose so I just thought I'd ask." He hated to lie to the boy, but he was at a loss to explain the question.

"If I see her, I'll let you know."

"I don't think you, will…just forget it. How can I help you?"

Robby paused, unsure how to ask such a tremendous favor.

"Mr. Scott, you remember my step dad, Earl?"

"Sure, we talked about him."

"Well, he's been acting crazy for a long time, and he's on drugs. My mother wants to leave him, but we're stuck. We need to get out of here, but we have no one else to call, and no where to go."

Carol, listening to the conversation from Robby's side, felt her face blush. It was insane thinking this virtual stranger would help them. She felt bad for Robby, being put into such a position of having to ask. Losing hope in the idea, she once again began racking her brain to come up with another idea.

"He's on drugs, huh? Robby, you and I both know you and your mom can't stay in that situation. Put your mother on the phone."

Robby handed the phone to his mother. She dreaded taking it. Fearful the man was going to chew her out for even having her son call.

"Yes sir, this is Carol Sinclair."

Robby felt elated hearing his mother use her former name. To him, it was a sure sign she had mentally distanced herself from Earl.

"Carol, I'm Fred Scott. We never met, but I know your son quite well. I told him to call if I could ever help, and I'm glad he did."

Now comes the bad news, she thought. I'm glad you called, *but...*

"I know enough about your situation to know you can't stay there. You want to get out, right?"

"Yes," she said, choking with emotion.

"From where I sit, I feel like you not only need to get out, you need to get some distance away. I don't know this fellow...Earl, but I get the sense he might not like it when you leave. And sometimes, people of his mindset don't to like to let things go. It might be better if you got out of that town. Maybe out of that state. The farther away the better. But you need someplace to go, am I right?"

"Yes," she said, again choking with emotion. She was overwhelmed with gratitude. Fred Scott had picked up on her situation without her having to say it. He was making everything easy, putting her at ease. A miracle was happening on the phone, and she was the recipient.

"I fell in love with your son the first time I met him. It would be an honor for me to help you, and don't go thanking me or anything. There's a blessing in this for me. It will take me a few days to set this up. I'll rent you a small place here in Joplin, Missouri. That's where we are.

And I'll help you get a job and get on your feet. When will you be ready to leave?"

"In ten days. As soon as Robby plays his last football game."

"Are you sure you can stay there till then?"

"Yes sir," she said, "Earl's getting worse, but we plan to tough it out till then. Are you sure your wife is okay with this?"

"She's a Christian Ms. Sinclair, and she don't play around with it. She's for real, and she loves the Lord Jesus more than she loves me. She'd divorce me if I didn't help you."

Carol couldn't help but laugh at this, more from relief than from humor. She stood there feeling as if the Red Sea had parted, allowing her to walk to freedom.

"I'll pay you back, Mr. Scott. I swear by everything I will."

"First of all, call me Fred. And secondly, I get paid back in blessings. Just watch over Robby until he plays that last game, then we'll get you out of there, okay?"

"Okay, I don't know what to say, except yes. This is a miracle for us, you realize that, don't you?"

"We're here to help each other. Give me your number and I'll call you a few days before it's time to leave. I'll have everything ready by then."

Carol read the number to Fred, said thank you, and hung up the phone. She stood there dumbfounded, looking at her son.

"What did he say?" Robby asked excitedly.

"He said we're moving to Joplin, Missouri right after your last game. It's a miracle, Robby. A miracle."

Robby looked at his mother. She was crying silently, tears running down her face in streams.

"Jehovah Shammah," he said, and hugged her tight.

***

From the moment he had crossed the Mississippi River Bridge, there arose in the dog a sense of urgency greater than anything he had previously felt. There was the desire to run instead of trot, and he often gave in to that urge despite his ever-increasing fatigue. Sleep became something he indulged in for shorter periods of time, resting not for hours, but for 30 and 40 minutes, before rising and resuming his march along the northern Louisiana border.

He reached the town of Monroe, Louisiana on the Friday of Robby's next to last football game. As the Monticello team was pummeling the White Hall eagles to run their record to 9-0, Buzz Saw had reached the intersection of Interstate 20 and U.S. Highway 82. He stopped for a moment at the juncture of these two roads, and then left his westerly path, heading once again north. Shortly after turning, the small dog crossed the border of Louisiana into southern Arkansas, and ran past a sign on the road that read, 'Hamburg 50, Monticello 80.' In a little over three weeks time, he had traveled 300 miles. He still did not know his destination, he only knew he could not stop.

***

On the Monday afternoon after his team's ninth victory, Coach Don Byrd stood on the sidelines watching his team go through the motions of their final week of practice. Their final opponent would be Dumas, a team that had posted only two victories that season. He was on the cusp of something long dreamed of, but so elusive: the undefeated season. He had never dreamed, when the season began, that he would be in this position, and he should have been elated. But there was uneasiness in his soul, and it related to something he had heard in the teacher's lounge that same day.

Tragically, a kid on the Dumas team had been involved in a car wreck over the weekend. He and his girlfriend had perished. Terrible, he had thought. Could have been one of my kids, one of my players. A young life snuffed out before it really even began. Upon hearing the news, he had breathed a prayer for the parents, but the coach in him had, at some point, began thinking how this might affect the attitude of the team he was facing. He had called the Dumas coach when he heard the news and was told the game would go on; would not be cancelled in the midst of the tragedy. So they would play. The question was: what would be the mindset of the kids they would be facing.

Byrd had faced situation like this before, and he knew it could swing wildly in either direction. The Dumas team would either come out in a state of mourning and grief for their lost brother, unable to concentrate on the task at hand. Or, it would motivate them to play the game of their lives. He felt guilty even thinking about it in these terms, but he was a coach, and his job was to prepare his team for what they would encounter.

At the conclusion of the Monday practice, he called the team together for a group prayer for the family of the player. He then addressed them concerning their opponent. He tried to explain to them the psychological ramifications of a tragedy on a team. Told them that despite a 2-7 record, they could be in for the fight of their lives come Friday. When the speech was over, he was not convinced he had gotten through to them. To his players, Dumas had only had two victories. His team had 9. On the faces of his players he read a confident look that said, how can we lose? It was a look that made sleep hard to come by that night, as he lay in bed wondering what they would face, come Friday.

For Robby, the week was a joyous experience. The team seemed relaxed and expectant as they went through the preparations for their final opponent. He knew life with Earl was coming to a close, and he had even found it in his heart to try to be friendly to his step dad, knowing he would be a distant memory in a matter of days. Earl had remained aloof and distant as ever, sitting by the window at the table when he was not out on business.

On the Friday of the game, there was a pep rally surpassing anything Robby had experienced thus far. A large banner reading, '10-0' was stretched across the gym, and as was the norm, the spirit group, in hopes of a victory, destroyed a paper machete bobcat with a baseball bat.

Robby's mother dropped him off at the field house, and as he entered the locker room, he was determined to see and experience everything one final time. He knew he would never be in this place again, and he wanted to relish every moment. He had not told anyone he was moving, fearing it would get back to Earl.

He and his mother had discussed their escape in detail. The Saturday after the last game would be spent quietly preparing. They were expecting a call from Fred Scott on Saturday, setting up the time when he would arrive Sunday. When Fred came to take them away, Carol hoped Earl would not make a scene. If he did, she would call the authorities to stand by, while she moved hers and Robby's clothes to the vehicle. All they planned on taking was their suitcases and her photo albums. He can have the rest, Carol had declared.

As Robby sat in the locker room suiting up for his last game, he noticed a difference in mood between his teammates and the coaches. The coaches were quiet and tense, acting almost as if they dreaded the trip to Dumas. His teammates were loose, loud and raucous. The cry, 10-0, and undefeated, was heard numerous times, and Robby couldn't help but be swept away with it. He was usually subdued in the locker before and after a game, preferring to let the more outgoing boys lead the horseplay. But now he joined in, wanting to make this last great game a memorable one. One for the ages. His last time to wear the Monticello blue

It is minutes before they will take the field. Coach Byrd steps into the center of the room and raises his hands for quiet. Once again, Robby notices his mood is in sharp contrast to everyone around him.

"We've come too far to let down now. You think that's a 2 and 7 team out there? This is their super bowl. They win this, and they can forget every loss they've had this season. Don't let down. Play hard through this game, and you'll have something to remember the rest of your lives. Let's pray."

The same prayer that has been recited before every game is spoken, and it is time to take the field. Byrd senses a lack of focus, even as they run onto the field. His players are horse playing and joking around as they enter the stadium. Then, they walk onto the field and it is then he sees them: black armbands. The entire Dumas team is wearing them in honor of their fallen teammate, as are the coaches. Byrd looks to the sidelines and sees the cheerleaders wearing them, too. He looks toward the stands and sees the majority of the home crowd with a black stripe on the right arm. There is emotional electricity in the air that would normally be lacking in a team with only two victories.

Monticello wins the toss and elects to receive the ball first. As the kickoff teams take their places on the field Byrd looks toward his receiving team. There is something off balance about the formation and a quick count returns 12 men on the field. Before he can call timeout the kick is sailing toward Ross, the return man, who brings it back to the 30 yard line. But the presence of the twelfth man has brought out the yellow flag of the official, and they are moved back to the 15 yard line. It is the type of error that typifies a lack of concentration, and he can only watch as the special teams coach grills the offending boy for his mistake.

He cannot allow it to stay on his mind for long, letting it draw his attention away from the task at hand. They begin the game as they usually do: handing the ball off to Owens. On the first play, a swarm of purple clad Dumas players buries the tailback, and they come out of the pile of bodies in high spirits. On second down, an option right is broken up as Bennett tries to make the pitch, almost resulting in a fumble. The enemy is penetrating the backfield, disrupting the play before it can develop.

It is obvious to Byrd what is happening. Wearing their black armbands, they are not playing for a third victory to end the season. They are playing for their friend, who they will never see again. Every play, every snap of the ball has been, in their minds, dedicated to their fallen brother. There is nothing he can say to his team to match this phenomenon. Grief is a powerful thing, and emotion can turn the whipping boy into a gladiator. The Dumas team is playing as a band of warriors, seeking to avenge the hurt in their hearts.

On third down, Bennett drops back to pass and is sacked, hit from two sides, both high and low. It is amazing he is able to hang onto the ball, and they are forced to punt. Byrd calls timeout and gathers his boys together on the sidelines.

"Do they have your attention now?" he screams over the noise of the band and crowd.

The faces of his players seem to say yes, but only time will tell.

Mercifully, the grief mentality of the Dumas defense seems not to have washed over to their offense, and after three plays they kick the ball back to the blue team. Watching on the sidelines, Robby is amazed at the emotion and intensity of their opponent. The talk at school all week has been how inept they are, how this game will be a blowout. But with Bennett, Owens and the offense on the field, the purple team seems to be everywhere, in the backfield on every play. On a third down pass play, Bennett has a receiver running open deep down field, but he is again cut down before he can throw. He comes off the field with mud and grass hanging off his facemask, berating his offensive line for their lack of blocking. It is one of the few times Robby has seen him without a smile on his face. The first quarter comes to a close in a scoreless tie.

To Byrd, the question is whether the opponent can maintain this level of intensity. Can play above their level of ability for four full quarters, relying on emotion? It becomes clear to him in middle of the second quarter that they have not yet reached a peak. During a routine dive play up the middle, Owens is rocked by the middle linebacker and the ball pops loose. Dumas recovers the ball at the Monticello 22 yard line, and they reach the 8 before running out of downs.

Field goals in the high school game are always questionable affairs, but the enemy kicker drills the ball through the uprights and Dumas leads 3-0. Byrd is relieved when the second quarter clock ticks down and his team heads to the locker room, but as he runs off the field he is at a loss as to what to do about what is taking place. Apart from the early mental errors his boys have made, it is not a lack of effort that has them at a deficit. It is the sheer, overpowering will of their opponent. He can only hope the spell they are under will fade as the game goes on.

In the locker room, his players seem to be in a state of shock. The laughter and jokes are gone. Bennett is limping badly from repeated, vicious hits by blitzing linebackers, and Owens seems to be in a daze, staring at the floor in front of him.

"You're gonna have to overcome the emotion they are playing with," Byrd tells them. "You're gonna have to reach down inside yourselves and find a way to overcome it."

As the third quarter commences, it becomes apparent nothing has changed. Dumas is, in fact, playing harder, feeding off their own growing confidence. Their offense begins moving the ball, and reaches the Monticello 30 yard line before it is stopped. On the sidelines, Robby notices a peculiar formation in the enemy offense. The flanker lined up directly behind the end. It is so unusual it catches his eye before the snap, and he watches as the Dumas quarterback drops back three steps and hits the flanker on a slant. It is just one of many plays on the long enemy drive, and it quickly passes.

Byrd's group takes over at their own fifteen yard line. The coach watches as Bennett drops back to pass, but he is feeling the pressure of the defense in his head now, as well as from the onrushing defenders. He has been hit so many times he cannot plant his feet effectively, and his pass falls incomplete. Three plays and out again, Dumas takes over at their own 40 yard line.

As Dumas runs a sweep to the right side, Robby watches as the starting left corner back for Monticello is caught in a cross block. At the moment of impact, a sickening sight ensues as his knee is bent backward in a direction it was never meant to bend. The boy stays on the ground, writhing in agony, and the training staff is called to cart him off the field. He is carried past Robby, his mouth open in a continuous scream, his eyes wide with pain.

Another enemy drive takes place, crossing the 50 yard line before Monticello manages to stifle it. The fourth quarter begins with the score still 3-0. Bennett manages to complete five straight passes, taking Monticello down to the Dumas 25 yard line. It is their deepest penetration of the game, but Byrd watches in frustration as Bennett loses the ball on an option pitch, and a Dumas defender comes out of the pile of bodies holding the ball aloft, jubilant.

The enemy has gained confidence all game, and it is reflected as they march down the field once again. Taking as much time off the clock as possible, they run the clock down to the 2 minute mark, before disaster strikes the blue team. Trying to break up a pass, the corner back that replaced the injured starter goes down in a heap, and does not get up. Again, a Monticello defender is helped off the field. The first, and second string cornerbacks are on the sidelines. From where he is standing, Robby does not immediately realize his situation, until Byrd calls out his name.

"Sinclair, you're in."

Robby looked around wildly for a moment, not recognizing what was happening. Byrd stepped to him and said, "Contain the corners, if they fumble the ball, fall on it. Don't try to run with it."

Robby looked into the coach's face for a moment, and despite the pain and strain of the game, saw the man was smiling. He then ran onto the field snapping his chinstrap.

He huddled up with the defense and felt conspicuous, as his uniform was spot less amongst their muddy, grass stained clothes. They took their positions and the ball was snapped. A run into the middle of the line netted 3 yards, but the clock continued to run, down to one minute now. As the Dumas offense broke the huddle the flanker and end lined up to Robby's side. Positioned five yards from the line of scrimmage, he watched as the receivers lined up in the odd stacked formation. He remembered the last time he had seen the enemy in this position. They had thrown a slant to the flanker, coming off the back of the end.

Robby took a step towards the center of the field, hoping they would repeat that particular pattern. The ball was snapped and the flanker stayed on the heels of his teammate till he was five yards down field, he then cut sharply in. Robby took two steps back, following the flanker all the way, ignoring the end, and to his amazement, the quarterback cocked his arm and rifled the ball his direction.

The third string Monticello cornerback, who had to this point not played a down all year, stepped in front of the enemy receiver and caught the ball cleanly. He found himself running toward the Dumas goal line before his senses could register what had happened. He did not remember precisely the moment he had gathered the ball in, nor did he remember taking off on his run. He only knew the ball was securely tucked under his arm, and his legs were churning to their utmost ability.

Unlike in his fantasies, he could not hear the roar of the crowd. There was, in his peripheral vision, a dim awareness that his teammates on the sidelines were leaving their feet and waving their arms, cheering him on. But it was strangely quiet in his world, with only his breath, and the muted sound of his cleats slamming into the soft turf being heard. He was running as fast as he possibly could, but desired to go even faster, so he consciously tried to lengthen his stride, stretching out like a cheetah in a National Geographic documentary, reaching for more ground.

There was the temptation to look back, to see where his pursers were, but that would cost him speed, and he would not allow that. He kept his eyes on the distant goal line, trying to pull himself with his legs, and with his eyes, willing it to draw closer.

Without looking sideways toward the painted yard markers, he knew he had reached the 20 yard line due to the fact that there were four, five yard stripes in front of him. A thought entered his mind: what would he do once he crossed the goal line? Would he spike the ball? Would he do some wild endzone dance like he had seen the professional players do? No, he decided, he would hand the ball to the referee and run back to his teammates, back to his coach. They would sing the fight song in the locker room, and on the way home, on the bus. They would carry Coach Byrd off the field, as they had done after the Star City game. It would be the grand conclusion to a once-in-a life time season. A season to remember.

He reached the five yard line, fifteen feet from everything he had dreamed in his boyhood fantasies. At once, there was a peculiar pressure around his waist. He felt his legs losing power, no longer driving him forward. Something was dragging him down, from behind, towards the grassy turf. He cast his eyes downward towards the grasping force around his waist and saw a pair of purple clad arms locked around his midsection. He pulled the ball from the crook of his arm and stretched it outward, towards the goal line, towards a victory, towards an undefeated season. His chest and face made contact with the ground, sliding several feet.

When his forward momentum ceased, he looked up from his prone position and saw he was a yard from the goal line. The Dumas player that had made the tackle was already up and running to receive congratulations from his teammates. Robby looked back toward the clock. He saw only zeros where the digits of time had been. The game was over. Slowly he rose to his feet, aware now that he still held the ball, which was strangely useless in his hands.

His team was slowly walking off the field. The purple home team, wearing their black armbands, was taking the center of the field, along with people who had left the stands to celebrate with them. Robby felt a temptation to walk in the opposite direction of his team. To go somewhere, anywhere. It felt like he was walking to a gallows, to his own execution.

He entered a locker room that was quiet for the first time this season. The only noise was the sound of cleats being removed, and the muted sound of several players sobbing into their hands. Robby sat down in front of his equipment locker. There were forty five other young men in the room, but he felt alone. For the first time this season, he had grass stains down the front of his knees where he had been pulled to the turf, but he felt none of the pride he once thought he would feel to be stained from battle.

Abruptly, unable to hold it in, he lowered his head and wept. The players around him seemed to ignore this as they silently stripped themselves of their equipment. No one spoke to him or even looked in his direction. Great spasms rocked his body as the closeness of the goal line flashed over and over in his mind, and he wished above all else he could have ran a little faster, or stretched out another yard.

Don Byrd saw the young man crying alone on the bench. The disappointment of the loss fell away from him at once, and he forgot his own heartache. He quickly walked to Robby and crouched down in front of him.

"Robby, listen to me. You didn't lose that game. You gave us a chance to win. You gave it your all. Week after week you practiced, even though you knew you might not play. You never quit. That's the mark of a winner. A winner doesn't necessarily always win. He just never quits trying. This will not be the defining moment of your life. You're a winner."

One by one, Robby's teammates rose up, walked to where he was sitting, patted him on the back and whispered encouragement, some of them still crying for what was lost.

Chapter 23

ON THE MORNING AFTER the game, Robby was able to look back, not with heartache, but with certain knowledge that he had given his all. Upon reflection, the team was able to admit they had underestimated their opponent, and the team shared the blame, as a whole, for the loss. He knew that as long as he lived he would see, in his mind, the goal line a scant three feet away as he lay helplessly on the ground. But he would not see this as a nightmare, but rather as a reality, and a life lesson: Never take anything for granted.

When he had showered and eaten breakfast, he began thinking of the future. He and his mother were in for a new experience, but he was certain it would be a change for the better. They were expecting the call from Fred Scott, and at 11:00 AM the phone rang. Carol ran into Robby's bedroom and answered it so she could talk in private.

Robby stood beside her looking at her face, trying to judge if the news she was receiving was good or bad. Seconds into the conversation he knew the news was good, as she was smiling and thanking him profusely. Carol hung up the phone and faced Robby who was anxious to hear what his friend had said.

"He said he's going to pick us up tomorrow evening at 5:00 PM. He rented us a two bedroom apartment, and his sister has a friend with a cleaning service who is going to put me to work right away. We're out of here, sweetheart. You did it. You and your friend. Earl won't know until the last minute, if he gives us any problem, we call the sheriff's office to stand by while we leave. Can you stand it here till then?"

"I think I can stand it here till then, mom," Robby said, excitedly.

In the kitchen, Earl's curiosity over who was calling his wife was a knife in his gut. He had been tempted to quietly pick up the receiver and listen, but was afraid she might detect a faint click when he picked up. When he heard her leave Robby's room and enter the bathroom, he picked up the phone and dialed * 69, which called back the last number calling in.

"Hello," said a man.

"Who am I speaking with?" Earl said.

"This is Fred Scott. Who is this?"

"Wrong number, sorry," said Earl, and hung up the phone.

So, that was it. The rooster was Fred Scott. She was seeing a black man. Earl sat there at the kitchen table shaking with rage, the sound of his gritting teeth audible to anyone who would have been standing nearby. She preferred a black man to him. An old black man. It was time for the get right lesson he had dug in the woods. Boy, was it ever time. Past time.

Not bothered with who might see, Earl poured a pile of methamphetamine onto the table, took a bill from his wallet, rolled it into a tube and snorted the pile in one sucking inhalation. He then threw his head back for a moment and called out to his wife.

"Carol, come in here a minute."

Carol walked into the kitchen and said, "What is it Earl?"

"I want you to take a ride with me, give me a hand."

"Is it important? I'm kinda busy," she said, warily.

"Yes, it's very important. We won't be long."

"Okay," she said, and went to tell Robby she would be right back.

"What does he want?" Robby asked.

"I don't know, but we don't want to make him suspicious. I won't be long, and we'll get what we can together for tomorrow."

Robby looked at his mother with a worried expression before she said, "Don't worry. He doesn't know anything. You didn't tell anybody did you?"

"No!" Robby said, emphatically.

"Then we have nothing to worry about, okay?"

"Okay," he finally said, but she could tell he did not feel good about it.

She walked back into the kitchen, and then she and Earl went out the door and got into his truck.

They pulled out of the driveway and she asked, "So, what are we going to do?"

Despite it being a cool day, she saw Earl had sweat running down his neck and cheeks. He was acting strangely, not looking at her at all.

"We're going to look at a new home."

"Oh, I didn't know you wanted to move," she said, nervously

"I'm not moving," Earl said, still looking straight ahead.

"I don't understand," said Carol. "You said it was a new home."

"You'll understand when you see it," he said, and glanced at her briefly, before returning his eyes to the road.

They had been on the highway for fifteen miles before Earl turned onto a county road, which presently turned into gravel.

"What's out here?" Carol said, finally unnerved by the silence.

"Good things," Earl said, and she noticed his eyes were bulging, as was a large vein in his neck. He seemed to be under a lot of internal pressure, like he might explode at any minute.

When they had traveled deep into the backwoods, Earl turned off onto a logging road, opened the truck door, and told her to get out.

"Earl, tell me what's out here."

"Walk that way," he said, pointing towards the brush.

"I'm not walking out into the woods," she said, shakily.

"Yes, you will," said Earl, pulling the pistol from under his front seat.

She stood looking at the gun, and then at the sweat running off his face. He vaguely had the same insane look he'd had when he kicked in the bedroom door.

"What are you going to do? Shoot me?"

"Walk," he said again, through gritted teeth.

She tried to put on her best brave face, and said, "Which way?"

"That way," he said pointing to the brush on the left side of the truck.

She began walking in the direction he had pointed, briars sticking to her clothes and scratching her arms. When they had walked about 50 yards he told her to veer right, and she saw the hole in the ground up ahead.

There was a moment when she considered running, but the gun in his hand made her toss this idea out. When she stopped 10 feet short he thrust the gun roughly into her back and made her walk right up to the lip of the grave. Now she stood looking down into the damp interior of the nearly six foot deep hole, a bag of lime resting neatly on the edge.

She expected to be shot in the back of the head at any moment.

"Leave Robby out of this, okay?" was all she could squeak out.

"Oh, he's in it. He's all the way in it."

"Why?" she said, tears beginning to course down her cheeks in rivulets.

"You've got a lot of nerve, asking me why. I should be asking you that. Why, Carol? Why did you betray me?"

"I didn't betray you, Earl."

"You keep lying and I won't just kill *you*. I'll leave you in this hole, then I'll go get the accomplice. Tell him we need his help out here. Then I'll bring him back. He'll look down in that hole just like you are. Except he'll see his mother laying there with her cheating head blown off. Then I'll put you two together, forever."

Her head was spinning, and she feared for a minute that she was going to fall into the grave. She took a step back, and he pushed the gun into her spine, forcing her back to the edge.

"I know about the old man. Tell me Carol, are you after his money, or do you just like old black men?"

She wasn't sure what to say, or what not to say, so she said, "He's Robby's friend. He's a good man."

"Oh, I bet he is. Good for you. Good to you."

"What can I do to save my son?" she choked out.

"Confess. And tell me about the relationship. Don't leave nothing out."

"There was no relationship, I called him. That's all," Carol said.

"You called him. That's all. You know, I didn't bring you out here to kill you Carol. I brought you out here to bring you to your senses. And to get to the bottom of the truth. I still don't think you've given me the whole story. But you will. I promise you that. There will be no lies in this marriage. Turn around and walk back to the truck."

Like a condemned prisoner who has been pardoned, she wheeled and retraced her path back to the truck with Earl on her heels. He motioned her back in the passenger seat, got behind the wheel, and pulled the truck back onto the dirt road heading back the way they'd came.

"What now?" she said after they had driven a ways.

"Now…we try this a different way," he said, not looking at her. "And don't think about jumping out of the truck, because I swear to God, I'll go get Robby and put him in that hole."

Up to that point she had not thought of jumping out, but she certainly would have now, had it not been for her son. They pulled back up in front of the house and he told her to get out, still pointing the gun in her direction. They entered the house and Earl made her go into Robby's room, where her son was busy putting clothes in a suitcase.

"Going somewhere, young man?" Earl said, motioning for Carol to sit on the bed.

The sight of the gun, and being caught packing the suitcase, left the boy speechless, and he just stood there looking at his mother.

"He thinks I'm having an affair with Mr. Scott," she finally said.

"That's crazy," Robby said, and Earl moved the gun in his direction slightly.

"He's not crazy," Carol said, afraid Earl might shoot her son. "He's just confused." She put a finger to her lips, instructing him not to say anything else.

"Nobody here is talking, I see," Earl said, "Well, I'm gonna give you some time to think on this. Stay right here." He pointed the gun at both of them and walked out of the room.

"I think I can take the gun away from him, mom," Robby whispered.

"You'll do nothing of the sort," she said, as Earl walked back in with a hammer and some long nails.

"Here's what we're gonna do," said Earl. "I'm gonna confine both of you to this room until I get some answers. When you get ready to tell me the truth, I'll be outside ready to listen."

With that, Earl stepped outside the room, slammed the door, and began nailing it shut. There was, inside the room, the loud incessant banging of the hammer, and

Robby counted six nails being driven into the door. Then, all was quiet.

Sitting on the bed, in this most outrageous situation, Carol felt nothing but relief. She and her son were alive. They had the spare bathroom that Robby used. Fred would be there the next day. The bars on the windows Earl had installed prevented any escape, so all they could do was wait. She got up off the bed and checked the phone, knowing Earl had taken it off the hook in the kitchen.

"He has it off the hook, but it's okay, honey. He's not going to kill us."

"Are you sure about that?" Robby said, taking a seat on the bed.

"I'm sure. He wants me to confess. We just have to wait here until Fred comes. It's still going to be okay."

***

On the Tuesday before Robby's last game, the dog had passed through the small town of Hamburg. The pads on his paws were raw and bleeding, but he did not allow this to slow him down. There was, to his senses, a presence with him, moving mostly ahead, sometimes along side. It was the same presence he had felt when he had entered into the realm of shadows. At times he strained to see it, but it could not be seen with his visual eyes, though it was undeniably present to his inner senses.

On the far side of the town, two dogs had fallen in behind him. He chose to ignore them, despairing to tarry even a single moment, seeking only to move forward. But they mistook his departure from them as fear of conflict, and they were determined to overtake him. When they drew close enough to be heard running behind him, he turned abruptly, ready to kill them both if they chose to fight.

They were not expecting him to wheel about, and they suddenly found themselves face to face with a snarling mad menace. To their eyes, it was like coming face to face with a devil, and they skidded on their back paws, yelping and screaming in terror. When they found their feet, they bounded away from him, running for their lives. Buzz Saw wasted not a second and turned back to his original course, resuming his pace.

On Saturday, he was beginning to pass houses on the outskirts of Monticello. He had never run with Robby through this particular part of town, so it was not familiar to him. He only knew he felt the leading taking him off the main highway, through residential neighborhoods, towards the northern part of Monticello, and Highway 147.

Robby and his mother spent Saturday mostly talking about the future and how their lives would be better once they were out of this nest of madness. They played gin rummy sitting cross-legged on his mattress, and later fell asleep side-by-side in their clothes.

Earl had spent Saturday doing drugs off a mirror that sat in front of him on the kitchen table. He had been awake for eight days, and had to continually take speed in order to remain vigilant. His pager buzzed in his pocket through the day, and even into the night, but he ignored it, wanting only to sit by the window and listen to the voices in the house.

She would confess eventually, he was sure of that. When the pressures of the room became too great she would call to him, and he would listen to her recount her decision to betray him. He would explain to her that this must never happen again. And if it did, he would be forced to end both their marriage, and her life. And not only her life, but also the thing she loved most in the world, her son. There would be no divorce. Not on her terms.

As the night moved into morning, he listened to the voices around him, ignoring their taunts. He had the situation in hand. He had acted. He was not his father.

Robby and his mother awoke on Sunday morning and spent the day looking at the clock and pacing the floor. She would walk around the bed for a time while he talked to calm her, then she would sit on the bed and he would take her place, the clock seeming to move ever so slowly towards 5:00 PM.

At 4:00 PM she ran out of things to discuss, and said simply, "Robby, I love you."

"I love you too, mom," he said.

"I love you more than...ice cream," she said, knowing he knew that was her favorite dessert.

"Well," he said, thinking hard to top her, "I love you more than...lasagna."

"Oh, really," she came back, "Well, I love you more than...garage sales."

This brought a smile to his face, since he knew she was nuts over her neighborhood shopping adventures. He knew he had to top her somehow.

After thinking a moment, he said, "I love you more than running."

That was it, he had won and she knew it, so she pounced down on the bed beside him and hugged him tight. At 5:10 PM, they heard the slamming of a car door outside the house. They both rushed to the door of the bedroom, suddenly desperately wishing Robby's bedroom window was facing the road instead of on the far side of the house. They could only listen as they heard footsteps walking onto the porch, and the sound of knocking.

Sitting by the window, Earl saw the Scott car pull up in the driveway and he jumped back from the window. It was her lover, coming to check on her. Coming right up to his house, despite the presence of his truck. The nerve of the man was incredible. Outrageous. Who does he think I am, Earl thought, as he stood behind the door? Does he think I'm just going to let him come in here and steal my wife? I should step out there and bash his brains in. But no, let him knock and go about his business.

Fred Scott had turned onto Highway 147 and drove past his house, grimacing at the state his property was in. Got to come back and clean that up, he concluded. Just as soon as I get Robby and Carol squared away. He pulled into the Sinclair driveway, and seeing Earl's truck, decided he would knock on the door and assess her husbands mood. If he was belligerent, he would pull his car off property and call the Sheriffs office on his cell phone so they could be safely escorted out. No muss, no fuss. I won't argue with him, he had decided. Let the officers handle it.

He was puzzled when the house showed no signs of life, so he left his vehicle and walked onto the porch. He was even more puzzled when he knocked and got no response.

In the bedroom, Carol and Robby heard Scott knocking and could not contain themselves any longer. They began shouting through the door.

"Mr. Scott, we're in here. We're locked in the bedroom. Please help."

Standing on the porch, Scott heard muted voices calling his name. Through two doors he could not make out what was being said, other than his name, which he could hear. On impulse, he reached for the doorknob, and finding it unlocked, twisted it open.

Standing behind the door, Earl saw the doorknob turning. The voices of his wife and stepson were loud and pleading in his ears, and he briefly considered reaching to twist the lock on the door, but instead reached across the counter and picked up a large kitchen knife. The fact that this man would enter his house uninvited was unthinkable, unpardonable and it made his blood boil. He had ever right to defend his castle, and unlike his father, he would do so.

Fred Scott pushed open the door and could now clearly hear Carol and Robby calling his name. He heard, 'in the bedroom,' and he stepped through the doorway, into the living room.

He moved into Earl's view, and now Carol's husband was looking at the man he knew as the rooster. The man who had made love to his wife. The man who obviously thought he was weak, thought he could walk right up into his house and take what was his.

Over the noise of Carol and Robby calling out to him, Fred Scott heard a noise that sounded like the growling of a wounded animal, and he spun to his left. Before his eyes could focus on the man standing behind the door, he saw an arm holding a shining silver object pass under his chin. He felt a stinging pressure run across his neck from right to left, and he staggered back. There was no sensation of pain, only a moment of confusion as he fell back wondering why he suddenly could no longer breath or speak.

Earl had cut the man's throat in one swift, drawing motion, just under the voice box, severing the trachea. Scott staggered back and a red line appeared across his throat. He was flailing his hands wildly, trying to speak, but the only sound being produced was roughly akin to someone shuffling a deck of cards. Scott grasped his throat with both hands and the blood began pumping out through the main artery running from the heart to the brain, pulsing between his fingers, soaking his shirt in seconds. He continued trying to call for help, able only to make the peculiar ruffling sound. He sank down to the floor in a squatting position, and then sat fully down, an astonished look on his face. He finally, slowly fell onto his back and appeared to convulse, his back arching up, before his chest heaved and he lay quiet, his hands still locked around his throat in a death grip.

Carol and Robby continued to call out from the room, but when no response came they simply stood with their ears pressed to the door desperate for any clue as to what was happening outside.

"What's happening," Robby said, and Carol shushed him, still trying to listen.

Earl sat down beside the body, still holding the knife. He hugged himself with both arms and began rocking back and forth, saying, "Oh, shit. Oh, shit. Oh, shit."

To Earl, it looked like the man lying there in a blood soaked shirt was trying to throttle himself. Upon death, the blood had ceased to pulse from the wound, but it continued to run off the body, collecting in a puddle near the shoulder. Scott's mouth was open in a silent scream, his tongue protruding and turning purple. His denture had fallen from its bridge, giving the open orifice a bizarre appearance.

Earl suddenly became aware he was still holding the knife, and he threw it to the floor as if it were a snake. Carol began calling for Fred Scott again, and Earl remembered his wife and stepson nailed in the bedroom. He got up off the floor and walked to the bedroom door.

Carol looked down to the bottom of the door and saw a shadow move under the opening where it met the floor. She grew quiet for a moment, and heard the sound of someone breathing in ragged gasps on the other side.

"Fred?" she finally said. "Fred Scott?"

Earl gathered himself and said, "Fred Scott has left the building. It's just you and me, babe."

Carol jumped away from the door at the sound of Earl's voice and backed up to the far wall.

"What does that mean, Robby's? What's he saying?" she said, breathing hard and beginning to hyperventilate.

"I think it means Fred went to get the police. We'll be out of here soon."

"No. No. If the police were coming he wouldn't stick around. I know Earl, he's afraid of the police." She was pressing herself against the wall, trying to blend into it and hide herself.

Robby, seeing her panic, went to her and took her hand.

"We're gonna be all right. You'll see."

"No. No," she said, the image of the grave Earl had showed her searing into her mind.

Robby was afraid she might faint, so he directed her to the bed, making her sit down. They saw the shadow leave the bottom of the door and heard Earl's footsteps receding.

Earl quickly walked to the shed and retrieved a roll of sheeting plastic. He cut off a large square with his pocketknife and carried it back into the house. He then spread the plastic on the floor beside the body of Fred Scott and crouched over the dead man, taking time to remove the man's car keys from his pocket. Placing his arms under the man, he drew the body towards himself in a bear hug, smearing the congealing blood onto the front of his shirt and face, and shifted him onto the plastic. He grabbed the edge of the plastic, pulled it over the body and began to roll the man up like a burrito. With the corpse wrapped in the sheeting, Earl went to the kitchen closet and found a roll of duct tape, which he used to seal the edges.

The voice of his mother was screaming in the house, screaming into his brain.

"Look what you've done, you miserable fool. Look at the mess you've made on the floor. Who's gonna clean that up? You're a worthless man. Worthless!"

Earl placed his hand to his ears and screamed, "Shut up, you bitch. Shut up!"

He ran to where he had dropped the knife and raised it in a threatening manner.

"I'll kill you, you slut. I'll kill you. Where are you? Stop hiding from me!"

Earl ran around the room turning over tables and breaking lamps, stabbing the knife in the air.

Carol and Robby heard the commotion coming from the living room and it threw her into a renewed sense of panic. She jumped down to the floor screaming, and tried to crawl under the bed, seeking anywhere to hide herself.

"Momma, momma, come here and look at this," Robby said, trying to lift her off the floor. She didn't seem to hear him at first, but he lifted her head up, looking her in the eyes.

"Come here. Look at this."

The words finally seemed to register in her mind and she allowed herself to be lifted off the floor. Robby walked her to the poster he had hung on the wall.

"You see this, Momma? You see this one?" he said pointing to the center of the poster.

"What does it say, Momma?"

"Jehovah Shammah," she croaked out.

"Yes. That's what it says. It means 'God is there'. God hasn't forgotten us. There's nothing Earl can do to us. The only power he has is fear. Don't give in to that fear. Jehovah Shammah. Say it, Momma. Jehovah Shammah."

"Jehovah Shammah," she said, barely audible.

"What does it mean, Momma?"

"God is there," she repeated, softly.

"That's right. In the fiery furnace...at the Red Sea... in the midst of the storm, whenever you need Him, God is there."

"But honey..." she began.

"No buts. He's not the God of if...He's the God of *when...when* you need Him, He *will* be there."

They heard Earl scream in frustration from the living room, and it seemed to frighten her again, but Robby pointed back to the center of the poster and led her back to the bed.

Earl had exhausted himself wrecking the living room and he sank into the recliner, regressing into a near catatonic state.

"Look at you sitting there," his mother said, venomously. "And you wonder why I sleep with other men. It's because you aren't a man. You're a worm. You're the belly of the worm. Lower than a snake's belly. God have mercy on me for marrying you."

Running full tilt, Buzz Saw had reached the outer limits of his 7 mile route with Robby, on familiar territory. Running this ground was like running again with the boy, and he was taken back, in his mind, to their days together. Carefree days. Days of sunshine and laughter. Lazy weekends and endless adventures, a lifetime ago, but being here in this place, he felt he was back there again.

The presence ahead of him urged his spirit on. His paws left bloody tracks on the ground behind him, but there was no possibility he would stop. He would run till death if necessary, and having no fear of death, this was not a concern to him.

Earl roused himself from the chair and, cursing his mother who still berated him from somewhere he could not reach, and went out the front glass storm door of the house to Fred Scott's car. He started the car and pulled it around behind the house, out of view from the street.

Carol and Robby heard the car crank up and pull into the back yard, and they moved to the window facing the backyard. Now, for the first time, they had some idea what was happening outside. They saw Earl exit the car and open the trunk. He then left the car and reentered the house through the back door.

"That's Fred Scott's car," Robby said.

This was not good and they both knew it. Robby glanced at his mother, but she now seemed beyond panic, staring open mouth through the bars on the window at the car with the open trunk.

"What's he doing? Robby said.

But moments later, it became obvious what Earl was doing. They could hear him dragging something through the hallway, and seconds later he emerged into view pulling the plastic shrouded body of Fred Scott. The body was barely visible through the sheets of plastic, but it was undeniably there, a dark mass present in the center of a long, cigar shaped bundle.

They saw Earl begin to load the body into open trunk and Robby had the presence of mind to move his mother away from the window. He looked to her, seeking to see if this latest horror would send her over the edge, but she seemed beyond shock, as she allowed herself to be guided back to the edge of the bed where he sat beside her.

"Momma, it's very important you listen to me. We've got to have a plan, and we've got to stick by it. Are you hearing me?"

She did not respond at first, only stared straight ahead.

Robby patted her hand and said again, "Momma, do you hear me?"

At this she nodded slightly.

"Momma, if Earl starts to come into the room, if he takes the nails out and starts to come in...I'll rush him..."

"Noooo..." she said, beginning to shake and look around wildly.

"Momma, listen to me," he said sharply. He was tempted to slap her like he'd seen done in the movies, but could not bring himself to strike his mother.

He patted her cheek instead, and said, "It's the only way. I'll rush him. You run by him and run up the street. It's about two hundred yards to the neighbor. He can only get both of us if you freeze and don't run. If you freeze and don't run, you can't get me any help. I can wrestle him until the police come."

"He'll kill you," she said wearily.

Robby knew it was very likely Earl would kill him, but he knew he must sell his mother on the plan to enable her to be saved, so he lied.

"No, he won't kill me. He's on drugs. I'm an athlete. I might kill him if he doesn't give up."

He was afraid he had stretched the limits of truth with the last statement, but she let it pass.

"He has a gun," she said.

"I have the element of surprise. He thinks we're gonna be afraid of him. What a surprise he's in for, huh?" Robby said, trying to sound confident.

"And he may not even come in. He might just take off and try to hide from the police. But they'll catch him. He's going to prison forever for this."

In the living room, Earl steeled himself for what was ahead. It would be an unpleasant scene, killing Carol and the boy, but there was no other way. If he fled leaving them alive, they would alert authorities. He had to have time to get across the Mexican border, then head south into Central America. He had plenty of money. He only needed time.

He would do the two in the bedroom, and then load them all into Scott's trunk. Take them to the grave that was already conveniently open. He would sink Scott's car in a water filled gravel pit that was close by, and make haste back to the house on foot. It would be at least a day before anybody missed the old man. By that time he'd be south of the border, trying to decipher Spanish. It might work. It had to work.

But first, he had to take care of business. Should he use the knife or the gun? The nearest neighbor was a good distance away, but they still might hear the gunshot and call the cops. No, better to do it quietly, just like with the old man. Open the door, do the boy first, since he was most likely to put up a fight. Then, on to the mother.

He walked to the kitchen table and, eschewing a mirror, poured a large mound of methamphetamine on the surface. He bent down and snorted the powder directly into his nose, then grabbed his hammer and knife and went to the bedroom door.

Being on Robby's running route had seemed to give the dog strength, and he loped in long strides, pulling the ground under him. Since he had run this particular road many times and it was no longer necessary to lead him in the direction he should go, the presence was moving only beside him, strong and steady. The familiar sight of the Highway 147 entrance came into view and Buzz Saw turned into it, willing himself to go faster.

Robby and Carol heard Earl's steps as he approached the door.

"Carol...Robby," he said, in a singsong voice, "Daddy's home."

With that, he began pulling the nails out of the door. Robby made his mother, who was stiff with fright, stand just to the right of the entrance.

"Remember our plan," he said, urgently. "Go get help. I'm counting on you."

Actually he was only counting on getting her out of danger, but he had to make her believe. The sound of the first nail being withdrawn reverberated though the room, and they heard it hit the floor on the other side of the door. Five to go, Robby thought. The second nail squealed in protest as it was dislocated, and a metallic sound was heard as Earl let it fall away.

Robby looked towards his mother, sure at any minute she was going to faint and doom both of them.

"Don't faint, momma, please don't faint," he whispered, as the third nail was pulled from the door.

"Jehovah Shammah, Jehovah Shammah, I call on you who is Jehovah Shammah," Robby prayed. "The God who is there, in the midst of the storm..."

The fourth nail seemed to hang for a moment, then gave way and clinked under the gap at the bottom of the door.

"I will not fear, for thou art with me..." Robby said, under his breath, and the fifth nail announced it's departure from the wood frame.

"You will not kill my mother, you son of a bitch," Robby said aloud, and he braced himself as the sixth nail was pulled free.

There was a moments hesitation, and then Earl opened the bedroom door.

Chapter 24

THE SIGHT OF EARL standing in the doorway covered with Fred Scott's blood made Robby gasp, and he was grateful his mother was to the right of the door, out of sight. But Earl was still blocking the doorway, and Robby knew he had to draw him in so his mother would have room to squeeze by.

He was looking at Robby strangely, as he said, "You're not gonna give your old step dad trouble, now are you boy?"

"Come get me, asshole," he said, and he hoped his mother would forgive him for cursing.

The knife glinted dangerously in his right hand, clean and free of the blood that covered him from his face to his waist. He was compulsively wiping it back and forth on the side of his pants.

Earl took a small step into the doorway and Robby, preparing to take hold of him, shouted at the top of his lungs, "Jesus!"

Running down the short stretch of Highway 147, Fred Scott's house first came into view, then Robby's. Suddenly the dog's joy knew no bounds, and he became fully aware of where he had been led. His life with the boy, all their times together, flashed through his mind in an instant. The past sufferings were forgotten, as was the underlying pain and fatigue in his body. He had come full circle. There was only he, and the boy, together again in this place.

As he approached the porch he heard the voice of his soul mate call out from inside the house. There was alarm in the voice, and terror. He was already running full speed, but the sound of Robby in distress gave him the strength to go even harder, and he propelled himself onto the porch and crashed into the glass storm door with force, shattering it.

Standing in the doorway, Earl Collins heard the glass of the door crash in, and time seemed to take on a peculiar, plastic quality; seconds stretching into minutes. There was no doubt, in his mind, what had taken place. Someone, somehow, had notified the police. They were, at this moment, in the living room with their guns drawn. A scene from the old I Love Lucy show flashed absurdly through his mind. Lucy had gotten in trouble, and Ricky, in his Cuban accent, was telling her, 'Luceee, you got a lot of 'splaining to do.'

Earl indeed had a lot of 'splaining' to do. There was the body of Fred Scott in the trunk, and he was covered in the man's blood. He had the knife in his hand. Game, set, and match. He would be tried for murder. But it was a crime of passion, he would argue. His wife was having an affair; he was defending his honor. And he was horribly hooked on drugs. Not in my right mind, no sir. Need treatment, not a life sentence. He was as much a victim as anybody. With any luck, he could draw a 20 year sentence. And the way the prison systems worked, he might even be out in five. He was a young man. Maybe all was not lost.

As he pondered all this, his senses were flooded by a sweet floral smell, and he searched himself to identify it…it was the smell of…roses. So strong it almost made him choke, filling the air around him, strong and sweet, strangely frightening in its intensity.

And there was, to his senses, a strong wind swirling through the house. He assumed it must be gusting in from the broken glass storm door in the living room, but the curtains in the room hung limp, in a becalmed state. Even the hair on his body was unruffled. It was as if he was standing in the midst of a gathering storm, a gale of near hurricane proportions, but the physical elements were untouched by it. Before he could decipher all this completely, he turned around.

A dark stain spread over the crotch and down the legs of Earl Collins as his bladder spontaneously emptied itself. There before him was the dog. Earl recognized Buzz Saw, though he looked much different from when he had last seen him standing in the field. He was horribly mangled, and earless. Deep, half-healed wounds ran the length of his body at every visible point. And beyond his physical appearance, there was a light surrounding him, like the corona of the sun during an eclipse.

Above all the things Earl Collins had to be afraid of, and he had plenty, it was the light that frightened him the most. He would have done anything, at that moment, to leave its presence, including run through the wall of the house had he been able. But he was frozen in place, holding the knife tightly in his right hand.

The voices that had besieged him in the house were strangely silenced, and another voice came ringing into his spirit, clear, calm, and authoritative in its finality.

"Touch not my anointed."

It was, to the dog, as if the room was filled from floor to ceiling by the pure, overpowering essence of evil, and on the other side of its source was Robby. There was no hatred of Earl in his heart. No lingering resentment for being taken away and abandoned. There was only the desire to remove the evil that was standing between him and his soul mate.

The dog left his place and, bounding upward, struck the man chest high. Earl swung the knife at the blur moving toward him and felt it make contact, bounce off a rib, and bury up to the hilt.

There was confusion in his mind as he felt himself falling backwards. Time still seemed stretched strangely out of kilter, and he found himself wondering how something so small could hit him with so much force. It didn't compute. Like something that shouldn't be, but is. Undeniable. Unavoidable. And, strangely detached, he found himself wondering about these things, as his flesh was ripped from his bones.

There was no great sensation of pain, only the wonderment of what was happening to him, what was happening above him. His world was filled with flashing white teeth, and the sound of his own demise voiced by the roar of the destroyer standing over him. He continued to look on in wonder at that which was above him, and seemed to be all around him, in all places at once. And he had time to consider if it really was a dog that was doing this to him. Had he mistaken it for a dog? Or was it a lion or...something else? Then his face was attacked, and his world went red with his own blood, then dark.

Standing in the bedroom, Robby was initially confused by the sound of the breaking glass. He then dived out of the way as Earl fell back and into the room. Years later, he would still not be able to accurately describe what he saw occur on the bedroom floor. To describe it would have been to accept it as reasonable, and it was not acceptable to the rational mind. Earl was there, and then most of Earl was gone. Amidst all this was a vast, raging roar of indignation coming from the small brindle form astride the man, as he ripped into him machine-like, from his torso to his face. Then all was quiet.

Robby found himself crouched against the wall, though he could not say when this had happened. He crawled to his mother, who was sitting where she had stood, to the right of the door. She was looking at the remains of Earl, and she was unharmed. The dog, still atop Earl, was lying motionless, the black handle of the knife visible just behind the rib. Robby went to him and, ignoring the gruesome scene under him, reached down and stroked the earless, scarred head. The dog seemed to linger for a moment looking up at Robby, wagged his tail twice, breathed a deep convulsive breath, and died.

Epilogue

STATEMENT OF CAROL SINCLAIR Collins, submitted from Detective Wesley Glover, Drew County Sheriffs Office, concerning the deaths of Fredrick Scott and Earl William Collins, whose bodies where recovered from a house located at the end of County Road 147 on November 28, 2006, at approximately 6:30 PM.

My son and I had made plans to leave my husband, Earl Collins, ten days ago. Earl was selling and using drugs. I admit I knew that, but I never saw any. Earl kept getting worse. One night he pointed a gun at my son. I knew I had to leave him, but didn't have anywhere to go. Robby was friends with Mr. Scott. We called him, and he offered to come get us the day after Robby's last game. We were suppose to go to Missouri with him. Earl overheard the phone call, or something. He took me out in the woods. He had a grave dug out there. He threatened to put us both in the grave. He thought I was having an affair with Mr. Scott, but I wasn't. After he took me into the woods, he brought me back home and put me and Robby in the bedroom and nailed the door shut. The next day Mr. Scott came to the house to pick us up. We heard Mr. Scott knock and holler for us. We couldn't get out of the bedroom, so we hollered back at him. I guess he came in when he heard us, and Earl killed him. We saw Earl pull Mr. Scott's car behind the house, and he put the body in the trunk. Then Earl broke some stuff in the living room. It sounded like he was cursing his mother. He was sensitive about his mother. He didn't like her. I knew Earl was going to come get us after I saw he had killed Mr. Scott. Robby said he would just leave, but I knew he would come get us. He already had the hole dug and everything. I thought we were dead. Robby told me to stand by the door out of sight, and if he came in to run get help while he wrestled with him. I didn't know what to do. I shouldn't have put my son in that situation. Now he was going to have to wrestle a crazy man, and he wanted me to run away. I didn't want to leave my son there, but I knew I had to get help like he asked me to do. My son has a lot of faith. He said God would help us, but I didn't believe it. I thought Earl would kill Robby, then come get me. I didn't know what else to do. Robby was brave. I've never seen anyone so brave. It broke my heart to see him facing the door while I hid, ready to run out and leave him there, but I didn't know what else to do. I'm ashamed of that, but it's the truth. Earl pulled the nails out of the door, just like I knew he would. He was gone crazy by that point. He had done killed Mr. Scott, so it didn't matter if he killed all of us. Robby kept saying, "Don't worry Momma, Jehovah Shammah is with us." Jehovah Shammah means "God is there," like in the Bible when he delivered all those people. It broke my heart to see him there with so much faith, and Earl was going to kill all that. (Interview was suspended at this point for approximately 5 minutes while Ms. Collins composed herself) *I'm sorry, where was I? Oh yeah, Robby was just standing there facing the door. And those nails were coming out. I'll never forget the sound of those nails being pulled out. Robby was telling me not to faint. Telling me I had to run get help. I didn't know if I could or not. I didn't know what to do. Anyway, Earl opened the door. I couldn't see him because I was standing to the right of it, so he couldn't see me. When he came in I was suppose to run. Did I already say that? Sorry, I'm still upset. Anyway, Robby said, "Come get me," or "Come in here," something like that. And I saw Earl step into the room. Robby hollered, "Jesus," real loud, and I just knew it was about to happen. I was gonna see my son killed, or I was gonna run off and leave him there. I'm not sure what I was gonna to do. Does that make any sense? I guess I never will know what I would have done, if God hadn't shown up. But He did show up. He really showed up. We heard the front glass break, you know, the storm door in the living room. And I looked behind Robby and there was someone else in the room with us, standing behind Robby. I could barely make him out. He was like, translucent. I could see through right through him, but he was there, as real as you are. Just standing there, shimmery like. I thought I was hallucinating, until I smelled the flowers. You can't hallucinate a smell, right? People see things all the time, but you can't imagine a smell. It was like you'd taken us and dropped us in the worlds biggest flower garden. I wish I had a perfume like that. I'd sell it and make a million bucks. It was about then that the wind came into the house. It was like a Kansas tornado. I was hoping it would pick up the house and take us all to Oz. I can tell you're looking at me like I'm crazy, but I'm just telling you what happened. And the* time. I looked at the clock on the wall and the second hand wasn't moving. I thought it had just gone dead, you know, like the battery had run down. But the digital clock beside the bed wasn't flashing either. And it runs on electricity. Time stopped. Can you imagine that? No, I don't guess you can. I don't think Earl saw the shimmery man, because if he had he wouldn't have turned around to see what broke the storm door. So, he turned around. I thought by that point I'd seen everything. I hadn't seen nothing yet. Lord, Lord… it was about that time we found out what broke the door. It was Robby's dog. He came home. He'd been missing since September. I don't remember a lot of what happened next. I wish I could tell you. Maybe I passed out, I don't know. I remember Earl falling back into the room. The dog was on him. There was so much noise. It was like sitting next to the tracks while a train goes by, inches from your body. Just a roar. Like I said, I think I passed out. I must have come to, and Robby made me go into the living room. He tried to keep me from seeing Earl, but there wasn't much left to see anyway. I saw that poor dog laying on top of what was left of him. We called the police and you showed up. That's all I can tell you. End of Statement.

Statement of Robby Sinclair concerning the deaths of Fred Scott and Earl William Collins, submitted by Detective Wesley Glover, Drew County Sheriffs Office.

Things got bad between Momma and Earl. He was doing drugs, and selling them. Momma wasn't involved in none of that, I promise you. We made plans to leave him. We were going to leave with Mr. Scott and go to Missouri. Somehow, Earl found out about it. He took

Momma off and scared her bad. Then he nailed us in the bedroom. We waited for Mr. Scott, but Earl killed him and put him in the trunk of his car. Then, he came for us. I wasn't gonna let him get my mother. He took the nails out of the door and came in to get me, get us. He had blood all over him, and you could tell by his eyes that he was plum crazy. He had a knife that he sits at the table and sharpens all the time. That's all he did there at the end, sit at the table, look out the window and sharpen that knife. Well, he was going to cut me with it, if he could, just like he did Mr. Scott. I wasn't worried about it. I was worried about Momma. I was scared she wouldn't run, and he'd cut us both up. We heard the front door break. I didn't know what did it. I could tell you a lot more, but you wouldn't believe me...(Interview was paused at this point, and subject was advised to relate the facts as they occurred). *Okay, Momma said she saw someone else in the room with us. I didn't see anybody else. It was like we were moving through molasses, you know. Everything slowed way down. It was like my heart was beating once per hour. It was windy. At first I thought it was going to blow me down, but it wasn't even pushing me back. Nothing in the room was moving around, like you'd expect with so much wind. I told you it wouldn't make sense. I smelled flowers. I thought it must have come in with the wind. It was strong, the flower smell I mean. Then Earl turned around, and I though about jumping on his back, but I never had time. Did I tell you I used to have a dog? Well, I did. But he came up missing. In September, I think. Earl took him off. I know he did. I asked God to bring him home, but he never came back. Until today, that is. Earl stabbed him with the knife, but he couldn't stop him. Nothing on earth could have stopped him. Earl had to die, and he was there to make sure he did. For some reason, I don't remember seeing much of it; as it happened I mean. Maybe it was so loud I had to turn my head. I don't know. The roar was everywhere around us. It pushed me against the wall, and held me there until it was over. When I was able to move, I went and checked on my mom. Then, I went and stood over Buzz Saw; that was my dog's name. He was alive, and he looked up at me. He knew me. I know he did, because he wagged his tail a couple of times. Then, it was time for him to go, because he'd done what he came to do. I got to pet him once more, and I could tell he liked it. Then, he closed his eyes and he was gone, just like that.*

The Detective punched the off button on the tape recorder and sat back. He reached for the breast pocket of shirt seeking a cigarette, knowing there would be none there. It had been years since smoking had been banned in the offices of the Sheriffs Department, and he no longer brought them into the building, preferring to leave them in his cruiser so as not to be tempted to light up where he knew he couldn't. But damn, he wanted one now; felt like he could eat one if given the opportunity.

He had statements from the mother and son, but there was still the report to write to the Prosecuting Attorney, and he had no idea how to go about framing it with so many questions left unanswered. He looked across the table at the younger Detective sitting there, waiting for him to fill in the blanks.

"Well, what do you think?" the young Detective finally said, breaking the tension of silence.

"Problems, problems," Glover said, looking toward the ceiling. "Scott murder is a slam dunk. Earl Collins prints are on the knife, on the plastic, on the trunk, on everything. After that, it all goes haywire. Coroner says the step father was 200 pounds plus before the attack. We find 125 pounds of him on the bedroom floor. He's almost half gone. Nothing left but skeletal remains, and the flesh where his back touched the floor. Where did the rest of him go? The damn dog didn't eat 75 pounds of human flesh. I can't present that to the Prosecutor."

"So, what do you think?" the young Detective repeated.

"Here's what I think: We know Earl Collins killed Fred Scott. Then, he stabs the dog. The boy goes ballistic; takes a chain saw to the stepfather somewhere outside the house. Then, drags the body inside, and lays the dog on top to make it look like the family pet did it. He gets rid of the chainsaw, squares his story with his mother, and calls us."

"So, that's what you think?"

His conclusions created more questions in his mind, and the last thing he needed were more questions. He'd spent his entire career listening to liars of one sort, or another. And his gut told him they were both telling the truth, or at least the truth as best they knew it.

"No," he said, with a sigh. "Is there anything you can add that I may have missed?"

"Did you notice the clocks?"

"What about them?" Glover said, with trepidation. He almost didn't want to hear anymore. Didn't want to hear anything else that might raise further questions.

"There were four clocks in the house. Two in the bedroom where we found Earl Collins and the dog. One in the kitchen, and one in Carol Collins bedroom. I noticed the two in the room where the body was didn't match the others in the house. They were eight minutes behind. Now, that in itself might not be anything significant. Except in light of what the mother just said on that tape.

"You think time stopped?" Glover said, evenly.

The young Detective weighed his response carefully and took a deep breath. He knew Glover was responsible for filling out a quarterly performance evaluation on him. He could imagine the evaluation filled out and signed, with the word "flake" conspicuous across the top. He would quietly be moved back to patrol, where he would languish for the remainder of his career, the only respite being a monthly trip to the department psychologist to see if he still had enough marbles to remain in a squad car. Or, he could just say what he felt, and damn the consequences. He decided the truth was the only thing appropriate.

"I think something strange occurred in that room, and that's putting it mildly. Whatever it was, it was a highly localized event. The windows in the bedroom were blown out with force. Not just broken, blown out. There wasn't a shard of glass on the floor of the bedroom, but we found pieces fifty feet away on the ground outside. No other windows in the house were affected, except the storm door the dog came through. And we know he entered the house by that means. We found his hair and blood on the broken pieces around the front door. Could the boy and his mother have concocted this hair brained story? Then, set the clocks back, knocked out the bedroom windows, broke the glass front door, and smeared some of Fido's blood on the pieces to make it all square up. Yeah, they could have done all that. But, I think it's even more of a stretch to imagine them doing that, than to conclude something else happened. Something we're never going to fully understand. I think Earl Collins came face to face with something he never expected to see. I think it came for him, and it took him, and now it's gone. And all the pieces will never add up, because we don't have all the pieces."

There. He'd said it. It was up to Detective Glover to decide how to swallow it. He fully expected the senior Detective to laugh hilariously, and he'd know his career was as good as over. Instead, Glover reached into the inner pocket of his jacket and slowly withdrew a clear plastic evidence bag.

"What's that?" the young Detective asked.

Glover unzipped the small bag and pulled out a cheap digital watch with a tattered leather band that appeared to have been ripped in half.

"We found this next to Earl Collins. The wrist band must have been bitten through during the attack, and it fell off his arm, which is probably why it wasn't destroyed along with him. Amazing really; it still works."

The young Detective sat looking at the cheap watch that could be purchased at any Wal-Mart for less than ten dollars, until the significance of it registered in his brain.

"It's eight minutes off, isn't it?"

"Eight minutes," Glover said, looking at the flashing digital time piece.

Final Report to the Drew County Prosecuting Attorney, concerning the deaths of Fred Scott and Earl William

Collins, submitted by Detective Wesley Glover, Drew County Sheriffs Office.

On November 28, 2006, at approximately 6:15 PM, 911 dispatch received a call from an address which was confirmed to be located at the end of Highway 147. Since two deaths were reported at the scene, Homicide Division was notified, as was the Coroners Office. I, along with my partner, Detective Kent Belin, proceeded to this address and met Deputy Steve Sloan waiting for us there. As we pulled up to the house, we noticed an adult female standing in the front yard with a younger male. This turned out to be the resident, Carol Collins, and her son Robby Sinclair. They informed us that there were two bodies located on the property. We immediately cordoned off the front entrance, and began an inspection. As we approached the front door we noticed a broken glass storm door. All the pieces were inside the entranceway, leading us to conclude it had been broken from the outside. Pieces of this broken front glass were sent to the State Crime Lab, and an analysis later revealed they contained traces of blood and hair which was canine of origin. There was a large area of congealed blood to the right of the entranceway. A sample of this was taken, and also sent to the State Crime Lab. There were several broken pieces of furniture in the living room, leading us to believe some sort of struggle may have taken place here. We proceeded to a rear bedroom where we observed a body laying inside the doorway. It was obvious that this person was deceased, as the body showed signs of tremendous trauma. A medium sized dog was lying on the upper torso of the body, with a black handled kitchen knife embedded in its torso. This dog was also dead. We had been told by Ms. Collins and her son that this body belonged to Earl William Collins, but the extreme nature of his injuries made visual identification impossible. A search of the body revealed a wallet containing a drivers license bearing the name Earl William Collins. There was also approximately 1/8 once of a powdery substance in a small plastic bag taken from a front pocket. Analysis of this substance by the State Crime Lab came back as Methamphetamine Hydrochloride. Through finger prints and dental records, this body was later confirmed to be Earl William Collins. There were two broken windows in this bedroom, and no signs of glass on the floor. The bedroom was otherwise undisturbed. We proceeded to the backyard of the house where we located a silver Buick Lesabre parked out of view from the front. An inspection of the trunk of this vehicle revealed the body of an African American male wrapped in plastic sheeting. The body was removed from the vehicle and confirmed to be deceased. There as an obvious wound to the throat area, and very little blood around the body, leading us to conclude he had been killed at another location, and moved here. There was identification in the pocket of this individual bearing the name of Fredrick Scott, and the license plate on the Buick Lasabre was also traced to the same. The blood taken earlier from the living room belonged to him. We could therefore conclude he had been killed in the living room, and placed in the trunk at a later point. At this point, the bodies were turned over to the Drew County Coroner, and Carol Collins, along with her son Robby Sinclair, were escorted to the Sheriffs Office to give a statement. After reviewing their statements, and the *available evidence, here are our final conclusions and recommendations: The State Crime Lab reports that the weapon used to kill Fredrick Scott was in all likelihood the same one used to kill the dog. The only prints found on this knife belonged to Earl Collins. His prints were also found on the plastic sheeting, and on the trunk and interior of the Buick Lesabre. We can therefore conclude with a high degree of probability that Earl Collins killed Fred Scott in the living room of the house, then wrapped the body in plastic sheeting and moved it to the trunk of the car, out of sight from the road. The death of Earl Collins is more problematic. Due to a large portion of body being missing due to trauma, the Coroners Office has thus far refused to sign a cause of death statement. All available evidence however, suggests that the dog entered the house by way of the broken front glass door and proceeded to the bedroom where he attacked and killed Earl William Collins. This is consistent with statements given by Carol Collins and her son, and I believe this to be true. Concerning their statements, it appears they have suffered some shared delusions, most likely as a result of the extraordinary nature of the events which occurred. Shared hallucinations have been documented in other cases that involved severe trauma, although I have never been personally involved with any, up to now. It is therefore my recommendation that the death of Earl William Collins be ruled Death By Animal Attack, and this case officially closed. If I can be of any further help to you, feel free to contact me.*

Robby buried his dog behind the house. The story made state headlines, and briefly, the national news.

But as the public has a short attention span, it was soon forgotten, and the media focused on other matters.

Throughout his life it would be a mystery to him where Buzz Saw had been, or why he had come home. The condition of his paws suggested he had traveled a tremendous distance, and the general state of his body made it apparent he had been through a horrendous experience.

Robby and his mother would sometimes discuss what they had seen together, but they could never come to any total agreement over the specifics of the final moments. It had seemed to happen in a blur, as if the horridness of it was somehow shrouded from their vision. There was, however, no doubt to them that God had arrived in the midst of their storm. However he chose to accomplish this was irrelevant. They accepted it as a miracle, despite what anyone else might think.

Friends from Don Byrd's church helped Carol find a job, and they remained in Monticello where Robby again played football in his senior season. He started at cornerback, and the team won eight games and lost two.

He declined opportunities to go to college, preferring to go to work and help support his mother. He was married at age 25, had a daughter two years later, and another three years after that. He was a faithful at his church, being present at every service, and generally in attendance every time the doors opened.

It was at a revival service shortly after his thirtieth birthday that his life turned a corner. The evangelist was preaching on the certainty of the resurrection, the witnesses to the living, post-crucified Christ, and the empowerment of the apostles after having seen him raised from the dead.

Robby sat in the service on this night with his family, and as the preacher related the many facts, and the Spirit moved through the service, it was as if a light came flashing into his soul, illuminating his inner man. The reality of it all came flooding into him, and he moved from simply believing with his mind, to believing with his heart. It was true…oh, Jesus…was the thought repeated over and over in his mind, and he wept for the sacrifice made, for the redemption given, and for joy at the knowledge of its fulfillment in his life.

Much like the early apostles, he was a changed man after this, and his life took on new power. He found, primarily, he could no longer not be a witness to the reality he had come face to face with. It was a natural progression moving into a full time ministry, and at age thirty three, he took over pastorship of a small church.

This was successful and fulfilling, but he was later called to abandon the comforts of this life and enter the mission field, where he and his family served in Haiti for 30 years. Upon his wife's death he returned to the United States, choosing to remain in the Monticello area, and served as deacon in a local church.

Throughout his life, running was a constant. Even as he celebrated his eightieth birthday his mileage never decreased, though his pace certainly was slower. Three months after this milestone, he laced up his running shoes and took to the road, running a familiar route.

He began the run feeling more fatigued than usual, but he felt like this would pass once he was well into it. At the two mile point, well before the "wall of pain" he was so accustomed to, his legs turned to lead and he had to fight hard just to keep moving. But he ran on, certain he could leave this behind, as he always did. Halfway through three miles, the pain and fatigue suddenly vanished so abruptly it was as if it fell away on the road behind him. So startling, and unusual was the sensation it made him gasp, but it was too wonderful to question for long. Instead, he went with the feeling, moving his legs and arms faster and faster, till he was sprinting down the deserted stretch of highway.

The thought briefly entered his mind that if anyone saw him, a man of eighty years sprinting like Carl Lewis, they would not believe their eyes, and the thought made him laugh out loud. As he ran ever faster, he searched his body for any pain at all, and found none. Even in the days of his youth he had never felt a sensation such as this, moving through the wind at breakneck speed, effortlessly. What's happening to me, he wondered, realizing that he was not even breathing hard.

He flew around a bend in the road and saw someone ahead on the side of the road. It was almost unheard of to see anyone else out here running, and as he neared he could see the stranger was wearing a gray jogging suit and appeared to be tightening up his shoes.

He slowed his pace self consciously and drew parallel with man, watching him from the corner of his eye.

"Hello Robby," the man said, putting the final loop on his shoe string and not looking up.

It had been twenty years, since the death of his mother, that anyone had called him Robby. He was known to everyone as Robert Sinclair, and had been since his middle twenties.

"Hello," he said, running a few steps past, but his curiosity overwhelmed him, and he stopped and turned around.

The man was tall, but otherwise nondescript. It seemed curious that there was no sweat evident on his running clothes, but Robert Sinclair brushed it off, concluding the man may have simply walked to where their paths had intersected .

"Do I know you?"

"Oh, you're very well known, and I've heard lots about you. All of it good, by the way," the tall man said, smiling.

"Well, thank you. It's unusual to hear someone call me Robby. I thought I left that behind a long time ago."

"Do you prefer Robert?"

"Uh, no. I guess not. Kinda makes an old fellow like me feel young again. No, Robby's okay."

He extended a hand of greeting to the stranger, and noticed the handshake was firm.

"I'm at a disadvantage. It appears you know my name, but I don't know you."

"You can call me Zack," the man said.

For Robby Sinclair, every opportunity to meet a stranger was an opportunity to share his faith; to bring another soul into the Kingdom. It had been this way as long as he could remember, and he moved into this mode as natural as one would take in the next breath, or exhale the last.

"Which direction are you headed?"

"I was going that direction, before I stopped to tie my shoe," Zack said, pointing in the direction Robby had been running.

"Well, you're welcome to run along with me, if you don't mind being seen with a very old man," said Robby.

"Okay, lets stretch the legs a bit," Zack said, and they set off at an easy jog.

It was refreshing to be running alongside someone else, hearing the sound of another's shoes striking the pavement, along with his. Robby felt an instant bond with his companion that was so unusual it rendered him mute for several minutes, before he found his voice and spoke.

"Wonderful day, isn't it?"

"It's a glorious day. Beautiful day to be running," Zack said, with enthusiasm, "and how are you feeling today?"

"I was feeling very tired earlier, even a little ill. It passed somewhere back there on the road. Now I feel...euphoric. That's the word for it. I don't think I have ever felt better in my life. And that's no exaggeration. Never better."

"Wow," said Zack, "to be alive on a glorious day like this, and feeling the best you've ever felt. I don't guess it can get better than that."

"No. I truly feel like I could run forever."

"Well, why don't we Robby? Why don't we just run forever?"

It was such a curious thing to say, Robert Sinclair laughed briefly, then casting a glance at his companion, saw he wasn't chuckling. It was almost like he was serious.

"I'm a very old man. Someday soon, I guess I'll just run off into eternity," was all he could think to say in response.

"How do you feel about that? Eternity, I mean?"

He was well accustomed to asking others about their eternal security, but it was strange to be on the other end of the question.

"I'm looking forward to it. So many of my friends have already crossed over. Most of them in fact. But judging from the way I feel today, it's liable to be a very long time before I can be there with them. I'm happy to stay here and work until Jesus calls for me, then I'm ready to go, whether it's today, or twenty years from now."

"So you wouldn't be upset if you were called home today?"

They had suddenly turned to a serious subject; from discussing the weather, to talking about life everlasting, it gave him pause to consider his response before he answered, wanting to be completely honest.

"Oh, no. I wouldn't be upset. You call it home. Only a believer would refer to it in that sense," he said, seeking an affirmation.

"Certainly, I'm a believer."

"That's great. I was going to witness to you anyway, so I guess I can save that for someone else."

"That's your calling. It's what you came here to do, and you've done a magnificent job," Zack said, matter of factly. "You've lived up to what was invested in you."

"It's very kind of you to say that. People tend to exaggerate things."

"I'm not relying on what others have said. I've been watching you for a very long time."

The reply stopped Robby in his tracks, and he stared at Zack for several long moments.

"Who are you?"

"Come see," said the tall man in the gray sweat suit, gently taking his arm and turning him back the way they had come.

Robby allowed himself to be turned around, and they jogged steadily back to the point where they had met, and then past.

"Where are we going? Robby asked, not feeling uneasy, despite the confusion he felt. The day had grown increasingly peculiar, but the strange man who ran just to his left did not give him the impression of one who would harm him.

"Just up ahead are the answers to so many of your questions. I promise you won't be disappointed."

They ran without speaking, rounded a bend in the road, and a white form clad in dark blue could be seen lying prostrate in the grass on the shoulder. Zack watched Robby from the corner of his eye, judging a reaction, ready to ease his fears if there were any, but his companion remained calm, even to the point where they stood over the body.

Robert Sinclair stood looking downward toward what had been his former persona, looking at himself lying peaceful in death in the grass on the shoulder of the highway.

"I was so old," he said, in wonder. "I guess this is where it ended."

"No," Zack said, softly. "This is where it begins. Everything awaits. Everything you've ever dreamed of."

For a brief moment Robby was hesitant to leave, not quite wanting to permanently break the connection with all he had ever known, but Zack's words filtered through to him and he realized that this reality was no more. It was time to step into his dreams, and claim what he had so often preached.

"Are you ready?" Zack asked.

Robby nodded, still unable to take his eyes of the old man lying in the grass.

"It's just a tent. A very old tent. Let me show you more."

Zack gently took Robby by the arm, and the present reality fell away. They were suddenly moving through a realm that was neither light, nor dark. As they moved, Robby was presented with a cinematic panorama that seemed to envelope them 360 degrees. He watched enraptured as a vision of his mother, obviously very pregnant, became visible.

The sight of his mother, who he had not seen for twenty years since her death, made him gasp.

"She's so beautiful," he whispered.

"Always has been," Zack answered. "And she always will be. She's anxious to see you. She sends her love."

A band of light could be seen encircling the pregnant woman, and Robby was about to inquire about it, but Zack explained before he could ask.

"I told you I've been watching you for a very long time. Me, and others with me. We had a hedge around you from the moment you were conceived. God uses each vessel as He chooses, and each life is significant. But you were imbued with the spiritual qualities of a soul winner. It was very important that you grow and reach your potential, not only for you, but for those who would cross your path. There were many souls at stake here, and eternal destinies hung in the balance. Unfortunately, it also made you a target for the enemy."

He watched as the scene progressed, from his years as a toddler, in the arms of his natural father, to his first day of school. Through all this time, the band of light never left him, encircling him protectively. And outside the light hovered a dark, formless shadow, sometimes near, sometimes lurking in a corner, unable to penetrate the protective hedge which surrounded him.

Significant sequences from his childhood came alive around him, each answering a particular question he had once wondered about, and bringing back a flood of memories from a time long since past.

The life review moved to his teenage years. There was an increasing tension apparent between his mother and father, a struggle between the two most important people in his life. Even though he knew how it all turned out, it was still painful for him to watch, when his father was no longer in the picture, and he and his mother were alone.

As he and his mother enjoyed a brief year alone together, and the darkness remained safely outside the shield of light around him, he could not help but wonder about the nature of evils purpose, and asked his angel about this.

"There is no doubt about the fate of Satan, when it's all said and done, I mean?"

"No," Zack answered, "His fate was sealed three days after Calvary. We all witnessed it. Every being in the spiritual realm can attest to it. The keys of hell and death were taken from him. He was stripped of any power. All he has are lies, but if he has a corporal body to work in, he can be very dangerous."

"Why is he so intent on taking others with him?"

"He believes if he can drag enough souls with him into the lake of fire, that God, in His mercy and love, will suspend his death sentence to avoid sending his creation there, also. It's his only hope, but it's a false hope. Above all else, God will fulfill His Word. In a desperate attempt to save himself, he is misleading millions, and billions towards eternal destruction."

The marriage of his mother to Earl enfolded before his eyes, and as he watched, the protective band of light was no longer visible surrounding him.

"We were very concerned at this point," Zack explained. "This marriage was not the will of God. She became one-flesh with an unbeliever, and it allowed the enemy to breach the hedge. And his drug use made him the perfect candidate for outright possession of his soul and body. We knew we had some time before he was fully conditioned for their purposes, but not much. So a plan was formulated, and our own weapon was introduced."

Robby watched as he, his mother, and Earl brought the small puppy home to the house on Highway 147. It looked so small and helpless cradled in his arms, who would have ever thought it could be so important in the grand scheme of things.

"That was your weapon," Robby said, without question.

"God uses the foolish things of this world, to confound the wise. Within him were all the spiritual qualities necessary to accomplish our purpose: Loyalty, courage, and boundless love. I left you for a time to accompany him into the physical world. I was with him as he fought to get back to you. Still, even with all his attributes, he would not have made it without the prayers of the saints… and the words of faith you spoke, on that day."

The scene from Earl's last day on earth enfolded. He and his mother trapped in the bedroom. The killing of Fred Scott. He watched himself, so young, and so long ago, facing the bedroom door while Earl extracted the nails and prepared himself to enter, snatching the door open with murder on his mind, and his face smeared with Fred Scott's blood. The maniacal look on his face made it apparent that he was completely given over to enemy. The dark shadow that had hovered near Robby was no longer visible; it had incarnated itself within Earl. Earl had become the darkness.

And as Zack and Robby watched, the destruction of Earl played itself out before their eyes.

"Even with all the power within him," Zack said. "It was your words of faith that brought the power to it's peak, and assured us the victory. Psalm 103:20 says, *'The angels of God, that excel in strength, that do his commandment, hearkening unto the voice of his word.'* Without faith, we can accomplish nothing in the physical plane. When you declared to your mother that God would be there, a thousand strong men could not have withstood the power that was brought to bear. And true to your words, He was there. The Holy One himself was present with us," Zack whispered, reverently.

"My mother was right. She said she saw him there, with us in the room."

Robby watched as his dog breathed his last breath, and it brought the pain back as fresh and sharp as it had been on that day, so long ago. To his surprise, tears filled his eyes and rolled down his cheeks.

"I'm sorry. I know there aren't suppose to be tears in heaven," he said, crying softly.

"Weeping may endure for a night, but joy cometh in the morning."

"Psalm 30:5. It's one of my favorite verses."

"And mine," Zack said, smiling.

"He gave himself for me," Robby said, as the scene faded away around them.

"That's what love does, in it's purest form. It gives all it has to give, and it never gives up. Till it does what it came to do. It never fails. Come see," Zack said, again taking Robby gently by the arm.

All at once they stood in a world where a blue sky was showing the first hints of morning. A translucent golden road lay beneath their feet, and ahead, on both sides of the road, was a vast multitude of people.

"They've been waiting for you," said Zack, and together they jogged between the outstretched arms of friends, calling out his name as he ran past. It took many minutes to clear this group, and it was joyous knowing they were here with him, in this place.

He was tempted to stop when he saw his mother smiling and waving to him, but she called out, "I'll find you in the city, I love you!" So he continued on, with Zack still at his side.

Up ahead, there was a shining city in the distance, and the sky seemed to be growing brighter by the minute. To the left of the city was a hillside, and the glow lighting the sky seemed to come from there.

"What would you like to do now?" Zack asked.

Without pause of thought, Robby said, "I want to see Jesus."

"Well, you're in luck. He's coming now."

In the never ending existence that we know as eternity, there was never another occasion for Robert Sinclair to ever shed another tear, or even feel the slightest hint of sadness, as a blazing eminence broke the crest of the hillside, and the morning of his forever dawned. So tremendous was the glory of his presence, that it illuminated the sky to the brightness of noon day, but somehow it was not impossible to look at. In fact, Robby found it impossible to look away.

Almost lost in the glory, but so very visible to Robby, was the small form of a dog, coming alongside the risen Lord, headed in his direction.

He ran strong towards the shining bright light, and the scent of roses filled the air around him.